MCCRARY'S JUSTICE

ALSO BY DALLAS GORHAM

The Carlos McCrary PI Mystery Thriller Series

Six Murders Too Many

Double Fake, Double Murder

Quarterback Trap

Dangerous Friends

Day of the Tiger

McCrary's Justice

Yesterday's Trouble

Four Years Gone

Debt of Honor

Sometimes You Lose

MCCRARY'S JUSTICE

CARLOS MCCRARY PI, BOOK 6

DALLAS GORHAM

ePublishingWorks!
...love what you read.

Book and cover design by eBook Prep
www.ebookprep.com

April 2022
ISBN: 978-1-64457-272-6

ePublishing Works!
644 Shrewsbury Commons Ave
Ste 249
Shrewsbury PA 17361
United States of America

www.epublishingworks.com
Phone: 866-846-5123

ONE

Liz Jenkins

L iz lay still as a corpse in the dim light, monitoring the fat man's chest as it rose and fell. Was he asleep yet?

Earlier, the springs had screeched in protest, the bed bouncing like a dinghy in a hurricane. The clock on her dresser had flipped over to *1:11* while he hammered away inside her and grunted like a pig at a trough.

Now his massive arm felt like a fallen tree trunk sprawled across her. The thick hair on his forearm scratched her naked skin like the bark of that ill-fated tree.

Her chest felt like a steel band had tightened around it. She fought back tears, struggling to overcome her helpless feeling. Her clothes were locked away in a closet. She never needed them except to dress for meals. The remainder of the time, she spent imprisoned in her room, languishing naked on the bed, waiting for the next john. Day after day, night after night, men violated her.

Liz wasn't a prostitute; she was a sex slave. She wiped away an escaped teardrop and swore she wouldn't be helpless much longer. Soon, very soon, she would be free, or she would be dead.

Tommy had told her to treat the fat man right. This john was an ambassador from some Latin American country, the Republic of San Something-or-other. But who knew? Tommy lied for the fun of it.

Liz had trembled when Tommy told her the ambassador had returned and the creep asked for her. For an entire night. Again.

Behind the john's back, Liz and the other captives called him Jabba the Hutt.

"Show him another good time, Liz," Tommy said, squeezing her breast hard enough to hurt. One more reason to hate Tommy. She wondered now what she had ever seen in Tommy.

Liz had almost protested, then she recalled the fat man's cellphone and kept quiet. Tommy kept his girls away from cellphones, but the ambassador was different. Tommy let him keep his phone. Jabba the Hutt was a big man in more than waistline. She wanted that phone. With a phone, she had a chance to reach the outside. A slim chance, but any chance was better than a slow death.

If Tommy caught her, he would make the other girls watch as he killed her. And she would not die quickly. The memory of Evelyn's death made her shudder. *Free or dead.*

Tommy had kidnapped six women over a few weeks, addicted them to drugs, and rented them out for sex. He called them *Tommy's Angels.* Now there were five. Three weeks ago, the women had witnessed Evelyn die by Tommy's order. "Angels, this is what we do if you try to escape." He had taunted the remaining five while he and three gang members raped and strangled Evelyn. "Don't make the same mistake she did."

Ironically, Evelyn's gruesome death rekindled Liz's burning desire for freedom—a desire that drugs and depravity had dulled to the brink of extinction. Since Evelyn's murder, Liz had only pretended to swallow the pills Tommy gave her every day. Once her captor turned away, she spat them out and hid them under the mattress. If all else failed, she had accumulated enough pills to kill herself. She hoped.

Tommy called her an angel, but Liz lived in hell with the devil. She would rather die.

There was nothing good about "good times" with the fat man. He provided drugs for them both, including blue pills for him. He appeared young enough not to need chemical help, but maybe he wanted to last extra long. He demanded rough sex in repulsive variations for an endless two hours. The previous times the drugs kept her from realizing how disgusting he was, but stopping the drugs let the reality of her situation sink in. She almost wished she had swallowed the last pills instead of tonguing them into her cheek. They would have made her pain and humiliation more bearable. The fat weirdo made her sore for days.

She shivered through the night, unable to sleep through the snores of the rancid, sweaty john. He kept the air-conditioning on its frostiest setting, and the room felt as cold as a meat locker. Still the stench of his sweat polluted the air. She stared at the ceiling in the icy room trying not to breathe the foul air. She dreaded the morning. He would awaken, swallow another blue pill, and rape her again. He always did.

He tipped her well, but no tip could compensate for the feeling of degradation. With no opportunity to spend money in captivity, she stashed the tip money in a plastic bag hidden in the toilet tank. If she escaped this brothel—no, *when* she escaped—she would need money to get home. The hope of escape gave her a reason to stay alive.

After an eternity, the john's breath slowed to a regular rhythm. His lips puffed ragged breaths. He rolled onto his side, and his bulky arm rasped like a cheese grater across her skin. The cheap mattress bounced like a bowl of Jell-O with his movement. Heavy musk from his after-shave mixed with the dirty socks smell of sweat and sex. She gagged and choked back the bile that rose from her empty stomach.

Tonight was her first opportunity to call for help since she had decided to escape or die, but did she dare move? What if Jabba the Hutt woke? Would he throw his disgusting body on top of hers, groping for her breasts with his slobbering mouth while he mounted her?

She scooched away from the ambassador toward the edge of the mattress. The bed shifted ominously, but he didn't wake. He snorted once and rolled over.

She used his movement to mask hers, and she inched closer to the edge of the bed. She wiped cold sweat from her forehead, careful not to jiggle the bed. The fat man squirmed onto his back, and she scooted enough to dangle one leg off the bed, reaching for the floor with her foot.

The clock on the dresser flicked over to *2:17*.

Do it before you chicken out. She shifted more weight to the foot on the floor and held her breath.

As gently as a lava flow, she eased the other foot off the bed and lowered it to the worn carpet, alert to the slightest change in his sleep. She began to sit up, but the springs vibrated and she froze. Her heart pounded like it would burst through her chest.

His snores halted. She froze. Jabba wasn't breathing. *Sleep apnea.* She had learned about it in a high school health class. *Don't panic. He'll breathe in a few seconds.*

The pressure grew in her chest. *Damn,* she was holding her breath. Jabba snorted like a pig and Liz exhaled. He resumed snoring, louder this time.

She sat upright, shifting more weight to her feet, and boosting her butt off the mattress. The springs remained quiet, and she breathed a silent prayer of thanks.

The john's clothes were draped over a chair in the corner. Slipping his phone from the belt holster, she eased toward the bathroom, keeping her focus on the sleeping john. The phone was different from the one she owned before Tommy imprisoned her. She fumbled with it in the dark. *How do I turn this damn thing on?* Her hands shook so much that she dropped it. Liz froze when it clattered on the tiled floor of the bathroom. *I'm a dead woman.* No one could sleep through that noise. Breathing deeply but quietly, she glanced back towards the bed. Jabba snored on.

Liz had another horrid thought. *What if his phone is broken? No, that's not the end of the world. I'll replace it in his holster and he will never notice. He'll be back someday with another phone. The pig always comes back. Always.*

The ambassador had listened to his messages earlier, and he hadn't noticed her peering over his shoulder. Now, she mashed every button on the phone until the light from the screen cast an eerie glow in the dark bathroom. She thanked God the phone still worked. *Free or dead,* she whispered, punching the messaging icon.

Carlos McCrary

My office phone rang. "Wilbur Jenkins on line one."

"Thanks, Betty." After scribbling the name on a notepad, I tapped the other phone button. "This is Chuck McCrary, Mr. Jenkins. How may I help you?"

"Are you the guy who shot that cop?"

The phone number of McCrary Investigations is listed. Who would hire a private investigator with an unlisted number? Hopefully, this wasn't another nut job calling to accuse me of murder. Such is the price of fame. Or is it notoriety? Sometimes the caller is a new client. Those are my favorites.

"I prefer to accentuate the positive and say I rescued a woman who was kidnapped by a crooked cop," I responded modestly.

"So, you are that guy?"

"That's me. How can I help?"

"I'm Will Jenkins. My daughter's been kidnapped. I want you to find her."

"Did you talk to the police?" There's no point wasting someone's money to do a job the cops do for free.

"That's the first call I made. They're working the case mighty hard, but they ain't got doodly-squat. He said to call you, and he give me your phone number. That Castellano fellow, he's the police detective that you sprung from that murder charge, ain't he?"

"He didn't tell you?"

"Maybe the lieutenant weren't too proud of that murder charge, even after he did beat the rap."

"Maybe."

"The main thing he said was that you might could find my daughter."

"Can you come to my office?"

Offering my hand, I said, "I'm Carlos McCrary."

My visitor switched his faded John Deere hat to his huge left hand so he could grab my hand with his right. "Wilbur Jenkins. Friends call me Will." His hand was scarred and calloused.

"And I'm Chuck." I handed him a business card. Maybe I should add a magnifying glass logo.

"The lieutenant, he already give me one of your cards."

Will's calloused palm matched his sunburned face. With his worn blue jeans, faded cotton shirt, and scuffed work boots, he reminded me of my father. His forehead was white below his thin brown hair. *A farmer's tan*, I thought.

I got him coffee and led him to my conference room. "What did Lieutenant Castellano say?"

"First, you oughta read these texts my Lizzie sent me early Tuesday morning." He handed me his phone.

The first text was sent at 2:22 a.m.

Daddy, held captive in Port City FL by white man named Tommy Flannigan, five foot ten, thirty to forty years, medium build, palm tree tattoo on left forearm, pierced left ear with diamond stud. Sex slave. DO NOT CALL OR REPLY TO THIS TEXT. HE WILL KILL ME IF HE LEARNS I USED THIS PHONE. It belongs to a john. Love, Binky

When I saw *sex slave*, my stomach clenched like a fist. It stirred a memory of my cousin Emily. No, not merely a memory; the two words stirred a dread and a fear.

The second text was sent at 2:25 a.m.

Four other girls held too, maybe more. Sex slaves. Jill from Chicago, Tawnya from Philadelphia, Delores from Shawnee, and Morgan from Cleveland. Don't know last names or any addresses. DO NOT CALL OR REPLY TO THIS TEXT. Binky

The last one was sent at 2:30 a.m.

Held in house with three stories, 30 feet wide 80 feet deep, on busy street with two lanes of traffic and parking on both sides. Sex slaves. Three gangsters. Scruffy, black, skinny, fifty. Vince, white, medium, forty. One big bald guy no name. DO NOT CALL OR REPLY TO THIS TEXT. Love, Binky.

Swallowing hard, I pushed away anxieties about my cousin Emily while I composed myself. "What did the police say?"

"I'll get to that in a minute. First thing I got to know is, can you find her?"

"Did she leave of her own free will, or was she kidnapped?"

"She went to Disney World. Her and her friend Jennifer."

"Jennifer?"

"She and Jennifer, they been friends since they was this high." He held his palm three feet off the floor. "Jennifer lives on the farm next to ours, maybe a half-mile down the road. Jennifer's parents give her a new car for graduation and the two of them decided to take a road trip to Disney World. I fought it, but Lizzie, she saved the money herself and she was legal age. There wasn't nothing I could do to stop her." He lowered his head. "We wasn't getting along too good, her and me, since her mom died."

Will didn't say anything else, so I prompted him. "She and Jennifer went to Disney."

He contemplated his hands in his lap. "She was so mad at me that she wouldn't return none of my calls. Three weeks later, Jennifer come back without her."

"Where was Liz?"

Will sighed. "At Disney, Liz and Jennifer met a group of young'uns on a high school trip from Brazil. Liz, she was real taken with one boy in the group. The Brazilians was going to visit Fort Lauderdale after Disney. Liz decided to go with them. Jennifer, she drove back by herself."

"Drove back to where? Where do you live?"

"Butler County, Nebraska. I'm a farmer. I grow corn."

"With you living in Nebraska, how did you learn about my gunfight with the cop who kidnapped that woman?"

"After the lieutenant give me your card, I Googled you. Just because I'm a farmer don't mean I don't use the internet. Then I Googled the lieutenant."

"Always a good idea to know who you're dealing with." I wrote *Butler County, Nebraska. Corn.* "How long since she disappeared?"

He swallowed hard. "A little over a year."

"Did she send you any letters, emails, anything similar?"

"Nope. Not even a postcard."

"Did she give Jennifer a note with the boy's name or address, maybe a phone number where you could reach her?"

"Sure. She didn't sneak off or nothing. She gave Jennifer the boy's name and phone number. But she made Jennifer promise not to tell me what she done until she—that is, Jennifer—until she got back home to Butler County."

He tugged a handkerchief from a pocket and wiped his eyes. "By the time Jennifer come home, the Brazilian boy, he was back in Brazil. I called him long distance. He said the last time he seen my Lizzie was at the Miami airport when the Brazilians was leaving for home."

"You hadn't heard from her before those texts?"

"Nary a word."

"Was her cellphone on your plan?"

"Yeah. After Jennifer come home, I called the sheriff in David City— that's the county seat. He attempted a phone trace, but Lizzie's phone wasn't on the network. The phone company said the last time her phone was used was in Port City a week after them Brazilians flew home. The Brazilian boy, he wasn't involved."

His eyes were moist. "I pay for her phone every month. I know it's lost or stolen or some such, but I keep hoping someday she'll turn it back on. The preacher, he says a faint hope is better than no hope, and I should live with faith."

"Are these texts the only clues?"

"That and the fact the phone was last used in Port City. Can you find her?"

"With so little to go on, it won't be easy. I'll do my best, but there are no guarantees."

Will sat straighter. "Mr. McCrary, I got one of the biggest farms in Nebraska, and if my Lizzie don't come back, I got no one to leave it to and nothing to live for. Corn prices are real good; I can pay."

"I figured that, but I don't want to raise false hope."

"I understand; no guarantees." He stuck out his hand.

We shook hands. "Of course, I'll help, Will. What's your daughter's name?"

"Elizabeth Marie Jenkins. Everybody calls her Liz."

"Date of birth?"

He told me and I added it to my notes.

Liz was nineteen. So young to be the victim of sex slavery. But any age was too young.

"Do you have a recent picture?"

He drew two wallet-sized portraits from his shirt pocket and studied them. "This one is her high school graduation picture. I snapped it after the graduation ceremony." He gazed at one and handed me the other. "Keep it. I got plenty more." His eyes glistened.

The world froze for a moment. It was his daughter's picture, but, except for the hairstyle, it could have been my cousin Emily. Sun-lightened, shoulder-length hair, pale blue eyes, and a wide innocent smile that knew no fear and saw no evil anywhere in the world. She looked like Emily when she smiled.

I swallowed hard and blinked. "You showed these texts to Lieutenant Castellano?"

"Of course. When the first text come in, my phone whistled like they do. That sorta woke me a little. You know how you kinda hear something in your sleep, but it don't, like, *register?* "

I nodded.

"The second text, the phone whistle woke me all the way. I was reading the second text when the third one come in. When I seen it—" His voice broke. He covered his face with his hands.

I gave him a tissue from the box of tissues on my credenza. You'd be surprised the number of clients who cry when they tell me why they need my help.

Will blew his nose. "I prayed for strength not to call her back then and there. She felt so close... so close."

I concentrated on Liz's photo again to avoid the sight of her father weeping. How did that innocent girl view the world now, a year later?

"I held that phone another half hour, praying my Lizzie would send another text. Then I called the airline and caught the first plane to Port City. I rented a car and I asked the rental clerk where the closest police station was. That's where I met Lieutenant Castellano. That was Tuesday afternoon late."

He pulled a paper from his shirt pocket and studied it. "The lieutenant, he ran the other girls' names through the missing persons' notices. There was nothing for that Jill girl or nobody named Tawnya, but that Dolores girl, Lizzie misspelled her name. It's not D-E-L; it's D-O-L. She gotta be Dolores Cherry from Shawnee, Oklahoma. That girl Morgan, she's Morgan Putnam from Cleveland. Their parents, they reported them missing a year ago. Lieutenant Castellano, he called the police in Shawnee and Cleveland. Nobody has no leads and the girls' parents, they ain't heard from them either. I promised them both I would contact them if I learned anything."

"The text mentions a man named Tommy Flannigan. Did the lieutenant find anything on him?"

"There's no Tommy Flannigan in the police records, the phone book, or nowhere else. This Tommy fellow, he must've gave my Lizzie a phony name. Over a hundred criminals named Tommy in Atlantic County fit his description. The lieutenant, he assigned two detectives to check out all them Tommys, but it takes time. Castellano says he's feared this Tommy, maybe he don't have no criminal record."

"What about Scruffy and Vince?"

"The lieutenant, he couldn't find nobody named Scruffy, white or black, with a criminal record. He did find a folk singer on Google. But he's white and seventy-three years old. Lives in Nashville. The lieutenant says there are two hundred crooks in South Florida named Vince. They're checking."

He slurped his coffee, now cold, and frowned.

"I'll call the receptionist for fresh coffee." I did. "Could the lieutenant do anything with the house description?"

"His computer geek, he ran it every which way through the property appraiser website and the Department of Transportation map database. He told the sergeants to brief every precinct for all the patrol units Wednesday, Thursday, and this morning. Nothing yet."

"What did he learn about the phone that sent the text?"

Will referred to his notes again. "It's a Washington, DC number. It took a couple of days, but yesterday the lieutenant learned it belongs to a fellow named Pablo Antonio Crucero Obregon. He's the ambassador from the Republic of San Cristobal."

"Did anyone interview the ambassador?"

"The lieutenant, he says the ambassador lives in Washington, but he's been in San Cristobal for the last three weeks."

"Somebody else is using his phone."

"That's what the lieutenant says. Maybe if we called the FBI?"

"Technically the girls are missing persons. Liz left home of her own free will. The evidence your daughter is held against her will is three texts sent from a phone with a diplomatic connection. That's not enough to involve the FBI. Sorry."

"That's what I figured. Lieutenant Castellano, he said the same thing."

"Okay if I call the lieutenant after you and I are through here?"

"You can call him now; I don't mind."

"I'll do it later. He and I need to discuss boring cop stuff."

"Nothing about my daughter's case will bore me."

"I'll call him later."

Betty knocked twice on the door and brought in fresh coffee. I nodded my thanks and she closed the door behind her.

Will cleared his throat. "Is there something you want to discuss with the lieutenant that you don't want me to hear?"

Sipping my coffee, I decided how to reply. "It would be a miracle if the cops found your daughter, or at least found her alive. That's why the lieutenant sent you to me."

"I don't understand. Why can't the cops find my Lizzie?"

"Jorge Castellano is a LEO—a law enforcement officer—sworn to uphold the law. LEOs obey state laws and the U.S. Constitution—search warrants, reasonable cause, Miranda warnings, and other things that protect people's rights."

"Okay, but so what? My daughter was kidnapped. Her life's in danger, not to mention the other girls." Will smacked the table with his palm. "We got to get a move on."

"The cops follow due process to obtain evidence, or the prosecutor can't use it in court."

"You mean that legal stuff I seen on the TV cop shows?"

"Right."

"I don't need to convict nobody in court. All I want is to find my daughter." His eyes glistened with unshed tears.

"Jorge knows that he has little chance of finding Liz by following due process of law. He sent you to me because I'm *not* a LEO. I don't care about due process. If necessary, I do things which are technically outside the law."

"Such as?"

I thought for a moment. "Even if I locate that three-story house Liz described. I would need to search the house to find her. I'm a private citizen and I can't get a search warrant. So, I might pick the lock or break down the door. If Liz or another of the captives were inside, nobody would care that I broke the law, because I freed them. You understand?"

"Yeah. Good P.R. makes you bullet proof."

"Right, but assume the girls are not there—say the kidnappers moved them somewhere else—then I wind up in jail if I'm caught in a B&E."

"B&E?"

"Sorry; I spend too much time talking to cops and lawyers. B&E means breaking and entering."

Will rubbed his chin. "You take big risks."

"Goes with the territory. Also, as a private citizen, I don't give Miranda warnings before I question a witness. I get them to talk to me however I can—whatever works."

Will caught the implications. "Jesus Christ. When you question somebody, and they don't answer you, what can you do?"

"Depends on who I question. If I'm *certain* it's a bad guy, I might... *persuade* them to cooperate."

"How?"

"Are you sure you want to know, Will?"

His stare transformed to ice. "I want my daughter back, whatever it costs, whatever it takes."

TWO

L ieutenant Jorge Castellano answered on the second ring. *"Hola, Carlos.* Did a man named Will Jenkins call you?"

"He just left. I'm gonna take the case. Thanks for the referral, I think."

"Good. You know our hands are tied, but you aren't subject to the same rules. You tend to, uh ..."

"Improvise," I said. "I prefer to say that I improvise."

"Well, that's better than admitting that you're a lawbreaker, I guess."

"Right. What did you learn about the names in the texts?"

"We're tracing every Vince and Tommy, but nothing's popped. I put two guys on it. Unfortunately, our records don't always include tattoos and identifying marks."

"The tattoo could be new anyway. Any luck with the house description?"

"We screened the property appraiser's data base for houses over six thousand square feet. There aren't many houses that size in the county and none in the area within three miles of the cell tower."

"How about the street she described?"

"Do you know how many streets in Atlantic County have parking on both sides?"

"Thousands of miles of streets."

"We briefed the patrol units in all precincts. We told them at morning muster to be on the lookout for three-story houses of any size on a street with two lanes of traffic with parking on both sides."

"That's the first time I've heard of a BOLO for a house."

Jorge chuckled. "I never thought of it that way. Anyway, nobody's noticed any building like that so far."

"I predict they won't. They don't have skin in the game."

"Maybe we'll get lucky."

"My ol' grandpappy always says, 'Wish in one hand and spit in the other. See which one gets full first.'"

"You and your ol' grandpappy stories. Is he even real?"

"Sure. Magnus McCrary. Next time he comes to Port City to visit, I'll introduce you."

"Magnus? That's his name?"

"Yeah, his father immigrated to Texas from Ireland. I think the name is from the Old Country. Anyway, enough about my grandfather. Tell me about the phone that sent the texts."

"We ran into a brick wall."

"How so?" I asked. "It's pretty simple to run a phone number."

"We got a warrant using the phone number and obtained the tower's location from the cell carrier. No problem until we asked to identify the owner. The phone's registered address is the Embassy of the *Republica de San Cristobal* in Washington, DC. We called the U.S. State Department to learn that it belongs to the ambassador, Pablo Crucero. We called the DC cops and the State Department. Pablo is not the guy. He's been in San Cristobal for several weeks for knee surgery."

"Who's using his phone? A family member?"

"Yeah. The ambassador owns four cellphones, all with diplomatic immunity, which means we can't get a warrant to do anything with the phone, like trace back its GPS locations. He has a wife, a thirty-year-old son, and a daughter who attends Georgetown University. The wife and daughter went with Daddy to San Cristobal, so the phone that sent the text may belong to the son."

"Jorge, you read the texts. This girl was kidnapped. Can't you do an unofficial GPS backtrack on the phone?"

"We're not on speaker, are we?"

"You know me better than that."

"We tried. The phone's GPS locator is disabled. Whoever this guy is, he's hiding something."

"Or maybe he just values his privacy. What's his name?"

"You're gonna love this, *amigo*. It's Antonio Ricardo Crucero *Calderone*."

"With my luck, this idiot is a distant cousin." My Mexican mother's maiden name is Calderone and my legal name is Carlos Andres McCrary Calderone, following the Mexican custom.

Jorge laughed. "San Cristobal is a long way from Mexico, *amigo*. If he's kin, he's an eighth cousin or some such."

"Where's Antonio now? Does he live in Port City or is he here on vacation?"

"Funny you should ask. We asked about the son and the embassy stonewalled us. A snooty embassy fart reminded me the ambassador and his family enjoy diplomatic immunity. The embassy would release no personal information, not even the son's whereabouts. And we can't question them without the father's permission."

"And you asked for permission?"

"Do cats have hair?"

"And their response was…?"

"Go pound sand. They used fancy diplomatic words to tell me to take a long walk off a short pier. That's why I told Jenkins to call you."

"Which cell tower did the texts use?" I wrote down the address and the name of the cellphone carrier. "Did you find pictures of the two girls you identified? Dolores Cherry and Morgan Putnam?"

"I'll email them to you."

"Thanks. Anything else to tell me?" I asked.

"The DC cops couldn't come out and say it, but one cop called them 'diplobrats'—that's what DC cops call the children of diplomats who ignore local laws. The mild offenders park illegally or break the speed limit, then tear up their parking citations and speeding tickets. The worst ones commit felonies, even drug smuggling or assault. They had a diplobrat commit murder once. All the cops could do was ask the State Department to declare the perp *persona non grata* and make his country recall the guy."

"Is that the situation here? Human trafficking or drug smuggling?"

"God, I hope not. We don't even know if he lives here, but his phone pings mostly on Port City Beach. If Antonio Crucero is a criminal, which we don't know, our hands are tied."

"But mine aren't."

"Exactamente, amigo. That's why I told Jenkins to call you. We'll keep working names from our end. If anything pops, I'll keep you in the loop."

"I may not keep you in the loop from my end."

"Of course, I need deniability. Next time you talk to Jenkins, tell him you saved my freedom and my career. Hopefully, you can save his daughter too."

Liz Jenkins

Liz sat on the edge of the bed and waited for the john to close the door behind him. Maybe he was the last one for the day. She was tired and sore from servicing a dozen men. She didn't bother to hope her day was over. Hope made no difference. Another stranger would come in the door or else Tommy would. One was bad as the other.

Liz washed in the bathroom before the next john appeared. She didn't bother to dress. Tommy would tell her when the john wanted to play dress-up. She returned to the bedroom and lay on the bed to wait for the next whoever—or *whatever.* It didn't matter, did it?

Some johns opened the door and walked in like they owned the place. The fat ambassador for example. Others knocked as if they needed permission to enter. They pretended this was a date even though she opened the door naked as Venus on the half-shell. Months ago, she told several johns that she was a captive. She asked them to call the police. They laughed, so they knew. Still, it was funny how many johns knocked.

Maybe they sought the illusion of a normal romantic relationship. Liz had lost her illusions long ago.

Benson Broady was her first romance. They had met at David City High School and dated for two years, he the basketball player and she the head cheerleader. She recalled their first clumsy love-making on the blanket behind the grain elevator. Benson was so sweet, so tender, so... romantic. Wasn't that the way love was supposed to be?

Benson enrolled at the University of Nebraska. She planned to follow him the next year. He drove out to visit her on weekends when he came home from Lincoln. They used the blanket behind the grain elevator again and again. She thought the sheltered space was their hideaway. She didn't understand why Benson's visits became less frequent. Then, before Thanksgiving they stopped. Maybe it was the weather cooling as autumn set in. At Christmas, he swore everything was fine between them. He had been busy, but he didn't call. If he came home on a weekend, she didn't know it. Easter weekend, she borrowed her dad's car, drove to David City, and confronted him in his living room. Benson confessed he was dating another girl, a freshman at the university.

That romance had been an illusion. Was it any different than the illusion the johns wanted? She sighed and regarded the door. That awful door that the parade of johns came through.

She never knew which john was the last until Tommy came in. He *always* opened the door without knocking. Of course, he did own the place. He would say her day's work was done, and he would screw her one more time himself. Every day.

She heard the doorknob rotate. No knock.

It was Tommy. "Hey, Angel. You had a good day today. I got compliments from three clients. They said they'd ask for you next time."

He called them *clients,* like they were somebody special. They weren't special to Liz. To her they were an endless drudgery of sweat, body fluids, and sore muscles. When a john complained about her sexual performance, Tommy would beat her. She sighed. At least Tommy wasn't going to beat her this time.

Tommy smirked. He never smiled; he smirked. "You know what I want, Angel." He shoved her back on the bed.

Once it was over, she dragged herself to the bathroom one more time. At least he was the last one for the day.

She stood under the hot water a long time in a vain attempt to scrub away the dirty sensation Tommy left her with. It didn't work. It never did, but she kept trying.

For her thirteenth birthday, Liz's mother gave her a pink flannel nightgown. Her mother died from breast cancer two years later, and Liz wore that nightgown every night. The nightgown let her pretend her mother was close, even though her father became more distant. She washed it so often, it faded almost to white. She packed it first for her trip to Disney World. It was her link to the home she loved before her mother died. Before Daddy changed.

Then she met Tommy. He was nice at first, and he seemed so sophisticated, so cosmopolitan. Tommy gave her a new phone to replace her old one. The old phone was so *last year* he said. They laughed and she threw the old phone into the Atlantic. She abandoned her old life, her old character. He partied with her, gave her drugs and alcohol.

Following a week as her lover, he asked her to have sex with a friend of his. She refused and he hit her. He brought her to this building and made her watch him burn her clothes in the alley behind. "Your past is dead, Angel. This is your future. I'll give you everything you need." He dragged her inside nude and locked her in this room for two days without food. She drank from the lavatory in the bathroom.

When he came back, she was so grateful that she met his demands. Better than starving to death, wasn't it? Now she wasn't so sure.

She returned to the bedroom where she worked and slept. Tommy had burned her nightgown. The only underwear he allowed his Angels was kinky stuff some johns told them to wear. The small chest of drawers overflowed with thong underwear, crotchless panties, pushup bras, and sex toys. The closet held a few normal clothes she wore for meals downstairs. The rest was a nurse's uniform, a maid's uniform, and see-through negligees in red, white, and pink for the johns. None of them felt comfortable for sleeping.

Liz sat on the bed and stared at the door. Tommy always locked it from the outside once he was finished. The bed was warm where she and her kidnapper had lain. She stood. She couldn't sleep yet—not on a bed still warm from the body of the rapist. She snatched tissues from the box on her nightstand, dried her tears, and blew her nose. She had slept nude for eleven months, but she never got used to it. She felt exposed and vulnerable, even when she lifted the covers over her head and made a little tent the way she did when she was a child.

Where is Daddy? Why hasn't he found me? He might be mad at me for leaving, but he's still my father. Did he change cellphone plans and get a different number? Maybe he didn't receive the texts I sent. A week had passed with no action. Her spirits fell further.

If Daddy didn't come soon, she would kill herself. Had she hidden enough pills for an overdose? How many would she need? If she tried to escape and failed, she would be tortured to death. No, it would be escape and rescue, or an overdose. Whatever she did, it must work the first time.

She flopped back on the bed. Daddy had two more weeks to come through for her. Two more weeks and she was through. For good.

Carlos McCrary

I had told Jorge that maybe Antonio Crucero disabled the GPS on his phone because he valued his privacy. In fact, I learned he was the opposite. Crucero was the eternal adolescent type who shared his personal life on social media without hesitation, bragging what a cool guy he was. It's like his whole life was one big "Mommy, watch me dive in the pool." Some people never outgrow that desire to attract attention.

Crucero had accounts on the first three websites I visited. I uncovered all the information the San Cristobal embassy wouldn't share with Jorge.

Crucero lived on Port City Beach in a rented apartment. He called himself Tony Crucero— very American. I got both license plate numbers from pictures of his Glacier Silver Metallic BMW sedan and his Torch Red Corvette convertible. Diplomatic plates on both—easier to park in loading zones and by fire hydrants. He posted the names and pictures of exclusive bars and nightclubs he frequented. More "Mommy, watch me." He was proud of the view from his waterfront apartment's balcony. He uploaded selfies of him with different beautiful women, his black hair blowing in the wind when it wasn't in a ponytail. The women appeared six feet tall; Crucero was five-foot-six. Diplobrat rated a three, maybe a four. The women were nines and tens. What did they see in him? The jerk needed more than money. Was it drugs? Diplomats had an easy time bringing drugs into the country. Or were these women professional escorts?

I filed that question away for future research.

Using the backgrounds and angles in the photos, I figured out where his apartment was and the approximate floor he lived on.

Saturday afternoon late, I staked out his building and waited for his Corvette or BMW.

Another gorgeous South Florida sunset lit the sky over the Everglades as Crucero's Corvette squealed down the garage ramp and headed south on Ocean Drive. The Corvette was fitted with very loud mufflers. It sounded like I was following a phalanx of Harley-Davidsons.

Crucero first stopped at the Pelican Roost, a fashionable thatched-roofed restaurant on an island in Seeti Bay, and a favorite on his Facebook page. He dropped his Corvette with the valet. Hopefully, I could stick a GPS tracker under his car, but if I failed, I needed my white Dodge Grand Caravan accessible to follow him when he left. I found a spot in the self-parking lot fifty yards from the rustic plank steps of the restaurant entrance. I backed in for a fast exit.

The Corvette was parked too close to the valets for me to stick the GPS tracker. Life is what happens to you after you make other plans.

I told the restaurant host that I was the first to arrive of a party of four. No, we didn't have a reservation. Yes, I realized it was Saturday night. Yes, we would wait an hour-and-a-half for a table. The host jotted down the fictitious name I gave her. "To signal your table is ready, Mr. Washington, this pager will vibrate and the red lights will flash like this." She tested the pager and handed it to me. "You can wait in the bar for your party."

The Pelican Roost seats all customers in the bar long enough to order a drink before giving them a table. Sure enough, Crucero slouched over a stool at the Tiki Bar, smack under a ceiling fan. His hair was longer than on his social media page. He was fatter in person than on the internet, maybe because he was sitting down. How did he manage to fit into a Corvette? His XXXL Hawaiian shirt made a vain attempt to disguise his bulk. He left three buttons open in the tropical heat. Three gold chains hung halfway down a chest that could double for a bearskin rug. He wore two rings on each hand. He had no visible tattoos. Not surprising, since his arms and chest were so hairy a tattoo would be invisible in the fur. He ordered a Coco Loco with a paper umbrella and a bougainvillea flower waving in the top. South Florida chic. The flower swayed in the breeze.

Crucero glanced at his heavyweight gold Rolex and scanned the crowded bar. Probably had an 8:30 reservation and his date was late.

Snagging a corner table, I ordered a club soda with a twist. Whoopee, it was party time for the hard-working private eye. The Pelican Roost was famous for its banana daiquiris. Too bad I was on duty.

As I sampled my yummy club soda, a six-foot blonde piece of arm candy walked into the bar wearing tropical sandals and a gold outfit. The neckline plunged to her waist and revealed the best cleavage money could buy. Miss Cleavage parted the crowd proudly with her chest as she strutted over to Crucero and presented her cheek to be kissed. She whispered in his ear and rubbed her assets on his arm. From the lack of tan lines on her chest and back, I surmised that she sunbathed nude, or at least topless. She perched on the barstool next to him, and Crucero grinned and squeezed her behind. Miss Cleavage ordered a white wine. Ten minutes later, they took a bayside table with a skyline view. Reservation or not, this guy had clout. Of course, he slipped the woman who seated him a fifty-dollar bill.

I surveilled Crucero and Miss Cleavage for an hour from the bar. The ceiling fan stirred the night air without conviction. It was so humid that I could work up a sweat hoisting my drink.

My pager buzzed and flashed. Leaning toward a party of four at the next table, I said. "Excuse me, my party hasn't arrived. Would you prefer a table now?"

They would.

We swapped pagers. "Tell them you're the George Washington party. Enjoy."

After another hour, I trailed Crucero and Miss Cleavage to an exclusive private nightclub with a velvet rope and a tuxedo-wearing bouncer at the entrance. Their parking lot was not well-guarded like the Pelican Roost's. After attaching the GPS tracker to the Corvette, I waited in my minivan. At

2:30 a.m. the couple staggered to his car. Crucero slipped his hand down the front of Miss Cleavage's dress as he helped her into the passenger seat, and she stroked his private parts through his slacks as he closed her door. Driving home, he weaved from lane to lane and narrowly missed causing two collisions.

THREE

My condo was a mile from Crucero's place. I hired an off-duty cop, Robby Gorski, to surveil Crucero's parking garage in case he used the BMW, but I figured he would use the Corvette again. Miss Cleavage seemed more Corvette than BMW. I monitored the GPS tracker from home. The Corvette moved shortly after noon on Sunday. Dismissing Robby with a reminder to send me a bill, I headed down to my Caravan.

Miss Cleavage must have arrived at the Pelican Roost in a taxi or Uber, because Crucero didn't drive her to retrieve her car. I caught the Corvette and kept it in sight. He and Miss Cleavage crossed the Beachline Causeway, top down in the South Florida sunshine. Crucero didn't speed. Maybe Miss Cleavage was reluctant to mess up her hair with the top down. He wore his hair in a ponytail, so he didn't worry about the wind. They drove to Coconut Grove. After recording Miss Cleavage's trendy address, I abandoned Crucero and his arm candy to enjoy their afternoon delight. What did a cover girl dish see in a short, fat blob?

Next, I drove to Crucero's apartment. He would be occupied for at least an hour while he climbed the Twin Peaks in Miss Cleavage State Park. From there it was an hour's trip to his apartment. I would monitor the Corvette's movements with the tracker app on my smartphone. Technology makes a PI's life easier when you ignore inconvenient laws about respecting people's privacy.

Crucero's apartment was in a rental high-rise, not a condo. The security was limited to a few cameras. Parking my Caravan in the loading zone, I removed a flower arrangement I had bought at Walmart and carried it to the reception desk. I held the bouquet high to obscure my face, but I could see the house phone. "Flowers for Tony Crucero."

"Just a moment." The receptionist grabbed a house phone and punched Crucero's apartment number.

Bingo. Apartment 1212.

He hung up. "Mr. Crucero doesn't answer. You wanna leave the flowers? I'll make sure he gets them."

"Sure." I set the flowers on the counter. "How about my tip?"

The guy shrugged. "You can come back later, or you can leave them. Your choice."

I left the bouquet. Let the poor schlub collect the tip from Crucero. *The jerk will stiff him anyway,* I thought.

After driving the Caravan back home, I switched to the sedan I had rented the previous day. Returning to Crucero's high-rise, I piggy-backed under the garage gate on the bumper of a resident's car and spiraled my way to the top floor and into an unassigned space.

I hiked down the ramps three floors until I located Crucero's BMW. After attaching another tracker to it, I stood behind a pillar to watch the keypad door lock. Another resident's car squealed up the ramp and parked. A woman clutched a Macy's bag and walked to the door. The door was too far away to make out the numbers, but I memorized her hand movements as she punched four digits on the pad. Top left, lower right, lower left, ending with a tap on the right.

Three possible combinations. The second one worked. The World's Greatest Private Eye on the job. I saved the code in my phone for future use. Most of these building managers wait a year or more before they change codes. Some of them *never* change codes. I never know whether another case—or this one—will bring me to these same apartments again.

Elevators always have security cameras, so I climbed the fire stairs to Crucero's floor. My loose jacket concealed my pistol in case I encountered an apartment resident. No point making myself conspicuous. My mouth was dry as I monitored the Corvette's GPS tracker again. Pre-action jitters, routine before a mission, even a simple B&E. Crucero was in Coconut Grove knocking boots with Miss Cleavage, having way more fun than I was. The stair door opened to the elevator lobby. It was as empty as the space behind the moon.

There were five apartments on the floor. A discreet brass plaque with an ornate coat of arms was mounted on his door, saying *La Republica de San Cristobal.* Some people display a college football banner; Crucero displayed his birthplace's coat of arms.

I photographed the plaque to show Wilbur Jenkins. Might make him feel better to know I was making progress.

It took me two minutes to pick the lock. My heart rate climbed a little higher. The last tumbler clicked and I twisted the knob.

As I stepped inside, the alarm system beeped. *Damn. I knew this was going too well.* The alarm would go off in forty-five seconds. The keypad was beside the door. I punched the disarm button. *Enter code* flashed on the screen. It's incredible how many people use *1-2-3-4* for their alarm code. If that failed, I had forty seconds to try Crucero's birth year, the last four digits of his cellphone, his birthday in both day/month and month/day format, both of which I learned on his social media, then the apartment number.

If those failed, I would run like a scalded dog.

"Who the hell are you?" A bulky man in a gray suit and striped tie came from further inside the apartment. *Bodyguard* was written all over him, plain as if it were tattooed on his forehead. Dark skin, black eyes, and beaked nose. Black hair parted in the middle and drawn tight over his ears. Probably had a ponytail at the base of his neck, but I couldn't tell from this angle. His features appeared chiseled from limestone, an Indian from southern Mexico or Central America. The Colt M1911A1 muzzle he leveled at me measured .45 inches in diameter. Pointed between my eyes, it seemed as black as a cavern and as big as a cannon.

A Special Forces instructor once told me, "When the balloon goes up, if you stop to blink twice, you might be dead. You may have less than a second to make a life-or-death decision."

My own gun was concealed beneath my jacket. If I tried to draw it, that .45 slug would shred a hole in me big enough to throw a baseball through. If I didn't reach for my gun, he might kill me anyway. Time for Plan C.

Lifting my hands to waist height, I replied in rapid Spanish. "I'm the maintenance man. Mr. Crucero reported his ice maker was broken."

Striped Tie responded in Spanish. "Where's your tool box?" He lowered the .45. Nobody fears the maintenance man.

"In the hall," I answered in Spanish. "I'll get it." Walking toward the hall, I seized a brass equestrian sculpture from the ornamental table beside the door. I hurled it at the gunman's head and dived out the door. He fired two shots that slammed into the wall and echoed in the marble-floored elevator lobby. The brass horse and rider must have hit him, because he didn't chase me when I sprinted to the fire stairs. Either that or he paused to enter the alarm code. I raced down five flights of stairs to the rental car.

Catching my breath, I let my heart slow to normal before I drove back to my own parking garage. I switched the fake license plates for the real ones. On the way to the airport to return the car, I tossed the baseball hat, surgical gloves, and fake eyeglasses into a dumpster behind a grocery store. The security cameras wouldn't help if Crucero reported the break-in, but I'd bet he wouldn't involve the cops.

How many solid citizens post an armed guard in their apartment? What was Striped Tie guarding that was so valuable? Jorge mentioned that some diplomats smuggled drugs. One thing for sure, Crucero was into something dangerous.

"Snoop, you got out of the hospital less than a month ago. You sure you're ready to work?" The previous month, my friend and mentor, Raymond Snopolski, aka Snoop, was shot multiple times attempting to prevent the kidnapping of our client. He had killed two of the four kidnappers before they gunned him down. I felt it was my fault that he had almost died.

"Doc Patrick approved me for light duty, bud." He spread a Port City map across my desk, then winced. "I gotta remember not to stretch my arms out for another two weeks." In addition to three shots to the abdomen and a grazing head wound, Snoop caught one in the shoulder.

"What are you working on?"

"I went online for cell tower locations near the tower that handled Liz's texts. I marked them here, here, here, and so forth." He leaned over the map. "This red circle marks the tower the texts came from. These X's mark other towers in range of the phone. From that, I determined the farthest distance from the first tower that Liz was when she sent the texts. That leaves this area which I highlighted." Snoop indicated a yellow line along three sides of a rectangle butted up to Seeti Bay. The bay shore marked the fourth side.

Snoop tapped the map. "She might be as far south as South 15th Street East and West over to the bay. She could be as far west as the East Carolina & Florida Railroad tracks. That's eight miles from the bay."

He drew a line with his finger. "She might be as far north as 75th Street, either NW or NE, from the tracks to the bay. That's six miles north of SW and SE 15th Street. That target area covers forty-eight square miles, bud."

"Yeah. And with 90 blocks between the north and south boundaries..." I lapsed into silence.

"And each street is eight miles long. That's, uh, 72 miles of east-west streets to search."

My stomach churned like I had eaten bad oysters. "You dropped a digit. It's 720 miles of east-west streets."

"Crap," Snoop said. "How many miles of north-south do we need to search?"

"About 480. The Seeti River cuts across that area, and parks, schools, canals, and such have no streets. That leaves a thousand miles or more of streets in the target area. Most of that thousand has *two lanes of traffic and parking on both sides.*"

I tilted my chair back. "I hoped Crucero would visit Liz again, but after he returned from Miss Cleavage's house yesterday afternoon, he drove to PCIA. After trailing the Corvette to long-term parking, I saw him buy a ticket on a red-eye to San Cristobal. He'll be gone a few days."

"We don't know that he's a regular at the house where they have Liz," said Snoop. "What if that was the only time Crucero ever visited the place?"

"He's still a lead. Once he comes back to Port City Beach, I'll ask him where he was on the night in question. I'll keep monitoring the GPS tracker anyway. Except for that cell tower location, Crucero's our best lead."

"Where's his BMW?" asked Snoop.

"He drove the Corvette to the airport yesterday. He left the BMW at home."

"Did you check it today?"

"No, he's still out of town."

"Humor me, bud. Check it."

Waking my tablet, I punched up the tracker app. "The BMW's rolling. It's gotta be the gunman with the striped tie who shot at me. I'll set someone on his tail. Get more coffee and I'll make a call."

Frank Bennett, another Port City cop I hired as an occasional operative answered my call. I gave him the login for the BMW's tracker app. By the time I explained the assignment, Snoop returned with coffee and a bonus.

"Where'd you get the sticky bun?"

"There was half a box in the kitchen. A civic-minded tenant was in the mood to share. Where were we?"

"Frank Bennett's on his way to tail the BMW."

"So, you and I comb a thousand miles of streets the hard way," Snoop said. "What would a girl from rural Nebraska consider a 'busy' street? 'Busy' is a worthless description. It doesn't eliminate any streets. There's no way to watch both sides of a street and travel 30 miles per hour while searching for a three-story house. That's two weeks' work."

"We can narrow the field. A phone in range of more than one tower will use the tower with the strongest signal, unless that tower is overloaded with calls."

"Four million people live in Atlantic County, bud. Cell towers are always congested. That's why I marked this whole area."

"But she sent the texts between two and three o'clock in the morning. So even though the phone was in range of other towers, the nearest tower had the strongest signal. At two a.m. it wouldn't be congested."

I drew another line halfway between the tower Liz used and each of the other towers. "This area is one-fourth the size of the maximum range." I tapped the red circle on the map. "We start there tomorrow and work our way outward."

Even though I had cut the target area by 75 percent, it was still 300 linear miles. Snoop drove, while I studied both sides of the road. Four eyes are better than two.

The morning sky was cloudless when we arrived at the base of the tower. The clouds would gather that afternoon and dump their rain. South Florida meteorologists recycle the same forecast for five straight months: high in the mid-90s, low around 80, 60 percent chance of rain in the afternoon with isolated thunderstorms. Yada, yada, yada from May to October every year. Except for the occasional hurricanes. Hey, no place is perfect, but South Florida comes close.

The tower stood at the rear of the parking lot of an appliance chain distribution center on NW 69th Street. The steel tower rose a hundred feet with two triangular antenna arrays stacked on top that reminded me of three-cornered hats.

Staring up at the tower, I imagined what a young woman—a girl actually—a year out of high school might feel while she sent those texts. A week had passed with no further word from her. Was she worried her message had not gotten through?

I shook my head. Such thoughts wasted time, energy, and emotion.

NW 69th Street is two lanes bordered by cyclone fences on either side. To the west, the street ends at a drainage canal. To the east, its two lanes dwindled to the vanishing point.

"Drive east until we come to a wider street." It was NW 23rd Avenue. "This street's wide enough. Hang a right." The pavement had no center stripe or lane markings, but it was wide enough for two lanes of sparse traffic to flow between the cars which had parked on both sides. Most houses in the blue-collar residential neighborhood featured waist-high cyclone fences in front and bars on the windows and doors. Ninety percent were one story; the others were two. None were three stories. Two miles later, we reached the line halfway to the next cell tower. "Drive three more blocks, then pull over and I'll mark the map."

We curved east on NW 39th Street. "Skip 22nd Avenue. It's two lanes wide. No parking on it."

We reached NW 21st. "Turn here." We rolled north on 21st Avenue, past 69th Street and continued until we hit a high school campus. After I marked the map, we continued one block east and headed south down 20th Avenue. We swept back and forth like plowing a vast field of houses and buildings, sweeping our gaze from one side of the street to another.

Two lanes of traffic and parking on both sides. Something danced in the back of my mind, a moth around a flame that I couldn't nail down. We skipped the two-lane and six-lane streets. We cruised every commercial street and every block filled with apartments. Liz said she was in a three-story house, but it might be a commercial building or a gentrified and converted warehouse loft.

We paused at four o'clock—the rain got so heavy we couldn't see. It hung on for two hours without slacking and we called it a day. Snoop needed rest and I wanted to research Google Street View to plan tomorrow's search.

The next day echoed the first but I told myself every street we eliminated brought us closer to the right house. Ever the optimist.

Arriving at the modest motel where Wilbur Jenkins was staying, I punched up the GPS tracker before I went to meet him. Crucero's Corvette was still at the airport.

"Come in, Chuck," Jenkins said. "How do things stand on the hunt for Liz?"

Lifting my phone, I showed him the picture of the plaque on Tony Crucero's apartment door. "Other than finding where he lives, I don't have much to report. Heavy rain stopped us early again. You hungry?"

We headed to a Cuban restaurant on Port City Beach. "Ever eat Cuban food?"

"Nope," Jenkins said, sipping a *Dos Equis*. "This here's not Cuban beer, is it?"

"It's Mexican. We don't have Cuban beer in the country."

"I drank real German beer once. Me and Mary Ann took Lizzie to Disney World for a week to celebrate her thirteenth birthday. We ate German food at Epcot. Real good. So was the beer." His gaze pointed over my shoulder, but I don't think he was aware of anything in the room. "That trip was the first time Lizzie had traveled out of Nebraska. First airplane trip. First time to stay in a hotel. Lots of first times there." He stared at the dark bottle of his *Dos Equis*.

His eyes filled with tears, and I looked away.

I ordered a selection of Cuban dishes to give him an abbreviated education in Cuban cuisine.

The server left our table. "Liz signed the texts *Binky*. What does that mean?"

"When she was little, Liz dragged this old blanket around until she was four. She called it Binky, so that was my nickname for her. There was a ton of TV hype at home about her disappearance. The week before I come down here was the anniversary of her going missing. The TV station in Omaha, they did something on the news about her still being gone, and lots of people contacted me claiming to be her. But none of them knew about her being called Binky, so I knew they was frauds."

"Do you receive many crank calls?"

"Emails, letters, and one greeting card, believe it or not. A psychic even offered to 'probe the aura' in Lizzie's bedroom." He gestured air quotes. "She said it was a bargain for a thousand dollars." He shook his head. "You wouldn't believe the nuts who contact me."

I made a note to search the Omaha news stories online. One of them might mention something that Jenkins had forgotten to tell me.

The first dish arrived, and he gestured at his surroundings with the *Dos Equis*. "This here's a real cultural experience for me. Thanks. Maybe tomorrow night we can try French food."

"Tomorrow I have a date, but I can recommend some restaurants near your hotel."

"You got a picture of your girlfriend?"

I showed him a photo on my phone. "Miyoki Takashi. I call her Miyo."

"Real pretty girl. Japanese?"

"Japanese-American. Both her parents were born in Japan. She was born in Miami. She's as American than I am. My mother was born in Mexico and I have dual citizenship."

"Are you serious about her?"

"Very serious. At least on my side."

"Do you love her?"

The moment he asked the question, I knew the truth. "Yes. Yes, I do love her."

"You told her yet?"

"No," I said, wondering why I hadn't. Was the big, strong private eye afraid of getting his feelings hurt?

Will laid a callused hand on my arm. "Take my advice, son. Tell the people you love that you love them. You never know when they'll be gone." His eyes glistened as he spoke.

"Thanks for the advice, Will."

"Pardon me for getting serious. This is merely a sociable dinner." He returned my phone.

"Don't mention it."

He slid a picture from his wallet and handed it to me. "You showed me your gal; I'll show you mine. That's Mary Ann. Only girl I ever dated. Only girl I ever loved."

The photo could have been of his daughter. "Liz got her mother's looks."

Will took the picture back and stared at it. "After Mary Ann passed, every time I seen Liz, it almost broke my heart. She's the image of my Mary Ann—her voice, the way she walks—everything. I would look at Lizzie and remember my Mary Ann. Then I would remember that she was gone forever and I'd be sad."

He stuck the picture in his wallet. "Things were not good between me and Liz when she disappeared. The preacher, he said I was avoiding Liz because she made me sad about losing Mary Ann. Maybe that drove a wedge between us. I get on my knees every night and ask the good Lord for one more chance to hug my Lizzie and beg her forgiveness."

My grandpa Magnus McCrary says, *Everybody has a story to tell. Often, the best thing to do is let them tell it.* Will's story was hard to hear, but he needed to tell it and I was available—Chuck McCrary, Private Shrink. Maybe I would add *Good Listener* to the list of services on my website.

We finished dinner, and I ordered Cuban coffee for two. "My colleague Snoop Snopolski and I spent the last two days sweeping the area near the cell tower. Nothing so far."

"I figured you ain't discovered no three-story house; you woulda told me straight off."

"Right, but we've eliminated 200 miles of streets where Liz *is not.* So we must be closer to where she *is.*"

"How much longer?"

"You don't cut down a tree with the first stroke of the ax. You chop until the tree falls."

He nodded. "Keep chopping, Chuck."

FOUR

Miyoki Takashi

The natural light from the clerestory windows in Miyo's penthouse faded with the afternoon showers. She shoved her easels into one corner and tidied up the workbench at the end of the great room.

She cleaned her brushes in the utility room sink and threw her clothes into the washing machine. Studying her body in the mirror on the door for stray paint smudges, she spotted a patch of yellow on her left elbow and another of ocher on her chin. They surrendered to the special linseed oil soap. Not bad for an entire day of painting.

After showering, she spritzed perfume between her breasts and on her abdomen. Chuck was coming over tonight. *These teal panties will show through the white silk shorts. Chuck will enjoy the preview of coming attractions.* Smiling to herself, she selected a filmy teal bra and a yellow silk shell—another preview for Chuck.

Miyo had begun cooking dinner when the doorbell rang. She smiled when she heard the key scrape in the lock. Chuck used his key, but he always rang her bell, saying he didn't want to startle her by entering unannounced. She had never met a man like him.

She reached the entry as the door swung open. "How was your day, big guy?"

"Another boring day of cruising back and forth like a street sweeper."

He held up a bottle of wine and pecked her on the cheek. The wine was typical; the peck was not.

"Pinot Grigio will go great with the fish tacos. I'll chill it in the freezer until we eat." She snatched the wine. "The rain's stopped. We can eat on the balcony and enjoy the sunset."

Chuck complimented the dinner and agreed the sunset was spectacular, but Miyo knew he wasn't feeling it. "How's the hunt for Liz Jenkins going?"

"We must be closer. We've covered over 300 miles where she isn't."

"Always the optimist." Miyo smiled and tasted her wine.

Chuck echoed her smile but it held little humor. "Liz could be a fraternal twin of my cousin Emily. The two are the same age."

"You never mentioned a Cousin Emily."

"I didn't?"

"No." Miyo remembered everything she and Chuck had talked about from the day they met. Another way Chuck was different from other men she had dated.

He twirled his wine glass in his fingers. He often did that while he thought. He wasn't even aware of the habit. Why did she notice so many little things about this man?

Chuck's brow creased. "Emily is a painful topic."

She ran her fingers across his forehead, smoothing the lines. "I don't understand."

He twirled his glass again. "Will Jenkins got some things off his chest last night, and it made him feel better. I have avoided the subject of Emily for three years and that hasn't helped."

Miyo held Chuck's hand. "Will it help if you tell me?"

He gave her an appreciative smile. "Maybe."

"Go ahead."

"The last time I saw Emily was the Christmas she was sixteen. I had recently made detective with the PCPD. Emily bought an original 1936 Dick Tracy Sunday comic on eBay. She framed it and gave it to me for

Christmas. Every time I walk into my office at home, I see it on the wall and think of her."

"I wondered about that comic strip. Emily sounds like a thoughtful young woman."

"Yes, she was."

Something about the way he said that made her breath catch. "Was?"

"Emily went missing three years ago."

"What happened to her?"

"We don't know. She didn't come home from school one day. By ten o'clock that night, my Aunt Carrie and Uncle Frank were frantic. They had called all her friends and no one had seen her since school let out. The Austin police found her car in the school parking lot. It was locked. She never made it that far."

He picked up his wine glass again and stared at it without seeing it. Miyo knew his mind was far away.

"I was so proud of my shiny new detective's shield that I asked for a week's vacation to go to Austin to find Emily. An arrogant know-it-all full of piss and vinegar who thought he could do a better job than the Austin cops."

He stared at his wine.

Miyo knew there was more, so she waited.

"I retraced every step the cops took. I re-interviewed her friends. I examined the crime scene photos—really just a crime lab work-up on her car. The only fingerprints were those of Emily and her friends."

He twirled his wine glass again.

"Like I said: She never made it to the car."

His eyes were moist. "I was no help at all. None. We never got a whiff of a clue to Emily's fate—*poof* like a cloud of smoke."

Miyo squeezed his hand.

"Is that why this thing has you tied in knots? Liz reminds you of Emily?"

Chuck sighed. "Right after I opened McCrary Investigations, an Illinois couple hired me to locate their teenaged daughter. It was an easy case—I pinged her cellphone and flashed her picture at teen hangouts near the cell towers until someone recognized her. But this case..." He lapsed into silence.

"What about this case?"

"This case gives me a chance to maybe *redeem* myself a little for not finding Emily."

Miyo brushed her hand across his cheek. "You did your best then, and you're doing your best now. No one can ask for more."

He held her hand and kissed the palm while a single tear brushed his cheek.

"My best wasn't good enough to find Emily. What if it's not good enough to find Liz either?"

That was so like Chuck, holding himself to impossible standards. "Of course, your best is good enough. You're the world's greatest detective, aren't you?"

She held up the Pinot Grigio bottle. "The wine is gone. Dr. Takashi prescribes a pitcher of Margaritas for you. Why don't you spend the night so you won't need to drive home?"

Chuck sat there, staring into the sunset. She didn't know what he was thinking, but he looked as if he had seen a ghost. "Chuck? Honey, did you hear me?"

"I have to go. You stay here; enjoy the sunset."

Carlos McCrary

I slid into the Avanti and slammed the door. I had to get out of there before I lost it.

What if Miyo was wrong? What if my best wasn't good enough? What if I couldn't find Liz the way that I couldn't find Emily, until it was too late?

Miyoki Takashi

Chuck called the next evening to apologize for his abrupt exit. "I'm embarrassed that my emotions got the better of me last night. Can I make it up to you, say, with that pitcher of Margaritas you suggested?"

"Do you promise never to run out on me again?"

Miyo couldn't believe she had said that. She had never cared before when a boyfriend pulled a lame ass stunt like that. She might never speak to him again, but she wouldn't have cared either.

"It's a deal," he said. "See you in a few."

The doorbell rang before she could hang up. Then the familiar sound of his key in the lock.

Five minutes later, Chuck handed her a Margarita. "The doctor prescribes a big gulp."

Amused by the switch in roles, she curled away to hide her smile. She should be furious but, to her surprise, she wasn't.

Chuck swallowed a long swig of his drink.

"Please, Miyo, let's sit on the couch. Will Jenkins gave me some advice at dinner the other night."

"Oh?"

Chuck set down his Margarita and held Miyo's hand. "He said I should tell the people I love that I love them, because you never know when they'll be gone."

Miyo knew what Chuck was about to do, and she was as powerless to stop him as an oncoming train.

"This is kind of sudden, sweety, but you deserve to know; I love you."

Other men had avowed their love. Miyo never treated them—or herself —seriously, but her feelings for Chuck were new, different. How was she supposed to handle his revelation? She wasn't even sure how she felt about him or their relationship. "What am I supposed to do now?"

"If it's any comfort, I don't expect you to say 'I love you' back. I didn't realize I loved you until Will Jenkins asked me. I showed him your picture and he asked if I loved you. If you only 'like' me," he made air quotes, "that's okay."

She kissed him. "I've had so many love *affairs* that I might not recognize real love unless it grabs me by the ears and shouts, 'Hey, it's me. I'm the real thing.'"

"You don't need to keep reminding me."

"Sorry. I'm not proud of it, but I'm not ashamed either."

"You said you might not know the real thing when you found it."

"It's just... maybe I don't understand the difference between love and lust."

"You're an artist. When you saw Michelangelo's *David* for the first time, how did that affect you? Love or lust?"

Miyo didn't respond for a second. She closed her eyes and smiled. "I went to Firenze and *experienced* that magnificent sculpture of David. I wondered how I would react if David came to life. How would it feel to caress that magnificent body? Whew, now that I recall it, I'm getting warm." She opened her eyes. "I guess that's lust."

"Was that what attracted you to me?"

"You were a *yes-ma'am-just-the-facts-ma'am* super-professional PI standing at my door. I thought the same thing about you that I did about the David statue except you were already alive, but fully clothed. I wondered what it would feel like to ring your chimes until you couldn't stand upright."

Chuck smirked. "In other words, you objectified David and me as sex objects."

That was a new thought. "We women complain when men treat us like sex objects."

He pointed his index finger in the air. "Bingo. Give that lady the prize."

"You're different from other men I've dated."

"Well, I am the world's greatest private investigator."

Miyo smiled. "Besides that. I get tired of every man I date. Often in a few days; occasionally the affair lasts a few weeks. One guy lasted three months."

"We've dated for five months. Are you getting tired of me?"

Miyo considered the question, then grinned. "I'm not tired of you at all. How about that? Of all the men I have known, you're not boring."

"That's high praise. That could be the slogan on my business cards. *Carlos McCrary: He's not boring.*"

Liz Jenkins

Liz stepped from the shower. She had scrubbed every trace of Tommy from her body, yet in her mind she smelled his breath, his sweat, even his semen.

43

She brushed her teeth twice, clenching her toothbrush with her fist. She was ready to explode at Tommy like a human time bomb.

She inventoried her assets: Desire to live free. That was it. Her liabilities were obvious: She had no weapons; Tommy outweighed her by fifty pounds; and she didn't know the first thing about fighting. Tommy wasn't her only captor either.

Tommy encouraged his angels to exercise. "Clients prefer a well-toned ass."

Following Evelyn's murder, Liz piled more weights on the Nautilus equipment the brothel provided. She grew stronger. In the last three weeks, she had worked more definition into the muscles of her arms and legs. She increased the speed and length of her treadmill runs. When she did get out the door, Tommy would never catch her. Her spirits rose along with the weights and distance she could handle. Was that an asset?

She knew her room was on the third floor even though she couldn't see out the frosted windows, and she recognized the outline of bars outside the translucent, wire-reinforced glass. Over the months of her captivity, she occasionally glimpsed the outside world through an unfrosted window on the second floor. Those windows had bars too.

She hoisted the corner of the mattress and counted the pills. She had enough for her last-ditch, end-of-all-hope final exit.

Liz had smoked a little weed in Butler County, but she had never seen heroin or cocaine until she got to Fort Lauderdale. She knew what Oxycodone and other drugs were from the television news her father watched every night during dinner. Anything to avoid talking to her. When she started a conversation, he would say, "Wait until the commercial." Following dinner, he would send her off to do homework.

Before her mother died, Liz and her parents talked at the dinner table every night. Her mother wouldn't let anyone bring a cellphone to the table. "This is one time of day we act like a family," her mother always said, "Let's not spoil it." She missed her mother so much, she felt that her heart had shriveled to the size of a walnut. Maybe a peanut.

After Mom died, Daddy avoided her. They went to church on Sunday but ate with other church folks at the Southside Cafe following the service.

Daddy talked to the other parishioners instead of her. Would Daddy try to find her? Did he even care that she was gone?

Carlos McCrary

It felt like I was pushing a lawn mower back and forth on the world's largest golf course. Two more days of marking the map. Two more days of dwindling hope and rising frustration. At least the afternoon rain was light enough that we worked late. Two more days spent wondering what was happening to Elizabeth Marie Jenkins while I was digging a ditch with a salad fork.

Two more evenings of being lousy company for Miyo. Two more days of telling a helpless father we had not located the three-story house.

The dashboard clock agreed there was not enough daylight to comb another section today. "It's seven o'clock, Snoop. That's enough for one day." I marked the map. A small sliver remained to scour. "We'll find it for sure tomorrow."

But we didn't. And the Corvette was still at the airport.

But the BMW was on the move. Of course, it had to be the gunman with the striped tie. Striped Tie worked for Crucero and he used his boss's car for the boss's business. But what business was Crucero in?

As I marked off the last street in the target area my attitude felt lower than a crab's basement. "We missed something. Let's eat lunch, Snoop. Maybe food and caffeine will stoke our brain cells."

My phone located the nearest Cuban restaurant. I displayed the screen to Snoop.

He smiled. *"El Unicornio.* My partner and I ate there when we patrolled this neighborhood twenty years ago. They made great milkshakes."

"You have lived in South Florida long enough to know that they're called *batidos. "*

"Maybe you could teach me the Spanish word for *smart ass.*"

Five minutes later he paused in the eastbound lane, turn indicator flashing, waiting to curve left to park. A line of westbound cars paraded past, blocking our way. Snoop waited for a break in the traffic. A pickup truck behind us yanked onto the unpaved shoulder and bounced past, kicking up dust from the sparsely-grassed area as it jostled across the uneven ground.

The truck bumped onto the pavement and sped away, barely missing a car parked on the unpaved area between the street and the sidewalk. *Two lanes of traffic and parking on both sides.* The something flitting across my mind jumped into focus.

Two lanes of traffic and parking on both sides. "Smack my head and call me Slappy. I'm an idiot."

"My shoulder's too sore to smack your head, Slappy." There was a break in the oncoming traffic and Snoop slipped into the lot and parked. He pocketed the key fob. "Okay, Slappy, why are you an idiot?"

"Two lanes of traffic and parking on both sides," I answered.

"Yeah, that's what the text said."

"She didn't say four lanes of *pavement.* She said two lanes of *traffic* and parking on both sides. I assumed that meant four lanes of pavement so the parking would be on the street instead of the shoulder. But analyze this street." I gestured to the street behind us. "It's a two-lane street with cars parked on both sides on the unpaved shoulders."

"Holy crap, Slappy. We skipped the two-lane streets."

"Liz's three-story house must be on a two-lane street."

"Can we eat lunch first? This place was my favorite years ago."

After wolfing down a plate of *pulpeta,* Cuban meatloaf, and *yuca,* I felt better, until I reviewed the tracker on the BMW. It had travelled all over Atlantic County from the Broward County border to the Miami-Dade County line in the south. What was Striped Tie doing?

Following another six hours of scouring two-lane streets, my head swam. Still, we had knocked out half of the two-lane streets. Tomorrow we would locate the three-story house, for sure.

For sure, right?

Snoop bumped into the lot and killed the engine. Lunch the previous day was so good we decided to eat dinner at *El Unicornio.* "That's the last of the two-lane streets."

The late afternoon sun streamed through the driver's side window and lit the map in my lap, taunting me. The colored highlights streaked the entire center of the map, spotlighting the brutal evidence of failure—*my* failure. "We are still missing something, Snoop."

"Well, duh, Sherlock."

"We covered every four-lane and two-lane street in the area. There is not a single three-story house. Not one. What are we missing, Snoop?"

"I'll bring the transcripts of the texts with us. Let's think again while we eat."

After we ordered, I studied the three texts. *"Four other girls held too, maybe more.* This operation has at least five girls. Let's say there's five. How many customers a day would come to the house?"

Snoop drank a beer; I was designated driver. "They need five or six customers per girl per day to cover their costs. Say, twenty-five to forty johns. But three stories—that's a mess of square footage. They have room for a bunch of women. There's gotta be at least twenty or thirty strange cars coming and going every day."

I dunked a strip of garlic bread in picante sauce. "If the house were in a residential neighborhood, neighbors would notice."

"I have a neighbor like that."

"Brothels operate well past midnight. The neighbors would complain. Jorge hasn't received any prostitution complaints for brothels in that area in the last year. So, the house must be in a commercial neighborhood with traffic at all hours."

"And it has a parking lot."

I recited the next clue. *"Held in house with three stories.* Since Liz is a captive, Tommy wouldn't let her wander around that house. She might jump out a window, so she's on the second or third floor, probably the third."

Snoop glanced up as the server arrived with a food tray. "The picadillo is mine." He waited until the server finished. "If I were Liz, I would jump from the second floor."

47

"She said *30 feet wide 80 feet deep.* Thirty feet is a normal width for a house, but eighty feet deep and three stories? That's a huge house."

"Maybe it's a converted commercial structure, bud."

"Also, we assumed the house was detached. It could be a commercial structure. Maybe in a commercial or industrial strip, or attached to a shorter building, maybe retail, on one side."

"But it doesn't have to be attached."

"No, of course not." I recited from the transcript. *"On busy street with two lanes of traffic and parking on both sides.* We covered that. *Sex slaves.* My stomach churns like a cement mixer every time I think about those girls."

Snoop reached a hand toward my forearm but stopped short. "Rule Three, bud. *Never get personally involved in a case.*"

"My cousin Emily is—or would be—Liz's age. In my mind, I see Aunt Carrie and Uncle Frank's faces whenever I call Will Jenkins to report our progress, or lack of it. I imagine how my aunt and uncle would feel if it were Emily in that brothel, y'know?"

We ate in silence for a minute.

I consulted the transcript again. *"Three gangsters. Scruffy, black, skinny, fifty. Vince, white, medium, forty. One big bald guy no name.* Three bad guys plus Tommy that we know of."

"She didn't describe the bald man's race like she did the others. Maybe he's mixed race or she didn't know how to describe him."

"He's not white, not black, not Asian. *Hmm.* At least we know he's big."

"And there are four of them."

"At least."

FIVE

The next morning, we continued the hunt. At three o'clock that afternoon, we found it.

"It's an old firehouse, Snoop."

The Mediterranean style building occupied a large corner lot a mile from the cell tower. Concrete blocks painted coral pink sealed the fire truck door on the left. The old door on the right was fitted with residential double doors in the center and framed with more coral pink concrete blocks. A half dozen late model cars parked in the adjoining lot.

Snoop slowed to a crawl. "Is that the house where they have Liz?"

"Maybe." I photographed the four visible license plates.

"It has two stories, not three."

"That's all you see from the front. That's why we didn't spot it the first time we passed by. Drive further."

He rolled fifty yards farther down the block.

"Stop. They built the ground floor double height to allow for big ladder trucks. See those windows cut in the side wall? The ground floor was converted to two stories. Thus, a three-story house from Liz's viewpoint inside and this cross street is two lanes with parked cars on both sides."

"All the windows are barred."

"Barred windows are typical Mediterranean architecture. Most Cuban neighborhoods have them. It doesn't mean they keep prisoners inside."

"And it doesn't mean they don't."

"Park at that appliance store, and I'll research the property."

The property appraiser's website said the building measured 32 feet wide by 84 feet deep. Close enough. The firehouse belonged to a Florida Land Trust, a legal entity that conceals the owner's identity. I had encountered a land trust on an earlier case. In that case I traced the ownership to the Trustee, but the hard-nosed attorney who was trustee had a don't-mess-with-me attitude.

"Circle the block and park at the convenience store."

Snoop selected a spot fronting the building.

I eyeballed the trackers on Crucero's cars again. "The Corvette is rolling. Crucero is back."

"Maybe he'll visit Liz again. Where's he going?"

"North on I-95. He wouldn't do that if he were going home."

I moved to the second row of seats to be less visible from the firehouse and called Jorge. "I have eyes on a building that might be the one." I gave him the address. "What about a search warrant?"

"What about probable cause, *amigo?* I can't get a warrant based on your say-so."

"Yeah, but I had to ask. Snoop and I will stake it out and note who comes and goes. This is me, keeping you in the loop."

Jorge laughed.

"Later." I didn't tell Jorge about the Corvette. It's illegal for private citizens, *i.e.,* me, to mount a GPS tracker on someone else's vehicle without their permission. Jorge wouldn't rat me out, but I never add more stress to a friendship than required.

I called Will Jenkins.

"Hey, Chuck. Do you have news on my Lizzie?"

"Maybe. Snoop and I discovered a building that fits the description Liz gave you. We have no proof it's the right one, but it measures 32 by 84 feet."

"Where is it?"

"I'll tell you after I get Lieutenant Castellano enough evidence for a search warrant. This building may be the wrong one. I called because this is the first lead we've uncovered."

I kept one eye on my tablet. The Corvette curved this direction.

"Where is the house? I have to see it."

"It doesn't work that way, Will. I know how badly you want Liz back, but you can't go off half-cocked and screw up the whole operation. At the first sign of trouble, the kidnappers might cut their losses and kill Liz and the other captives so they can't testify. We can't risk that. I'll text you the address before Lieutenant Castellano executes the warrant. You can be there to give her a big hug once they rescue her. *If* it's the right building. Fair enough?"

The silence on the line was so long that I wondered if Will was still there.

"You say you know how much I want Lizzie back, but you *can't* know until you have your own daughter."

"I hope to do that someday, Will. Maybe Miyo is the right woman, but that's another story. It's hard to be patient, but you've waited a year. Give me a little longer." I said good-bye.

"Snoop, call three more operatives. Get them here ASAP in their own cars. We're going to tail people."

He grinned. "Rule Two: *When in doubt, follow somebody*"

I laid my camera with the long lens on the console between the front seats and observed the building. A typical stakeout—time passed with the speed of a snail crossing a driveway.

Snoop made a half-dozen calls from his list before he recruited two operatives available to join the stakeout on short notice. "Robby Gorski and Morris Martinez are all I could get, Chuck. They'll be here within the hour. I'll be the third guy. Janet can bring my car and she'll Uber back home. That way, we'll split up if someone leaves the target before the new guys get here."

"Are you healed enough?"

"I can't chase anybody on foot or get into a fistfight, but otherwise, yeah."

"Thanks."

A late model blue Lexus curled into the firehouse lot. I photographed the license plate. The driver peered around to see if anyone was watching him. He wouldn't notice me in my second-row seat, and Snoop pretended he was talking on the phone. The driver looked like a guilty husband. Or was that wishful thinking? I snapped several photos. He wore blue chinos and a pink Polo shirt. His temples flashed a little grey, but his face looked unlined through my long lens. Late thirties or early forties.

Trying not to think about Liz, I waited for something to happen. From my time in the Army, I knew how to wait, but this time it didn't sit well to wait for probable cause. Crucero's Corvette had stopped where the BMW was. Crucero was meeting Striped Tie. He wasn't coming here, at least not yet.

Emily—I mean Liz *might be captive in that building,* I thought. *God knows what she's going through, and I'm sitting here waiting. Still waiting.*

Rule Sixteen ran through my mind: *Sometimes you have to do something, even if it's wrong. At least you'll know you tried.*

I would interrogate a suspect. One of the brothel customers was a good enough suspect to start. "Snoop, take the camera inside the convenience store and get something to eat. Get a table by the window and photograph everyone. I'll trail the next guy who comes out."

Fifteen minutes passed. I drummed my fingers on the armrest.

Two men walked out together, laughing and joking. The middle-aged one was pudgy and balding and more than half-drunk. His polka-dot tie hung loose around his neck. The younger man wore a dress shirt with no tie, navy blue sport coat, and khakis. From his body language, I imagined he was the huckster and the older man his customer. Or maybe his sucker. Maybe they visited the firehouse for entertainment in the form of booze and broads. Or maybe that was more wishful thinking.

The younger man I thought of as Huckster sat behind the wheel of a black Cadillac Escalade. Sucker lurched around to the passenger side.

Opening the van door, I peered in the convenience store window. Snoop lifted the camera in one hand and gave me a thumbs-up with the other. I took the driver's seat and cranked the engine.

The afternoon commuter traffic snarled the streets. The throng of vehicles hid my van from Huckster's view. He was too busy schmoozing

Sucker to glance in his rearview mirror. The traffic crunch meant I risked getting marooned at a red light if I hung back too far.

My guts did a tap dance watching the Escalade run a yellow light and speed up the I-95 entrance ramp; I was mired on the crossroad. I drummed my fingers on the steering wheel and waited for the light to cycle. Jumping ahead of the car to my right, I made it first up the ramp.

A minute later I recognized the Escalade ahead, stuck in traffic, a dinosaur in a tar pit. Traffic was gridlocked, so I checked my tablet.

The Corvette was underway again. Crucero was headed in the direction of the firehouse. My gut told me Huckster and Sucker were routine customers. Crucero, on the other hand... If he was going to the firehouse, I should be there. I wove my way through the vehicle scrum to the shoulder and scrambled my way to the next exit.

I called Snoop. "The Corvette is headed your way. I dropped the tail on the Escalade and I'm coming back."

"This is the place, bud. I got good pictures of the big bald guy that came out to receive a liquor delivery. He's big as a giant football player. I think his shirt was Samoan. He's six-four, maybe six-five, and three hundred pounds easy. Perfect for a whorehouse bouncer."

"How are Robby and Morris doing?'

"They arrived after you left and each followed a customer. I let two more go because I wouldn't abandon my post in case Tommy, Scruffy, or Vince come—wait a minute. Someone's coming out. He fits Tommy's description. Let me look through the telephoto. Yeah, there's the palm tree tattoo. Hot damn, I got a good picture of him looking into the setting sun. Get your ass over here, bud. We have enough for the search warrant."

I coasted into the convenience store lot at 7:00 p.m. Robby's car was gone, but Morris had returned and parked on the far side.

Snoop got up from the booth inside and I focused on the firehouse.

Crucero's Corvette was in the lot. I called Morris. "If the man driving that Corvette is the next one out, don't tail him unless he has someone with him. I know who he is."

"Got it. I emailed you a report on the other car I followed. You want me to interview the driver?"

"Not yet, Morris. Maybe later. Good work."

Snoop got in the passenger side. "The Corvette arrived after we talked. I didn't call since you were on your way. It was Crucero. He carried a briefcase and a suitcase inside. Beats me how he stuffed those things in the rear of a Corvette, but he pulled them out like a rabbit from a hat. He's been in there ten minutes. We gonna take them down?"

My gut wanted to charge across the street and kick those double doors open. My gut wanted to run in and pistol-whip the first thug I saw until he told me where Liz was held. My gut would run upstairs and kick that door down. My gut would shoot Crucero between the eyes, laugh at his brains splattering the wall behind him, and drag his body off Liz. My gut wanted to pick her up like a fireman rescuing a child from a burning building.

My gut wanted it so bad that my stomach ached.

But I also have a head. This was one time I had to listen to my head instead of my gut.

"We can't take them down yet, Snoop. We have no legal justification for what is essentially a home invasion. Even if we did, we don't know what opposition we'd encounter. It kills me to say it, Snoop, but we take one step at a time. The first step is to get evidence of probable cause for a search warrant. You accomplished that with your photos of the kidnappers."

Jorge examined the top photo of the stack. I had rousted my friend from a late dinner at home and insisted he meet me at the precinct. Liz and the other captives shouldn't spend a second more than necessary in that prison. My gut and my head agreed on that.

"This is Tommy, the kidnapper?" he asked.

"He and the bald guy both fit descriptions Liz gave. Do you recognize either of them?"

"I don't recognize Tommy, but I'll get a guy from Organized Crime to run facial recognition. Since we know his first name, we might get a hit."

He flipped to the next photo. "This guy, I do know." He flipped open a file on his desk. Even upside-down, the mugshot was the same guy.

"His name is Losefa Ponalelie Topati, aka Lucifer. He got the nickname when he played college football. He played dirty. He's a bad guy with a rap sheet long as Melania Trump's shopping list. Attempted murder, DUI, assault—you name it. He's long on muscle and short on brains. He's as mean as a hungry dog fighting for a bone." He pushed the file across the desk.

I flipped through the pages. "He played defense for the Denver Broncos."

"Not quite. Denver drafted him in a late round fifteen years ago. They cut him because he kept committing personal fouls in practice. He head-butted his own teammates. Our profiler says he's a psychopath. Or is it a sociopath? I can never keep those straight. Whatever. He's a nut-case whacko, literally on steroids. Don't tackle this guy in a street fight. That's where the attempted murder charges came from."

"There's more than one?"

"Three over the last ten years. He's sent three gang-bangers to the hospital, and they were tough guys. They recovered, but none of them cooperated with the cops. Lucifer said the fights were self-defense and we couldn't prove otherwise. He's walked on every arrest except the DUI. For that, his license was suspended for 90 days. No one will testify against the weirdo."

"I'll keep that in mind if I cross his path."

"Don't cross his path without a gun—unless you're in Superman mode." Jorge flipped to the next photo. "Well, well. Antonio Ricardo Crucero Calderone."

"Do me a favor, *amigo*. Don't use that matronymic name. It makes my skin crawl to think that thug might be a distant cousin. Yeah, that's him. He's either a regular customer, or he's involved in this another way."

"Either way, we can't touch him." He scooted the photo toward me. "Keep it; we can't use it."

"You have enough for the warrant?"

"You bet your ass. This was worth a trip to the office at midnight. Yeah, we'll visit the judge first thing in the morning. Get a good night's sleep. I'll call you once we get the warrant. We'll hit the building tomorrow afternoon."

Tomorrow afternoon meant one more night in hell for Liz Jenkins and the others.

It bothered me no end to wait, but that's life.

———

The convenience store was busy at 2:30 a.m. when I bought my drinks and a foot-long. My van was one of a half-dozen vehicles in the lot. The firehouse's front windows had been dark since midnight. If I were a kidnapper, I wouldn't hold my captives in a room with a window visible from the street either.

After chugging an energy drink, I tossed the can in the litter basket of my Caravan. I finished the last bite of the foot-long. Wadding the sandwich wrapper into a ball and crushing it in my fist psyched me up, pumping the adrenalin for action. Crucero's Corvette was gone. He must have stopped at the bordello to get his rocks off. Then he went home to catch up on his business, whatever that was.

I pitched the wrapper in the basket with the energy drink. My mouth was dry again. Showtime.

Patting my bulletproof vest under my shirt, I popped the door. I walked down the sidewalk across from the long side of the firehouse. Dim lights shone behind three third-floor windows on the north side. The windows were barred, and behind the bars they were frosted. A window on the second floor glowed in the night. From the street level, all I could see was the ceiling fan. Liz was behind one of those windows. What was happening to her while I waited?

In case anyone was spying from a darkened window, I continued to the next street and passed out of sight. Crossing the street, I came up behind the firehouse to the alley at its rear.

The sole feature on the east side of the ground floor other than the electric meter was a metal fire door flush against the back wall. It had no outside handle. The fire escape had a six-foot landing beneath another featureless steel door on the second floor.

The top landing stretched beneath four dark windows on the third floor. In the dark I couldn't tell, but I would bet the windows were wire-reinforced glass. We couldn't make a rescue through there either.

A steel ladder continued to a flat-roofed area that served air-conditioning equipment I had spotted on my daylight reconnaissance.

Creeping down the alley, I came to the vacant lot next door. An ancient cyclone fence surrounded it, collapsed in two places from corrosion and neglect. Stepping over the ruins of the fence, I wove my way through the bushes, hedges, and trees that had sprouted. Nature abhors a vacuum. The concrete foundation of the long-gone building sprawled at the rear of the lot, a lonesome tombstone for the extinct business. Saplings grew in the ancient foundation's cracks.

The shadow of the trees was my perfect hiding place, invisible from the firehouse. Three more third-floor frosted windows glowed on the south side of the firehouse. Was Crucero with Liz behind one of those windows earlier? Was someone else raping her now? I shuddered.

Emily's image came to mind unbidden. Was she captive in a similar building? Or did she lie in an unmarked grave? Despite Rule Three, I was personally involved.

Another second-floor window glared. Maybe an office. The "entertainment" might be on the third floor. Perhaps Tommy thought the dim light was more romantic for his johns to do their thing with the captive women. Three lit windows on the other side plus three lit windows above me meant there were six women inside. Or someone left a light on. It was pointless to speculate.

A sliver of light flashed across the alley behind the firehouse and widened to a wedge. Someone had opened the fire door.

I duck-walked through the weeds and bushes to the rear fence. Rising to a squat behind a hedge, I peered down the alley. The stench of a cigar assaulted my nose.

The steel door opened at an angle. The cigar smoker was on the opposite side, holding it open.

There had been eight cars in the lot. Liz's texts identified four bad guys. If each had a car, there could be four or more customers inside. If I took out one bad guy, that improved the odds twenty-five percent. If there were four bad guys. If the smoker were alone. If I sneaked up on him. If I jumped him without warning the others. Too many *ifs*.

But the smoker hadn't talked to anyone else. He was what my Special Forces combat instructor called a *target of opportunity.*

After stashing my backpack behind a bush, I stepped over the fence. Flipping a mental switch, I morphed into a homeless person. Part of the transformation was slumping to make myself smaller as I shuffled up the alley. I positioned my video camera on the ground and aimed it at the back door. Stepping forward a few yards, I saw the smoker. It wasn't Crucero or Tommy, and it wasn't Lucifer. Thank goodness. From what Jorge said, I shouldn't tackle him unarmed.

The smoker fit Liz's description of Scruffy. Black, skinny, and fiftyish. The handle of a revolver peeked from his belt.

Stumbling to where he would notice me, I spoke slurred Spanish. "Sir, could you spare a dollar? I haven't eaten all day." I shuffled closer with my hand out.

Scruffy sneered. His retort was in Cuban-accented Spanish. "Get the hell out of here, you bum. This is no neighborhood for you." He propped the door open with a foot, jammed the cigar in his mouth, and eased his hand toward the revolver.

I flinched but didn't back away. The hallway behind him was empty. I needed to get two feet closer. I shuffled to my right.

He reached for the revolver then stopped. A homeless bum posed no danger. He leaned toward me, but he didn't release the door, and I stood out of reach.

I shuffled closer. "Please, sir, I mean no harm. I'm a veteran, and I'm hungry. Can you spare a dollar?" I reached out with my hand.

"Go to hell. I'm going inside." He threw the cigar into the alley.

Jerking him from the doorway, I snatched the revolver from his belt and clubbed him on the temple with the butt. He fell to the pavement, a red streak on his temple oozing blood. I jammed the revolver into his throat. "Make a sound and you're dead. I may be homeless, but I'm a *person* and a combat veteran. You had no call to be mean. I *served*, man. I *served.*"

His eyes grew big as golf balls. "Hey, I'm sorry. Let me give you a couple of dollars. Hell, I'll give you a twenty. Don't shoot."

Stepping back, I lowered the revolver.

———

Jorge acted pissed, but I knew better. "First you haul me away from my dinner table so I miss my bedtime, then you haul me away from my breakfast at seven in the freakin' morning."

"*Amigo,* we'll all sleep late once Liz Jenkins and the other girls are safe. It's customary to say 'thank you' to someone who brings you a present." I pushed a stick drive across the desk. "Here's a video of the man Liz described as Scruffy holding this weapon." I slid Scruffy's revolver across the desk.

"We have the warrant. I didn't need this."

"That's great news. If you had texted me that, I wouldn't have called you in early. I figured you could use more evidence."

Jorge inserted the stick drive and played the video. "Nice move there on the revolver." He handed the drive back. "Erase that; it's evidence of assault."

"Then why erase it? You can add assault to the charges against Scruffy."

"*Amigo,* he's not the one doing the assaulting. Resting his hand on the butt of the gun isn't assault. You're the aggressor here."

"Picky, picky, picky."

"Erase the video, smartass. I'll look up the weapon. If it's unregistered, we'll get him on a weapons charge. If it's registered, it will help us identify him."

"When do you execute the warrant?"

"SWAT team will gear up at one o'clock. I'll meet you near the firehouse at two p.m. I'll text you the assembly point. We'll hit that target harder than a tornado in a trailer park."

SIX

There were eleven cars in the firehouse lot. One was Crucero's BMW. *Hot damn.*

The SWAT team assembled in the parking lot of a vacant store. I parked my Caravan beside a SWAT truck. I recognized a head of familiar flaming red hair.

Renate Crowell was the top crime reporter for the *Port City Press-Journal.* In this era of shrunken newspapers and internet and television news on the rise, she had to be tough as a combat boot, dedicated as a Mormon missionary, and smart as an encyclopedia. If the *Pee-Jay* ever folded its tent, she would be the last one out the door.

Renate was pointing a microphone at Jorge. "Who is the target of the raid, Lieutenant Castellano?"

"It's not a raid. We are serving a search warrant." Jorge glanced my way with a relieved expression. "Chuck, will you please... uh, deal with Ms. Crowell. I have work to do."

She gave me a smile. "My favorite sleuth. How's it hanging?" She lowered her microphone, but she didn't switch off the recorder. She hoped I wouldn't notice.

"Hello, princess. What brings you here?" I nicknamed her the Princess of the *Pee-Jay.*

"My snitch at the courthouse told me Lieutenant Castellano obtained a warrant to bust a prostitution ring and raid a real-life, honest-to-God bordello. You know how rare that is in the twenty-first century? What's your role in this, handsome?"

"Bystander. Can we go off the record?"

"Do I get an exclusive when this thing is ready to publish?"

"Sure."

"We are off the record." She clicked off her recorder and stowed the microphone.

"This is bigger than a prostitution bust, princess."

Naming the people on the warrant, I filled her in. Once the suspects were booked and arraigned, this much and more would be public information. For now, this was one way to keep Renate from wedging her way into the raid, creating one more bystander to worry the cops.

She waved her notebook. "Ten years ago, the *Pee-Jay* sent photographers with me. Today, I snap pictures with a phone, and I provide the phone. The pickings are mighty slim, handsome. I'll eat the crumbs that fall off your table. And I mean that however you interpret it." She winked.

"Snoop will be here in a minute. Maybe he'll have a crumb or two for you."

"Why is that old warhorse here? Has he recovered from his wounds?"

"Almost. He's gonna take my Caravan for an assignment. He'll arrive in a Toyota and exchange it for my van. You can interview him while you wait for me to return."

"Humph. Snoop won't tell me a bloody thing. He's friendly as a crossing guard and as informative as a stone."

"Stick around, princess, but stay here. I'll brief you once the danger's over. You'll make deadline for tomorrow's edition."

"I'll wait in my car over there. You have my number, though you never call." She grinned. Or was it a leer?

"Okay, lover. I'll be patient. You won't call me for a date, but I know you'll call me for business. I'll eat the crumbs."

"This may be a whole cake."

Jorge keyed his radio. "Go, go, go."

Two SWAT cops swung the battering ram at the front doors. Two more would be jimmying the rear fire door with a giant crowbar. The battering ram bounced off. "It's reinforced. Okay, hit it again. Go, go, go."

Two more bangs and the doors gave way. Six men in assault gear ran through the broken doors. Jorge had dispatched six more to the alley for a simultaneous breach.

"Port City police," the armored cop in the lead shouted. "On your knees, hands where I can see them."

I followed on their heels. The cop had been shouting to an empty room. Four men ran up the stairs. Two others headed toward the rear of the ground floor.

The first cop twisted the doorknob. "Port City police. On your knees, hands where I can see them." He led the heavily-armed rush through the door. Two more SWAT cops came in the rear door.

It was a normal kitchen with appliances and a sink ranked along one wall. Two women sat at the table. I recognized Morgan Putnam from the picture in the PCPD file. A man who matched Vince's description gawked at five guns pointed at him. He raised his hands. "Don't shoot."

Maybe Lucifer and Tommy were upstairs with Scruffy.

"On your knees," Jorge yelled. "Fingers interlaced on top of your head." He lowered his weapon. "You ladies are safe. Where are the other captives?"

A SWAT cop handcuffed Vince and read him his rights.

Morgan Putnam said, "The kidnapped girls are with clients. Third floor. The local whores work the second floor." She pointed to an elevator.

One cop used a fire department key to disable the elevator. Jorge nodded his thanks and faced his team. "You two climb the rear stairs. You two take the front. I'll guard this bum and stay with the women."

Taking a chair from the kitchen table, I sat across from the two women. They were shaking like palm fronds in a hurricane. "You're safe. These men are Port City police. I'm Chuck McCrary, a private investigator hired by Liz Jenkins's father. Where can I find Liz?"

"Liz's room is the last one at the back on the west side, third floor. She went up with Ambassador Tony."

"Ambassador?" I asked.

"That's what we have to call him, at least to his face. Tony is a short fat slob with a greasy ponytail. Between us, we call him Jabba the Hutt. He'll be pounding away on Liz and grunting like a pig. Shoot the bastard for me, will you?"

"Thanks." Bolting through the rear door, I rushed up the back stairs three at a time.

Nearing the third floor, I caught up with two SWAT cops who had preceded me. The other two must've peeled off to clear the second floor. "First door on the right is Liz Jenkins's room, Gary. Okay for me to go first?"

Gary and I graduated police academy together. "Sure, Chuck. Your turn to be the hero. You earned it." He lowered his weapon and waved me ahead.

At the end of the hall, another cop entered from the front stairs. Between us, a pudgy middle-aged man stood in his underwear, khaki pants and blue Polo shirt draped over his forearm, shoes in hand. He was punching the elevator button over and over with his other hand.

I pounded on the door three times. "Liz, your father sent me. He's downstairs. I'm coming in." I jammed the door open.

The fat naked man sprawled atop Liz, his ponytail bouncing with his motion. *"Casi, casi, casi,"* he grunted in Spanish. *Almost, almost, almost.* Crucero was so focused on hammering Liz, he didn't hear me knock or open the door.

Liz spotted me and beat her fists on Crucero's chest.

He continued to pound away. *"Casi, casi, casi."*

Charging across the room, I seized Crucero's ponytail and yanked his head back. His hands clutched Liz's shoulders in his frenzy. I wrenched again and he wouldn't let go. Throttling him around the neck with my other hand, I crushed his windpipe, cutting off his air.

He released Liz's shoulders and clutched at my hand.

After dragging him off the terrified woman, I threw him against the wall. His head punched a hole in the drywall with a satisfying crunch, and he crumpled to the floor.

I eyeballed Liz. "Are you okay?"

"Yes, yes. Did Daddy send you?"

"Yes. He told me he would give everything he owned to get you back. He's downstairs waiting for you."

She rolled off the bed and headed for the door. "I knew Daddy would come through. I knew it."

"Whoa there, Liz." I stole a blanket off the bed and draped it across her shoulders. "Let's cover you first."

She peered down at her naked body. Her chest was scrubbed raw from Crucero's abrasive chest hair. Her face reddened, then her whole body flushed, and she clutched the blanket around her. "I have clothes in the closet."

I looked the other way while she dressed.

Crucero moaned, rubbed his head, and levered himself to a sitting position. His naked gut hung over his lap. His glassy gaze roamed the room, then clicked into focus, riveted on Liz behind me.

Jabba the Hutt leering at Princess Leia.

His glance cut to me. "You can't arrest me," he said in accented English, "I have diplomatic immunity." He stared at Liz and laughed.

Keeping my gaze on Jabba, I sidestepped between him and Princess Leia. "You dressed yet, Liz?"

"Not quite."

The naked bear of a man glared at me, his face red. He struggled to his feet. "I have diplomatic immunity." He tried to dodge around me. "You can't touch me."

"Watch me." This time I listened to my gut.

I kicked him in the balls hard enough to make a sixty-yard field goal. He doubled over, and I kneed him in the forehead. He fell into the wall again, bashing another hole.

"You can turn around. I'm dressed."

Liz wore faded blue jeans and a threadbare tee-shirt with an obscene slogan blazoned across the chest. The tee-shirt had been laundered so often it had faded to light gray. It was obvious she wasn't wearing a bra.

"Let's wrap you in this blanket too." I draped the blanket around her shoulders. "Your father shouldn't see you in that shirt."

She peered down at her chest. Her body reddened again. "I could change shirts."

"Let's not make your father wait any longer than he has to. Wrap in the blanket."

In the corner, Crucero struggled to his feet. "You can't do this to me; I have diplomatic immunity. I'll have your badge for this."

"I don't need no stinkin' badge," I said in my best *Blazing Saddles* imitation. I kicked his family jewels again, hard enough for an extra point this time.

He fell to the floor and scrunched into a ball.

"I'm not a cop, asshole, and I don't care whether you're a diplomat. To me you're a kidnapper and a rapist. Get up again and I might kill you."

He peered up, eyes wide with fear for the first time. "If you're not a cop, what are you?"

I leaned close enough to smell the Scotch on his breath. He shrank back against the wall.

"My name is Carlos Andres McCrary *Calderone,* cousin. I'm something you've never seen before. I'm your Karma."

I helped Liz down the front stairs.

Will Jenkins waited at the bottom. "Binky!" He rushed to her side and wrapped his arms around her. Tears streamed unnoticed down his rugged cheeks. "I was feared I'd never see you again, Binky." He patted her back and stroked her hair.

Liz's tears spilled onto the blanket. "Oh, Daddy, I'm so sorry. I'm so awful sorry."

"There's nothing to be sorry about, honey. I pushed you away, and I been regretting it ever since. Can you ever forgive me, sweetie?"

"Like you said, Daddy, there's nothing to forgive."

Two more women came down the stairs, escorted by SWAT team members. "Are you two Dolores and Jill?" I asked.

"I'm Dolores Cherry," said a tall brunette.

"I'm Jill Kimbrough," said the shorter woman.

"Lieutenant Castellano wants a doctor to examine you all. Tawnya and Morgan already went in an ambulance. There's another ambulance outside for you."

Liz gazed my way, still huddled in Will's embrace.

"Liz, I can take you and your father in my Dodge Grand Caravan. It doesn't have red lights and a siren, but you might be more comfortable than in the back of an ambulance."

Liz glanced at her father, who nodded. She looked at me. "Okay. Thanks."

Two uniformed cops led Tommy Flannigan and Vince, handcuffed, down the stairs.

Where was Lucifer?

Another SWAT cop followed with two more women, both in handcuffs. One had a full sleeve of tattoos.

Jorge emerged from the kitchen/dining room.

The SWAT cop reported to him. "These are the women from the second floor. They worked here by choice. They're the pros."

"Read them their rights, then book them for prostitution," Jorge said, "and accessories to kidnapping."

A uniformed cop led Crucero down the stairs. The cop had let Jabba get dressed. He wore a turquoise guayabera and yellow chinos, hands cuffed behind his back.

"You can't arrest me; I have diplomatic immunity."

"Yeah, sure," the cop replied in a level voice. "We'll straighten that out at the precinct. You can call your embassy or your lawyer or anybody in the whole wide world. Sir."

Crucero stumbled on the bottom step. He caught his balance, then he spotted me. "You. What the hell are you doing here?"

"In case you haven't noticed, cousin, I'm everywhere." I stepped toward him. "Tell me once more that you have diplomatic immunity, and I'll kick you in the nuts so hard your parents will never have grandchildren."

He jumped behind the uniformed cop. He was short enough but twice as wide as the cop. "Keep that lunatic away from me. He assaulted me. You heard him confess. I want to press charges."

"Yes, sir," the cop agreed, "You do that, for sure, sir. We'll handle all that down at the precinct." He winked at me before he led Crucero out.

I followed with Liz and Will.

Snoop waited at the curb beside my Caravan. All four doors were open.

Liz spun to Tony Crucero and Tommy and Vince, huddled in handcuffs on the sidewalk. She shivered. She clutched her father's hand and slipped into the second row of seats.

I closed the Caravan doors and stood by the front passenger seat.

Crucero glared at me with reptilian eyes. "I will remember you, *cousin*. You are a dead man."

I winked at him. "Wanna bet?"

As Snoop drove us away from the curb, I had a disturbing thought: I had not seen Lucifer Topati anywhere in the firehouse.

Lucifer

Red and blue lights flashed in the distance. Losefa Ponalelie Topati, aka Lucifer, eased his foot off the accelerator. Were those lights at the firehouse? He let the sedan coast until his speed dropped below the limit.

Topati's trunk was full of groceries for the bordello. Did he have any contraband in the car? Oh, crap, his steroids were in the glove compartment. If the cops searched the car, they would discover his stash. He considered throwing them out the window, but steroids cost big bucks. What if the flashing lights were merely a traffic stop? Maybe he was paranoid. He knew steroids did that. No need to panic.

He eyeballed the speedometer and glanced in the rearview mirror. He was good for now. Calm down.

As usual, Tommy Flannigan gave him a wad of cash and a grocery list before he went to the store. As usual, Topati skimmed some cash. Tommy always asked for a receipt and demanded the change, but he never counted the money Topati returned to him. Tommy was stupid. Tommy deserved to be strangled for stupidity. Topati imagined his hands around Tommy's scrawny neck. He wanted to squeeze the life out of him.

The car rolled closer to the police lights. They were in front of the firehouse. Bad news, patrol cars and SWAT trucks.

67

Was that Tony Crucero in handcuffs on the sidewalk? Panic seized him. If Tony Crucero wasn't there to tell him what to do, how would he know? Without Tony, Topati would be a boat with no rudder and no harbor.

Keep it together. Tony always said he had a *Get Out of Jail Free* card.

Topati had no friends and few acquaintances. He had managed to stay in college long enough to become eligible for the NFL draft. His agent handled his NFL contract negotiations and everything else about his life. After the Broncos cut him, he attacked his coach. It required four Bronco teammates to tug him off. His agent dropped him like he had the plague.

Topati bounced from job to job following his abortive NFL career.

Tony Crucero discovered Lucifer working as a bouncer at a Polynesian-style waterfront bar. Topati beat a bar patron so brutally that the manager called an ambulance for the unfortunate drunk. The manager fired him on the spot, and Tony trailed Topati from the bar and offered him a job.

After that, his life revolved around the bordello and handling unruly johns. No one got unruly more than once.

Topati coasted past the firehouse. More SWAT vehicles on the side street. The whole damned Port City Police Department had descended on the firehouse. How could Tony combat that?

His breath caught in his throat. He scanned his rearview and side mirrors. No one was behind him, but that didn't mean they wouldn't give chase. His palms slicked with sweat on the steering wheel.

He had fifteen thousand dollars in skimmed cash hidden in his flophouse apartment. He had a week's supply of groceries for ten people in the car. With his appetite, that would last him four weeks. He could hibernate until the heat cooled.

Maybe Tony's *Get Out of Jail Free* card would work. He would wait a day and call Tony.

He cruised through the intersection and disappeared down the street.

Carlos McCrary

Snoop and I escorted Liz and Will to the hospital and returned to retrieve Snoop's Toyota. I locked my van and walked to Renate's car. "I'm all yours."

"Promises, promises."

I gave her the bare facts on the raid. She asked follow-up questions, most of which I answered. I didn't tell her my client's name or Liz's name. The arraignments and arrest reports would give her enough names to give her story authenticity.

"There's another angle that hooks into a series of stories that could win you a Pulitzer Prize." I knew that would get her attention.

"What's that, handsome?"

"Abuse of diplomatic immunity. The cops arrested the son of the ambassador from the Republic of San Cristobal in the raid. He was caught naked in the act of raping a kidnapped woman."

"Caught by whom?"

"Can you leave my name out of it?"

"I'll call you 'someone close to the case.' Fair enough?"

"Thanks. To continue, the son shares his father's diplomatic immunity. The son's involvement is more than as a customer. His name is Antonio Ricardo Crucero." I omitted the *Calderone* matronymic.

"Spell *Crucero*."

I did.

"How is he involved other than being a customer?"

"Not clear. The CSIs are processing the crime scene. If they find his fingerprints anywhere but in the bedrooms, we'll know more. The hook for your story is that he's a rich, pampered rapist and an accessory to kidnapping, but he can't be prosecuted."

"I like the 'rich' angle. The editor loves to stick it to rich people."

"Yeah, I noticed."

"Is diplomatic immunity the reason he can't be prosecuted?"

"Bingo. The DC cops have seen diplomats or family members commit felonies: assault, drug smuggling, even murder. They escape with no consequences other than being expelled from the United States. You might write a series on it. The DC cops call these bums 'diplobrats.'"

"No. 'Diplobrats' sounds cute and cuddly. Give me another name for them, one deadly and dangerous."

"How about 'diplofelons' or 'diplocriminals'?"

"Diplofelons, diplofelons. That sounds sexier than diplocriminals."

Renate gave me a high five. "What else can you tell me about this Crucero diplofelon?"

"His apartment has a sophisticated security system, but the burglar alarm is not hooked up to the police. When he's not there, he has a big, mean-looking armed guard on duty."

"You speaking from personal knowledge?"

"I'm psychic."

Barney's restaurant isn't across the street from the North Shore Precinct, but it might as well be, judging from the cops and former cops who eat and drink there.

Jorge waved me over to a booth. He edged a mug of Port City Amber Ale toward me and shoved a thin file across the table. "Crucero was out of jail before dinner time."

I picked up my mug. "Don't worry. We'll meet again."

"Amigo, you don't intend to do anything illegal, do you?"

"Moi? Perish the thought. What's in the file?"

"It's what my CSI guys have ascertained so far."

The file contained an inventory of stuff confiscated in the office on the second floor: $85,000 in cash, 600 grams of cocaine, 450 grams of heroin, 95 pills of various addictive drugs. The CSIs had not yet cracked an industrial-sized safe in the office.

"Jeez, Jorge, with $85,000 in cash and a big drug stash in the office desk, think how much they must keep in that safe."

"It'll take time to open it. The CSIs will contact the manufacturer with a court order, unless Tommy gives them the combination. All Tommy says is he wants a lawyer. His real name is Thomas Henry Finch. We had his fingerprints in the system from the time he worked as a valet car parker at a condo on Port City Beach years ago. He has no other criminal record."

"He'll come around," I predicted. It was a safe bet.

A server approached and we ordered. After she left, I opened the file again. "Whose fingerprints have you found?"

"We found too many for fast solutions. We didn't bother to print the bedrooms. The DA isn't interested in prosecuting johns other than the three we arrested onsite."

"Liz told me the johns knew the girls were prisoners. In the past, she has asked several of them to call the police and they laughed at her. All of them are accessories to kidnapping."

"I didn't know that." He sent a text. "I texted the CSIs to dust the bedrooms. The DA will prosecute anyone who ignored the victims' calls for help."

"Wanna bet?" I asked. "Not if any of them have political connections."

"So young and yet so cynical."

"Thank my years of experience as a police detective and a PI. And a voter."

"If the DA bails on any of the guilty johns, I'll leak the fingerprint evidence to your pal Renate the news-shark."

"That might work. She's good at pointing fingers," I said. "What about the cars in the lot?"

"We hauled them to the crime lab. Our guys are on them closer than hair on a dog."

"And Crucero's BMW?"

"It has diplomatic plates. Can't touch it. It's still in the lot as far as I know."

"I suspect Crucero owns the human trafficking operation and whatever else you find in that safe. In fact, he might own the whole building. Tommy Finch fronted for him. Did you get Crucero's fingerprints to compare with the prints you found in the office?"

Jorge lifted his hand, fingers spread, and waggled it. *"Mas o menos."* *More or less.*

"What does that mean?"

"In accordance with regular police procedure, we fingerprinted Crucero when we booked him. We had not confirmed his diplomatic status, so it was legal to do that."

"Okay, that's the *mas* part. What about the *menos?*

"Crucero's lawyer came in, and he got the State Department of the freakin' U. S. of A. on the phone. A diplomatic prick in Washington told me to destroy the prints. Or, in our case, delete them from our computer system since we don't use paper fingerprints anymore."

He set down his beer mug and reached in his coat pocket.

"I, of course, being a sworn officer of the freakin' law, obeyed the State Department prick's orders to the letter."

He handed me a stick drive with a stick-on label that said *Jabba the Hutt*.

"I deleted Crucero's prints from our system. Completely. One hundred percent. Gone."

I pocketed the drive.

"You'll let me know once you finish processing the office?"

"Of course not. It's against department policy to share files with a mere civilian. Now gimme that file back—that file which you never saw—and we'll eat."

SEVEN

F ollowing Liz's examination by the doctor, the District Attorney gave
her the afternoon off. Assistant DA Mendoza interviewed Liz in her
office the next day, which was a Friday.

While Liz was with ADA Mendoza, her father checked out of the
modest hotel where he stayed while Snoop and I hunted for Liz. He rented
a two-bedroom suite in the Port City Palace, the five-star hotel that had
been the headquarters for the Super Bowl earlier that year. I knew the hotel
well from a previous case involving one of the Super Bowl quarterbacks
and his kidnapped fiancée.

Then Will, Snoop, and I went fishing. We all needed a break.

Saturday morning, I met Liz and Will in their suite.

"Lizzie will be out in a minute." He pointed at the breakfast buffet he
had ordered from room service. "Help yourself. I'm going first class for my
Lizzie. She deserves to be pampered after the rough time she's been
through."

Liz saw me and smiled. The innocent, farm-girl appearance emerged
from hiding and lit up the room. I told her fish stories during breakfast.

Once we finished, I poured her a fresh coffee. "Now that ADA
Mendoza has interviewed you, I have some questions. Is that okay?"

"Sure, but until four weeks ago, I was whacked out on drugs. My time with Tony and the other clients—I mean *johns*—is blurry until the last four weeks."

"I understand, Liz. I don't expect you to be accurate. This is for my information only. What business is Crucero in?"

"Tony—he said to call him Tony—me and him never discussed business. It was *slam-bam* without the *thank-you-ma'am.*"

"How did Crucero make his money?"

"Us girls never discussed money with the johns. Tommy handled the money. Occasionally, a john gave me a tip though. Oh jeez, I hid over four thousand dollars in a plastic bag inside the toilet tank in my bathroom. It's still there. Can we go back and get it?"

"The cops confiscated it and entered it into evidence. I'll ask Lieutenant Castellano to get it back for you."

"Don't you worry about money none, Lizzie. I'll give you all you need."

"Did Crucero mention working a job?"

"Nope. But he did tip me pretty well. That's kinda funny—not *ha ha* funny, but *weird* funny. I had four thousand dollars hidden away, but no way to spend it. None of us girls did."

She pivoted to Will. "I was saving to pay my way home once I escaped."

"What did Crucero do when he wasn't with you? Any hobbies or outside interests?"

"It's a waste of time to talk about this, Chuck. Ms. Mendoza told me she can't put Tony on trial for anything. He has this *Get Out of Jail Free* card where the law can't touch him."

"It's called diplomatic immunity. It protects him from the law. However, I am no longer a cop. The bum's diplomatic status will not protect him from me."

Liz grinned. "You're going to stop Tony on your own, aren't you?"

"The way I see it, if I don't stop him, no one else can."

"Binky, if Chuck obeyed the laws, he wouldn't have never found you. You'd still be locked up in that... that *cell*. Or, worse, you'd be dead."

"You broke the law to find me?"

"I broke several."

"And you couldn't have found me otherwise?"

"I might have located you legally, given enough time. We'll never know. I do know that my not-so-legal shortcuts helped me find you quicker than otherwise. I helped the police get a search warrant a little sooner."

She picked a sweet roll and chewed, peering out the window at the view.

"I want information about his weak spots, his vulnerabilities. Anything you remember that he told you or let slip."

Liz swallowed and blotted her lips with a napkin. "I may not know much, but what do you want to know?"

"You sent those texts from Crucero's phone?"

"Yeah. I snuck it out of his holster once he went to sleep. Then I slipped it back in."

"His phone requires a password. How did you unlock it?"

She smiled. "Tony always listened to his messages after he, uh, after he finished with me, but before he went to sleep. The night I sent those texts, I peeked over his shoulder when he used his phone. I memorized the password."

"What was it?"

"You have his phone?"

I reached in my pocket and flourished it. "Ta-da."

"Where did you get that phone? Oh, I get it." She giggled. "You stole it when you rescued me."

"What's the password?"

She told me. I didn't need to write it down; it was an obscene Spanish word. Unlocking the phone, I laid it on the table.

"Did Crucero ever bring anything with him to your room?"

"He brought his phone. I don't know that it's important, but he was the only john Tommy let bring his phone."

"It is important, but you should tell me every detail you remember about him and let me determine what's important."

"Okay. Tony always brought drugs for me and him, which he kept in a pill box thing in his pocket. A couple times he brought a suitcase and a bag you hang suits in to keep them from getting wrinkled. He called it a carry-on bag."

"Why did he need a suitcase *and* a carry-on bag?"

"He was on his way to the airport to fly back to San Cristobal. He wore a guayabera and blue jeans, but said he needed to change into a suit and tie to travel. Something about his image as a diplomat. When he came to my room, first thing he, uh, he took off his casual clothes and packed them in the suitcase."

"That's good. What else was in the suitcase?"

She shook her head. "I'm sorry. There wasn't anything but clothes."

"Let's do a mental exercise, okay?"

"Okay."

"Close your eyes. Look with your mind's eye. You're safe with us, but pretend that you're in that room with Crucero and his suitcase. Are you there?"

"Yep." She shivered and wrapped her arms around herself.

"With your eyes closed, observe him opening that suitcase... See him pack his clothes in it... Tell me what else you see."

Liz's eyes popped open. "I see money. It's in paper bands like it comes from a bank. It's hidden under his clothes in the suitcase."

"And he was on his way to the airport?"

"Yeah, he—that's it. It was the next-to-last time he brought a suitcase."

"Great. Tell me about the last time."

"He brought one the day before you and Daddy rescued me."

I didn't tell her that Snoop and I had been there. It was complicated to explain why I had not rescued her then. I kept my mouth shut.

"Did he bring the carry-on bag?"

"Yeah."

"What happened?"

"Tony had flown in from San Cristobal and he came straight to the whorehouse 'cause he said he missed me. He wore a suit and tie when he came in. It was like he wouldn't wear that suit any longer than he had to." She glanced at her father and her face and neck bloomed pink. "He took off his suit and stuffed it in that hanging bag. Then he—" She lowered her gaze to the floor.

Will patted her hand. "It's okay, sweetie. We understand."

She smiled feebly. "After... afterwards. He opened that suitcase to put on a sport shirt and khakis. But when he opened the case, there were packages inside."

"Drugs?"

"Cocaine. Must have been ten or twelve packages lined up flat in that suitcase. Come to think of it, there was empty space at one corner, like he removed a package before he got to the whorehouse. Tony said he brought them in every week or two from San Cristobal." She rotated to Will. "He was high, Daddy, or he would never say something like that. He seemed proud of himself."

Crucero's phone vibrated on the table. The screen said *Lucifer.* It rang with the sound of a jungle drum.

I raised my finger to my lips. "Shush. This may be important."

They nodded.

"Hello."

"Tony, it's Losefa. Where are you?"

"At home. Where are you?"

"Who is this? Where's Tony?"

"He can't come to the phone. He's in a meeting. Where are you?"

The phone went dead.

Lucifer

Following his narrow escape from the SWAT raid on the bordello, Topati drove to his apartment in a daze. He huddled in a ratty recliner, his mind clenched tighter than a fist, rousing only to eat or use the bathroom. When he slept, nightmarish SWAT teams invaded his dreams, broke down his door, and stormed his apartment with guns drawn. Had the ancient Samoan gods sent the dreams to show him his future? Or was it the steroids?

Friday afternoon late, his mind unclenched enough to watch television. The Six O'clock News featured Tony Crucero's handcuffed perp walk into the North Shore Precinct of the Port City police. The announcer said the cops released Tony from jail because he was a foreign diplomat. Was that his *Get Out of Jail Free* card?

Whatever it was, it worked. Tony was free. Maybe Topati would survive.

Topati's mind stirred at a glacial pace. He would sleep on this development. This time he slept in his bed. Maybe the ancient gods would send him another, clearer vision.

He awoke Saturday morning. The gods had not sent him a vision, but he had not suffered any nightmares. At least not that he remembered.

He ate lunch on the dinette table in his tiny kitchen and agonized about his circumstances. Topati knew his limitations. He was not a thinker; he was a muscle man. Without Tony, he had no future.

Tony would know what to do. For the first time in two days, Topati switched on his phone and called Tony.

On the third ring, Tony answered. "Hello."

Relief flooded his mind. Everything would be okay.

"Tony, it's Losefa. Where are you?"

"At home. Where are you?"

That wasn't Tony's voice. "Who is this? Where's Tony?"

"He can't come to the phone. He's in a meeting. Where are you?"

Panicked, Topati disconnected.

The gods had cursed him again. He had to escape.

Carlos McCrary

I punched up the call log on the phone. Lucifer's call was at the top of the list. I tapped *View contact.* His address was in Uptown, a blue-collar neighborhood north of downtown.

First, I forwarded Lucifer's contact info to Jorge Castellano's phone, then I called him with my own phone.

"Jorge, I just sent you Lucifer Topati's address. I'm on my way there, but I'll be ten minutes. He's gonna rabbit. Can you get a patrol car there ASAP?"

"I'll have the nearest patrol on the way within 90 seconds. I'll come too." He disconnected.

"Liz and Will, you heard what I said. I have to run. I'll call you later."

"Go, Chuck," Will said, "Nail the bastard."

I made it in nine minutes.

The parking lot was half full of older vehicles. Three people stood chatting at one end of the lot. A timeworn maroon Ford Taurus was backed into its spot, unlike the other vehicles. Its open trunk fronted the sidewalk. The same Taurus had been parked at the firehouse during our stakeout. Topati was its registered owner.

Rolling through an empty spot on the third row, I parked the wrong way on the second row. If necessary, I could give chase without backing up.

I did not lock my Caravan. There would be no time to unlock it if I came back at a sprint.

As I crossed the lot, Lucifer tottered down the stairs lugging a box of groceries. His Samoan shirt, shaved head, and sheer bulk were unmistakable. Jorge was right; I shouldn't tackle this guy alone. He was taller, which gave him a longer reach than I had, and he out-weighed me by a hundred pounds, most of it muscle.

I caught my breath. Lucifer was immense. It would be like fighting with a truck, maybe even a locomotive. But if I held back, he would drive away before the cops arrived. Somehow, I had to hold him until reinforcements arrived.

I reached for my sidearm. My heartrate increased. The fight-or-flight effect began.

Two cars down from Lucifer, a young woman was buckling two children into car seats. Both her back doors were open.

With civilians present, I didn't dare pull a gun. Nothing to do but play the hand I was dealt.

I stepped to his open trunk, stood by the bumper, and waited for Armageddon. It would be like attacking a redwood tree with a hand axe, except this tree moved with the speed of an NFL player.

Lucifer halted six feet from me, his hands occupied with the groceries.

Skipping a half step forward, I flexed my knees and angled my shoulders.

Lucifer dropped the box and raised his hands. Before the box hit the sidewalk, I launched my best right cross straight at his nose. I brought that punch up from near the sidewalk, traveling a million miles an hour with power like a tank.

Lucifer twitched his head and my fist missed his nose and struck his cheek. It felt as solid as punching a bag of cement.

His hand snaked faster than a rattler's strike and clamped my right wrist tight as a vise. He twisted my arm away like sweeping aside a cobweb.

I followed with a left cross to his midsection under my trapped right arm. I have broken bad guys' ribs with that punch. This time it felt like I had punched a sandbag. The flesh over his ribs gave a little, then stiffened like there was a brick wall underneath.

Lucifer hauled my right arm up and out and wrenched me off balance. He threw his right arm around my neck and tightened it like a tourniquet. He bull-snorted and hoisted me with the chokehold like I was a ragdoll. He tightened his arm and cut off my breath like slipping a plastic bag over my head.

My wrist felt encased in concrete. So did my lungs. Throwing my left arm across the choke hold, I fumbled for his fingers, fighting to find a grip. My fingertips found his hand, but his volleyball-sized fist was clenched tight as a prison door. Yanking on his thumb, I might as well try to peel the bumper off an eighteen-wheeler.

My vision blurred. I released his thumb and grasped his belt, snapped my head back, and slammed the bridge of his nose with a crunch.

He grunted but his grip never loosened. The guy was as relentless as a landslide. As I began to lose consciousness, I snapped my head back again. Another crunch. This time he yelled.

Bending my legs, I kicked backward at his kneecaps. It felt like my heel hit a lamppost. My vision blurred and darkened. I kicked again and something loosened.

Sirens screamed in the distance as I lost consciousness.

I woke with an oxygen mask over my nose.

"He's coming around."

My eyes flickered open. Lieutenant Jorge Castellano stared down at me. "You get enough sleep, *amigo?*"

The EMT removed the mask and nodded to Jorge. "He'll be okay."

"Thanks," I said. "Are you sure?"

The EMT smiled. "As far as I can tell, he didn't choke you long enough for any brain damage."

"With this guy," Jorge said, "no one could tell."

He gave me his hand and helped me to my feet.

"Witnesses told us Lucifer was busting your chops pretty good before you got saved by the bell—or I should say, the sirens. Lucifer heard sirens, dropped you faster than a hot skillet, and bolted."

I glanced at where Lucifer's sedan had been parked. The spot was empty, groceries scattered across the sidewalk. A crime scene tech snapped pictures.

"When we find him, we could charge him with attempted murder, except the woman who witnessed the fight said you hit him first."

"You know the guy, Jorge; he's a freakin' giant, or maybe a giant freak. Would you let him throw the first punch?"

"Not in a month of Sundays. You didn't pull your gun because of the civilians?"

"Yeah. What happened after I passed out?"

"Why didn't you step aside and wait for us cops?"

"Lucifer could drive away before you got here," I said. "I wanted to hold him for you."

"Well, you saw how well that worked out, hot shot. Why didn't you just follow him in your minivan, which is conveniently parked over there?"

Follow him? I felt gobsmacked. The truth was that, in the heat of the moment, following the suspect did not occur to me. I must have panicked and my mind must have frozen. *Follow him? McCrary, sometimes you act too stupid to be a Private Eye.*

"Truthfully, Jorge, following him just didn't occur to me. I tried to play superhero and stop him with my bare hands. Sometimes I think it's a wonder that I'm still alive. What happened after I passed out?"

Jorge pointed up the street. "Two patrol cars approached Code Three while you and Lucifer duked it out. The cops found you unconscious on the sidewalk and groceries scattered like confetti. Witnesses said Lucifer dropped you when he heard the sirens, jumped into his car, and drove off like a bat from a campfire. One witness videoed most of the fight with her phone. I'll play it for you later." He grinned. "Or I could send the video to your phone so you can watch it over and over."

"Never mind. You needn't remind me how bad he beat me. Why didn't your guys tail him?"

"They didn't know it was him. Wasn't until they stopped that they learned they'd missed him. First thing they did was call an ambulance for you. That reminds me: How'd you get Lucifer's address? We came up empty."

I slapped my pocket and held the phone up. "Crucero's phone. Lucifer called for Crucero while I was interviewing Liz Jenkins. His address was in the contacts."

"Put that away. I never saw it. Crucero came to my office yesterday and demanded we return his missing phone. Claimed it disappeared when we arrested him."

"I'll send you an email with the call log and address book. From an anonymous, public-spirited private citizen who happened to find the phone."

"And I'll email you the cellphone video of Lucifer beating you like a drum. You could use a little humility."

EIGHT

"Flamer, I need you to chase down the ownership of a property." I gave him the old firehouse's address. "A Florida Land Trust owns it."

Flamer21 was my computer guru and online researcher. It still feels uncomfortable to use a gay slur, but Flamer was the only name he ever gave me. Go figure. I had met him in person just twice. We normally communicated via phone or email. He has a Key West phone number, so I wasn't sure where he lived, but he could uncover facts even I couldn't learn.

"Chuck, I can't break a Florida Land Trust. Unless maybe I hack the law firm that's the trustee. *Hmm.* Don't get your hopes up."

"I found one clue that might help: The trustee firm or its personnel cross paths with the embassy of San Cristobal or a bad guy named Antonio Ricardo Crucero Calderone." I gave him Crucero's home address and social media addresses.

"Calderone, huh. He your cousin, hot shot?"

"God, I hope not." I told Flamer what I suspected. "Dig up what you can on Losefa Ponalelie Topati."

"Spell it."

I did, then gave him the address I had come from. "He's a minor league criminal, mostly muscle. Ignore anything on his football career; that's ancient history. Nowadays, his main digital footprint may be his rap sheet. Find out all you can."

Snoop walked in with more coffee as I was gazing out the window to Bayshore Drive. Traffic was sparse for a Saturday afternoon. Maybe they were all at the beach.

"This couldn't wait until Monday?" he asked.

"You're retired. Every day is Saturday. Besides, I pay you. If you were home, Janet would make you mow the lawn or plant tomatoes or something equally fun."

"Maybe I should be grateful." He scooted a few sheets of paper across my desk. "These addresses match Crucero's phone contacts. I'm still working the call log and the cell towers they used. Haven't gotten to the international numbers yet. They'll be tougher."

"Forget the foreign numbers. Jorge will give them to Interpol and DEA."

Snoop lifted his cup halfway to his lips. "Who's the client now, bud?"

"Huh?"

"Who's paying you to do this work?"

"I'm doing this on my own."

"You sure you want to go this route?"

Clasping my hands together in a *Namaste* pose, I bowed to him. "What is 'this route' of which you speak, Obi-Wan Snopolski?"

Snoop was my partner after I made detective. He was the wise cop with thirty years' experience. He taught me more about detective work than I learned for my master's degree in criminology at the University of Florida. He mentored me for a year until his wife talked him into early retirement.

He set the cup down without taking a sip. "What is the mission? What does victory look like? When is it over?"

"One question at a time, Obi-Wan. The mission is to wipe out Crucero's drug operation."

"Then what? Let's say you remove one bucket of shit from a cesspool. The cesspool is still there. It still stinks to high heaven, and you risk getting shit all over you."

When I laughed, Snoop scowled. "It's not funny, bud. You saw what happened with this Lucifer nut. He came *that* close to breaking your neck. Drug people are dangerous, and there are a lot more of them than there are of us."

"You watched the cellphone video. I broke his nose and he limped when he ran to his car."

"That's not the point. You rescued the damsel in distress. Hell, you rescued *five* damsels. Five young women are free now because of you. Take the win, run a victory lap waving the flag, then move on to the next case. Eliminating Crucero would have the same effect as pouring an extra bucket of water over Niagara Falls."

"You mean someone else will replace Crucero in the drug ecology. Nature abhors a vacuum."

My old friend spread his hands. "My point is: Where do we stop? This guy has more connections than a spider's web. And those connections have connections. And *those* connections have still more connections. You can't bail out the ocean."

"You said 'we' and 'us.' This is my fight. I didn't ask you to be part of the takedown. Once you get me those addresses, you can go home to Janet and the girls. In fact, go home now, if you want. You haven't broken any laws. Yet. But if you stay with me on this, you will. That's not something you should jump into until you fully recover."

Snoop scoffed. "My body may be unable to help with the takedown for a couple more days, but I'm in this fight, sure as sunrise. I'll do skull work and surveillance. You can hire the young guys like Robby and Morris when you need muscle."

"Robby and Morris can't provide muscle, only surveillance. They're full-time cops and I will step *waaay* over the line on this project. Involving them in anything illegal would ruin their careers. If this blows up in my face, I have to take the heat alone."

"What about me? I'll be involved in the illegal stuff. Doesn't it ruffle your feathers that I might have to skate on the dark side?"

"Nope. You're not a cop anymore; you retired and your pension is secure. Another thing, your two daughters are about Liz's age. I noticed your expression when we rescued Liz Jenkins. It wouldn't be right not to let you help, if you want."

"I want."

Antonio Crucero

The previous summer, one of South Florida's frequent thunderstorms hit Tony Crucero's apartment building with a lightning bolt that fried his computer along with half the electronics in the building. Following that disaster, Crucero powered down his computer and unplugged it at the end of each use. He backed everything up in the Cloud.

Too bad he couldn't back up the $485,000 in cash or the thirty kilos of cocaine in the safe at the firehouse. Maybe his lawyer could say it was part of his consulate for San Cristobal? He dismissed the notion. His law-and-order father would disinherit him for that.

While he waited for his computer to boot, he admired his new smartphone. The goddamn police stole his old phone even though they denied it. Piss on them; the manufacturer wouldn't break the password for the authorities. No one would ever know what was on his old phone.

He couldn't ask his Washington embassy to apply pressure to get the phone returned, because his father would learn about his arrest. The old man was suspicious of his actions already, always lecturing him about his obligation to represent his beloved *Republica*. The old man believed in that patriotism bullshit, but Crucero sure as hell didn't.

He pulled the phone's USB cable from its box and plugged the phone into his computer. In five minutes, he had restored his contacts.

He opened the address book. The bordello was kaput and his employees were in jail, except Al Tegumbre. He might as well delete the entries.

He used his new phone to call a girlfriend. "Hey, babe. It's Tony Crucero. I bought a new phone, and I called so you have my new number. How about dinner at that new Asian fusion restaurant tonight? Don't worry, I guarantee I can get reservations."

Crucero seldom read newspapers other than international soccer scores, but before his date, he watched a segment on the Saturday Six O'clock News about the raid on the bordello. As a result, he made an early night of it with his date and spent the night alone in his apartment.

He went to breakfast at Denny's and bought the Sunday *Port City Press-Journal.* He scoured every page but saw no mention of the SWAT team invasion of his private bordello.

Following breakfast, he returned to his apartment and accessed the newspaper's website. He read the article in the Friday edition with a photo of him in handcuffs on his perp walk into the police precinct. His picture flashed on the screen and his stomach knotted. In the confusion of the raid, he had not realized there were photographers there. If he believed in God, he would have prayed his father would not see the newspapers.

He had called the embassy in Washington on Thursday night to get released from jail. It was a matter of time before his father learned about his fiasco. He could curse his bad luck, but there was nothing he could do. That ship had sailed.

He read the news article. Tommy Flannigan's real name was Finch. Funny people, these Americans. He studied the sections on Vincent Scarpatti and Scruffy Valdez. He studied a follow-up article in the Saturday edition about the men's arraignments. Something in the article tickled his memory. Bail denied for Tommy, Vincent, and Scruffy. It made no mention of Lucifer's bail status. He stared at the newspaper in disbelief; there was no mention of Lucifer's arraignment either. Was it possible the cops didn't arrest Lucifer?

He plugged his smartphone into his computer and restored the address book entry for Lucifer Topati.

Carlos McCrary

After wiping down the weight bench, I slung the towel over my shoulder and stepped back for Tank Tyler. I'm six-foot-two and weight 225 pounds, but Tank makes me look like a 98-pound weakling.

Thomas "Tank" Tyler fastened two more 25-pound disks on the bar. "Let me demonstrate how a real man works out."

Kennedy Carlson, owner of Jerry's Gym, was spotting us both. "Okay, Tank, now you're showing off."

Tank smirked at me. He was six-foot-six and out-weighed me maybe seventy pounds, all muscle. He winked at Ken. "Coach, you're jealous you didn't get a chance to coach me when I played in the NFL." He pumped the weights without apparent effort.

Ken laughed. "I was strength coach for the Steelers, and I coached three Hall of Famers, but I would've enjoyed coaching you too."

Tank continued the exercise. *"You* can *coach* me *now,* bro," he said in time with the weights' rise and fall.

"Hell, Tank, you know more about fitness than I do."

"There's *nobody... knows* as *much* as *you* do, *coach.*" He pumped the weights in time with his conversation. Tank pumped iron for ten more reps.

"Now you made me feel puny." Ken was the personification of *Mr. Clean,* right down to the white tee-shirt and gold earring, except his eyebrows were brown instead of white. He said it was good marketing.

Tank gave the weights one more thrust and let them down to their rests with a soft click. His caramel-colored skin glistened in the fluorescent lights. He sat upright. "And that, coach, is how an NFL defensive lineman works out." He wiped down the cushion and lifted a hand to Ken for a high-five.

Ken smacked his palm and walked off shaking his head.

"Let's hit the sauna," Tank said. "We need to talk."

Tank and I always begin on the bottom sauna bench where the temperature is cooler.

"What you want to talk about, bro?"

Tank cut his gaze to two other men seated on the top bench. "It'll wait."

I took the hint. We spent the next few minutes discussing the Port City Pilots' chances at the playoffs. Our baseball team was in their usual end-of-season slump, but there was still hope for the post-season. Miracles can happen. Always live with hope.

The other men abandoned the sauna. Tank spread a towel on the top bench and sat on it. I did the same.

"I read in the *Pee-Jay* about what a hero you are. How you rescued those five women who were kidnapped when no one else knew they were missing."

"Renate got that part of the story wrong. All the families knew the women were missing, but they didn't know they were in Port City."

Tank wiped his face and head with a towel. "Making allowances for

Renate's journalistic exaggeration for maximum newsworthiness, you did a good thing there, little bro."

"Thanks. If that's all you have to tell me, you didn't need to wait until we were alone." It was definitely hotter up there.

"Don't be impatient. Let a brother ease into the subject, not jump into it like a cold swimming pool."

"Go ahead. Slather more compliments on me. I promise they won't go to my head."

"Too late for that, bro. Anyway, I know what you plan to do."

"Is that so? And what do I plan?"

"You're going to, uh, *remove* that SOB Crucero."

"He has diplomatic immunity, big brother."

Tank guffawed. His giant body shook like a mountain in an earthquake.

"The *diplofelon.* That's what Renate called him and his kind. The law can't touch a *diplofelon* because of a treaty."

He slid into the corner. "But no one is immune from McCrary's justice."

"What makes you think I want to tag Tony Crucero?"

"Puh-lease, little bro. This is your big bro Tank you're talking to. Even if Bigs Bigelow hadn't told me, I know you too well. I backed you on that Monster Moffett takedown when Snoop was in the hospital. I know how you think." He tapped his temple with a forefinger the size of a bratwurst.

"I never discussed this with Bigs."

"Bigs is as good a detective as you're gonna meet. You think Bigs can work for Jorge Castellano and not know what's happening? He would need to be as blind as a cave fish."

"Okay, let's say I want Crucero's scalp—which I do not admit. So what?"

Tank wiped his head again. "Bigs says you need help. That's why he came to me."

"Go on."

"I want in. Before you say anything, hear me out, okay?"

"You have the floor, or the bench."

Tank didn't laugh. Some people don't appreciate my sense of humor.

"Let's consider facts. First, I do your tax returns and I manage your investments. I know your financial capabilities."

"This is true."

"You rescued the damsels in distress, collected a nice fee, and now you don't have a client. In other words, no one will pay you to put Crucero out of business."

"Also true, if I wanted Crucero."

Tank raised a finger. "You need manpower for surveillance, research, and security backup. Plus, maybe money for travel and out-of-pocket expenses, if the case requires it."

"It will. That is, it *would*, if I were after Crucero."

"You could finance this yourself, but it might impoverish you. You shouldn't blow your retirement fund to run down one criminal—assuming you could bring it off."

"I'm young, Tank. I could lose every cent, and it wouldn't bother me. My condo is paid for; so is my boat. I have another thirty years to earn money. Look at the bright side: If I get killed, I won't need a retirement fund."

Tank made a *who-you-kidding* face.

"I'm serious, Tank. The money isn't important."

"Please, Chuck, don't ever say money isn't important. That offends my sensibilities as a CPA and financial advisor. Money is *always* important, but sometimes your goals are more important than the money. To you, holding Tony Crucero responsible for those girls' kidnapping and abuse is more important than the money it would require."

"I get your point. And I'm willing to pay the price because there's something I never told you."

"What's that?"

"It's a long story. We'll roast like two Thanksgiving turkeys if we don't get out of this sauna."

Tank rose off the bench. "Let's go to my house for dinner and chit-chat. I'll call Cook and ask her to whip up chicken enchiladas."

———

Tank and I propped our feet on twin hassocks around the pool of his mansion on Pink Coral Island. He had earned millions in the NFL, invested wisely, and built an investment management firm with a dozen or more employees to manage other people's fortunes. Tank wasn't a billionaire, but he was in shouting distance.

Tank managed my investments, modest as they were. My portfolio was a pimple on his portfolio's butt. Thankfully, he's a friend as well as my CPA.

A sliver of sun peaked through the evening clouds and reflected on Seeti Bay, painting the twilight with a vivid palette, heavy on reds and golds.

Tank lifted his Sangria glass. "To justice."

We clinked glasses. "Down with the evildoers."

Tank grinned. His teeth gleamed in the twilight against his brown skin.

"Tell me this long story, bro."

My wine glass clinked softly on the glass-topped table as I set it down. "My cousin Emily may have suffered the same fate as Liz Jenkins."

I told him the story. Telling it again eased more of the weight off my shoulders.

"That's why I want Crucero. It's personal."

Tank lifted his glass. "If ever a man deserved to die, it's Tony Crucero. Why not kill him? That seems easier."

"Two reasons: First, the people he sells to would still be there. I want more impact than removing one man. Second, he's a diplomat. If he's murdered, the FBI will investigate the case. I'm good at covering my tracks, but nobody's good enough to risk having the FBI chasing them."

"If you somehow manage to reach Crucero, you can't beat *all* the bad guys. There are too many."

"I know I'll have to draw the line somewhere. I can't clean up all of South Florida. But, yeah, I'll hit Tony Crucero and the first circle of people he sells to. That much is doable."

Tank refilled our Sangrias and watched the sunset fade. We had emptied the pitcher.

Tank's butler materialized, a genie whose lamp was rubbed. As always, the old man wore a pale blue guayabera, dark blue Bermuda shorts, and sandals. He must have a closet full of identical outfits. "Would you care for another pitcher of Sangria, Tank?"

"I'm good, Gregory. How about you, Chuck?"

"I'm good."

"Very good, sir. Give a shout if you need me."

Gregory walked away.

"Every time I see him, I think of Bruce Wayne's Alfred."

"And every time you tell me that, I remind you that I don't have a Batmobile."

I finished my drink. "It's been nice, bro, but I have a big day tomorrow."

"Not so fast, Kemosabe. I have my own story to tell."

"If it's a long one, you'd better ask Gregory to fix me a coffee. Make it iced coffee."

"Good idea. I'll join you. This story takes a while to tell."

By the time Gregory served the iced coffee, it was full dark. Across Seeti Bay, the lights of the mainland glowed on the right and Port City Beach on the left.

"Gregory, we won't need you anymore tonight. You've had a long day, my friend."

"Very good, sir. I'll see you for breakfast. Will Chuck be joining us?"

Tank regarded me. "You're welcome to stay. I have eight guest rooms."

"Thanks, but I have an early day tomorrow. I'll head home, Gregory. Good night."

The old man tottered to the bungalow where he lived.

"My story is different from yours," Tank said, "but it's the same. You remember I have six brothers and two sisters."

"You're second youngest?"

"Right. I used to have *three* sisters. My oldest sibling was my sister Eugenia. She was twelve years older than me—than *I,* I meant to say. She graduated from Florence High School and took a part-time job in Birmingham. She went to junior college there to learn to be a legal secretary."

"Go on."

"Eugenia got in with the wrong crowd. She started partying, got pregnant, and dropped out of college."

I didn't know what to say, so I grunted.

"Her baby was born addicted to cocaine."

"Oh, God. The poor baby."

Tank waved it off. "I was eight years old. Momma went to Birmingham to be with Eugenia when the baby came. It was four weeks premature. Three days in neonatal intensive care unit before the baby died. Momma got Eugenia to name her Esperanza."

"Esperanza is Spanish for *hope*."

He swung his feet off the hassock and stood. "I know. That's my momma, always looks on the bright side. Esperanza."

He paced the pool deck. "At the time, I knew none of this. Hell, I was in third grade in Florence. Daddy said Momma went to Birmingham to help Eugenia with her baby. But they came back for a funeral. Such a tiny coffin." He held his hands three feet apart and stared at them while he brought his emotions under control. His voice broke when he said, "I'll never forget that tiny coffin."

He gazed toward heaven and took a few long breaths. "Three weeks following Esperanza's funeral, Eugenia died of a cocaine overdose. We buried her beside Esperanza."

Tears traced shiny tracks down his cheeks. "This Tony Crucero guy, he's a cocaine dealer. That's why I want in. I'll pay the tab to bury him six feet under, and, if needed, I'll back you with muscle and guns like I did before. If you need me to, I'll even pull the trigger."

I considered that for a few seconds. "Thanks. You're the banker, but I call the shots. This is my most dangerous mission since Afghanistan."

Tank wiped his cheeks with a napkin and threw me a mock salute. "*Our* most dangerous mission."

"First thing you do is learn to shoot a sniper rifle."

Tank's face broke into a feral grin. "Ooh, I like the sound of that, bro."

NINE

Robby Gorski

R obby Gorski sat in his eight-year-old Camry and waited for the traffic light. He didn't worry he would lose the trail on the man Chuck called *Striped Tie*. The GPS tracker would guarantee that. Mid-afternoon, Striped Tie steered into a Mexican Restaurant for a late lunch.

As Robby trailed Striped Tie into the restaurant five minutes later, he switched on his phone's video camera. It was recording while he walked past Striped Tie's table. He would extract a still photo off the phone later. Robby sat at the counter and ordered a *pan dulce* and a *cafe con leche*. He paid for his order when it arrived, leaving a good tip. Chuck had taught him to be ready to scram without waiting for the bill, and to tip generously because the servers needed the money, but not extravagantly because an operative shouldn't be memorable.

A half-hour later, Striped Tie thrust his plate away, finished his *Dos Equis,* and scraped his chair back. He dropped some bills for the server and exited.

Robby walked past the vacated table, jammed his finger in the neck of the bottle, and slipped it into a plastic bag. DNA and fingerprints both.

Morris Martinez

Morris Martinez lost Crucero's red Corvette in the second mile on I-95. Crucero wove through the Sunday afternoon traffic at 80 mph like the world was one big video game. Crucero had immunity from traffic cops, but Morris didn't. He slapped his steering wheel in frustration. Neither he nor Chuck had been able to switch out the dead battery on the GPS tracker Chuck had stuck under the Corvette.

He made the next exit and called Chuck. "This is Morris. I tailed Crucero to Miss Cleavage's cottage. He carried a briefcase inside. After he left her house, I lost him. The jerk hit 80 mph on I-95 and punched his Corvette harder than a stock car race. I didn't dare stay with him. Even without the danger to other traffic, he would have made me."

"You made a good decision, buddy. Use that list of his hangouts I gave you. You might pick him up again. Maybe you can replace the tracker device."

At the second place Morris searched, he located the Corvette. The car was accessible, so he replaced the dead tracker battery with a fresh one.

At sunset, he tailed Crucero home.

Carlos McCrary

Robby's email hit my inbox an hour after I reached my office Monday morning.

Striped Tie's name was Alfonso Luis Tegumbre Pedroso and he hailed from Guatemala. His American name was Al Tegumbre. Robby included his rap sheet: armed robbery, ADW, attempted murder, possession with intent, and lesser sins. He spent eleven years in Gentryville State Prison in the Florida Everglades. Gentryville Prison was like graduate school for career criminals.

I was surprised when Tegumbre's parole officer reported that he had kept his nose clean for the two years he had worked for the Republic of San Cristobal at their Port City consulate. As far as I knew, San Cristobal didn't have a consulate in Port City, but I remembered the plaque on the door of Crucero's apartment. Could it be? I punched the internet. No listing. Flipping further back in the PO reports, I found it. The consulate's address was Tony Crucero's apartment. That explained the San Cristobal coat of arms on Crucero's door. It made Crucero's apartment the sovereign territory of the Republic of San Cristobal and immune to a search warrant. How nice for his drug boutique.

I called Robby in the field. "Nice work. Put a looser tail on Tegumbre. That guy's as dangerous as an alligator with a toothache. Log every stop he makes, but don't get within fifty yards. Use the telephoto to shoot whoever he does business with, but, for God's sake, don't let him spot you, or little Tess might wind up an orphan. In fact, do you want off the case?"

"Don't worry, boss. He'll never make me."

Flamer's email arrived Tuesday:

The old firehouse/bordello property trustee is Horatio Gustavo Mendoza. Nickname "Harry Mendoza." Dual citizenship USA and San Cristobal. Why are we not surprised? Mendoza is a partner in Herkimer, Klein, Lewandowsky & Cornish. Law firm has offices in DC and Port City and is registered lobbyist for La Republica de San Cristobal.

Losefa Ponalelie Topati has one DUI and a suspended driver's license. That's it.

Flamer attached Mendoza's resume from the law firm's website. Mendoza graduated from Georgetown law school in DC. On a hunch I Googled *Pablo Antonio Crucero Obregon*, the ambassador. He attended Georgetown with Harry Mendoza. The international old boys' network in action.

That Saturday, my condo association was throwing a pool party for kids. Since I had no children, I invited Robby and his wife Gisela and two-year-old Tess to the party.

Miyo was visiting her parents in San Francisco over the Independence Day weekend. She had invited me to go with her, but I needed to stick close to the Crucero case. We agreed to both go on Labor Day weekend. I was happy as a bee in an orange grove.

Clint Watkins, my semi-ward, came home from school for the long weekend. I grilled burgers for the adults and a hot dog for Tess. Clint was transitioning between child and adult, so I made him both. At seventeen, he ate enough for two people anyway.

Clint burst into my life by helping me solve a double murder. His mother had been an addict for his entire young life with no apparent desire to quit. He had lived hand-to-mouth on the streets. It wouldn't be right to send him back to the foster care system, so I obtained her written consent to enroll him in Port City Preparatory School as a boarding student. He liked Port City Prep fine, but my condo was home.

Following lunch, Gisela escorted Tess to the condo pool for the party. There would be ice cream.

Seeing Tess made me a little jealous of Robby and Gisela. My relationship with Miyo was ready for the next step, an exclusive relationship. When she traveled to New York or Chicago on gallery business, she dated other men. She never kept that secret. Now that she knew I loved her, I hoped her viewpoint would change.

Clint cleared his throat. "You and Robby gonna talk about this case?"

"Yes. But don't let us bother you. Go to the pool with Gisela and Tess, or watch TV, play video games, whatever you want."

"You told me you were in high school when you decided to be a PI."

"Yep."

"My senior year starts soon. It's time to consider a career before I go to college. If it's okay with you and Robby, I'll sit in to learn a little more about the private investigator business."

Robby shrugged. "Okay by me."

"Take a seat, Clint. You sit and listen. I'll answer any questions once Robby and I finish. Make notes if you want, so long as you shred them after we talk."

I spread the Atlantic County map on the dining room table. It was a twin of the one Snoop and I had used to hunt for Liz.

"These lines are the routes Tegumbre drove this week. I drew them from your logs, Robby. Notice on Monday, he stayed in the area from

Barranca Bay to the EC&F railroad tracks. On Tuesday, he went from the tracks to the Everglades south of the airport. On Wednesday, he was in the area from Humboldt Springs to the Everglades north of the airport. Thursday, Seeti Lakes west of I-895, and Friday to the Mixmaster and down the beaches to the cruise port."

Robby peered at the map. "He covered the whole county in five days. It's a delivery route."

"Crucero bragged to Liz Jenkins that he brings cocaine from San Cristobal every week or two in his baggage. My airport contacts say he often checks a big trunk as baggage. It's marked as a diplomatic pouch and U.S. Customs lets it in without inspection. Tegumbre delivers product to dealers all over Atlantic County."

"If he has such a great way to bring in drugs, why does he stay in Atlantic County. Wouldn't he expand to Miami or Fort Lauderdale?"

"Tuesday, I'm meeting with Sergeant Wilma Leonard of Organized Crime. Maybe she'll know."

Monday, July 4th, Independence Day, Clint and I went fishing.

We anchored offshore to enjoy the sunset. Gentle swells rolled under the *Gator Raider Too* making it hard to keep our balance. The beer didn't help my balance either. I leaned against the counter in the galley while I taught Clint how to make ceviche with our catch. We hadn't caught much, so the dish was skimpy, but I had packed sandwiches. Be prepared.

We unfolded a camp table on the back deck.

"Dig in, Clint. Fireworks at nine o'clock."

Clint swallowed a bite of his sandwich.

"This case you're working, Chuck. Who's the client?"

"The labor is on my own dime. Tank bankrolls the expenses."

"Why? What's his interest?"

"A member of Tank's family had a bad experience with drugs. Tank takes Crucero's drug trading personally. He and I agreed the world would be better off with Tony Crucero gone."

"You and Tank are judge, jury, and executioner?"

That was a tricky question. After considering what to say, I told Clint the truth. "Pretty much."

"Won't you feel guilty killing him in cold blood?"

"No more than I would for stepping on a scorpion. Actually, less guilty: The scorpion doesn't have a choice; Crucero does."

Clint stared at the half-eaten sandwich in his hand. "Okay. Let's say that Crucero deserves to die and you and Tank elect yourselves to do it. You could be charged with murder."

"If we mess up, yeah."

"You're the one who always says, 'Eventualities tend to eventuate.' What if you get charged with murder again—especially if you're guilty this time—where would that leave me and the rest of the family? Your parents, grandparents? We've all gone that route with you before when you were charged with two murders. You don't want the family to go through that again. Especially if you're guilty, which you would be."

"Tony Crucero is an accredited diplomat and killing him would cause international repercussions. The FBI would get the case. Anyone who would bet their life or their freedom that they could fool the FBI would be stupid. I have made a few mistakes in my life, but I am not that dumb."

"So, *you* can't pull the trigger."

"Remember: You *squeeze* a trigger; you don't *pull* it. I'll arrange for someone else to *squeeze* the trigger. Either that or Crucero attacks me with witnesses and I kill him in self-defense. And I can't count on him to have the balls for that."

"So how are you going to make Crucero attack you?"

"Haven't figured that out yet, but something will turn up. I'll stir the pot until it boils."

TEN

Sergeant Wilma Leonard lifted her paper cup. "I like you, McCrary, because you bring me cappuccino."

"And I thought it was my movie-star good looks and boyish charm."

"Mainly it's the cappuccino."

She situated the cup on her battered desk. "What brings you downtown?"

"There is a drug distributor in Atlantic County named Antonio Ricardo Crucero. I intend to put him out of business."

"Is he the guy in the *Pee-Jay* article? The one you caught in a whorehouse with his pants down?"

"I caught him with his pants *off*. He was raping my client's daughter at the time. I found her in time to drag him off her and kick him in the balls as hard as I could. Unfortunately, that is the only punishment for rape, kidnapping, and accessory to murder that he will suffer."

Wilma's big, warm laugh filled the whole room. "The follow-up article said he was involved—excuse me, 'allegedly' involved—in the drug trade. Were you the anonymous source?"

"Yeah. Renate Crowell got wind of the bust. She wanted to witness the building breach firsthand to write an 'I was there' account. To get her to stay out of the way, I promised an exclusive in-depth interview. I learned last week that Crucero uses a Florida Land Trust to own the building where the five women were captive. He's involved to the tip of his greasy black ponytail."

"Was he behind the kidnappings?"

I rocked my hand back and forth. "He knew the women were captive even if he didn't orchestrate the abductions. He was at least an accessory. With the bordello for a tenant, he profited from coerced prostitution."

"Nice guy."

"Jorge's CSIs opened the safe there and confiscated half a million in cash and thirty kilos of coke."

"Was it Crucero's?"

"Tommy Finch, who's doing back flips to cooperate with the DA, claims the whole operation belonged to Crucero, including the women, the money, and the drugs."

"Okay, I got that," Wilma said. "Why tell me?"

"I want you to help me eliminate Crucero."

"He's a diplomat. We can't touch him."

"I know."

"What do you expect me to do?" she asked.

"Crucero employs a gunman named Al Tegumbre—full Hispanic name of Alfonso Luis Tegumbre Pedroso. He's from Guatemala. He's on parole from Gentryville for attempted murder and ADW. The last two years he's worked for Crucero as a gofer, bodyguard, and general bad guy. He's paid by the Republic of San Cristobal at their Port City consulate."

Wilma arched an eyebrow. "San Cristobal has a consulate here? Where?"

"Tony Crucero's apartment."

"That makes it sovereign San Cristobal territory."

"And immune to search warrants in the United States," I said.

"You said Tegumbre's a gunman. If he's on parole, he can't own a gun."

"That's true, but as long as he drives a car with diplomatic plates, no cop has probable cause to stop him."

Wilma spun her cappuccino cup in a circle with her index fingers. "Okay, we both know what I *can't* do for you. Tell me what I *can* do."

"Tegumbre runs a regular drug delivery route covering Atlantic County. Crucero imports cocaine in a diplomatic shipment from San Cristobal every week or two."

I referred to the Atlantic County map I had shown Robby Gorski. "Here's the route Tegumbre drives to deliver the drugs. Tell me who he's delivering to."

Wilma leaned over the map. "These stops in Humbolt Springs are the Teddy Sanson gang's territory. Port City Beach is Sasha Eisenfeldt's gang. Oklahatchee is Daquon Petrie's territory."

"Hold on. Let me write these on the map."

"The near north side from the Seeti River to Oklahatchee is Makenlee Tucker's territory."

I wrote his name on the map.

"Hernando Hernandez runs the territory from west Port City out to the Everglades. Down in Corcoran Heights, Alex Tremaine's outfit is the only WASP gang in Atlantic County."

I finished posting the gangs' names. "We have two Cuban gangs, one Jewish, two African-American, and one Anglo. Atlantic County can be proud that the diversity of our criminal gangs reflects our city's ethnic makeup."

"Yeah, we're the poster child for inclusiveness."

"For that much territory and as little cocaine as he imports, Crucero is merely a mid-level supplier?"

Wilma rocked her hand back and forth. "Maybe he's not ambitious. How many employees does he have?"

"Tommy Finch, Vincent Scarpatti, and Scruffy Valdez are in jail. That leaves him Al Tegumbre and Lucifer Topati."

"He can't run a drug operation with two employees. Hell, Chuck, Crucero couldn't run one with five. The real drug gangs would steal his lunch money and give him a wedgie."

"So, he stays small time and imports drugs from San Cristobal for a lucrative hobby."

"Crucero is such small fry that we never heard of him until the bordello bust," said Wilma. "Even without his diplomatic status, we have enough on our plate with the six real gangs."

"Who runs Fort Lauderdale?"

"Broward County is the Garcia gang's territory. They ran out the Cubans, the Jews, the blacks, and the Anglo gangs."

I snatched my notepad. "Tell me about them."

"Garcia is a common surname. We can't always identify who the gang's members are. It's like a criminal gang named *Smith*. The Garcias are a franchise of the Garcia cartel in Sinaloa, Mexico. They imported over a hundred gunmen from Mexico. A *hundred* guns. They invaded Broward County seven years ago, won a bloody gang war with the Cuban Mafia, and captured the drug business up to the Palm Beach County line. Didn't you hear about that?"

"I was in Gainesville. I was too busy in college to pay attention to news from anywhere outside Gainesville. I mainly followed sports news."

Wilma nodded. "By the time you graduated and moved to Port City, the gang war was over. Any Cuban Mafia the Garcias hadn't murdered migrated to New Jersey."

"What about Miami-Dade County?" I asked.

"The Ochoas control Miami Beach. The Taylors command the area from the Miami River north to the county line. The Jacominos own Hialeah. The Cernan gang owns the territory from the Miami River south to Homestead. If your Crucero guy moved on either county, his diplomatic immunity wouldn't stop a bullet."

"I know the Ochoas, the Taylors, and the Jacominos. Why haven't I heard of the Cernan gang?"

Wilma spelled it for me. "They're new. Andrej Cernan runs the whole Miami-Dade operation from Switzerland."

"Why Switzerland?"

"Maybe he's learning to yodel. He's ethnic Bosnian, by way of Slovenia. Cernan was an *apparatchik* in the Yugoslav Communist Party. The Slovenes agitated for independence in 1987, and he and his cronies took advantage of the distractions to loot the public treasury. Andrej stole 45 million dollars. Once Slovenia declared independence in 1990, Andrej fled to Switzerland with his wife and daughter. He developed an organized crime network in the former Yugoslav republics. He delegates local operation to communist cronies. Today he rakes in more than 45 million dollars every year."

"That's over twenty years ago. Why haven't his local guys declared their own independence from him?"

"He's short-tempered, ruthless, and cruel. He makes bloody examples of anybody who crosses him. One trick is called the *barbed-wire necktie.* You get the picture?"

My neck tingled like I had shaved too close. "Remind me to stay out of Switzerland."

"Andrej Cernan is careful not to break any laws in Switzerland." Wilma slurped her cappuccino. "A couple years ago, he expanded into South Florida."

"How does he run a gang in Miami from six thousand miles away? Does he know more former communist leaders here?"

"Nah, he has something better, his daughter Alena. His daughter is bad as he is. Maybe worse."

"That's gotta be rare—a woman running an organized crime gang."

"It's practically unheard of. Alena Cernan attended the best Swiss finishing schools. She knows which fork to use at an embassy dinner and she speaks five languages."

"How do you spell it?"

"A-L-E-N-A."

I wrote it down. "And she's a gang leader?"

"She's more ruthless than her father. If I told you the ways she killed the local gang leaders she replaced in Coconut Grove, it would give you nightmares."

"Worse than a barbed-wire necktie?"

"The most recent method I heard from a buddy in Miami is the *gasoline enema.*"

"Jeez." My butt puckered.

"Alena invaded Miami three years ago to build the Cernan network in the Land of the Free and the Home of the Brave. She brought Serbian muscle with her. Their surveillance photos looked like a squad of Hitler's Aryan soldiers. My friends in Miami-Dade's organized crime unit call them the Blue-Eyed Devils."

"You have their pictures?"

Wilma stepped to a gray file cabinet behind her and fished out a manila folder. She tossed it on her desk for me. "Help yourself."

There were a dozen photos of Alena's thugs. Buzz-cuts, broken noses, and scars. Eleven of the twelve had blue eyes. "Can I have copies?"

"Photograph the pages with your cellphone."

I did and slid the folder across the desk. "These guys stick to Miami-Dade?"

"Coconut Grove and south to Homestead. Yeah. Alena keeps an uneasy truce with three other Miami-Dade gangs. But she's paranoid about encroachment."

Lucifer

The Samoan waited for Tony Crucero at the Denny's in Humbolt Springs. After two weeks of loss and confusion, Tony would restore order to his universe. He drummed his fingers on the table beside his half-empty cup. He scratched his neck. His new beard itched like crazy.

Crucero's BMW rolled into the lot and parked. He headed for the restaurant. The BMW's headlights flashed as Tony locked the doors.

Topati stood so Tony would spot him.

Tony waved the hostess over. "Can we eat at that table instead?"

"Of course, sir. I'll tell your server."

He moved to the table and grabbed the chair by the wall. Topati sat to his right. The hostess gave them menus and left.

"Always get a table in the back, Luce, and sit with your back to the wall."

Topati felt relieved the rebuke wasn't more severe. Tony called Topati *Luce* when he was pleased. He called him *Lucifer* when he did something wrong.

"Sure thing, boss."

"Did you rent a new place the way I told you?"

"Yeah. Ground floor with parking in front and back and a rear exit like you said. 3326 NW Malta Drive in Oklahatchee."

Tony handed his phone to Topati. "Enter your address in here. You're back on the payroll. The cops are hunting for you for sure. Stay out of sight. Let your beard and hair grow in more, so you'll be hard to recognize. I'll have an assignment. For now, Luce, watch a lot of TV."

Carlos McCrary

Jorge paid for lunch.

"What's the occasion, *amigo?*" I asked. "We usually go Dutch."

"I'm paying it forward like that old movie said. Ten days ago, a public-spirited citizen sent me the call log and address book from a drug dealer's phone. I don't know who that anonymous citizen was, so I bought your lunch to pay it forward."

He handed a stick drive across the table.

Shoving it my pocket, I asked, "What's on it?"

"The names and addresses for every number Tony Crucero talked to that we could identify. Maybe we learned stuff you didn't know. When we couldn't name the caller or the callee, we gave you the cell tower the other end used."

"Thanks. Did you GPS a location for Lucifer's phone?"

"Nah. It's an old model without GPS, but when it wasn't pinging the cell tower near the old firehouse, it pinged a tower in Uptown near that dumpy apartment where he tried to kill you. Since then, it's pinging a tower north of Oklahatchee Airport."

"He's rented a new apartment in that airport neighborhood. Send detectives to canvass the area with a photo. Ask the locals if they've spotted him."

"We don't have the resources. We issued an arrest warrant for an accessory to kidnapping and entered his description in the system, but with our budget, that's all we can do."

Over the remainder of the week, Tegumbre repeated the route he had taken the previous week. Robby Gorski determined that his territory stretched from the Broward County line down to the Miami-Dade County line. At every stop, he hauled a briefcase inside or met someone at the door. Later he brought the briefcase back to his car. Two repetitions of the route suggested a pattern. Crucero ran a Drugs-R-Us store, free delivery included.

One exception to Tegumbre's Atlantic County route was a trip made the second week to Miss Cleavage's cottage in Miami's Coconut Grove section. He carried a briefcase in and came out empty-handed. Was she involved in Crucero's network? If Crucero was her supplier, it explained why a knockout babe hung out with a creep like Crucero.

I assigned another operative to Miss Cleavage. Within twelve hours, we identified her. She was Alena Cernan, the Serbian-born daughter of crime boss Andrej Cernan.

Small world.

ELEVEN

W alking out of her Coconut Grove cottage, Alena Cernan didn't look like Miss Cleavage. Quite the opposite: low-heeled dark blue pumps, pin-striped matching blue slacks with a wide white leather belt, and a modest white silk blouse with long sleeves and a high neck. Her large blue burlap purse with a long shoulder strap completed an image that announced *Entrepreneur of the Year*.

An hour earlier, I had parked my Grand Caravan half a block away behind a Ford sedan and sat in the rear. Concealed behind my tinted side windows, I snapped pictures through the untinted windshield. There must be eighteen bazillion white minivans in the world, which effectively makes mine invisible.

Her black Mercedes S600 sedan stopped at the curb pointing the wrong way. Alena garaged the Mercedes off an alley behind her cottage. The previous night I had picked the garage door lock and mounted a GPS tracker on the big sedan.

A black Suburban with tinted windows parked behind the Mercedes. I photographed its license plate.

A big man in a bad suit jumped from the Mercedes and opened the rear door. Behind the sunglasses, I recognized Viktor Kokot from Wilma's folder. His shoulder holster made his jacket hang askew. His frumpy suit looked *made in Serbia.* So did he. Light brown hair and wide shoulders. The difference between him and the suit was that one had a crew cut and the other was badly cut. Viktor's brow and nose looked like he had been on the wrong end of numerous fights.

Despite her business attire, Alena descended the porch steps with a fashion-model strut. She spoke to the driver, then entered the sedan like stepping into a royal carriage.

Viktor opened the trunk. He removed a bulky cardboard box, balancing it between his arm and hip while he closed the trunk. He placed the box on the seat next to Alena and closed the door. Returning to the driver's seat, he powered the Mercedes from the curb. The Suburban trailed at a respectful distance.

They curved out of sight. I booted my GPS tracker app and followed the parade.

Forty-five minutes later, the Mercedes exited the turnpike and headed west through the heart of Homestead, a small city south of Miami, and into the countryside. The S600 angled south on 195th Avenue. Row crops, mango groves, avocado trees, and native plant nurseries lined the two-lane rural streets. I turned into the entrance to a nursery at 195th Avenue and 312th Street and referred to my paper map. Why did they drive to the boondocks?

On my screen, the blip for the Mercedes swung west on 326th Street. The land was filled with agriculture and an occasional farmhouse. I passed auto salvagers and produce processors, both banished from town. The occasional strip center was anchored by a Mexican restaurant or bar and a *tienda* Mexican store. Many migrant workers lived in nearby trailer parks. The S600 continued west, then stopped.

The Mercedes parked on the sandy shoulder ten yards east of the entrance to Jose's Auto Salvage. The Suburban stopped thirty yards to the west, bracketing the sliding gate between it and the sedan. Four men in bad slacks, knock-off golf shirts, and ill-fitted sports coats stood guard like they expected an attack on the junkyard. It didn't take a trained eye to assess the bulges the weapons made under their jackets. From their skin and hair color and their bad taste in clothes, they were more Blue-Eyed Devils.

Continuing past the auto salvage, I reached Buddy's Berry Farm across the street. A sign beside the palm-thatched fruit stand advertised fresh strawberries and fruit milkshakes in various flavors. Customer vehicles reflected a cross-section of South Florida citizenry. An old Saturn had a Conch Republic bumper sticker from the Florida Keys. I parked between a pickup truck with Michigan plates and a camper on the back and a shiny sedan with a *¡Viva Mexico!* window sticker and Mexican plates.

Wooden picnic tables under canvas umbrellas sprawled at each end of the open-air fruit stand. A dozen parents and children sat at the tables enjoying strawberry shakes. One father slurped a blueberry shake, obvious through the clear plastic cup. His daughter held an orangecolored shake, looked like mango.

A guardrail separated the fruit stand from the parking area. The rail could have been the hitching post in a western movie, except it was steel pipe painted traffic-stripe yellow. Sidestepping around the rail, I waited under a sign that said *Order here.*

The shopkeeper stood at the shake machine and filled two plastic cups with frozen pink deliciousness. She finished the order and handed the two shakes to a man farther down the counter under the *Pick up order here* sign. She rang the sale and stepped over to me. "What can I get y'all today?"

"A large strawberry shake, please."

"Full disclosure: It's past the fresh strawberry season, but our frozen fruit shakes are almost as good."

"That'll be fine."

The shopkeeper about-faced to make the shake, and I stepped to the back of my Caravan.

As I pulled out my telephoto-equipped camera, my heart rate increased. Alena Cernan and her gun-toting entourage had not driven to the back of beyond for a picnic—or a strawberry shake. This might be the first stop on her distribution route.

A gate in the concrete block wall screeched open, and two men in straw hats, dirty tee-shirts, and cowboy boots walked out. One wore grease-stained overalls. The other wore faded blue jeans. Maybe one was Jose.

Standing between my Caravan and the Mexican sedan, I started the video camera.

A small airplane engine roared behind me. There was a grass airstrip north of the fruit stand, but I had never seen it used.

A tricked-up red Lexus with flashy hubcaps and extra chrome trim bumped onto the grassy shoulder a block east of the junkyard. It flashed its headlights once.

The men from the salvage yard waved at the Mercedes. They walked over and stood beside the Suburban.

Viktor approached them. Both extended their arms, and he frisked them. He nodded at the guard closest to the Mercedes. The guard was featured in the photos in Wilma's surveillance folder: Hugo Horvat.

In the Green Berets, we didn't wear rank insignia in the field. If a Taliban or Al Qaida terrorist spotted officer's brass, it made him or her a sniper's target. Most of us were sergeants. If we wore insignia at all, it was an embroidered emblem invisible from more than a few feet away. Yet we knew when a ranking officer approached, even one we had never met.

A leader exhibits an *attitude of altitude* that his or her own people perceive even when the enemy can't. It's often visible, not in the leaders, but in the men and women who report to them, in their body language as they interact with the leader. Hugo Horvat was treated this way. Even Viktor respected this guy.

Horvat acted like the Chief of Security, or whatever the equivalent was in Serbia or Slovenia or wherever the hell he came from.

Viktor opened the rear door of the Mercedes, and Overalls ducked in. Viktor left the door open and stepped back. He kept his hand inside his jacket and his attention focused inside the Mercedes.

Overalls slid from the car and stuffed an envelope in his pocket. He and Blue Jeans reentered the yard with a wave at the Chief of Security. Their boots kicked up a small dust cloud that followed them through the gate. The gate screeched closed again.

Viktor glanced toward the Lexus, then leaned into the Mercedes to speak with Alena. He closed the door without latching it. He made a call.

The Lexus bumped onto the street and approached. It bounced off the pavement and steered into the sand parking area. It stopped by the Suburban, a respectful distance from the Mercedes.

A thin young black man with abundant dreadlocks exited the driver side, leaving the door open.

Viktor motioned him toward the Suburban.

Dreadlocks extended his arms to either side, revealing sleeves of tattoos vivid against his light brown skin. The tattoos would identify him when I shared my video with the narco cops.

Viktor paid no attention to the strawberry farm—it was a part of the landscape that had become background noise.

He frisked Dreadlocks and wrenched a switchblade from his pants. He flicked it open and waved it in the man's face. His body language was clear: *What's this, smart guy?*

Dreadlocks raised his palms in protest.

Viktor closed the knife and tossed it into the Lexus through the open door. He pointed Dreadlocks toward the Mercedes.

Viktor opened the door, gestured Dreadlocks to get in, and followed the same routine he did with Overalls: Stay close, focus your gaze inside the Mercedes, keep hand near gun.

"Sir, your shake is ready."

A yellow biplane taxied to a stop fifty yards behind the fruit stand.

I picked up my shake. "A biplane landed behind you."

The shopkeeper glanced over her shoulder. "Yeah, he's an antique airplane nut. Lives somewhere near Sebring. He flies in every week or so for a shake. You'd be surprised how many people fly in."

Opening the Caravan's rear door, I stuck my shake in a cupholder. From the rear of my van, I saw Dreadlocks exit the Mercedes. I videoed until he drove away.

I called Snoop. "I'm at Buddy's Berry Farm on SW 326th Street."

"Lucky guy. Janet and I bring the girls every February for strawberry milkshakes. You know strawberry season is over, right?"

"That's not why I'm here."

"You there for a mango shake?"

"For once, just shut up and listen. Alena Cernan and four of her crew have set up shop down the street."

"You mean Miss Cleavage?"

"Today she dressed like the *Wall Street Journal* is interviewing her for their 'CEO of the Year' award. She's in a Mercedes with a four-man armed escort in a black Suburban." I gave him both plate numbers. "She opened for business at Jose's Auto Salvage. I'll need backup if the two vehicles split up."

"I'll need an hour and a half to get there, bud."

"They may not stay that long. After they close up shop, I'll text you where to meet me. There's nothing west of here but the Everglades, so they'll go back the way they came. There's a traffic light at 195th Avenue and a Mexican restaurant and *tienda* in a strip center on the corner. Wait for me in the parking lot. After Cernan's vehicles drive past, I'll be a mile behind them. Can you do it?"

"I'm walking to my car. I'll text once I get in position."

I nursed a strawberry shake at a table. Two more cars wobbled across the sandy strip and stopped next to the Suburban. Two more drivers were frisked and two more transactions took place under Viktor's watchful supervision. From the shade of the umbrella, I photographed the license plates and drivers with my cellphone. The Michigan pickup beside me drove away, leaving the Caravan exposed. I didn't risk the video camera or the video feature on my phone; I was too visible at the table. I had pressed my luck staying this long.

Hugo Horvat

Horvat ambled over to Viktor Kokot. His face pointed at Viktor, but he cut his gaze to the fruit stand. "Don't look," he said in Serbian, "but that man in the white Dodge Grand Caravan across the street is worrisome."

Viktor began to swivel, and Horvat clutched his arm. "Don't be stupid. I don't want him to know I am watching."

"Why tell me?"

"Help me observe him without him noticing. The Caravan arrived less than five minutes after we did. Other vehicles at the fruit stand come and go, but the Caravan is still there." Horvat tugged a crumpled cigarette package from his jacket and lit one.

"Maybe he's eating lunch? They sell hamburgers and hotdogs."

"Maybe, but he never looks over here. A normal person would look, if just in passing." Horvat puffed on the cigarette.

"That is your job. I am a driver."

"The man never turns his back. He watches from the edge of his vision."

"Is he police?" Viktor asked. "A stakeout? If the people at the fruit stand are suspicious, perhaps they called the police."

"No. He arrived too soon after we did to have responded to a phone call."

"If he is a cop, how did he know we were here? I guarantee no one followed us."

Horvat shrugged. "As you walk around, observe without him noticing. He used a camera earlier. And perhaps he uses his cellphone camera even now."

"Are you sure?"

"Of course not. That's why I need your help."

"If you're not sure, why does this peasant concern you?"

"Alena pays me to be paranoid."

Carlos McCrary

As I tossed my empty cup in the recycle bin and ordered a mango shake, thunder rumbled from the Everglades. I glanced at the anvil-shaped clouds forming to the west. In the rainy season, we were due for a thunderstorm within the next hour.

The Chief of Security glanced my way when I returned to the fruit stand for my second shake. Not good.

"You videoed those people at the junkyard," the shopkeeper said. "What is that about?"

If the shopkeeper had noticed me, the odds were that the Chief of Security had too. Also not good.

"Don't point," I said. "I don't want them to spot me. I'm with Miami-Dade County Building Code Enforcement. We received a complaint that the salvage yard is violating zoning regulations."

"Zoning? What violation?"

"The yard is zoned for wholesale auto parts distribution and scrap metal sales. We suspect they sell used auto parts to retail customers. They don't have enough parking spaces for retail requirements. See those two cars over there?"

"Yeah. So?"

"If they're retail customers, that's a violation of regulations."

"I'm a milkshake jockey, but my IQ's higher than room temperature. Those guys ain't dealing auto parts. They come here every week selling drugs. Everybody knows that." She smirked. "You're an undercover cop or I'm the queen of France."

"France is a republic."

"Exactly."

Fifty minutes later, a Blue-Eyed Devil shifted his weight from one foot to the other. Horvat consulted his watch.

Viktor had made five more phone calls. Five more cars had driven down the road and bounced to a stop on the sand. The customers took turns in the Mercedes and climbed out a minute later with their envelopes. The last customer had left fifteen minutes ago.

The instant drug boutique was about to close shop, and Snoop was a half hour away. I called him. "They're about to roll. They'll take 195th Avenue north to 312th Street. That's the only turnpike entrance for ten miles. Have you reached that exit?"

"My GPS says it's fifteen more miles."

"Don't bother to come here. Once you exit, pick a spot where you can turn either direction and wait."

Horvat stared at the fruit stand. Or was he staring at me? Hard to tell behind his sunglasses.

The nape of my neck tingled as the hairs rose. *Barbed-wire necktie* came to mind, followed by *gasoline enema*. My heart rate increased.

Viktor circled the Mercedes and opened the driver's door. He waved at the guards and three men walked toward the SUV.

But not the Chief of Security. Horvat spoke to Viktor. His posture indicated he was consciously not pointing. But his chin twitched my direction. I imagined the conversation going like this: *There's this guy across the street. He took pictures of us. And he's drunk a bunch of milkshakes like he's on a stakeout.*

Viktor Kokot listened. He began to curve toward me but jerked to a halt like his boss had told him not to look.

Horvat gestured another Devil over to the Mercedes, who sat in the front passenger seat. Horvat spoke to him, then closed the door. He slapped the Mercedes roof twice, and it gunned off with a cloud of dust. The Chief of Security had split his force to respond to this new threat—me. *Crap, I hate it when that happens.*

Horvat returned to the Suburban.

The remaining two Devils waited in the back seat. Horvat handed the second guard the key fob and the guard sat in the driver seat. Horvat took the passenger seat. The SUV backed away from the wall in a tight rotation. It curved 180 degrees and stopped at the concrete block wall, its nose toward the street.

Pointing my way.

Horvat's gaze focused on me tighter than a targeting laser. It felt like a red dot had flashed on my forehead.

"Floorboard it, Snoop. I've been made." I smiled for the benefit of the gunmen observing my every move.

"GPS says I'm twenty-five minutes out, bud. What's your situation?"

"Three gunmen in a Suburban are gazing this way. A half-dozen families are at the berry farm. The bad guys are vultures waiting for me to run so they can tag along and pick my bones."

"Call the cops and wait until they get there."

"These predators won't wait that long. This parking area is a security nightmare; I can't allow a gunfight around these kids and their parents."

"Head toward and I'll meet you when you get closer to Homestead."

"I admire your confidence, Snoop, but that won't work. I won't bring the gunfight any nearer to town than it already is. More innocent people to get hit by a stray bullet. Even if I stay on the rural roads, people are working the fields."

"Call the cops, bud."

"You ever see that bumper sticker that says, 'When seconds count, the police are minutes away'? No cops. I'll lead the Blue-Eyed Devils into the Everglades. They expect me to escape toward Homestead. I'll catch them off guard and be a quarter-mile down the road before they can crank their Suburban."

"I'll call the Homestead police and tell them you're headed west on 326th."

"No. Don't call them. By the time they catch us, the fight will be over. I'll be dead or the Devils will. It's better not to waste a day giving the police a statement."

"You're the boss, boss. If they kill you, can I have your boat? And your season tickets to the Pelicans?"

"You can take my barbecue grill, too. I'll leave the line open, but I'll be too busy to talk. Get here ASAP." Smiling again for the benefit of the watching gunmen, I slurped the end of my mango shake and tossed the empty cup in the recycle bin.

"Have a nice day, officer."

No point in denying it; she wouldn't believe me. "And the same to you, ma'am."

Backing out far enough to peek around the cars on either side, I scanned both ways down the two-lane road. A stake bed truck approached from the west, a load of sabal palms hanging out the back.

Waiting for the truck to pass, I grabbed four extra Glock 17 magazines from my glove compartment. Rule Nine: *You can never carry too much firepower.* I stuck two in my pockets on each side and grasped the steering wheel at ten and two o'clock. Ready to roll.

As the truck passed and blocked the gunmen's view, I hit the gas and squealed backwards across the pavement, clearing the truck by six feet. My back tires bounced onto the dirt shoulder across the road as the truck passed in front of the Suburban, blocking their way. I spun the wheel, slammed the gearshift into drive, and floored the accelerator. My front wheels gripped the asphalt like Velcro and wrenched me around, tires screaming in protest. Fishtailing down the road toward the Everglades, my Caravan gained speed with every screech of the tires.

117

My driver's side mirror framed the Suburban. After the truck passed, its tires spun up a huge dust cloud.

I had jumped two hundred yards ahead by the time the SUV bounced on the edge of the pavement. Its front end sprang in the air and came down with a crash. Its rear tires threw sand, and it clawed onto the pavement. The SUV fishtailed and straightened.

By then, I had a quarter-mile head start.

Row crops, fences, orange groves, tropical plant nurseries—all spun past my windows in a dizzy kaleidoscope. A farm worker trailer park whizzed by. The table-flat land stretched to the horizon. In the distance, thunderheads climbed toward the stratosphere.

Ahead, a pickup rumbled down an unpaved side road trailing a dust cloud. Flashing my headlights, I screamed through the intersection at 70 mph. A truck depot came into view, its aluminum gate propped open, welcoming a truck slowing on the road ahead.

The Suburban gained on me.

A half mile ahead, an eastbound sedan approached. I swerved to the other lane and roared past the slowing truck. Its horn substituted for the driver's finger. I steered to the right lane to miss the oncoming sedan.

The SUV wouldn't have space to pass the truck. If the SUV forced the issue, it would run the sedan off the road. I hoped. Otherwise, a head-on collision would kill a bunch of people, most of them innocent.

I flashed my lights to warn the sedan. The speedometer signaled 80 mph.

Behind me, the Suburban swung out to pass the truck, which had begun its wide right turn.

The sedan flew past me, its horn protesting like the truck's had.

I clenched the wheel as if my strength of will could force the sedan to the grassy shoulder to miss the careless reckless SUV.

The Everglades lurked two miles ahead, and the road was clear. In my mirror, the truck, the kamikaze Suburban, and the eastbound sedan appeared fated to reach the same spot at the same time.

I gripped the wheel harder. If Alena's Blue-Eyed Devils met the real devil, that was okay. But the innocent people in the truck and the sedan did not deserve this.

"*Noooo. Noooo*," someone yelled. I realized it was me.

As the sedan swerved onto the grass shoulder, the SUV ripped off side mirrors as it closed the gap.

The red speedometer needle danced past 90. Glancing back at the SUV, I had no clue how fast they were gaining, but my Caravan was made for families not for racing. I stomped the accelerator so hard my calf muscles began to cramp. Easing the pressure on the accelerator, my speed held at 90-plus.

The Caravan became airborne where the street ended and became a one-lane dirt road. My cellphone on the passenger seat sailed into the air and bounced on the floorboard. Everything loose in the cabin flew like a flock of shorebirds. The van hit the dirt and bounded into the air again, bucking like a bronco fighting to throw a cowboy. I fought for control on a rutted track designed for swamp buggies, not minivans.

I stomped the brake. The rear wheels crabbed to the right. Releasing the brake, I jammed the steering wheel into the skid. The drift lessened. Gravity and friction slowed the van. It was too dangerous to hit the brakes again. If the Caravan rolled over, I was dead. Even if the seatbelt and airbags saved my life, the Devils would be on me before I could unbuckle and climb out.

All I saw in the mirror was my dust cloud. The driver would have noticed that my van bucked when the pavement ran out. Maybe he slowed before they hit the dirt. Maybe I would get lucky and the driver would roll the SUV. Maybe I'd win the Florida lottery.

Slowing to 55, the Caravan bounced and leapt across the ruts, fighting me for control. The Suburban had better suspension. They would drive faster over the dirt track.

The casuarina trees I bumped past marked the end of cultivation. The land beyond teemed with bushes and trees planted by birds and wildlife in the century since the first farmers dug the drainage canals.

Ahead, the low green line of the Everglades angled away toward the southwest, marked by the six-foot berm that holds back the waters during the rainy season.

The berm marked the territory of alligators, eagles, panthers, and pythons.

The Suburban's headlights flashed in my mirror, glowing through the dust. The berm was a half mile ahead. At 55 mph, I would reach it in 33 seconds.

With the SUV traveling, say, 70 mph, I had less than a minute before they rammed my bumper. Their three-ton Suburban would smash my two-ton Caravan like an NFL lineman sacking a high school quarterback. If they hit me off-center, my van would roll. I had wrestled the steering wheel earlier to keep all four tires on the ground; I wouldn't press my luck again.

Whoopee, I would make it to the berm with ten whole seconds to spare —maybe. I had less than a minute to plan and ten seconds to act.

Captain Ramirez's words came back to me: *Always be polite and respectful, but make a plan to kill everyone in the room if necessary.* I made kill plans every day as an intellectual "what if" drill.

Not this time. This was not a drill.

TWELVE

As I raced west, the Everglades angled closer from my right. Cypress trees and live oaks reared their crowns above the berm.

Standing on the brakes, I skidded up a dust cloud designed to hide my next maneuver. I shifted into *Low* and climbed the berm's steep slope. After bouncing across the twin ruts worn by swamp buggies, I eased down the far side, stopping with my tires inches from the water. The Caravan canted at an angle it was never designed for.

The Everglades is often called a river of grass. It's 100 miles long, 60 miles wide, and often inches deep. Occasional hardwood hammocks rise a foot or two above the water, but 90 percent is swamp, sometimes dry during the winter once the rains stop. In the dry season, the gators dig down to the water, making gator holes in the sand. This was the rainy season. Patches of open water and a vast sawgrass prairie that appeared to be dry land but wasn't.

Fighting gravity, I shoved the door open. I rolled to the side and the door crashed shut. The Suburban's V-8 engine grew louder. I crawled up the berm on my belly.

The SUV burst through my dust cloud and hurtled past. The brake lights flashed once. The Suburban slowed, then stopped.

I imagined the one-sided discussion Horvat had with the driver: *You idiot, he was right there. How could you lose him?*

I knew my way around in the Everglades. The Serbs were city boys who might have seen gators on television but never faced a modern dinosaur nose-to-snout.

The water in the Everglades was two feet deep this time of year. The berm stood four feet above the water and my van reached six. The Devils would stop to reconnoiter, and they would spot the windows sticking above the berm like a beacon. Time to relocate.

Crabbing west past the Caravan, I heard a small splash. A mirror-smooth patch of water churned by a twelve-foot gator. At that size, it must be male. Bull gators are territorial and I was a trespasser. He swam away, his snout and eye bumps trailing a wake of ripples. He would return to protect his territory. *Oh, great. Keep one eye on the gunmen and one eye on the bull gator.*

Rising to a crouch, I scampered parallel to the dirt road. Forty yards down the way a hardwood hammock butted against the berm, inches above the wet-season waterline. The bull gator's hole was near the hammock. Gumbo limbo, mahogany, and oak trees grew on the hammock in the field of sawgrass. When I reached the gumbo limbo, I straightened up until I could see over the berm.

As I considered my options, I eyeballed the gator.

The SUV bobbed over the rough track like a series of speed bumps. I didn't shoot inside the vehicle because of its skipping motion. No point in giving away my location. The driver was visible through the windshield, but the others were hidden by the tinted windows.

My Glock 17 was deadly inside fifty yards. Once the Suburban stopped, I could pick the gunmen off one by one when they exited the vehicle. *If* they exited one at a time, which I knew they wouldn't do. If I were doing this, I would tumble all three or four killers out simultaneously and roll away in the tall grass.

The killers wore shoulder holsters at the salvage yard, but they might carry an arsenal in the Suburban. Lord knows, Kalashnikovs are cheap enough. If they fired back with AK-47s, I would be outmanned and outgunned. I'm good, but I'm not crazy. My odds of success in a shootout were forbidding.

The engine stopped. The sound of the transmission clunking into park broke the stillness. The cooling engine ticked and clucked.

The rumble of distant thunder shook the ground to announce an afternoon rainstorm.

The driver's door thumped open. The warning bell *ding... ding... dinged.* He pulled the key from the ignition, laid it on the dashboard, and exited the SUV. The crown of the Blue-Eyed Devil's head peeped above the vehicle. He didn't have any horns.

He grasped the luggage rack and heaved up to stand in the open door so that he had a 360-degree view. He peered ahead where the dirt road diminished to the vanishing point. He spun to the left, surveying a landscape flat as a pool table and covered with trees and bushes. I could be hiding anywhere.

His head scanned like a radar antenna. He stopped again to examine the landscape opposite me. Then he switched hands on the luggage rack to revolve back toward the east. His head rotated like a faulty lighthouse beacon, stopping every few degrees as he surveyed potential hiding places. He would stop his sweep search when he spotted the van, but even if he finished the circle, he wouldn't spot me in the hammock.

I hid in the shade of a stand of hardwoods with my eyes above the berm. His gaze would glide past me if I didn't move. In the Afghan mountains, I once waited motionless for eleven hours while 150 Taliban combed the countryside for me. I could outwait a few Serb city boys.

The driver pointed at my minivan and yelled something in a language I didn't recognize. Two more doors flew open and the two other gunmen spun out, AK-47s at the ready. So there were only three gunmen. Relatively speaking that was good news since the SUV could have held four or more Devils.

Whoopee, only three people were trying to kill me. My heart rate boosted. Showtime.

Not forgetting the gator, I turned. The bull gator stopped ten feet from the berm. His eyes and nostrils peeked above the water, equidistant between me and the Caravan.

Thunder boomed, louder this time. The gator ignored it.

Horvat shouted words that sounded like gravel tumbling in an empty barrel. The Serb behind the Suburban replied with something that resembled a coughing spasm. Maybe they spoke Klingon.

The three shooters formed a skirmish line toward my Caravan, Horvat in the middle. He waved them forward through the thick grass toward the berm.

Sidestepping down the slope, I crept into the deeper shadows in the center of the hammock. From my new position, their heads rose above the berm. I spotted the man on the north end through a space between a live oak and a mahogany. I aimed my Glock as he advanced up the slope.

His shoulders rose into view, then his chest. He sidestepped; I shifted my position to keep him centered in the gap between the trees. I lined up the white dot on the Glock's front sight with the slot in the rear one. His waist came into view, then his knees. He was sixty yards away. Any target beyond fifty yards is a toss-up, but I wanted the Serbs to believe I was on the north side.

Slowing my breath, I let my heart rate decelerate. Aligning the white dot with the center of his chest, I imagined my sniper mantra from my rifle training in Special Forces: *Easy squeezy; nice and easy.*

The gunman reached the berm's summit.

I squeezed off two rounds, *bang-bang.* The second one hit his shoulder. Lowering my aim four feet, I squeezed off two more while he fell. The fourth round punched a hole in his chest.

Horvat fired a burst from his AK-47. Leaves and bark flew into the air eighty yards to the north. He dived onto his stomach and disappeared, rolling off the crest of the berm and down toward the Caravan.

The third man ran toward the Caravan and ducked by the grill, thinking he had shielded himself from the shooter behind the van.

He was an easy target, but he crouched between me and the Caravan. If I shot him, the bullets would go through and hit my radiator and motor. Tough to drive home with a shot up motor.

Horvat shouted in that strange language. His henchman retorted and edged downslope. He waded into the shallow water. When he stepped in the water, he confirmed my theory: The Serbs didn't know squat about the

Everglades; they didn't realize the swamp was full of gators. Man-eating gators.

He waded toward the rear of the van. If he moved far enough, I could take a clear shot without hitting the Caravan.

Cutting to another gap in the trees, I kept him in sight.

He was thirty-five yards away. I had my clear shot.

The bull gator skimmed beneath the water, trailing smooth ripples silent as sunset.

Leveling my sights at the center of the gunman's back, I lined up the white dot with the rear slot. Every Western movie I had watched as a kid flashed through my mind. Code of the West: Don't shoot a man in the back. Those three men were stalking me with Kalashnikovs. *Code of the West, my ass.*

Slowing my respiration again, I slipped into sniper mode. *Easy squeezy; nice and easy.*

I fired two rounds. The first hit his shoulder; the second caught his kidney. His body splashed into the swamp, spreading ripples toward the sawgrass. And the gator.

Horvat fired another burst at the ghost he figured was hiding in the northern trees. He still didn't know where I fired from. He would figure it out once he realized where his last man was standing when I shot him.

Time to relocate again.

The bull gator paused when the gunman fell into the water. Then he moved again.

Horvat called to his man. It sounded like *Bojan.* That would be Bojan Matic. Horvat called again, louder and faster, "Bojan, Bojan," his voice an octave higher. He fired two more bursts into the trees. The gator didn't react.

Easing closer to the hammock, I observed Horvat on the Caravan's other side.

He stretched flat on the grass and searched under the Caravan. From his angle, he might spot Bojan's hand where it reached toward the water's edge. It would be only seconds until he figured where my shots came from. I expected him to empty his AK-47 into the hammock where I was hiding.

Horvat crawled toward the Caravan. He disappeared behind it, and I sprinted across the berm and hit the dirt on the far side of the Suburban.

Lightning flashed in my peripheral vision, and I counted seconds. At *five-thousand-five* the thunder boomed. The lighting was a mile away. The wind brought the smell of rain. A tropical thunderstorm moving at thirty mph would strike in less than two minutes.

Three of the SUV's doors hung open. I leaned in the rear door and looked over the seat back. The fourth AK-47 lay there along with extra ammunition. I snatched the Kalashnikov and threw it into a thicket of brambles and palmetto. I clicked a fresh magazine into my Glock.

An AK-47 fired two long bursts. *bra-a-ap, bra-a-ap.* The echoes faded to silence, and I heard the unmistakable sound of Horvat ejecting the empty magazine. More than once, my life depended on knowing that the enemy had paused to reload. I heard the *cli-click* as he inserted a fresh magazine, followed by another *bra-a-ap* of automatic rifle fire.

Lightning flashed, and three seconds later the thunder rolled across the Everglades like an echo from the AK-47. The storm was a little over a half mile away.

Thunder masked the crunch of my steps as I sprinted back down the dirt road.

Inch by inch, I slinked up the berm. Halfway to the top I spotted Horvat's head as he crouched behind the Caravan. His attention focused on the hammock where I had hidden two minutes before. Horvat made an easy target, but he had squatted beside the Caravan's fuel tank. If I shot him, best case, the bullets would punch through him and shoot a hole in the tank. Worst case, I might *ka-boom* the fuel tank. Not a great way to get home in either case, plus the smoke from the gasoline explosion would be visible for miles.

I snuck to the first man I had shot, not twenty yards from Horvat. I found his Kalashnikov and lugged it back down the berm. I chucked it into the tall grass at the bottom.

The west wind stirred the sawgrass and brought the smell of rain.

Inching up the berm, I held my Glock in a two-hand grip, ready to fire.

Deja vu all over again. I needed to draw Horvat away from my Caravan or get a different angle on him.

Beside me, the dead man's cellphone rang. *Crap.*

Horvat spun toward the sound and spotted me. *Double crap.*

I sprang and rolled down the berm.

Horvat's Kalashnikov raked the air where I had been. I dashed toward the Suburban and sheltered behind the rear tire. If he climbed the berm, I counted on him to hesitate before shooting his own vehicle. He wanted to get home too.

Ironically, Horvat was on the Everglades side of the berm hiding behind my Caravan and I was on the dry side hiding behind his SUV. If either of us advanced, the other would shoot the first head that peeked over the berm. Stalemate.

The thicket where I threw the extra Kalashnikov would make a great hiding place if I burrowed in the weeds under the palmetto fronds. However, snakes love those thickets too.

What other options were there?

Horvat couldn't remain behind my Caravan because it offered no protection if I came back over the berm from that direction. He would assume I had abandoned the hammock he sprayed with bullets.

As a city boy, he would hide downhill from the Caravan, standing in the water near Bojan's corpse. And the bull gator.

Crawling back up the berm, I peered under the Caravan. Horvat crouched on his knees in the water looking north.

I waited. Waited. Minutes passed. I wouldn't shift my gaze to my watch. Maybe ten minutes. I still waited. Then it came. Finally. The thunder.

The *bo-o-om.*

With the sound, I slipped back into the hammock again and hid among the dense foliage. I peeked through the undergrowth.

Bojan Matic sprawled face down in the water. Horvat knelt in the water between his dead henchman and my Caravan, his back to me, forty yards away.

The thunderheads fell silent. Perhaps they were gathering strength for the imminent storm.

Bracing my left palm underneath my gun hand, I spread my feet in the

Weaver shooting stance. A dead oak branch snapped under my left foot. The crack sounded loud as a firecracker.

Horvat leapt to his feet. Time flowed in slow motion. Horvat's movements jittered like a series of still photos fanned by a finger. Ballplayers say the game slows down and the action speeds up. It felt like that. Horvat spun in my direction, squeezing the trigger while he rotated.

I imagined individual bullets tracking toward me, stitching the surface of the water with instant geysers. The shots marched across the gator hole and raked the dirt, parading in my direction.

I rapid-fired as fast as I could squeeze the trigger. I don't remember how many times I fired or if my shells hit him. I kept squeezing.

I felt the dreaded *thwack* of a gunshot to my left forearm. The Glock fell from my hands into the underbrush. I was back in Afghanistan fighting the Taliban. I lunged into the hammock empty-handed.

I had not brought my Browning .380 in its ankle holster. That mistake could be fatal.

Lightning blinded me. Thunder claps deafened me.

I rolled down the hammock's far slope and hid behind an ancient gumbo limbo.

Like turning on a giant waterfall, the rain gushed in sheets, torrents, buckets. The air was so wet I could scarcely breathe. Lightning strobed on my forearm. The blood washed away, replaced by more blood flowing from the jagged wound.

Clamping my palm over the bullet hole, I scanned for Horvat, blinking the deluge from my eyes. Crouching behind the gumbo limbo, I couldn't see a thing. The rain beat on the jungle loud as a snare drum, so I could not hear footsteps. Leaning into the tree, I used my legs to force myself to a standing position, the gumbo limbo bark snagging and ripping my shirt. My arms felt like they weighed a thousand pounds.

Horvat might come at me in a flash. The torrent of rain and its noise masked his movement. I peered toward where I thought the Caravan was. Foliage hung down from the wet branches and blocked my vision. With my

128

wounded arm bracing my other hand, I swept the greenery aside. The Caravan materialized through the downpour. It was as unreachable as if it were a mile away.

Any second I expected Horvat to march toward me like the Grim Reaper, but brandishing a Kalashnikov instead of a scythe.

Horvat didn't come. Where the hell was he?

In my weakened condition, if I ran, I might bleed to death, or Horvat could follow and cut me down from the rear. But my spare revolver was in the Caravan's gun safe. That and my first aid kit.

Stumbling toward the Caravan, I half fell, half crawled over the berm.

Then Horvat was there, standing thigh-deep in the swamp. Blood marked his shirt and pants where two of my shots had hit their target. Dark mud smeared his thighs above the water. None of that mattered. Horvat had won.

I was as good as dead.

He leveled the AK-47 at my belt buckle. Wading toward me, he staggered through the water. In a heavy accent, he asked, "Who the hell are you?"

If he wanted to question me, I had a few more seconds to live. If I could lure him closer... I raised my hands and blood spurted from my wound.

Horvat shrieked when the bull gator clamped onto his calf. His rifle fell from his hand and splashed into the swamp. The gator dragged him screaming toward deeper water.

Keeping a wide berth from the gator hole, I staggered to my van. The bleeding wound would kill me if I couldn't plug the hole.

The bull gator dragged Horvat's body into the swamp. Bojan's body had fallen in the water, so the gator could haul it away anytime. If the gator wasn't hungry following a dinner of fresh Horvat and Bojan, there were the panthers, the vultures, the bears, and the insects. Also, the Burmese pythons, newcomers to the Everglades who ate most of the native wildlife. The biggest stretched over 18 feet.

Reaching the Caravan's rear hatch, I popped it open and plopped on the back deck, fighting to keep my balance on the slope. At least I was out of the rain while I rummaged for the bandages. I tightened a tourniquet above my biceps to stop the blood flow and prepared an Israeli emergency pressure bandage. It's not easy to apply a bandage with your teeth and one hand, but I managed.

With a wary peek at the gator, I waded into the water and fished Bojan's cellphone and wallet from his pockets. Had the phone survived immersion? I pulled the Glock 17 from his shoulder holster. The wallet held $450. Spoils of war. Feeling under the water, I swept my free hand back and forth until I located his Kalashnikov. I hoisted it butt-first and let the barrel drain, then tossed it onto the berm and plunked the Glock beside it.

You never know when you'll need a weapon that can't be traced to you.

Lumbering to the first man I had shot, I retrieved his wallet and cellphone. His name was Edvard Oblak—another face from Wilma's file. Another $600 in spoils. Compared to my life, $600 is peanuts, but I wasn't about to let the money go to waste. The wildlife that would claim his body couldn't spend it. His Glock 17 would replace the one I lost in the hammock. After dumping Oblak's body into the swamp, I retrieved his Kalashnikov from where I had hidden it and tossed it near the first one. I didn't search for Horvat's Kalashnikov, and there was no way I was gonna fight that gator for his wallet and his Glock. The odds anyone would stumble across either weapon or any of the bodies were astronomical.

Within a week or two, the Everglades would digest every trace of the gunmen.

Weakened from hunger and loss of blood, I couldn't open the driver's door on the uphill side. After making sure the gator was occupied working on Horvat's body, I waded to the passenger side of the van. Gravity helped open the door. I didn't try to close it.

"Chuck, is that you? What's going on?"

My cellphone lay forgotten on the floorboard. "Snoop, I've been shot. Where are you?"

"Just passed the berry farm. Four more miles to the Everglades. You need an ambulance?"

"No. It's a deep graze to my forearm. The bullet missed the bone and the artery. I stopped most of the bleeding, but it needs stitches. Come to the end of the road. Continue a half-mile past where the pavement stops."

"How about the, uh, the other parties?"

"They had an unfortunate accident." Grasping the wheel with my right hand, I struggled over the center console to the driver's seat. "If you'll excuse me, I have work to do before you get here. I'll keep the line open." I fired the engine and eased the Caravan up the slope, wheels slipping in the wet grass. The Caravan coasted down the other side and gravity slammed the passenger door closed.

"Was that a gunshot?" Snoop asked.

"No. The passenger door slammed shut. I'll explain later."

After parking behind the Suburban, I flipped the air conditioning to *iceberg.* Wolfing down three energy bars, I guzzled a liter of water. After finishing the snack, I still felt limp as a wrung-out dishrag. Getting shot does that to you.

I fished out Bojan's and Edvard's cellphones. Edvard's was still on. I ran a translation app on a few words in texts he had sent. They were Serbian. There was notepaper in my map compartment. Using the same translator app, I composed and sent a Serbian text on Edvard's phone. I removed the battery and the SIM card and slipped the pieces in an evidence bag, labeling it *Edvard Oblak.* Later I would ask Snoop to analyze its call log, address book, and texts.

The rain slackened to a desultory dribble and the thunder shifted toward the Atlantic coast.

Bojan's cellphone worked also, and I sent another Serbian text message, then removed the battery and SIM card and placed the phone parts in a second evidence bag.

Snoop's Toyota grew larger in my mirror. He stopped behind me and got out. He opened my door. "Where are the bad guys?"

Gesturing toward the Everglades, I said, "Gator bait. The bodies won't be found. Collect their weapons: two AK-47s and a Glock on the other side of the berm."

"In a minute, bud. Let me examine that wound. That bandage is on wrong. I'll replace it." He applied a fresh bandage from the first aid kit. "It's obvious you never had medical corpsman training."

"What did you expect, *Doctor* Snopolski? I applied it with my teeth."

"You're grumpy when you're wounded, bud."

He replaced my bandage with his more professional one.

"That'll hold you until I get you to the ER."

I told him everything. "There's one more AK-47. You'll find it in those brambles. Wipe my fingerprints off, then stick it and the other weapons in that Suburban. Also, these." I shoved the dead men's cellphones and components into his hand. "I don't want them with me when we go to the ER. We'll come back and get them later."

I tilted the driver's seat back and shut my eyes while Snoop followed my instructions. The pain in my arm throbbed in rhythm with my heartbeat.

In ten minutes, he returned. "What are we gonna do with the Suburban? The water is too shallow to dump it."

"I know the perfect place."

Snoop said, "You gonna fasten your seatbelt or you need me to help?"

I clicked it with my right hand.

"You locate the nearest hospital on the GPS. I'll get us back to civilization." He wheeled the Toyota into a three-point U-turn and bumped down the dirt road.

"Drive to Cedars of Lebanon."

"Are you crazy? That's gotta be sixty miles. We need to tend to that wound ASAP."

"I'll live. The ER will file a GSW report. I don't want it filed in Homestead. It's too close to the scene of the shootout. Take me to Cedars."

"If we abandon your van and the Suburban that long, someone may report them before we get back to retrieve them."

"Life is full of gambles."

"We could drive to the Homestead ER, and we'd get back here faster than driving to Port City and back. We'd save three hours."

"Cedars of Lebanon, Snoop. It's my wound and my choice."

"You gonna stay with the *shot myself cleaning my gun* story?"

"Unless you think of a better one."

"The guys at the North Shore Precinct will hear about it, and they'll yank your chain something awful."

"Such is life, my friend."

It was a rough eighty minutes in Snoop's Toyota. I dozed a little, but my arm hurt like a toothache.

THIRTEEN

Alena Cernan

"What does this mean, Jakob?" Alena Cernan asked in Serbian, leaning across her desk and shoving her cellphone under the man's nose.

Jakob Zupan repeated the message aloud in Serbian: *"Crucero send the man in Dodge Caravan. He not bother us again."*

He replied in the same language. "He means he questioned the man and disposed of his body."

"And this one. What does it mean?" She swiped the screen and held it toward Jakob again.

"He work for Crucero. He not a problem again. The same thing. They captured the man, questioned him, and killed him."

"And where is Hugo? And Bojan? And Edvard?"

"I don't know, Ms. Cernan. They went together."

"And why did these messages come from Bojan and Edvard instead of Hugo?" She shook her cellphone at Jakob. "Hugo is the boss. He should be the one who sends me this information."

Jakob shifted his weight from one foot to the other, hands clasping and unclasping. Jakob was a simple man, good with a gun, his fists, a knife—or

133

barbed wire. Especially barbed wire. He was no thinker, but who else could she talk to? Viktor, her driver, could barely read.

Her father had transferred Niko and Tomaz back to Switzerland once she won the gang wars in Miami-Dade. She was used to discussing things with Gregor and Tomaz, but they were gone. The other men were working elsewhere. She was short-handed until the three missing men surfaced.

It was six o'clock—midnight in Zurich—too late to call her father, who was always drunk by ten o'clock.

Why should she worry? Her three gunmen had been gone only a few hours. They caught the man, questioned him, then killed him. That was clear from the text messages. Naturally, they needed to dispose of the body. That would take time.

Maybe they chased the stranger beyond cellphone coverage. No, that couldn't be. They had enough signal to send text messages.

But why didn't they answer their phones? Where were they?

Cernan's throat ached and she felt her heart thumping overtime. *Where are my men? What has happened to them?*

Carlos McCrary

Rebecca Tinsley, ER nurse at Cedars of Lebanon Hospital, gave me a hard look.

"Would you believe I was cleaning my gun?" I said.

She arched an eyebrow. "You expect me to believe that, Chuck?" She removed the old bandage. "Whoever wrapped you up did a good job."

"That was Snoop. He's over there, but don't compliment him or he'll get a swelled head."

"Hey, Snoop," Rebecca said. "You did a great job bandaging your idiot friend. How about you? Your shoulder healing okay?"

"A couple more weeks and I'll be good as new, Rebecca. Thanks for asking."

Rebecca switched back to me. "I have to report GSWs."

"So report it."

"How are your ribs? They heal all right?"

"Yeah. You did a great job." The last time I saw Rebecca was to get my ribs taped. During a shootout with bad guys, a couple of bullets hit my armored vest and broke some ribs. This bullet wound to my arm was more deadly but less painful than the broken ribs had been.

She lowered her voice. "How did this happen, really? You can tell me."

I matched her tone, *sotto voce.* "To tell the truth, there were these three bad guys." I glanced around like I was prepared to tell her a great secret. "You know what a Kalashnikov AK-47 is, don't you?"

She narrowed her eyes. "It's a Russian machine gun, right?"

"Right. See, these three bad guys chased me. In a big black SUV. And they all carried these AK-47s."

Rebecca leaned back. "Three guys with machine guns just like the movies, huh?" She injected my arm with the local anesthetic, maybe a little rougher than required.

"Ouch. Yeah. The shooters trapped me on a lonely, deserted road."

"The road was lonely *and* deserted. Isn't that redundant?"

"Hey, it's my story, Becky. Anyway, we got into a fierce gunfight and I caught a stray bullet."

She arched the eyebrow again. "From an AK-47?"

"Sure, why not?"

"And what happened to the bad guy?"

"Bad *guys,* plural. There were three of them."

"Okay, what happened to the *three* bad guys?"

I grinned. "I killed all three single-handedly."

"Uh-huh. And what happened to their bodies?"

"Truthfully, that is a mystery to me."

"Okay, smart ass, don't tell me. I still need to report GSWs."

Rebecca bent over the wound and concentrated on her stitches. Above her head, I winked at Snoop.

We thanked Rebecca, checked out, and returned to the scene of the gun battle. It was twilight, and I wouldn't drive the Suburban with its side mirror hanging by the cable. It was too recognizable to any Blue-Eyed Devils lurking in the vicinity. Better to wait until the wee hours.

I idled the Suburban to trail's end. This far from civilization, if it hadn't been seen by now, no one would spot it before we returned after midnight.

We locked it and Snoop ferried me back to my Caravan. He trailed me home, then stood watch in my condo while I slept like I was in a coma.

Snoop shook me awake at one a.m. "You got three hours' sleep, bud. You sure about moving this soon?"

"I'll nap. You drive."

Ninety minutes later, the Caravan shook like an earthquake and woke me when Snoop bumped down the end of the pavement.

Snoop touched my shoulder. "Help me watch. It's dark using just the parking lights." We crept along the bumpy dirt road until we came to the black Suburban and stopped.

The air in the Everglades was clear, and the night was so dark that far from the Miami lights that the Milky Way stretched across the sky, a silver highway to heaven.

The police need a reason to send divers into the drainage canals of South Florida. Usually someone witnesses a car roll off the road and the divers search for victims. They comb the canal in both directions from the accident. Often, they recover other vehicles missing for years or even decades.

Three weeks earlier, two hunters near the Everglades saw an ancient sedan veer off the road and plunge into a canal. The hunters dived to rescue the driver, but the car sank out of sight, and they couldn't locate it in the murk. They called 9-1-1. Police divers recovered the car with an 85-year-old woman's body behind the wheel, seatbelt fastened. Her family had reported her missing. She suffered from dementia and had stolen the car keys.

The Sheriff towed eleven more vehicles from the canal, nine of them stolen.

When I read the story in the *Pee-Jay,* I noted which canal they searched. You never know when you'll need to dump a car. Or an SUV.

The newspaper said divers had not entered that canal for thirty years. It wouldn't be searched again until someone else rolled into it. I could be an old man before that happened.

I drove the Suburban past an abandoned service station standing at civilization's edge. The road faded into darkness beyond the headlights. The Suburban's remaining side mirror showed my Caravan's headlights a hundred yards back, where Snoop followed me. There were no other lights in sight at 3:30 a.m.

I stopped by the canal with the SUV pointed at the water. After slipping the transmission into *Park*, I buzzed the driver's window open a few inches. Anyone recovering the car in the future might think the driver had been a smoker. I wore nitrile gloves but I wiped any place I might have touched anyway. Can't be too careful.

Snoop parked the Caravan behind me.

First, I flicked the lights off and unfastened my seat belt. Then I shifted into *Drive* and stepped from the vehicle, leaving it in gear. As the Suburban lurched onto the shoulder, I slammed the door.

The gravel crunched under its tires as the black vehicle coasted toward the black water. The crunching lessened when the front wheels reached the wild grass beyond the shoulder and stopped when the back wheels found the grass. The bank of the canal sloped downward and the SUV gathered speed. It surrendered to the inky water with hardly a splash. The engine ran while bubbles escaped around the hood, then clattered a death rattle and fell silent.

Ripples spread across the surface, faintly reflected in the Caravan's headlights. Then they were gone. The Suburban disappeared like it had never existed.

FOURTEEN

I was first off the plane at *Aeropuerto Internacional de San Cristobal.* No cooling breeze blew from the adjacent Caribbean Sea. The humidity hung in the air, limp as wet sheets on a clothesline. The tropical sun baked the concrete apron and plastered my long-sleeved *guayabera* to my sweaty back. I wore sleeves to hide the large adhesive patch that covered the bullet wound on my forearm. The angry red scar would fade in time. They always do.

I picked the Caribe Real, an elegant hotel in the heart of Santa Maria, the capital of San Cristobal. Bypassing the taxi queue, I hired a limousine. I wanted to project a certain image at the Caribe Real.

After registering, I followed the bellhop to my room. After I tipped him, I asked where a lonely man could arrange a date. He said Umberto, the concierge, knew everyone in town.

Umberto stood behind a counter in the lobby. I spoke to him in Spanish. "The bellhop said you know everyone in town."

"Yes, sir. How may I help you?"

"I should like to meet an experienced woman who knows how to keep a man's interest, not an immature teenager with no imagination."

"Yes, sir. I know such a woman."

Hiring a prostitute was distasteful, but the quickest way to get the information I wanted without arousing suspicion was to ask a local who was close to the underworld. A prostitute with some years of experience should fit the bill.

"It is good you came to me, sir. Picking up a woman on the street or in a tourist bar is dangerous. You might get mugged or worse. Desiree has a clientele of the best people in Santa Maria. She is popular with the locals but not as expensive as girls with lesser talents because Desiree speaks no English. Most tourists prefer a girl who speaks English. I shall enquire if she is available."

I showered and changed into a fresh guayabera.

Forty-five minutes later, an attractive fortyish woman knocked on my door. Her grey eyes sparkled with intelligence. Subtle makeup expertly concealed the hint of crow's feet at the corners of her eyes. She wore a white silk blouse and a flowered native wrap-around skirt like one I saw in the airport gift shop. She wore no bra, and her blouse was tucked in tight at the waist. A small straw purse hung over her shoulder on a gold chain.

I ogled her chest long enough to demonstrate that I appreciated the view.

"Come in," I invited in Spanish. "I am Carlos."

"My name is Desiree," she responded in the same language.

"Shall we go onto the balcony? There's a nice view of the Caribbean, and it's shady and private there. Would you care for a drink?"

"Are you Mexican?"

Most of Latin America speaks Spanish the way most of the United States speaks English: Each region has differences in their common language. A Texan doesn't speak like a New Yorker, and a *San Cristobalero* sounds different from a *Mexicano*. Different cadence, different vowel sounds, different slang and idioms.

"You have a good ear, Desiree. I live near Mexico City. Would you care for a drink?"

"White wine would be nice."

I uncorked a Pinot Grigio and jammed it in an ice bucket. She appraised my suite.

"Bring the glasses and slide the door open," I said. "I'll carry the wine bucket."

She ran her fingertips across my shoulders as she passed behind me and glided toward the glass sliders like she was on rollers. Her hips rolled like swaying palm trees, and her gentle perfume infiltrated my nose. She was exactly what I ordered. She even had a flair for accents.

We ducked under a blue canvas awning and sat in chairs at a glass-topped table.

She tugged her blouse free from her waistband. "I want the breeze to caress my skin."

She unbuttoned her top button and smiled at me. It was difficult to keep my gaze on her face. Then I thought, *Why bother?* and enjoyed the view.

We chit-chatted our way through her first glass of wine. I led the conversation and listened more than I talked. I learned local idioms and slang terms for the beach, a traffic accideent, a nightclub, and a rock band. We discussed local politics, the corrupt police force, and the local gangs, both juvenile and organized crime.

I poured her a second glass.

She raised it. "To new friends and lovers."

I toasted with my half-full first glass. "New friends and lovers."

"Umberto, the desk clerk, said you wanted a date."

"Umberto is correct."

"While I enjoy our conversation, I have to make a living. Let's settle financial matters before we spend more time discussing local news."

She unbuttoned the next button.

"Or before we do anything more…" She leaned over to rub my thigh and let her blouse gape open, "…exciting." She smiled and undid another button.

"Okay."

"One thousand pesos per hour. Two thousand total, and we'll do anything you fancy. *Anything.* Umberto said you asked for an experienced woman who could keep your interest."

She grinned and finished unbuttoning her blouse. "I know many ways to keep your interest."

"Wonderful. For now, the day is young and I want conversation. I'll give you the first thousand now and the second thousand before things get more exciting."

Desiree stuffed the two five-hundred-peso bills in her purse, and I noticed the small pistol she carried. Smart girl.

Halfway through her third glass of Pinot Grigio, I asked, "If I wanted to buy cocaine, who would I go to?"

"You can get anything from Umberto. He knows everyone in town."

"And if I wanted more than that? Say, an entire kilo?"

"Ah. I understand. You are a dealer?"

"I am many things. Who would I approach for a kilo or more?"

"I don't travel in such circles, but I believe Don Francisco de Pilon is involved in such business."

"And how would I reach Don Francisco?"

"As I said, I do not travel in such circles, but my *padron* would know." She used San Cristobal slang for *pimp,* literally a stallion or stud horse.

I handed her two more five-hundred-peso bills.

"Let us talk to your *padron.*"

Desiree stowed them with the other bills. She shrugged out of her blouse and draped it over her purse.

"We can talk to my *padron* after I demonstrate why an experienced woman is better than young girls." She rubbed my thigh with one hand and reached for my belt buckle with the other.

I grasped her hand on my belt and stopped her.

"Any other time I would be delighted. You are as beautiful as a painting in the Prado in Madrid, but I do not mix business with pleasure. Please keep the two thousand pesos, on account for future services."

She slipped her hand from mine and sat upright on the lounge, shoulders back, chest pointing at me.

"Don't you want me? I can make you very happy."

"I am sure you will, my dear. You are a very desirable woman. But business first."

"No man has ever refused me before. Are you gay? If you are, I won't tell anyone."

"Oh, no. You are alluring and delectable. I merely wish to conclude my business first."

She patted the bulge of my pants.

"I believe you." She smiled. "We will get together soon, yes?"

"Yes, I promise."

Desiree and I strolled across the square. Afternoon shadows from the cathedral shaded the lion's head fountain in the center. A handful of children splashed in the water under the watchful supervision of mothers or nannies. I wondered if their fathers were at work.

"If you go for a walk later, stay near the shopping area and the beach toward the north. Don't walk south; cargo ship crews and local rough characters frequent that side. It's not suitable for tourists."

"Thanks for the advice. I'll be careful."

Whitewashed walls blazed so brightly I was glad for my sunglasses. We sat at an outdoor cafe table under a multicolor umbrella and ordered two white wines.

Ten minutes later a tan man wearing a fake Rolex, a blue Polo shirt, and pressed blue jeans entered the square from a side street. One on the north side. He sat at our table and drank from Desiree's glass without asking.

Macho man, marking his territory. I didn't like him.

"You wanted to talk to me, *senor?*" he asked in English.

I answered in Spanish. "I am Mexican. You don't need to speak English."

"If you speak English, I prefer it for business; Desiree doesn't understand a word."

I faked a Mexican accent. "My English, it is fair. I want to buy a large amount of the cocaine. Desiree says Don Francisco de Pilon is in that business. I hope you can arrange an introduction for me."

"If I know this Don Francisco, and if he is in this business, why would I do that, *senor?*"

I lifted my wine glass toward my lips. "Sometimes a man does not require a reason. He does something because it... *¿Como se dice divertir?*"

"Amuse."

"*Si, si.* It *amuses* him. Are you such a man?"

Desiree's *padron* laughed. "I like you, Carlos. You have style. I am Esteban."

"¡Mucho gusto!" We shook hands.

"To introduce you to Don Francisco de Pilon involves certain, uh, risk."

"What risk?"

"Don Francisco is an important man—that is no secret. Also, a rich and powerful man— everyone knows that also. If I introduce you as a possible customer, and he discovers you are, uh, not what you appear." Esteban spread his hands.

"It would be bad for us both."

"¡Exactamente!"

I handed him my Carlos Andres Calderone business card—the one with the Mexico City address. "I'm interested in, uh, diversifying my investments. I want to meet with Pilon to discuss business opportunities."

"What's in it for me?"

I plucked a coin from my pocket. "This is a Mexican *Centenario* 50-peso gold coin."

"I am familiar with those."

"It contains 37.5 grams of gold. If you're used to pricing gold in U.S. dollars, that's a little more than 1.2 ounces. It's more than you'll make off Desiree in two weeks. You get me a meeting with Don Francisco de Pilon, and it's yours. And I'll give Pilon one for a, uh, *¿Como se dice senal?* A *token?* Yes, a *token* of goodwill."

Esteban reached for the coin, and I closed my fist around it.

"You get the *Centenario* when you get me to Pilon."

"Don Francisco is a busy man. It is not easy to arrange a meeting."

"I am a… *paciente,* a patient man. This is a small country. If you know Pilon, you should be able to get a response within twenty-four hours."

I laid my hand on Desiree's. "I shall pass them pleasantly."

It seemed like I hadn't lied when I promised to see Desiree again. I had intended not to hire a prostitute for the second time in my life, but I had a role to play. I had played worse roles. The next day, I hired a limo for

Desiree to show me the sights of Santa Maria. She kept us to the town's north side except for one trip to the ancient Spanish *castillo* ten miles south.

That evening, Esteban approached us while we dined at *El Paraiso,* a beachfront restaurant, as the sun set over the Caribbean.

"Hola, Don Carlos." This time he stopped a respectful distance away.

I had been upgraded from *Senor Calderone* to *Don Carlos.* My phony Carlos Andres Calderone Mexican identity and website must've impressed him.

"Please join us, Esteban."

He sat but waved the server away. "I won't stay long," he said in Spanish. "You and Desiree enjoy this lovely evening in the paradise of the Caribbean. Don Francisco has invited you to lunch at his estate tomorrow. As a token of goodwill, you may keep Desiree for the night with my compliments."

Without consulting her, this pimp donated the services of a working girl who was trying to make a living. That rubbed me the wrong way.

I faced Desiree. "Perhaps you are tired of me and would prefer time on your own?"

"No, Carlos. I would love to spend the night."

"Excellent."

I asked Esteban in English, "How do I get to Pilon's house?"

"I will pick you up at your hotel at one o'clock. Don't forget to address him as Don Francisco, not Pilon."

Tomaz Kopitar

Tomaz Kopitar's spirits soared. He climbed the steps to Alena Cernan's house in Coconut Grove. In seconds he would be near the woman he had secretly loved for years. He had been gloomy when Andrej Cernan summoned him back to Switzerland after he won his last gang war in Miami. Neither she nor her father knew of Kopitar's obsession with her.

He rapped on the doorjamb.

"Come in, Tomaz. It's good to have you back," she said in Serbian.

"I prefer to live in America, and Florida has a better climate than

Switzerland or Serbia." He glanced at the two men leaning against the wall before returning his attention to Alena. He continued in English, "and I enjoy working with you."

Alena shook his hand and his face flushed. He hoped she hadn't noticed.

She waved him to a seat.

"You've met Pavel, and Niko you remember from when you worked here before. He arrived yesterday."

Pavel Struna bowed. Niko Iva waved a hand in greeting.

"Congratulations, Tomaz. You are my new head of security."

"Head? What about Hugo? He was head of security when I went back to Switzerland."

"Hugo disappeared five days ago. He spotted a stranger taking pictures where he shouldn't. He wanted to question him. He and Bojan and Edvard chased the man, but they never came back. Father sent you, Pavel, and Niko to replace the missing men. For five days I have had only eleven men."

Bad luck for Hugo, of course, but with Tomaz as head of security, perhaps Alena would consider him to be more than a simple hired killer.

"Father is sending more men next week."

"We can make do until then," Kopitar said.

"The missing men texted me that Tony Crucero sent the stranger."

"Who?"

"Tony Crucero."

The name sounded Hispanic. Kopitar did not trust anyone who was not Caucasian. He considered most Hispanics to be *ukrste,* Serbian for crossbreed.

"Who is Tony Crucero?"

"Antonio Crucero. He is a wholesaler I met after you and Niko went back to Europe. He supplies me with a few kilos of coke each month."

"From the name, I assume he is Hispanic? You cannot trust this man. He is a crossbreed."

Alena slapped Tomaz, producing an angry mark on his cheek. "Don't give me any master race crap, Tomaz. The man is a fat hairy pig who wears too much cologne, but he gets me into the most exclusive clubs."

Kopitar fought the mental image of a crossbreed rutting between his Caucasian beauty's legs.

"You're sleeping with him? How very American you've become, Alena."

"It's not your concern, Tomaz. You obey orders. *My* orders."

Tomaz shrugged. "Why would this supplier send a man to follow you?"

"Who knows? He's a diplomat who brings in cocaine each month. He is one of several suppliers, and I sleep with him to keep him happy. Besides," her lips twisted into a smile, "his tongue is ten centimeters long. It works for us both."

"Does he plan to compete with you? Invade our territory?"

Alena's blue eyes looked glacier-cold. "If he starts anything, I'll cut his balls off with a hacksaw and stuff them in his mouth."

That was encouraging. She had merely a physical attraction to the crossbreed's sexual talents. Given the chance, Kopitar would gladly satisfy Alena that way. "What else do you know about this stranger?"

She handed Kopitar a slip of paper. "This is his van's license number. Find him."

Carlos McCrary

Esteban waited at the entrance to the Caribe Real in an old Land Rover so dirty and faded I couldn't decide whether its original color was brown or gray—maybe the color was *gravy*. The dented passenger door groaned when I opened it.

"Good morning, Don Carlos. Slam it hard or it won't latch."

On the second slam, it latched. I reached for the seat belt and saw the end was cut off at the floorboard bracket. Esteban wasn't wearing one either. So much for vehicle inspections in San Cristobal.

A half mile east of town, the road degenerated from old and pot-holed to rutted and barely passable. Esteban pointed through the windshield. "Don Francisco's castle is there."

A limestone citadel perched atop a craggy mountain a thousand feet above. Two towers stood sentinel at each end of the wall. It was more impressive than it looked on the Google Earth aerial view I had studied in my hotel room earlier. Desiree told me where Don Francisco de Pilon lived. We made a virtual tour of the grounds on my computer. She filled in details from visits when she entertained at the estate.

"Have you entertained Don Francisco?" I had asked.

"I do not discuss clients with anyone. You understand, I'm sure."

Esteban drove twenty-five bone-crunching minutes zigzagging up the mountain. He stopped at a steel bar painted optic orange that stretched across the gravel road. A circular paved area large enough for a truck to turn around widened beyond the bar. A guard in a military-style hat and scuffed black combat boots slouched in a wooden chair smoking a joint. His khaki uniform resembled U.S. Army surplus from World War II. He was dressed like the Santa Maria cops except for the lack of badges and brass. He took one last hit, flicked the joint to the ground, and picked up a Heckler & Koch MP7 leaning against the wall. He sauntered to the car.

"Esteban Canizares and Don Carlos Calderone to see Don Francisco."

The guard spoke into a handheld radio, repeating what Esteban said. He stared at us for maybe a minute before the radio squawked. *"Pronto."* He snapped to attention and listened. *"Muy bien, señor."*

He stepped to Esteban's window. "Don Carlos will walk to the house. You go back to town."

He hoisted the metal bar and Esteban swung the Range Rover in a tight circle. I handed him the *Centenario* and got out. A puff of dust trailed the Range Rover down the mountain.

The guard slung his MP7 over one shoulder, laid his radio on the chair, and frisked me. He pivoted toward the security camera mounted by the double-doored gate and gave a thumbs-up.

Metallic scrapes and bangs reverberated from the twin steel gates. They creaked outward with a groan of corroded hinges, pushed by two more armed guards that could have been clones of the first guard.

As I walked through the gates toward a three-storied mansion, I was reminded of a *parador* historic hotel where I stayed in Spain when I was a teenage vagabond one summer. Whitewashed stucco walls, Spanish tile roof, and ornately carved double doors. A limestone sidewalk stretched fifty yards to the mansion's entrance. Neat bougainvillea hedges in a variety of colors guarded the walls beneath each ground-floor window.

"Wait," one clone said. They shut the steel gates behind me and locked the bolts with the same *scrape bang* I heard earlier.

I had walked into a fortress. Or maybe a prison. The overhead sun reflected off the steel gates, reinforcing the heat. Again, my shirt clung to my back. If not for the mansion and gardens, I could have been in a hellish Latin American prison yard.

The clones stepped away five yards to form an equilateral triangle with me. They unslung their identical MP7s and aimed them at me. "Hands up."

A young man in a light green guayabera, gray slacks and woven leather sandals opened the mansion's carved front doors and stepped onto the porch. Closing the door behind him, he walked down the stone sidewalk. He reached the driveway and stopped between the two guards.

"You sure know how to make a man feel welcome," I said in Spanish.

He frowned. "Who are you and why are you here?" he asked in English.

"I do speak English, but I prefer Spanish."

He repeated the question in Spanish.

"Carlos Calderone. Would you care to see my passport?"

"Yes." He gestured to the man on his right. "Pepe, bring it to me."

"It's in my back pocket."

As Pepe shifted his weapon to his other hand, the other clone's weapon drooped toward the ground. Pepe passed me close enough that I could snatch the machine gun from his hand and kill the other guard before he knew what had happened. After that, his boss would be an easy target. That kill plan would work, but I wasn't there to start a war.

Pepe took my passport and handed it to the man.

"Where is the matronymic?" he asked, referring to the mother's surname on most Mexican passports.

Calderone was my mother's maiden name, and I obtained my Mexican passport without my patronymic McCrary.

"Not everyone uses his matronymic. In my case, it's a personal matter of no interest to you."

"And if I were interested?"

"I would tell you it's a personal matter."

He closed the passport and tapped it on the fingers of his other hand.

"You didn't fly from Mexico. You flew in from Port City in the U.S.A."

That was not a question, so I didn't comment.

He pressed the point. "What do you say to that?"

"Your man in the Immigration Department or the Caribe Real Hotel told you that. What's your point?"

"Why do you wish to meet Don Francisco?"

"Your man outside frisked me; he found no weapons. Okay for me to lower my hands?"

He bowed his assent.

"I wish to discuss business with Don Francisco."

"What business?"

"That is a matter between Don Francisco and me."

"We investigated you, Mr. Calderone. Your businesses are legitimate. You own a mine in Chile, a ranch near Mexico City, and a casino in New Jersey. Don Francisco has no interest in acquiring any such business. What is your interest in Don Francisco?"

"I also own a piece of a Bahamian casino."

"Big deal, I missed one. Don Francisco doesn't want a Bahamian casino either. My point is that you are a business man—a legitimate businessman. Why do you want to meet Don Francisco?"

"Are you Don Francisco?"

"No."

"I don't wish to be rude, but my business is with Don Francisco. I was told he had invited me to lunch. Perhaps I was misinformed, or if he changed his mind, that's his right. Call me a taxi and I'll go back to my hotel. Your choice."

He waved at Pepe. "You and Jesus return to your posts."

Both men walked away before he stepped over to me.

"I hope you will forgive the, uh, unorthodox welcome, but we are cautious. I am Federico, Don Francisco's son."

We shook hands.

"No problem, Don Federico. I am cautious also."

"Father is by the pool. We shall walk through the garden."

Federico led me north through the garden that surrounded the house. The rectangular estate covered the entire mountain top, two-hundred-plus yards from east to west and a hundred yards from north to south. Steep cliffs plunged hundreds of feet on three sides. The thick wall where I entered protected the west side. We paused at an overlook with a view of the Caribbean and several neighbor islands.

We curved at a waist-high stone wall bordering the garden where it ended at the cliff. A limestone sidewalk traced the wall the length of the northern side and the other two sides. I had not seen the wall from the Google Earth overhead view.

I had studied Google Earth for an emergency escape route in case this meeting blew up. There wasn't a good one. Craggy rocks to the east made a goat path down the mountain, or for a man running for his life. I had counted three armed guards and there would be more. For the first time in a long time, I had no realistic plan to kill everybody in the place.

I didn't care for the odds.

Federico pointed at an island. "With binoculars, you can make out the ruins of a Spanish fortress on Swallow Island. The Spaniards built it to protect the approach to Santa Maria. Ah, here we are."

The sidewalk widened to form a limestone deck surrounding the swimming pool. Four fiberglass tables with matching chairs and lounges were arranged on three sides.

The deck led to a loggia on the mansion's north side. Two more guards dressed and armed like the other three stood in the shadows in the loggia. That made five. My odds were getting worse.

A poolside table with a blue canvas umbrella was set with three place settings. A slender middle-aged man with salt-and-pepper hair stood by the table. He wore a white guayabera, white slacks, and white leather sandals.

"Mr. Calderone, Don Carlos, welcome to my home." He grasped my hand in both of his and shook it. "You met my son Federico."

"He was most gracious following the initial welcoming ceremony." I smiled. "Don Francisco, it is a pleasure and an honor to meet you."

He gestured at the chair fronting the ocean. "Please sit, Don Carlos. Would you care for something to drink?"

"What are you having?"

"Sangria, but we have anything you would care for."

"Sangria is fine."

A man wearing a white jacket and black slacks set a silver tray with a pitcher of sangria and three glasses on a wheeled cart. He reached for the pitcher, but Pilon stopped him.

"We will pour, Ernesto."

We chatted about deep sea fishing, the Mexican *futbol* league, and the dangers of hurricanes on San Cristobal. Ernesto served a luncheon of chicken enchiladas and ceviche, with *flan* for dessert.

I let my third glass of sangria sit without tasting it.

Ernesto came back to adjust the umbrella when the sun migrated across the sky.

Pilon passed a box of Cuban cigars.

I declined. So did Federico.

Pilon laughed and selected one. He passed it beneath his nose and inhaled. "I don't care what the doctor says. Since I must die eventually, let it be from something I enjoy."

He lit the cigar with a gold lighter and examined the end. "Tell me, Don Carlos, what brings you to San Cristobal?"

I clunked a gold *Centenario* on the table.

"First, to present you with this small token of respect, Don Francisco."

He glanced at the coin, but didn't touch it. "Thank you, Don Carlos."

"I am hunting for investment opportunities. I hope to create business relationships to expand and, ah, diversify my businesses."

Pilon puffed his cigar and studied the glowing end.

"Don Carlos, you've never gotten so much as a speeding ticket. Why are you here?"

"I got two speeding tickets and some parking tickets." I smiled. "As I said, I wish to diversify into other businesses. May I be candid?"

"Of course."

"I have done well, yes. Some people would envy my success. But, you, Don Francisco," I gestured at his mountain-top estate, "I can't do anything this grand in my legitimate businesses. Too many taxes, too many regulations," I paused before continuing, "too many laws."

Pilon knocked cigar ash into a ceramic ashtray. "You have a proposition?"

"The Garcias control the drug traffic in Broward County, Florida—that's Fort Lauderdale and its suburbs."

"Yes, yes, I know. They are not seeking a partner."

"They have a supplier whom you are familiar with," I said. "In fact, he is your customer: Antonio Crucero."

His eyebrow twitched. "You are mistaken, Don Carlos. I know the Crucero family, of course. Pablo Antonio Crucero is our ambassador to the United States. He is married to a Calderone. Are you related to Pablo's wife?"

"Not to my knowledge."

"I don't know his son Antonio. I have met him once or twice."

"Whatever you say, Don Francisco. My sources tell me Antonio imports cocaine into Port City in diplomatic baggage. He distributes it to dealers in Miami-Dade County, Atlantic County, and to the Garcias in Broward County. But Antonio is not ambitious. Some in Port City call him lazy. There are limits to how much cocaine he can bring in—political limits. He has not tapped far into the South Florida market."

"Even if that were true, what's the point?"

"Palm Beach County is wide open. I want to provide additional product to the Garcias and, in return, ask them to help me organize Palm Beach County. Instead of Antonio selling them one or two kilos a month, I can sell them ten kilos a month. But first I must prove myself in Palm Beach."

"Why Palm Beach? Why not Port City or Miami?"

"I have certain, contacts in Palm Beach."

"And how would this involve me?"

"I understand you can import unlimited amounts from South America into San Cristobal, but the bottleneck is locating people to smuggle it into the United States."

"Assuming this were true—and I do not say it is—but, assume I could import this product from South America, how would you get it to the States?"

"That is a matter of proprietary interest, Don Francisco. It can be done. Let's leave it at that."

"How much product can you handle?"

"Forty to fifty kilos a month."

That was twice the amount Tony Crucero smuggled into the States every month.

Pilon glanced at Federico. "Let us discuss your proposal. I shall give you an answer tomorrow."

He wedged his half-smoked cigar on the ashtray and stood. "Thank you for the *Centenario*. Javier will drive you to your hotel."

Pilon's Mercedes had seat belts. And air conditioning that worked.

Desiree and I enjoyed the sunset at *El Paraiso*. As we lingered over brandy, Esteban appeared again.

"Don Carlos, your meeting with Don Francisco went well?"

I did not invite him to sit.

"Esteban, I do not wish to be rude in your employee's presence, so I say this in English. My dealings with you are over. You did me a service and I paid you handsomely. I shall continue to enjoy Desiree's company whenever I am in San Cristobal. If I need you again, I shall tell Desiree. If not, we need never meet again."

He returned a blank stare.

"Good-bye, Esteban. As the Americans say, 'Have a nice life.'"

FIFTEEN

The next morning, I was at the beach with Desiree when my phone signaled a text:

Javier will pick you up at 12:30. Francisco de Pilon.

I paid off Desiree, walked her to a taxi, and told her I was leaving San Cristobal. She made me promise to call her next time I returned. I hated to lie to her; being a hooker didn't make her a bad person. At least she had an honest job. I handed her into the cab. I pushed a *Centenario* into her hand and told her it was a gift and not a fee. She didn't owe Esteban a commission. She cried when I paid the driver and shut the door.

I returned to my hotel and rested until noon.

At 12:31 my room phone rang. Pilon's driver waited in the lobby.

The trip to the mountain fortress was less white-knuckled this time. As we approached, the steel bar rose and the gates opened.

Javier stopped the Mercedes at the front sidewalk. Federico approached from the house.

"Don Carlos, welcome again. Please come with me."

He led me to a foyer that would make Queen Isabella or King Ferdinand proud. A wrought-iron chandelier hung from a twenty-foot vaulted ceiling between hand-carved oaken beams. Ancient tapestries hung above the ornate doors. A baronial double staircase curved up either side of the atrium. An authentic suit of armor stood guard on a pedestal in a corner.

Federico noticed me admiring the room.

"Father collects Spanish antiquities. A conquistador wore that armor when Cortez invaded Mexico in 1520. Come with me."

He led me into a wood-paneled parlor. Ancient, edged weapons hung on the walls: pikes, broadswords, a mace. At one end of the forty-foot room, double windows displayed the garden with the Caribbean glittering in the distance.

"Have a seat. Father will be right down."

I collapsed into a leather couch that sighed as it molded to my body. My stomach growled. I had not eaten lunch, but there was no table set for food in the room.

Footsteps sounded on the tile floor. I stood when Pilon entered from the foyer.

"Don Carlos, thank you for coming. Have you eaten?" We shook hands.

"Don Francisco, thank you for inviting me. No, I have not."

"Excellent. Come with me."

Double French doors in the far corner led to the loggia overlooking the pool. A table and chairs had been relocated from the poolside. "It's a bit windy today to eat by the pool, and it might rain. I hope this is agreeable?"

"Of course. Thank you."

The same two guards were posted in the loggia. I wondered if they had moved in the last twenty-four hours. Maybe they were training to be human statues and work as buskers in Santa Maria on their day off.

Today's small talk was friendlier, more intimate, jovial. While we ate, the clouds gathered and it began to rain. Following lunch, Ernesto served brandy.

Pilon hoisted his glass. "To new friends."

We toasted as the rain passed and the sun came out.

"I understand from Esteban that Desiree has entertained you in Santa Maria."

"Desiree showed me around the tourist sites, beaches, and shops, yes."

Pilon winked at me. "Desiree is quite famous in Santa Maria."

"Oh?"

"Yes. Years ago, I engaged her to entertain at parties here and in Santa Maria. When we were younger, I spent many happy hours in her arms. In fact, I engaged her services again for a gift to Federico on his fifteenth birthday."

"Yes," Federico said. "Desiree and I spent an unforgettable weekend together. I trust she has lost no skill over the last twelve years."

"Desiree ages like fine wine. I promised her I would call again, assuming I have reason to return to San Cristobal."

Pilon smiled. "Well said, Carlos. May I call you Carlos?"

"Of course."

"And you shall call me Cisco."

"And I am, of course, Federico."

Whoopee. We were gonna be BFFs.

"Carlos, we accept your proposal. We will provide twenty kilos a month to begin, at market price. In a few months, we'll increase the quantity. I'll have the first twenty kilos ready tomorrow. Is that acceptable?"

"It takes time to establish a transportation network. If you agree, I will return in three weeks for the first twenty kilos."

"That long? I'm disappointed at the delay."

"This is my first venture into this type of business. I have cemented my contacts in Mexico and the United States. But there are certain logistics with customs officials in both counties to coordinate. Certain payment methods to test. A new business needs start-up time."

"Mexico?"

"Yes, all my operations are controlled in Mexico."

Pilon waved a hand. "Of course, of course."

He glanced at Federico, then back to me. "You must demonstrate good faith. More than a *Centenario*. Buy one kilo to prove you are a serious man. Thirty thousand U.S. dollars."

I didn't want to act eager, so I hesitated.

"That is acceptable, Cisco, but I don't travel with that much cash unless I know I will need it. I will wire the money to Santa Maria tomorrow or the next day. What bank do you trust?"

156

"In Santa Maria, I trust everybody. But, yes, there is a preferred bank. Federico will give you bank wire instructions. You will deal with him from now on."

He stood and lifted his brandy glass.

"To new friends."

I carried my beer to the balcony. Sailboats paraded in the harbor. The rain returned and swept across the water toward the mountain citadel. It was an hour earlier in Port City. There might be time to wire the money today. I used a special cellphone to call Mexico.

"Hola, this is Corregidor," Uncle Felix said.

"Corregidor, this is Traveler. This line may not be secure."

"I'll keep that in mind."

"My friend will call you in five minutes. Tomorrow, send thirty packages to the *Banco Popular de Santa Maria.* Text me to this number once you know if you can do it tomorrow. The next day would be okay, but I would prefer it tomorrow." I gave him the bank code and Pilon's account number.

Felix recited the information, and I disconnected.

Using the same phone, I made another call.

"Hello."

"Tank, this is Carlos Calderone."

"What can I do for you, bro?"

"This phone is supposed to be secure, but I wouldn't stake my life on it so I'll be vague about things and give you clues to others."

"My best game is football, but I play other games. What do you need?"

"Wire $30,000 for me, today if possible."

"Where to?"

"Don't say anything more than yes or no. Do you recall meeting my relative who lives in Mexico? The one who wears a uniform?"

"Yes. I have his business card."

"Good. Call him. He'll give you wiring instructions. Can you send the money today?"

"Maybe. It's almost cutoff time. I'll get on it after we hang up."

The sun sank low in the west. The golden reflections from the harbor flashed on the underside of my balcony awning. I debated eating at *El Paraiso* again to celebrate a successful trip. I relished their grilled grouper, but it was Desiree's favorite restaurant. If she was there with another customer, she would know I was in town and she would expect me to call her tomorrow. I would have to do that to stay in character, but spending time with a prostitute, even a nice one like Desiree, rubbed me the wrong way, no pun intended.

Instead, I strolled from the Caribe Real to the beach. I ambled left and passed *El Paraiso*. Outdoor restaurants and bars lined the beach. Continuing south, I came to *El Fogon, The Stove*. The restaurant displayed a barbecued shrimp platter on a table beside the entrance along with their menu. The shrimp smelled delicious.

The aroma of barbecued shrimp lured me inside. *El Fogon* had a Spanish tile floor, a thatched roof, and waist-high stone walls that let cooling breezes blow from any direction. An opening in the beach wall led to chaises and umbrellas on the beach. An attendant was folding the umbrellas and stacking lounges in the thickening twilight.

This neighborhood didn't look bad. Besides, the barbecued shrimp beckoned.

A second glass of Pinot Grigio went well with my barbecued shrimp. Then the text arrived.

Package to be sent tomorrow. Will text when it leaves here. Corregidor.

As I toasted myself with the Pinot Grigio, I imagined Snoop saying: *Don't break your arm patting yourself on the back.*

Next door was another open-air restaurant. I gazed through it to the other side. There was a bar with a half-dozen large television screens. A sports bar would be a good place to practice my San Cristobal accent and slang. If things worked out the way I planned, I would need to pass as a *San Cristobalero* soon.

After paying my tab, I dodged through the twilight crowd, walking down the sidewalk to *La Tribuna Barra Deportes, The Grandstand Sports Bar.* The streetlights had not come on.

I ordered a beer and listened to the locals talk for a half hour. One television broadcast a *futbol* game between San Cristobal and a Puerto Rican team. The locals fell behind one to nothing early in the first half. I rooted for the locals in my imitation San Cristobal accent.

A man wearing a faded Pittsburgh Pirates baseball cap came in and sat beside me at the bar. I recognized the *P* logo on the front.

"Are you from Pittsburgh?"

From his expression you would have thought I asked him if he was from the moon.

"Your hat—it's the Pittsburgh Pirates American baseball team."

He removed his hat and studied it. "I found the hat on the beach. A tourist must have lost it. You don't speak like an American."

"I watch American baseball on satellite TV."

I retreated to the restroom for a smartphone internet search on the local soccer team.

As I returned to my seat at the bar, one of the human statues who had guarded Pilon's loggia entered the restaurant. The tattoo on his neck gave him away. He walked in with a man wearing a soccer jersey like the San Cristobal team. Tattoo and Soccer Fan sat at a table in the rear.

At half-time, I swiveled my barstool to the man in the Pirates cap and pointed at the TV screen. "Enrico Fuentes is my cousin." Fuentes was a player on the San Cristobal team.

"You from Ponce?" he asked. Fuentes was from Ponce, a smaller city on San Cristobal's south coast.

"Yeah. I crew on a charter fishing boat."

"What brings you to Santa Maria?"

"I'm here to shop for my own fishing boat."

We talked for the rest of the game. If he suspected I wasn't from Ponce, he hid it well. I figured he was a plant sent in by Pilon's guard, Tattoo, but Tattoo may not have told him who I was or where I was from.

In the second half, Enrico had an assist and San Cristobal tied the score. Pirates Cap and I high-fived. The game ended one all, and my new fake friend left, along with Tattoo and Soccer Fan. I stayed to catch the post-game program, still absorbing the local idioms and slang. I hoped they would interview Cousin Enrico, but they didn't.

The sidewalk was deserted for a block in either direction by the time I left *La Tribuna*. The few streetlights were far apart and half had burned out. Heading back the way I came, I ambled down the sidewalk on the gloomy street.

A half-block ahead, two men emerged from a narrow alley: Tattoo and Soccer Fan.

Glancing to my rear, I saw two more men exit from another alley and curve in my direction. The first was average in every way, except he wore a leather jacket and it was still 85 degrees at eleven o'clock at night. Leather Jacket kept his right hand in his pocket.

When I was in the Army, I'd encountered tough guys in Germany who wore leather jackets. Guns were hard to get in Germany, so bad guys often carried knives. A leather jacket sometimes stops a blade that isn't razor sharp. Was it the same in Santa Maria?

The other man was my barroom buddy, Pirates Cap. Small world. The Pirate nickname fit him in more than one way. When he picked the barstool next to me, I had figured it for a setup. I was disappointed that I was right.

Four men appearing at the same time? Rule Seven popped into my head: *There is no such thing as a coincidence,* followed by Rule Fourteen: *When you think someone is out to get you, they probably are.* The question was: Who?

Pilon had not sent them. If Pilon wanted me dead, he would let me return to his fortress for the cocaine, kill me, and bury me in his garden to fertilize his Bougainvillea. No muss, no fuss, and goodbye Carlos.

No, the guard was in business for himself. After the robbery, he couldn't let me live. If I recognized him from his neck tattoo and told Pilon, the mobster would have him killed because of the affront to his hospitality.

Therefore, as the World's Greatest Private Investigator, I deduced that I wasn't supposed to survive.

Tattoo must have asked Pilon's driver, Javier, which hotel I was staying in. He might have recruited Pirates Cap, Soccer Fan, and Leather Jacket for muscle. He would have promised them this would be easy.

Tattoo and Soccer Fan didn't glance in my direction. Maybe they thought if they pretended not to notice me, I wouldn't notice them until it was too late. They crossed the deserted street and stopped on the sidewalk. Pretending to talk to each other, they waited for me to approach.

Tattoo was forty pounds overweight and had probably never fired a shot from his MP7 in anger. He assumed I wouldn't recognize him. After all, who notices servants in uniform? He observed me at lunch with Pilon, so he knew I was rich and figured I wouldn't fight. Amateurs.

I glanced back.

The men behind walked down the center of the street, Pirates Cap in the lead.

While making my kill plan, I calculated angles and speeds, lighting and locations. Stepping off the curb, I angled toward the alley where the first two men had come from. My pace remained the same, but I lengthened my stride.

The first two men pivoted to me.

"Hey, you," I hollered. "You dropped something."

I kept walking. I was halfway across the street.

Tattoo stopped and gazed at the sidewalk behind him.

"Where?"

"There."

Walking faster, I was nearly to the opposite sidewalk.

Fast footsteps thumped behind me. A backward glance showed Pirates Cap and Leather Jacket running toward me. "Stop him," Pirates Cap shouted.

Sprinting the last fifteen yards, I reached the alley. A glance up the narrow walkway confirmed it was deserted. Less than six feet wide, it was built before the automobile age. I spun in the alley and confronted them. No one could flank me and they could approach only two at a time.

The four men skidded to a halt three or four yards away. Tattoo advanced a half step. "Give us your money, tourist, and we'll let you go."

"My name is *El Vengador,* you fat pig." I used the Spanish word for *avenger.* A little psychological warfare *machismo* couldn't hurt.

Thirty yards up the street, a couple walked out of a bar. The man spotted the five of us in the mouth of the alley, clutched his date by the arm, and yanked her back inside.

Tattoo stood a little straighter and sucked in his gut. "Your money, tourist. *Now!*"

Four amateur thugs versus one of me. To me, this was a target-rich environment.

"My sainted grandmother made me promise to warn someone before I hurt them, even a fat Porky the Pig. I will send all of you to the hospital or the morgue. Walk away while you still can."

Tattoo laughed. "Can't you count, tourist? We are four and you are alone. Don't die protecting your money. You can make more money, but not if you're dead."

He glanced to his comrade.

"Show him, Miguel."

So Leather Jacket's name was Miguel. Miguel removed his hand from his leather jacket. *Click.* The four-inch blade flashed in the dim light. He waved the switchblade, an ugly grin on his unshaven mug.

"I will cut off your balls, tourist."

"There may be four of you, Porky, but those two don't count."

I peered over his shoulder at Pirates Cap and Soccer Fan.

"How much did this fat piggy promise you? A hundred pesos? Five hundred? Porky told you to come along and act tough, didn't he? He lied. Five hundred pesos won't cover your hospital bills if I let you live, or your funerals if I decide to kill you. Think about that when the fight starts, but think fast. If you stop to blink twice before you run, I will come after you faster than the devil himself. I will catch you and kill you both."

The two men exchanged a glance. My trash talk made them nervous. Putting four people in the hospital might cause waves. Two people, not so much.

Tattoo half-stepped toward me.

"Enough stalling. Give us your money *now,* before I run out of patience."

"Porky, I will chop you down like a machete hacks a vine. I will drop you and Miguel to the street like two sacks of shit. Then those two will run away, and I'll kill you both. Last chance."

Miguel snarled and stepped forward, leading with the knife.

Instead of retreating, I sprang at him. Seizing his knife hand in my fist, I clamped his fingers like a vise so he couldn't drop the knife. It became *my* knife, not his; he just didn't realize it yet. But he would soon enough.

Jerking him toward me, I kneed him in the groin. I slammed my right palm against his elbow, forcing it up as I yanked his knife hand down.

Miguel screamed as I bent his elbow the wrong way. I felt the ligaments pop as the cartilage in the elbow exploded.

Twisting his knife hand up, I stabbed Tattoo in the stomach, pushing hard to shove the four-inch blade through the fat. I could have gutted him by jerking the blade sideways, but I wanted to wound him, not kill him.

Tattoo held his stomach with both hands and stumbled backwards. Blood oozed between his fingers.

I kneed Miguel in the face, breaking his nose, then released his arm and let him fall to the sidewalk.

I threw a left jab to Tattoo's throat then a hard right to the solar plexus. He doubled over and fell on his side in front of Pirates Cap and Soccer Fan.

They stared down at the bleeding guard, eyes wide, and stepped back.

I kicked the guard in the temple and challenged Pirates Cap and Soccer Fan. I scooped up the knife. "Now you both will die."

It was melodramatic, but it worked. They ran like scalded dogs.

Miguel moaned and rolled to get up. His nose was broken. A kick to the face would punch the bones into his brain, killing him. I kicked him in the stomach instead. That would keep him down but let him live.

I used his shirt to wipe my fingerprints off the knife.

Tattoo moaned. I stomped his right hand, crunching the bones. I wiped the knife again on his shirt. He should survive the stab wound, but he wouldn't rob anybody for a long time.

I stomped both Miguel's hands in case he was ambidextrous with a knife.

I hiked up the alley. The area was hilly, but I figured it would let out on a street a block back from the harbor. At the top of the alley, I moved to the sidewalk again. I stopped at a storm sewer, broke the knife blade, and chucked the pieces in the hole.

Ten minutes later, I reached my hotel, having learned I could pass for a *San Cristobalero.*

———

Felix texted me the next morning:

Packages shipped.

It would take a few hours for the Mexican wire to clear in San Cristobal, so I returned to *El Fogon* for lunch. This time, I took a table on the beach. The server wedged a beach umbrella in the sand next to the table. I ordered barbecued shrimp and watched the pelicans and gulls swoop and dive. Families cavorted on the beach. Maybe I would bring Miyo once this crazy mission was over.

I dozed in the chair following lunch. My phone woke me.

"Carlos, it is Federico. Your items arrived. Can you dine with us at seven?"

"Of course. Thank you."

"Javier will pick you up at half past six. And Carlos," he added, "bring an empty briefcase."

———

Don Francisco and Federico both greeted me at the foot of the sidewalk. They wore matching white guayaberas and linen pants, but they weren't headed to a First Communion celebration.

"Carlos," said Pilon, "thank you for coming."

"With pleasure, Cisco."

We shook hands. Like I said, BFFs.

Federico took my case and handed it to the driver.

"Javier will handle this for you, Carlos."

Javier avoided eye contact and had not spoken to me on the ride to the citadel. I gave no indication he fingered me to the would-be muggers.

We ate poolside again. Long evening shadows stretched from the table to the loggia.

A new guard had replaced Tattoo. No wonder Javier acted skittish. I didn't tell the Pilons about the attempted mugging. I wanted them to consider me a rich business owner, not a trained street fighter. Besides, if I told Cisco, he would have Tattoo and Javier both killed. Being a snitch should not be a capital offense.

Dinner was served as the sun fell behind the offshore islands. Pilon served several unfamiliar local dishes, but I recognized octopus in one. It was delicious. Maybe it was the garlic; maybe it was the sunset.

Following dinner, we relocated to a table near the cliff to enjoy our brandy. The twilight remnants painted the sky in pink and gold, and Santa Maria sparkled below us. It would be romantic if Miyo were with me. Being surrounded by guards armed with machine guns made it less so.

Pilon dismissed the servers. "The money arrived from your bank in Mexico this afternoon."

"Good."

"Javier has your briefcase, with your kilo of product in it. He'll give it to you when you leave."

"Fine."

"We'll contact you in three weeks about the twenty kilos. We'll tell you the price before you come down."

"I thought the price was thirty thousand U.S. per kilo."

"That is today's price. With many commodities, prices rise and fall." Pilon shrugged. "You can say no if the price gets too high."

I didn't respond.

"And next time, bring cash. U.S. dollars."

"Cisco, I understand cash is important. It's difficult to smuggle such amounts out of the United States. Banks report to the government when customers withdraw large sums. Wiring money is better."

"You can bring cash from Mexico or Chile or your Bahamian casino without such reports."

"For such sums I need 72 hours' notice."

"Agreed." Pilon stood. "As I said, you deal with Federico. We may not see each other the next time you return. Safe journey."

Federico bid me good-bye when we reached the Mercedes.

"Once you return to your hotel, you will find a surprise from father and me."

As I opened the door to my suite at the Caribe Real, Desiree's familiar perfume permeated the air, but she wasn't there to greet me. She left identical notes on the bar, on my bedroom door, and taped to the TV screen. She made sure I got the message: *Come out to the balcony. Alone.*

I locked the cocaine in the room safe in my bedroom closet and opened the balcony door.

An ice bucket with a bottle of Pinot Grigio and two glasses waited on the table. Desiree lounged on a chaise wrapped in a colorful peasant skirt and a smile. She rose to her feet like a flower blooming. She held out her arms and made a dancer's pirouette. "Surprise."

After Desiree gave me her best performance on the balcony, I sent her to the bedroom for an encore. I promised to join her once I made a phone call. She stopped in the bedroom door to blow me a kiss, then left it open behind her. I closed the balcony door.

"Corregidor, this is Traveler."

"Hola, Traveler. You receive the package I sent?"

"Yes, and I received the item I was expecting. I'll be on the morning flight."

"Are you bringing the item with you?"

"In my briefcase. Meet me at the gate."

"I don't like this, Traveler. Wiring money is one thing. Bypassing customs is something else."

"We discussed this, Corregidor. I told you what it involved."

"Okay. We proceed as planned."

I exited in the middle of the passenger scrum. Uncle Felix waited at the gate in Mexico City, his Mexican Federal Police uniform starched stiff as a statue, and his brass shined mirror-bright.

"Come with me, *gringo,"* he said in English. We spoke English in Mexico and Spanish in the United States. He carried my briefcase and led me toward the terminal.

Felix led me through a door marked *Personal Autorizado Solamente*. He flashed his badge, spoke to people, and in fifteen minutes we stood at baggage claim awaiting my suitcase.

My mother was the oldest of five children; her brother Felix was the youngest. Uncle Felix was just a few years older than I, more of a big brother. As a child, I spent a month every summer with my Mexican grandparents. Felix and I became as close as brothers. I admired him when he entered the Mexican Federal Police, and I followed his example with the Port City Police.

Felix patted me on the shoulder. "Mother is thrilled you're here. I took the day off. Carry your own bag now that we're through Customs; it wouldn't look right for a *Federale* Major to lug a civilian's suitcase."

Once we reached his car, he said, "There is a kilo of cocaine in this briefcase."

"Yeah."

"Jesus H. Christ. You got a *Federale* officer to help you smuggle cocaine into Mexico. I lost count of the laws I broke in the last fifteen minutes."

"Just keep telling yourself it's for a good cause."

Felix merged onto the freeway and headed north to his mother's and my grandmother's ranch. My Uncle Sergio ran the ranch. Sergio would buy out his siblings once *Abuelita* passed away. Until then, she owned everything. It's nice to have a family you trust.

"What will you do with that crap, *gringo?*"

"I plan to set up Crucero for a confrontation with the Garcia gang in Fort Lauderdale."

"That means you must smuggle it into the U.S."

"I thought you might help me."

"What? Do you lay awake at night thinking of ways to get me in trouble?" Then he smiled. "Maybe I know someone who could help you."

"Why don't you call him?"

"Too easy for someone to overhear on a cellphone. Wait until we reach the landline at the ranch."

SIXTEEN

Diego Calvo chugged his tequila, wiped his mouth with his sleeve, and belched.

"I'm supposed to smuggle a goddamn kilo of cocaine into Dulles International Airport in my diplomatic luggage?" Calvo gestured toward me with his chin.

"Yes," Felix said.

The three of us sat at a quiet table in an expensive restaurant in La Zona Rosa in Mexico City.

"How pure is it?"

"That's not relevant."

"It's good stuff?"

"It makes no difference if it's pure as the driven snow or just ordinary crap, Diego," Felix said. "You smuggle it. You don't snort it."

Calvo regarded me with lidded eyes. For a moment I thought he was falling asleep. He was on his second tequila and our lunch hadn't arrived.

"If the goddamn ambassador gets wise to it, I lose a cushy embassy job. Why should I accept that risk?"

I told Calvo about Crucero's drug smuggling and sex slavery operations.

"Do you have a daughter?"

He paused for a moment. Maybe he didn't know if he had a daughter.

His cheeks cracked into an impression of a smile. "Two by my wife and one by my mistress."

Felix had warned me about Diego Calvo. "Diego's father works for the Ministry of Transportation. There are rumors he accepts kickbacks from highway contractors. His father keeps a mistress, which does not speak well for his character."

I had asked Felix if he knew anybody else we could use, but he didn't. Bad vibes emanated from Calvo, but Felix and I had no other option.

"I wrecked Crucero's sex operation, but that won't stop him from doing it again. Those girls were someone's daughters."

"My daughters are safe here in Mexico."

Calvo made a movement with his mouth exposing his teeth. It was supposed to be another smile, but it held no humor or goodwill. His teeth were perfectly aligned, bleached, and capped. Teeth to grace a toothpaste ad. Teeth impossible to afford on a sub-minister's salary.

Felix said, "You would help Carlos bring an evil man to justice and keep him from abusing more women in the future."

Calvo waved a manicured hand. "Evil is for the priests to handle. That is an American problem, not a Mexican one. It's expensive to maintain a wife and a mistress. What's in it for me?"

He rubbed two fingers across his thumb in the universal *show me the money* symbol.

I glanced at Felix. "We're wasting Diego's time."

I leaned forward to rise, but Calvo grabbed my arm. "Wait, my friend. I didn't say I wouldn't do it; I merely asked for a small consideration. My lifestyle is expensive. Doesn't hurt to ask, does it?"

He made that mouth movement again, but wider. Supposedly a grin.

The server arrived with a heavily laden food tray and a wooden serving rack. While he served our lunches, Calvo chugalugged his tequila and thumped the glass on the tray.

"Bring me another, a Margarita this time since they're paying." He gestured at Felix and me.

We waited for the server to leave.

"Will you do it?" I asked.

"Where is the, uh, stuff?"

"In a safe place. When do you travel to the U.S. next?"

Calvo mumbled around a mouth full of food. "Three days."

We concluded the arrangements, and Felix pressed his hand on Diego's forearm. "Diego, don't forget that I am a major in the Mexican Federal Police. And this man," he tweaked his chin in my direction, "is a trained killer. Google him before you consider double-crossing us. We both have long arms and long memories."

He gripped Calvo's arm. "Are we clear?"

Once again I wished we had had an option.

Tomas Kopitar

Kopitar stopped at the curb in front of Alena's house. He dreaded this summons. He had not located a man whose license number he knew. He trudged up the sidewalk, climbed the steps, and knocked twice on the doorjamb.

Alena opened the door and stepped back. God, she looked good. Kopitar ached for her with every breath in his body, but to her, he was another hired thug.

She sipped from a cut crystal glass. Scotch maybe? He hoped she would offer him a drink. He preferred Scotch.

"Shut the door, Tomaz."

He did and glanced at the rattan chair, waiting for an invitation to sit.

"It's been over a week, Tomaz. What have you learned about this stranger and about my missing men?" She paced the living room.

"Our police contact traced the license number. It's a white Dodge Grand Caravan registered to a shell corporation. The address is a post office box. It's a dead end. Let me ask Tony Crucero about the stranger. If he knows something, I'll get the answers." Kopitar clenched his fists unconsciously, eager for a chance to put that *ukrste* in his place.

Alena stopped pacing.

"If we asked Tony about the man, he would learn that we know he sent the stranger. It's better he doesn't know we spotted his man. We might lose Tony for a supplier."

"There's always cocaine available and people to sell to us. I can make Crucero talk." He had seen Crucero's picture. If the crossbreed died in the process, even better.

Alena smiled without mirth. "He wouldn't be good for anything after that."

Kopitar valued his duty to Alena and her father above his personal antipathy toward Crucero. Something didn't sit right with this whole affair of the missing men. "Alena, tell me again: Why do you think Crucero sent the stranger?"

"After Hugo chased him toward the Everglades, Bojan and Edvard both texted me that they caught him. They must have questioned him, because they knew Tony Crucero sent him."

"Did Hugo send the text?"

"Bojan and Edvard sent them. There were two texts."

"Are they still in your phone?"

Alena leaned over to get her phone from the cocktail table. Her blouse draped open and Kopitar caught a flash of nipple. Instantly, his loins stirred. If only she would consider him as a man...

She handed him the phone. He inhaled her perfume.

Kopitar read the text aloud. *"Crucero send the man in Dodge Caravan. He not bother us again!"* He raised an eyebrow at Alena. "Bojan sent this?"

"Yes. Read the one from Edvard."

"He works for Crucero. He not a problem again. This came from Edvard's phone?"

"Yes."

Kopitar handed the phone back. "You should have told me this sooner. I can't say about the text from Edvard's phone, but Bojan did not send that first text."

"Yes, he did. It came from the number that's in my phone contacts."

"It came from his phone, but someone else sent it."

Alena sat on a rattan couch and studied the message again. She crossed her legs, and her skirt hiked up her thighs.

Kopitar was further aroused. If he could plunge between those tanned legs, he and Alena could have beautiful blond, blue-eyed children.

"Sit down, Tomaz."

Kopitar sat on a matching rattan chair. He tried not to stare at her legs.

"Would you care for a drink?"

"Whatever you're having, Alena."

"Scotch. You know where the bar is."

Kopitar tore his gaze from Alena's legs and walked stiffly to the bar, hiding his erection.

"Why do you say Bojan didn't send the text?"

He poured two fingers of Scotch and added ice. He remained standing behind the waist-high bar.

"I trained Bojan. He would not send any text if Hugo were there. It was not Bojan's position. Bojan would contact you only after something happened to Hugo."

"Okay, but Hugo is gone so something did happen to him. So Bojan sent the text."

"Not quite. Bojan wouldn't send a text; he would call you for instructions. The fact that he didn't call and did send a text means Bojan did not send it. All three men are dead. The stranger sent the texts with their cellphones."

Alena tapped her lips with a forefinger. "Why would he do that?"

"To make you suspicious of Crucero."

"Again, why? What would he gain?"

Kopitar hated to defend the *ukrste,* but his loyalty to Alena's father trumped his antipathy toward Crucero. "The stranger wants you to believe Crucero is your enemy."

Alena set her drink down.

"So, the stranger is Tony's enemy and wants to use me—or my men—to get back at Tony."

She reached for the cellphone. "That gives me something I *can* ask Tony about and keep doing business with him."

And that *ukrste* would fuck his beloved Alena again. And again. And again.

———

Kopitar glanced at his watch. Had the hands stopped moving? What was taking the crossbreed so long to respond to Alena's summons? Did the man have so little respect for her?

Alena peered past Kopitar's shoulder and saw Crucero's Corvette through the living room window. "He's here."

Kopitar stood.

"No, I'll let him in, Tomaz."

She opened the door and threw her arms around his neck. Wearing high heels, she was eight inches taller. "Tony, it's good to see you." She kissed him, oblivious to the effect she had on Kopitar.

Crucero returned her kiss and wrapped his arms around her, giving her buttocks a firm squeeze. Kopitar stared at the crossbreed's hands and seethed with hatred.

"Tony Crucero, this is my head of security, Tomaz Kopitar."

Crucero gave Alena's buttocks a final squeeze before he released her and extended his hand to the Serb. Kopitar felt like the crossbreed had crushed his heart.

"Pleased to meet you, Tomaz."

"And you."

They shook hands.

"Tomaz and I are drinking Scotch, but you can have anything you want. And anything else." She smiled and stroked his arm.

"Scotch is fine, Tomaz. Thanks."

The ungrateful interloper assumed Kopitar would fix his drink. He considered ignoring Crucero's order and sitting down, but he would not embarrass Alena.

Crucero pivoted to Alena. "What is so urgent you can't wait until our date this weekend? Are you that horny? Not that I'm complaining."

Alena led him to the couch and snuggled in beside him. She hooked her elbow through his, rubbing his arm with her breast. "Tomaz wants to ask some questions before he leaves us."

Kopitar handed the cocktail to Crucero before returning to his chair.

Crucero swirled the glass. "Sure, Tomaz. Ask away."

"We hunt a man who drive white Dodge Caravan, five years old. This is license number."

He handed Crucero a slip of paper.

"Why do you ask?"

"I hunt for this man."

"Why?"

Kopitar peered at Alena. He wouldn't disclose her interest; that was her decision to make.

Alena rubbed her hand on Crucero's thigh. "He followed me recently."

"You have his license plate. Should be simple enough to ascertain who owns the car. What's the problem?"

"We traced the license plate to a dead end. A shell corporation owns the van. The address is a post office box." She stroked Crucero's thigh. "I thought you might know who he is."

"Why would I know a guy who followed you? If he's a stalker... Oh wait, you can't call the cops, can you? You can't afford to attract attention."

"No. Tomaz and I will handle this with our people, but first we must find him."

"Why ask me?"

"He may have some connection to you. Perhaps he is also your enemy."

"Alena, you're freaking me out a little."

Kopitar said, "Read the license number and recall if it is familiar, please."

Crucero glanced at the paper and handed it back. "I never pay attention to license plates. Show me a picture of the man or the van."

"I no have photo of him. This photo I download from internet is not same van, but is same model and year." He handed an 8 x 10 photo to Crucero.

Crucero studied the picture. "There are a million white minivans and they all look the same, but this one—oh shit." He handed the photo to Alena.

"This guy, is he a white man, 190 centimeters, thirty years old, clean shaven, maybe a hundred kilos?"

Kopitar thought back to the description Viktor had given him. "Yes.

Short dark brown hair. Tan skin. Perhaps he is Latino like you." Perhaps he was *ukrste* like Crucero.

"I know the guy, and, yes, he hates my guts. I want to kill that bastard so bad it makes my teeth ache. You say he followed you?"

"Yes."

"Why would he do that?"

Alena glanced at Kopitar.

He shook his head and spoke in Serbian. "Don't tell him our men are missing. It makes us appear weak."

"What did he say?" Crucero asked.

"Tomaz said he will kill him for you. Who is he?"

"Apparently, he's my cousin."

Lucifer

Losefa Topati stopped shaving after he went to ground. Four weeks later, he sported a respectable beard and a bushy crew cut. He studied his image in the mirror. Should he shape his scruffy beard into a goatee? The cops were hunting for him. The Feds wanted him. The DEA, the NRA, and the IRS too, for all he knew. Everyone was out to get him. He studied his visage from one side then the other. He grinned and turned on the hot water.

Ten minutes later, he admired his handiwork. Except for the sideburns, he resembled Vladimir Lenin with his bushy eyebrows. He wiggled his eyebrows and laughed at his reflection. Vladimir Lenin. Maybe he should add a baseball hat.

An hour later, his new cellphone rang. "Yeah, boss."

"I have a job for you, Luce."

Topati remembered to pick an empty table at the rear. Tony would sit in the chair by the wall. Topati settled on a chair with its back to the kitchen door. Satisfied with his thorough, but slow, thought process, he smiled and waited for his leader.

Tony drove the Corvette this time. He accepted the chair Topati had left for him. "I like the Vandyke beard, Luce. Don't wear a Samoan shirt. Wear a guayabera and no one will recognize you."

Topati basked in the glow of Tony's approval. "Thanks. I look like Vladimir Lenin. He was a great leader, you know."

Tony gave him an expression he couldn't read and started to open his mouth. Topati thought he had said the wrong thing. "Lenin, he didn't take no shit from no one and neither do I."

"Yeah, whatever. Let's order breakfast."

Once the server brought their orders, Tony handed over an envelope. "This week's pay."

Topati shoved the unopened envelope in his pocket. He didn't count it. Tony would never cheat him. He wouldn't dare. "Thanks."

"Do you have a gun?"

"No." Topati avoided guns. Once he held a Colt .45 pistol, but it frightened him with its hard steel and heavy weight. He preferred his violence hands-on and personal.

"That's okay. Al will get you one."

Topati swallowed hard but said nothing.

"But you do know how to shoot, right?"

Topati had watched people shoot guns on TV many times. Cops, killers, cowboys, Indians. They pointed and pulled the trigger. How hard could it be? "Sure, I know how to shoot."

"I have a job for you."

Carlos McCrary

Saturday afternoon I landed in Port City and called Snoop and Morris to meet me at the office.

While I was out of town, Snoop continued to tail Al Tegumbre on his rounds. Snoop had a handle on his routine and thought he knew who Tegumbre's contact was with the Garcia gang.

Where I-895 met the Ronald Reagan Turnpike near the Broward County line, there were blocks and blocks of blue-collar rental apartments. Tegumbre met a customer there each week, who drove a car registered to a

Broward County construction company. "The construction company is rumored to have mob connections," Snoop said, "so I think the driver is a member of the Garcia gang."

"Thanks, Snoop."

Morris had tailed Alena Cernan and her Mercedes whenever he was off duty from the PCPD.

"What do you have for me, Morris?"

"Miss Cleavage added a new dark green Suburban a week ago. It has dealer plates so it's not in the DMV database. The black Suburban has been missing for two weeks. We are overlooking action somewhere. Also, I haven't seen..." he referred to his notes, "...Hugo Horvat, Edvard Oblak, or Bojan Matic in two weeks. Maybe they went somewhere in the black Suburban. You should assign another operative so we can track both the Mercedes and the green Suburban until we determine where the black SUV and the three missing Devils went."

They went to hell, I thought. "Alena dumped the black Suburban. She no longer owns it."

"Are you sure? After I saw the green SUV, I ran a DMV report on the black one and no change showed. As far as the DMV knows, Cernan LLC still owns it. There's something fishy about its disappearance."

Snoop smiled but didn't say a word.

"I investigated it, Morris. They sold it in an off-book transaction. Forget the black Suburban. It's out of the picture."

"Okay. What about Hugo Horvat, Bojan Matic, and Edvard Oblak?"

"They left town, maybe to Switzerland."

"Hmm. That explains this next item." He shoved a set of pictures across my desk. "Sorry, Snoop, I brought just the one set."

He turned back to me.

"Three new Devils appeared at the same time the green Suburban showed up. Those are their photos."

"You know who they are?"

"Nope. Run the pictures by Wilma Leonard on Monday. She might recognize them."

"She let me photograph her file on the Devils. I'll see if the new guys are in there first."

SEVENTEEN

Miyoki Takashi

Miyo's doorbell rang, and she heard the familiar key in her lock. She rushed to her door and opened it as Chuck twisted the handle. "Welcome home, world traveler." She stepped into his arms and clutched his body against hers. His lips were warmer than the South Florida heat accounted for, or maybe it was her lips.

"Did you miss me," she said, "or is that a gun in your pocket?"

"You noticed."

"I'm horny and you're available. If I'm treating you like a sex object, I may as well take advantage. We are celebrating tonight. Besides, you've been gone a whole week. Can you spend the night?"

"I never say no. What are we celebrating besides my return and the end of your dry spell?"

"The Ronaldrick Galleries in Hollywood asked me to do an exhibit next month."

"In Hollywood? Never heard of them."

"Not Hollywood, *Florida* silly; the *real* Hollywood, in California."

"Don't let the Hollywood Florida Chamber of Commerce hear you say that. However, that's wonderful news. You deserve the best."

She made an exaggerated curtsey. "Thank you, kind sir. Mix Margaritas and I'll finish the salad. I'll be out four seconds after you fill the pitcher."

Later, Miyo lazed in bed with her head on Chuck's shoulder. She nuzzled his neck. "That's a better celebration than drinking a Margarita."

"You celebrate the same way whether it's sunset, National Woodpecker Appreciation Day, or the arrival of the mail."

She sat up in bed, snatched a throw pillow, and tossed it at his head.

"How did your trip to San Cristobal go?"

"Pretty well. I met the local crime boss."

Chuck told Miyo about the view from Pilon's mountain fortress and the beautiful gardens.

"Pilon's the supplier Crucero buys his cocaine from. I got on Pilon's preferred customer list and bought a kilo of cocaine to prove my sincerity."

She sat up on the bed. "You know I nearly died from a heroin overdose." Her throat felt sore and her head swam when she recalled the incident.

"You told me Gracie called 9-1-1, and EMS rushed you to the hospital in time. That must have been awful for you."

Poor Gracie. She had been Miyo's best friend since childhood. Later, she got hooked on drugs and blew a successful career as a New York City supermodel. Chuck had rescued her from a kidnapper, but he couldn't rescue her from drugs. Miyo wasn't about to let that happen to her.

"That's why I stick to alcohol and not much of that. I won't even smoke a joint. I hate for you to get mixed up in cocaine. That crap kills thousands of people every year."

"Don't worry, sweetheart. I'm doing this to stop Crucero's cocaine ring. No one will get high with this cocaine. It's bait for the Garcia gang. Once I'm through, I'll destroy it."

"Don't flush it down the toilet. Cocaine might seep into the ground water or the ocean."

"I'll give it to the Port City police," Chuck said. "They destroy unused prescriptions and street drugs."

"I heard about the Garcias on the news. I don't want you mixed up with them either. They are more than dangerous; they are *freaky* dangerous. Like *insane* dangerous."

"Being a PI isn't limited to missing persons, insurance fraud, and wandering spouses, honey. Occasionally I target bad guys. I plan to put Crucero down like a rabid dog. That's dangerous. You knew that before we first dated. Hell, you know what I did to that maniac from New York City who held Gracie's family hostage. That case was how we met."

She rested her head on his shoulder again and draped her arm across his chest. "My first attraction to you—no, my *second* attraction to you—was hero worship."

"What was the first?"

"Lust. Michelangelo's statue of David, remember?"

"If you ever get serious about me the way I am about you, you'll need to accept who I am."

Ever since Chuck professed his love, Miyo had analyzed her feelings for him. He was in a dangerous business. Could she accept living in fear that he might not come home? She would need to ponder that.

"I do accept who you are, and I am serious about you, that's why I brought it up."

"How serious are you talking about?"

Miyo had never intended to spend the rest of her life in the artificial world of art gallery shows, casual sex, and hobnobbing with glamorous but shallow people. Since she had learned more about Chuck and his world, that aspect of her life—she thought of it as the *New York glamor part*—seemed superficial. She loved painting, but a successful artist didn't need to jump into bed with other people in the business to promote her career. The art should speak for itself. Was she thinking of settling down? How serious was she about Chuck?

"I know the difference between lust and love." She touched his cheek. "I love you."

Chuck put his hand over hers and pressed it to his cheek. "I love you too." He brought her palm to his lips and kissed it.

Her pulse quickened. "Then show me."

"Again?"

Miyo smiled with lidded eyes. "Aren't you *up* for it yet?"

Chuck stood and swept her up in his arms. "Let's go."

Later, Miyo rolled off and lounged on her side circling her finger through the hair on Chuck's chest. "You asked me a few weeks ago if I were ready for an exclusive relationship. *Monogamous* you called it."

"That offer still goes."

She rubbed his chest with the flat of her hand. "You didn't ask me the difference between love and lust."

"I figured you'd tell me when you felt like it."

"Lust is treating someone like a thing—a sex object we talked about once. Until I met you, I did that with every man I ever dated. Lust is one-dimensional. That's why sex can get boring; because the other person is a one-dimensional participant."

"And love?"

"To *love* someone is to treat him or her like a person, in three dimensions. The last few months, I've come to appreciate your other facets. You are three-dimensional to me." She touched his hand. "I love you."

"I love you too, and I love to hear you say you love me, but what does love versus lust have to do with my offer of a monogamous relationship?"

"Since I know you for a multi-dimensional person, I know how important faithfulness and fidelity are to you."

"And…?" He let the word hang in the air.

"Providing you still want to, I will accept that exclusive relationship."

A frown raced across Chuck's face and disappeared. "Okay. I still want to be exclusive, but you need to know something that happened in San Cristobal."

Chuck told her about his encounters with Desiree.

Miyo didn't say anything.

Chuck sat up on the bed. "Well?"

"Thanks for telling me, lover. I know that was uncomfortable for you."

"Uncomfortable for you to hear too, I'd bet."

She patted him on the cheek. "I don't see a problem with it."

"Why not? She's a prostitute."

"For one thing, we had not agreed to be exclusive before you went to San Cristobal so it's no biggie."

"But now, if I return to San Cristobal for any reason, I might need to spend time with her as part of my cover."

She fell silent. "Let's fix a pitcher of Margaritas and talk it through. I'll make the Margaritas. You wait on the balcony."

Later, they returned to Miyo's bedroom and she stretched across Chuck's chest drinking the last of her Margarita through a bent straw.

"The way I view it, you didn't have sex with Desiree."

"But I did. Several times."

"No, you didn't. Carlos *Calderone* had sex with her, not Carlos *McCrary*. You were playing a part." She licked a little salt off the rim, then licked his cheek. "There's a difference. I will believe that you were not doing it because you wanted to have sex with her. You did it because those people in San Cristobal expect it of Carlos Calderone the gangster—that man *would* patronize a prostitute."

She finished her Margarita. "By the way, that new move we did with the lounge cushions on the balcony, did you learn that in San Cristobal?"

"I'll never tell."

"Wherever you got the idea, it was remarkable. We should practice a few more times and make it a permanent addition to our dance card."

She licked a fleck of salt off his shoulder.

"What if I need to go back to San Cristobal."

"I would be dishonest if I said I was okay with it. If we choose monogamy, you being with another woman—for any reason—scares me, but you seemed okay with the idea of me dating other men before I agreed to monogamy."

"It wasn't like I had a choice. From the get-go, I knew your terms to have a relationship. That was better than not seeing you at all."

"Your job can require you to play a part." Miyo said. "It's part of me accepting your chosen profession."

"You know I'll avoid doing that if possible."

"I know. So long as you don't come home with an STD, do what you need to do to play your role. I'll tell myself that Carlos Calderone is doing it, not Carlos McCrary." She smirked. "Besides, you might learn something else you can teach me."

She laid her hands on his cheeks and kissed him. "I love *you,* and you love *me.* Now let's forget the prostitutes and the gangsters, and you tell me about San Cristobal seen as a tourist. Did you get to see any of it?"

"I toured Santa Maria, the capital. It's a beautiful city. It reminds me of Puerto Vallarta. Have you ever been to Puerto Vallarta?"

"I haven't. Why don't we go there?" She rubbed his ankle with her bare foot.

"We could stop in Mexico City on the way, and you could meet the Mexican side of my family."

"Yes, we could."

"How about October?"

"I have a show in Chicago the first week of October. Other than that, I'm flexible. We can fit it in, as long as we're still going to San Francisco for Labor Day too."

"Right."

Miyo rolled onto his chest.

"Did you notice I am stark naked?"

"Am I so forgettable? I noticed your nakedness enthusiastically and expertly a half hour ago on the balcony."

"Yes, you did."

"And an hour before that right here."

"Yes, you did." She kissed his neck. "But did you observe I'm *still* naked?"

"You are? With you lazing on my chest, all I can see is the ceiling."

She planted her hands on the bed on either side of Chuck's head and did a pushup. She drew her knees up and sat astride his waist. "Now can you see?"

"Oh, my yes. You are in fact naked as a peeled peach."

"What do you intend to do about it, big boy?"

"This."

Carlos McCrary

Monday morning, I headed straight to Wilma Leonard's office from Jerry's Gym.

She smiled when I walked in. "It's Chuck McCrary, bringer of cappuccino."

"I also brought you more information."

She sipped her cappuccino, and I spread Morris's photos of the new Blue-Eyed Devils on her desk.

"I identified two of the three men from your file. We never spotted them with Alena Cernan until a week ago. Maybe they had gone back to Europe."

"Maybe. My buddies at Miami-Dade Organized Crime tell me the Cernans, both father and daughter, shuffle two dozen different thugs in and out from Europe. They come in on tourist visas, so they stay six months."

"Their gang is a revolving door. What about Alena? Does she depart the USA every six months?"

Wilma spun her chair around and lifted a file from the cabinet behind her. "Alena Cernan obtained permanent resident status as CEO of Cernan LLC, a real estate management company."

She tapped on a photo. "That's Tomaz Kopitar, and this guy is Niko Iva." She twisted to her computer and accessed it. "Iva returned to Switzerland and then came back here four days ago on a tourist visa."

"What about Kopitar?"

She did her magic with the computer again. "Not in the system." She slid her keyboard aside. "The system isn't perfect."

"Maybe the third man arrived with Niko Iva. Can you access the U.S. immigration security cameras when Niko arrived and see if this guy arrived at the same time?"

"*No problemo.* Ever since that San Bernardino massacre the Feds give us access to their security cameras."

Wilma retrieved her keyboard and scanned security videos on her monitor. She swung her monitor so we could both watch. "This is the third man."

She tapped more keys. "Pavel Struna, also admitted on a tourist visa. Does that help?"

"It's more than I knew before. Thanks. I owe you one."

"You owe me a damn sight more than one." She laughed. "Go get 'em, tiger."

Lucifer

Another white minivan glided into McCrary Investigations' parking lot. This was the fourth one Topati had counted so far, but two were not Dodges. Tony had determined McCrary's office address from the McCrary Investigations website and sent Topati to stake it out. He had arrived at 7:30 that morning, three-and-a-half hours earlier. He was tired, hungry, and he needed to pee.

He compared the license plate to the paper in his hand. Yes, that was McCrary's van. The driver was the man who attacked him at his old apartment. His pulse pounded in his temples when he recalled the fight. Why was McCrary pursuing him?

He had fought with Carlos McCrary and beaten him, and he hadn't even known it. Wait until he told Tony.

Topati photographed McCrary and the van's license plate. He waited two minutes for McCrary to get to his second-floor office, then he used the restroom on the first floor.

Carlos McCrary

I called Jorge.

"Our old friend Lucifer Topati was parked in my office parking lot when I arrived. He's in the same maroon Ford Taurus he drove four weeks ago."

"Not the sharpest knife in the drawer, is he? I'll send two black-and-whites to arrest him. Can you keep him on ice until they get there?"

"I gotta catch a plane to Washington, and I should leave now. He'll tail me to the airport. Can your guys pick him up there?"

"Are you taking the Pelican Freeway?"

"Yeah. I'll use short-term parking; I expect to be gone two days."

"He might peel off when you turn into the parking garage. I'll set a roadblock at the airport exit."

I didn't glance toward Lucifer while I walked back to my Caravan. I cruised a little below the speed limit to give Jorge time to set the roadblock. Once I curved into the airport entrance, Lucifer stayed on the Pelican Freeway.

A missed opportunity because I had a plane to catch.

EIGHTEEN

D iego Calvo met me at a sushi restaurant a block from his embassy in Washington. It was a big, noisy room crowded with people of all races, dressed in styles from around the world. I ate at a sushi restaurant in Port City once, but it wasn't so elaborately decorated. I recognized the ornate Sake flask on the table. Calvo finished his small *choko* cup as I arrived and refilled it.

"Sit, my friend. Let me pour you a Sake. One does not pour one's own Sake, at least not the first cup. Another person at the table is supposed to serve you."

He filled my *choko* to the rim, spilling a little.

"You weren't here to pour mine, so I didn't wait." He giggled. I thought diplomats didn't giggle. It was twelve-thirty and Calvo was drunk.

My briefcase was not visible. Must have been under the table.

The geisha-costumed server bowed like in the movies. Calvo ordered for us.

The server walked away. "Fine ass on that girl."

He giggled again. "You come to Washington often?"

"I was here once before."

"On vacation when you were a kid?"

"No, when the president awarded me the Bronze Star and a Purple Heart."

"That's right; I had forgotten. I Googled you, like Felix suggested. You're a goddamn Green Beret war hero."

He was jovial when I arrived. Now his tone reeked of sarcasm. Maybe he wasn't a happy drunk.

"I'm no hero. In that situation, any man in my unit would've done the same. I survived, although some didn't."

"You're pretty goddamn tough, aren't you?"

The hostility in his voice told me something wasn't right. "You have my briefcase?"

His focus flicked to one side. "Yes."

"Give it to me."

He reached beneath the table and the case nudged my foot. I pulled it closer.

"Got it. Thanks."

I lifted the briefcase onto my lap and glanced at the lock. The seal I had affixed to the latch was disturbed. Someone had opened the briefcase, broken the seal, and smoothed the ripped edges back together. The tear was almost invisible. Almost.

"Someone broke my seal."

"There was... There was a, uh, incident with the goddamn case. It wasn't my fault. It wasn't my goddamn fault."

"Does that mean I will find the contents undisturbed once I open the case? The seal was damaged, but not removed?"

"Not exactly. My boss, the ambassador."

He spread both hands like he couldn't find the words. "He asked what was in the case. He's my goddamn boss, for God's sake. What else could I do but share it with him?"

"You promised this would be in your personal luggage. Does the ambassador often display an interest in your personal luggage?"

"I had no choice, I swear." Calvo peeked both ways and lowered his voice. "I swear on my children's lives; I'll pay you back. Don't kill me."

Whether the ambassador was involved was irrelevant. Calvo double-crossed me, and he would pay the price—but not in money.

I gave him the deadeye cop stare.

Calvo's hands trembled.

"He took only half, I swear. He cut the other half. It's still good quality. I'll pay you back. How much? Name your price."

"You can't repay this with money."

Whatever Calvo did with the stolen cocaine, he wouldn't have it on him, even in a public restaurant. It pained me no end, but I could do nothing about it.

I stood with the briefcase and walked away.

Calvo shouted after me. "It wasn't my goddamn fault."

It wasn't prudent to carry concealed weapons in Washington; the cops were alert for crazy people with mass murder on their minds. I had locked both pistols in my hotel room safe and walked to the restaurant unarmed except for the ceramic knife strapped to my left forearm.

Washington being a hotbed of various three-letter federal agencies and other foreign intrigues, I assumed my hotel room was under surveillance. It would be bad for a video to surface of me with a briefcase full of cocaine, assuming Calvo had not stolen all of it. I didn't dare open the case yet.

I checked out, rented a car at the hotel, and headed for I-95 South. A roadside park near Richmond, Virginia was my first stop.

I unlocked the case.

Calvo had opened the cocaine package and resealed it, but it hefted like one kilo. Calvo had cut the cocaine.

Someone once said revenge is a dish best served cold. I added Diego Calvo to my *to-do* list, but I left that for the future.

A thousand miles and a day later I wheeled the rental car into the condo garage at sunset and parked in a visitors' spot. I felt like I had run two marathons, back to back.

Lucifer had had two days to spot my van in the airport parking garage and attach a GPS tracker. I had driven twelve hours that day. I didn't feel like crawling under the van to locate a tracker. I decided to send someone to collect the Caravan in the morning.

I called Miyo.

"I just arrived home, and I had a shitty trip. I need cheering up from the woman I love."

"I love to hear that. I'll be there in forty-five minutes. Shall I wear a cheerleader outfit?"

"Forget the outfit, but bring your pom-poms."

Miyoki Takashi

Miyo followed Chuck's example and rang his doorbell before she inserted her key. When she twisted his sturdy deadbolt, she reminded herself again to get a more secure lock for her condo. The only problem was finding one that complemented the other hardware on her door. Chuck had promised to install it; all she had to do was find one that met her artistic standards. She should do that soon. Maybe the next weekend.

She opened the door as Chuck reached the entry, threw herself into his arms, and kissed him. She kicked her sandals off. "I have been so bloody proper today that I feel like going barefoot. In fact, I may go barefoot all over. You want to see my pom-poms now?"

"As much as I love to see you *au naturel,* if you sit with me by the grill, keep your clothes on. There's danger of sparks—I would hate for your lovely body to get an owie."

"Would you kiss it and make it better?"

"I'll do that, owie or not."

As they passed through the kitchen on the way to the balcony, Chuck poured her a Margarita.

Chuck hoisted the lid on the grill and flipped the steaks. Sparks flew but he stood between Miyo and the grill. They bounced off his apron harmlessly.

"What made you blue, lover?"

"Two things." He told her about Lucifer tailing him to the airport.

"This Lucifer person, he works for Tony Crucero?"

"He was a bouncer at the bordello with a history as a brawler. He's sent people to the hospital with his bare hands."

"Wasn't he arrested at the whorehouse?"

Chuck lowered the lid on the grill. "He wasn't there at the time, but I located him later." He told her about his fight with Lucifer.

"You mean he would have killed you if the cops hadn't used their sirens?"

"It does my bruised ego no good to admit this, but, yes, he had me like he was strangling a puppy. Then the cavalry arrived and scared off the attacking Indians—I mean Samoan."

"It's not funny, smart guy. You might have died if they hadn't arrived."

"I won't minimize the danger of my career." He held both her hands in his. "I had passed out from lack of oxygen before the cops scared Lucifer off. The fact is that I would have died if they'd arrived two minutes later."

Miyo shivered. "I told you that I accept you as you are, and I meant it, but if someone killed you, I'm not sure I could survive."

"Thousands of cops' wives and husbands, and military spouses, and firefighters' spouses confront that threat every day. It goes with the territory."

"I know," she whispered, tears rolling down her cheeks.

He wrapped his arms around her. She leaned her cheek against his chest. Miyo heard the powerful beating of his heart, steady as a clock.

She also heard the steaks sizzle and smelled the smoke from the meat bursting into flame. Chuck ignored it and held her.

She raised her gaze. "It's Cousin Emily, isn't it?"

One cheek was dry where it had pressed against Chuck's chest. Her other cheek felt wet. He kissed the tears away.

"And all the other Emilies out there. A man can do only what he can do. But if he does that each day, he can sleep at night and do it again the next day."

"Albert Schweitzer?"

"I think so. I can't save everybody, but I can save somebody."

"Schweitzer again?"

"No. An amateur philosopher named Carlos McCrary."

She smiled. "Enough with the tears, my love. Let's live one day at a time. If those other wives and sweethearts can accept the risk, it's possible that I can too. Besides, I came over to cheer you up."

He refilled their Margaritas, threw away the first steaks that were charred to a cinder, and threw two more on the grill.

Miyo stood on the windward side of the grill. "You told me two things made you blue. What was the other one?"

"My trip to Washington went into the toilet. My Mexican smuggler stole half the kilo. He cut the remainder with something to make up for the missing cocaine. Then he dared me to do anything about it."

"What will that do to your plans for the Garcias?"

"I'll test the remaining cocaine and figure out what to do. I'll come up with something."

"When do you meet the Garcias?" she asked.

"I'll approach one of their gang members tomorrow to arrange a meet with the boss."

"I would remind you to be careful, but that would be redundant."

"Careful is why I'm alive." He forked the steaks. Juice flared from the coals.

"Excuse me for being pissy, but you were being careful when Lucifer nearly killed you. A lot of good that did."

"Point taken. I can't foresee every risk."

"What payback do you have in mind for what's-his-name, the Mexican double-crosser?" Miyo licked a bit salt off the rim of her Margarita glass.

"Diego Calvo."

"You say his name like it's a curse word."

"It is a curse word now."

"Yeah. So, what about Diego Calvo?"

"Revenge is a dish best served cold." He smirked and drank his Margarita.

"Wow. You quote Albert Schweitzer and Star Trek on the same day."

"Star Trek?"

"Star Trek II, The Wrath of Kahn, that revenge remark. It's a Klingon proverb."

"It sounds like Shakespeare."

Miyo shook her head. *"Star Trek* trivia is my hobby."

"You are a woman of unplumbed depths."

Miyo felt a stirring between her legs. "Speaking of unplumbed depths, you've been gone for two days. I want to show you my pom-poms."

"The steaks might burn. It's unlucky to burn four steaks for one meal."

"Let the steaks simmer; I've simmered long enough." She unbuttoned her blouse. "How about a quickie to hold me until dinner."

"You deserve more than a quickie. Keep your shirt on. No, wait, take your shirt off; I'll move the steaks off the grill and finish them a little later."

Miyo winked. "Maybe a *lot* later."

Carlos McCrary

I sent Snoop and Pedro Martinez, Morris Martinez's cousin, to the airport to get my Caravan. Pete was a Cuban-American PI who lived in Miami-Dade County.

I Ubered to my office. Lucifer wasn't in my parking lot when I arrived.

Snoop returned with my Caravan. The good news was Topati had not stuck a GPS tracker on it. Like I said: Lucifer Topati wasn't the sharpest knife in the drawer.

Snoop had not been able to fasten a GPS tracker on the Garcia man's car either. While I flew to Washington, I assigned a two-man leapfrog tail. Pete Martinez had worked with Snoop. Pete snapped a telephoto of Garcia's man then trailed him into a Mexican restaurant where he got the subject's fingerprints the same way we got Tegumbre's prints.

Snoop placed a batch of surveillance photos on my desk. "Welcome home, bud. Here's the batch we took since Monday. And the Garcia man's fingerprints."

I flipped through the photos. "Tell Pete that's a good job on the fingerprints. Where did you snap this photo?"

Snoop compared the time code to his log. "Pete took it at a Denny's in Humbolt Springs." He looked again. "That guy with Tegumbre seems familiar. Should I know him?"

"That is Lucifer Topati. He grew a beard. I spotted him Monday before

I flew to DC. I've expected him to tail me ever since, but he's a no-show today. Makes me wonder where he is."

Snoop's eyebrows rose. "Jeez, it didn't occur to me. Yeah, that's the guy I photographed at the firehouse stakeout. It's hard to tell with the baseball hat and beard."

"This is the first picture we've had since he grew the beard. Congratulations on that. Crop his face, blow it up, and make a comparative with the one from outside the bordello. Send it to our operatives for a BOLO for him."

"Will do."

"Lucifer's kept me under surveillance and maybe you or the other operatives who come to my office. Tony Crucero threatened to kill me. Maybe he delegated the hit to Lucifer."

"We could run a sting on him, lead him out to the Everglades the same as we did those Chicago hoods, then hold him for the cops."

"Maybe. In any event, tell our operatives about the hair and beard. Also, email the photo and where you snapped it to Jorge Castellano. All kinds of cops want this guy. Maybe they'll get lucky and save us the trouble. I'll give the photos and fingerprints to Wilma Leonard tomorrow afternoon."

Lucifer tailed me to the North Shore Precinct. He had not been in my lot earlier. Had he been staked out in the Bayshore Parking Garage across the street? When I turned into the precinct parking lot, he kept going. Maybe being that close to the cops made him nervous, especially if he was waiting for an opportunity to kill me.

Wilma was walking toward her door, purse in hand, when I got to her office. Her gaze tracked me up and down. "At least tell me you brought cappuccino."

"Sorry, Wilma. I was running late when I left my office and didn't stop on the way. It was close to five o'clock and I didn't want to miss you."

"Ten seconds more and you would have. Can this wait until tomorrow?"

I didn't say anything.

"For God's sake, give it to me." She set her purse on her desk and sat down.

"Who is this guy?" I laid down a telephoto shot of the suspect. "He works for the Garcias. Antonio Crucero's delivery man, Al Tegumbre, sells him cocaine every week."

"Why come to me? Broward County has an organized crime department."

"Frankly, the Garcias are so successful in Broward, I think they have a mole in the Broward OCD."

She hooked a wayward strand of hair behind her ear. "Things have happened in Broward to make me wonder. They could have a bent cop up there."

"Here are three addresses we tailed him to." I handed her a sheet of paper. "The first is the Port City apartment where he got his delivery. The second is a house in Fort Lauderdale, maybe where he lives. The third one is a commercial building in west Broward. It might be the gang HQ. I didn't bother to run plate numbers until I learn more about this guy. Here are his fingerprints. We got them off a water glass. Can you help?"

"I can access NCIC the same as the Broward cops. Sure, I'll help. Call me after lunch tomorrow." She clutched her purse and stood beside her desk.

I didn't move.

"Del is waiting for me. It's my birthday tomorrow and he's treating me to my favorite restaurant tonight."

"If your birthday's tomorrow..."

"He couldn't get reservations for tomorrow. I'll get your information tomorrow morning." She stepped toward the door. "Tonight, I belong with Del."

"Happy birthday, Wilma."

I hoped Lucifer would tail me again after I finished at the precinct but he no-showed.

No one tailed me on the drive to Miyo's apartment.

"The suspect is Salvador Ramon Ortiz Garcia," Wilma had told me. "Charged with assault, ADW, conspiracy, yada, yada, yada. All arrests and no convictions. No one will testify against him. Ortiz's mother is a Garcia. That's what makes him a loyal gang member."

I sat in my rented Honda sedan a hundred yards from Ortiz's house. The SUV parked in his carport was registered to his wife. Gangsters have families too. He lived in a conventional house in a middle-class neighborhood in western Fort Lauderdale.

At six p.m. Ortiz's company car rounded the corner a block away.

I flashed my headlights before he reached his driveway. It would not be good to surprise him. Starting my Honda, I rolled up the street to his home.

Ortiz parked in the carport beside his wife's SUV.

I parked on the grass between the street and the sidewalk and got out. I waited beside my car with my hands visible on the roof.

He studied me for a moment from the shadows between the two vehicles.

I wore a guayabera and straw hat from San Cristobal. He couldn't see them from where he stood, but my pants and sandals came from the same store.

Ortiz wore a blue denim jacket that bulged on his left side. He made a phone call. He pocketed his phone and walked to the sidewalk on the other side of my car.

"You want something?" he said in accented English.

I spoke in my San Cristobal Spanish. "Yes. I want to meet your boss."

Ortiz switched to Spanish. "I have no boss."

"As you wish. Where can we talk?"

"What do we talk about?"

"I have product to sell. Quite a lot, and I can get more."

"What product?"

"Snow." I used San Cristobal slang for cocaine, *la nieve,* snow. Ironic since the nearest snow to San Cristobal was hundreds of miles away in the Mexican mountains.

"It doesn't snow in Florida."

I didn't say anything.

"I am a construction foreman; I'm not interested in cocaine."

"As you say. You have heard of San Cristobal?"

"A republic in the Caribbean."

"It snows in San Cristobal. The kind that never melts."

I waited for Ortiz to consider that.

Finally, he nodded.

"Do you know El Mirador on Sunrise Boulevard?"

"I have a GPS."

"Meet me there in fifteen minutes."

He walked toward his house. Kiss the wifey and the 2.3 kiddos before discussing business. Hard day at the office assaulting and battering.

I made it to El Mirador before Ortiz did. I picked a corner table and sat against the wall—an old habit from my days in the Special Forces. I ordered Cuban coffee and mango pastelitos.

Four more customers arrived, two to a car. All men, all wearing jackets that bulged on the left. They sat twenty feet away, two at a table in a triangle fronting me.

Ortiz arrived ten minutes later. He ignored everyone else in the restaurant and walked straight to my table. He sat to my right, giving the four other "customers" clear shots at me.

"Who are you?"

"Carlos is as good a name as any."

Neither of us offered to shake hands.

"You are from San Cristobal?"

"Sometimes."

"How do you know me?"

"I have connections in the Palm Beach County Sheriff's Office." I shoved the pastry platter toward him. "Enjoy; they're mango."

Ortiz picked one. "I'm listening."

"I ask the Garcia family to help develop my connections in Palm Beach County into a business."

"You in the construction business?"

I smiled and said nothing.

"And in return for me helping you establish a construction business...?"

"I will discuss it with your boss."

He started to speak and I lifted a hand.

"Don't tell me you have no boss, Salvador Ramon Ortiz Garcia; I know better. This deal involves millions of dollars and ten or more kilos of snow each month. With due respect, for that big a deal, I must meet the real boss. If not, forget the whole thing."

I nibbled a pastelito and chased it with Cuban coffee.

"Wait here."

Ortiz stepped to the table where the first two gunmen sat. He leaned toward one man. They spoke in low tones for a minute.

The other gunman approached me. Ortiz sat at the other table.

"I am Jose Jeronimo Garcia Garcia."

Garcia Garcia. Both his father and mother were Garcias. That didn't mean their relationship was incestuous. Franklin D. Roosevelt married his distant cousin, Eleanor Roosevelt. It did mean that Garcia's criminal genealogy was generations deep.

It is hard to translate the nuances of the Spanish word *el jefe.* It is often translated as *chief,* but it includes boss, leader, manager, and commander.

"Nice to meet you, chief." I called him *jefe* as a sign of respect.

Garcia didn't offer to shake hands either.

"What is your proposition?"

"I have contacts in the Palm Beach County Sheriff's Office, loyal men who protect me from the police. These men are high enough in the Sheriff's Office to deflect suspicion and to warn me every time the cops plan a raid."

I indicated the pastry platter.

"Would you care for a pastry, chief?"

Garcia bit off a chunk. "I own a construction business and do not need protection from the police."

I waited. He spoke for the benefit of any wire I was wearing to record our conversation.

"As a matter of curiosity, how did you acquire these men?"

"I have planned this move for three years, Don Jose. I may blackmail one. I might intimidate another. Some are simply greedy. Shall I say more?"

"I run a legitimate business and have no need for police protection, but you may say anything you wish. It's a free country."

"I can provide twenty to thirty kilos of snow a month. I need a distribution network. The Garcias have a reputation in these areas. I want to learn from the Garcias and have you consult to develop my network in Palm Beach. For this I will give you fifteen percent of the profits for five years."

I drank my Cuban coffee.

"Carlos, if you want tips on the construction business, we can continue this conversation in my office."

I dropped a few bills on the table. "After you, chief."

Garcia led me to the parking lot.

I stopped beside my car. "I'll follow you."

"No. You come with me in that van." He gestured to a shiny blue windowless Ford Transit parked nearby.

This was crunch time. Until now, I had controlled the situation. Garcia knew I was armed. Although out-numbered, I could walk away and he would let me. He didn't want a gunfight on the streets of Fort Lauderdale. If I got in that truck, my control evaporated faster than rainwater in the desert. He could wiggle a finger and I would never get out alive. My body would never be found.

"Sure thing, chief."

Ortiz opened the side cargo door. The inside appeared brand new. The black artificial leather seats were unmarked. The cheap rubber floor mats showed no wear. Parked in the Florida sun, the interior was over a hundred degrees. The fumes from the overheated upholstery reeked *new car smell* on steroids.

"Get in," Ortiz said.

"It's hot as a pizza oven in there. How about flipping on the air conditioning?"

Garcia gestured to another man who opened the driver's door and climbed inside. He cranked the engine and switched the AC to max.

Garcia rode shotgun and I climbed into the back.

Ortiz followed me and closed the cargo door with a *clunk*. "Raise your arms."

I complied without protest. He frisked me and removed my Glock. He missed the knife strapped to my left forearm, but I didn't expect to need it.

"Empty your pockets. Place everything on the seat."

I did.

"Unbutton your shirt."

I undid the shirt, and Ortiz checked my ribs and back for a wire.

"Sit over there."

I buttoned my shirt and tucked it in before I sat.

Ortiz slipped a black cloth bag over my head. "Sorry about this, Carlos. Security."

"No problem, Salvador. If our positions were reversed, I would do the same."

The truck began to roll.

I kept track of turns the best I could. We travelled west, which positioned us near the Everglades. Maybe twenty minutes later the truck stopped. The transmission clunked into park. The engine killed. The cargo door rumbled open and snapped to a stop.

"Mind your head getting out."

Hands gripped my arms to guide me from the truck. Stepping down, I felt a soft surface beneath my feet. No, not soft. It was firm on part of my shoe sole and springy on part. They were honeycomb grass pavers—concrete grids with holes to let grass grow. I heard the roaring sizzle of distant traffic. If this was where we'd tailed Ortiz earlier, it was the Sawgrass Expressway.

We walked eighteen paces and stopped. Footsteps climbed to a porch.

"Four steps, Carlos. A handrail on your left."

A key chittered its way into the keyhole. A deadbolt lock opened with a metallic *snick.* Sounded like a steel door.

"One step, Carlos."

I stepped. A deadbolt *thunked* into place behind me, but I didn't hear a key. That meant it had a twist knob to lock and unlock it from the inside. Good to know if I needed to make a fast escape.

Someone unlocked another deadbolt ahead. This door sounded wooden, an interior door for a house or office.

I stepped into a carpeted room. The door closed behind me. No one locked it.

Ortiz removed the cloth bag from my head.

Garcia waved to a table and chairs. "Make yourself comfortable, Carlos. Something to drink?"

"Coffee if you have it."

Garcia waved at one of his henchmen. "Coffee. Make enough for the men."

He squared up to me. "What is your proposal?"

"As I said at El Mirador, I have sources for up to thirty kilos of cocaine a month. I need distributors. You can advise me how to develop a network. For this I will give you a commission of fifteen percent of the profits for five years."

"You are talking about a partnership. That means fifty percent forever."

"That can't work, chief. My other partners won't agree. Instead, I can offer you a sweetener. Fifteen percent for five years, and I get you access to another ten kilos of cocaine at the market price each month. You can sell it here in Broward County, assuming we are still in Broward County."

"What other partners?"

I spread my hands. "Just as Ortiz was my go-between for you, I am a go-between for other people. These people have money and political connections."

Garcia glanced up when the coffee arrived, his expression as unreadable as stone.

"You say you have access to large amounts of cocaine. You claim you have political connections and money. Why have I never heard of you?"

I gave him the same story I gave Francisco de Pilon about diversifying my investments.

Garcia tossed my passport to me. "Your passport is Mexican, but you speak with a San Cristobal accent."

"You recognize my accent because it is similar to your supplier Tony Crucero, yes?"

Garcia's eyebrows rose a millimeter.

"Who is Tony Crucero?"

"Please, chief, let's not play games. I know the pig. His full name is Antonio Ricardo Crucero *Calderone*."

This time Garcia made no attempt to hide his surprise.

"You didn't know that, Don Jose?"

"It never came up. You are related?"

"My father is from San Cristobal," I said. "I spend a lot of time there. Tony is a cousin."

"But you called him a pig."

"Calling Tony a pig is a compliment to Tony and an insult to pigs."

"You had a bad experience with him?"

"More than one. The man has no honor. It would be typical for him to cheat you."

"Cheat me how?"

"I don't know what method he would use. I know his character, or lack of it. Regarding my family, often he denies he knows us; other times he lies about us. He is scum, or else he's crazy. Maybe both."

I waved a hand. "That's not relevant to this discussion. I can offer fifteen percent of the profits for five years and another ten kilos at the market price each month. Do we have a deal?"

"Twenty-five percent for ten years and the extra ten keys of coke per month."

"Deal."

This time we shook hands.

Garcia called Ortiz to the table. He gave me a burner phone programmed to call another burner that he handed Ortiz. "Salvador Ortiz is your contact with us. You shall communicate with these phones. How soon can you provide a sample?"

"Day after tomorrow."

We made arrangements to meet.

Garcia shook my hand again. "I regret we must continue our security procedures until we gain experience with you. You understand, Don Carlos."

"Of course, Don Jose."

I glanced at my watch before Ortiz slipped the black bag over my head. Thirty minutes later, I was back at my rental car.

Now I had to hope the cocaine that Diego Calvo had cut was still usable. If not, all the risks I had taken were worthless.

NINETEEN

I rapped on Wilma Leonard's office doorjamb.

"Come in, Chuck. Sit down. Ziggy Townsend is on his way over. He's the expert on cutting drugs. Let me have it."

I placed my briefcase on her desk and popped the latch. "There's a kilo, but it's been opened. My courier from Mexico stole half and cut the rest. I need to learn what he cut it with." I shoved the plastic-wrapped package across the desk.

"Ziggy will analyze it. Here he comes." She stood. "Doctor Sigmund Townsend, meet Chuck McCrary. He's our undercover man."

Ziggy was middle-aged, balding, and wore a white lab coat over blue jeans and sneakers. With his rimless glasses, he could play an eccentric medical school professor on a television series.

We shook hands.

"Wilma tells me you have a line into the Garcias."

"Yeah. I offered to sell them ten kilos a month. They want a sample."

Ziggy hefted the package. "It's about one kilo."

"My Mexican courier admitted he stole half and cut the remainder. It was pure when I gave it to him. I need to know whether the stuff is poisonous. I promised the Garcias quality drugs."

"From what I hear, they are bad people to cross. They stuff their victim's balls in his mouth after they kill him."

"I heard the same thing, and I'm fond of my balls. I need you to tell me what condition my cocaine is in, before I give a sample to the Garcias."

Ziggy pulled a paper evidence bag from his lab coat and unfolded it. He inserted the package and crimped the top. "I'll analyze this and report to Wilma. You and she decide what to do."

"Sure thing, Ziggy. Thanks."

Wilma waved me into a chair. "I have your cocaine." She laid the repackaged dope on her desk.

"Three hours is fast turnaround."

"This case is hot. Everybody wants to nail the Garcias."

She handed me a sheet of paper. "Ziggy says the cocaine was cut fifty percent with benzocaine with chemical markers from Mexico."

"Benzocaine?"

"You don't know squat about the drug business, do you, kid?"

"I didn't work drug cases when I was a detective. Those were worked by more experienced detectives. And my PI cases have never involved drugs before. Why do you ask?"

"Most cocaine from Latin America is cut with benzocaine or other crap even more harmful before it gets to the U.S. This batch is no worse than the other crap the Garcias are used to. Even after your courier cut it, 50 percent is good purity for cocaine, and benzocaine is a common thing to cut with."

She shoved the drug package across her desk.

"The Garcias will be happy with this sample. Your balls will be safe. Don't accept less than fifty thousand dollars for it."

"I don't intend to sell it. It's for bait. I'll let them test a sample, then I'll call the cops before delivery. I'll give this back to Ziggy to destroy."

Salvador Ortiz answered the burner phone on the fourth ring, *"Hola."*

"I have the snow."

"You recall the restaurant where we first met?"

"Yes."

"Bring it there tomorrow at 3:30."

"I'll be there."

Tank drove a rental car and parked four rows back in El Mirador's parking lot. I asked him to video every vehicle license plate in the lot before he parked. If I got killed, at least he would have clues for the Fort Lauderdale police.

I spotted him from the corner of my eye before I walked inside.

Ortiz sat at the table we used three days before, a pastelito platter before him. His back was to the wall.

I sat beside him, back against the sidewall and picked up a pastelito. "Thanks, Salvador. These look delicious."

"I don't see a briefcase."

"I didn't bring it." I took a bite.

"Why not?"

"We need to work out the details first."

"What details?"

I licked my fingers and wiped them on a napkin. "The first detail is the quantity and the quality of the product. The sample is a full kilo. It is 50 percent pure, cut with Mexican benzocaine. I presume that quality is at least as high as the product you normally get."

"Of course, we'll test it, but if it's good as you say, that's acceptable quality. What other details?"

"Is that Cafe Cubano for me?"

Ortiz waved a yes.

"The next detail is the price: sixty thousand dollars." I tasted the Cuban coffee.

"I can go to forty thousand—once we test it. We need a quality guarantee."

205

"I'll bring you the package, and you take a sample to test. You test it, then we'll talk again about price."

Ortiz opened an old-fashioned flip phone and punched a number. *"Hola.* He didn't bring it. He says it's one kilo, 50 percent with 50 percent benzocaine. He wants sixty. I offered forty. He offered to let us test a sample."

Ortiz listened. He regarded me. "How do we get the sample?"

"In the employee parking lot of the Paradise Suites Hotel on Palm Beach."

Ortiz relayed my words, listened, then said, "We can come up to forty-five. That's a good price."

I shook my head. "This is first quality product, purer than you usually get. Sixty is a good price. But don't worry, my friend. Test the sample. We'll talk price after that. Tomorrow at 3:30 p.m. in the employee lot at the Paradise Suites. I'll drive the same car I used today."

It was off-season. The multi-story parking garage at the Paradise Suites was half full, or half empty if you're a pessimist. The employee lot butted up against it and covered ten acres. Someday, the resort would develop the land. For now, it was employee parking. The five rows nearest the hotel were full. The half-dozen rows by the street were empty.

I parked my rental in an empty row and waited. My phone chirped with a text from Tank:

In position. Have you in my sights.

I had bought a Rock River Arms Varmint rifle, 5.56 mm with a suppressor. A nice weapon, semi-automatic, with a thirty-shot magazine, accurate to 400 yards. Tank practiced with it at a 200-yard shooting range near the Everglades. I hoped I wouldn't need backup, but I breathed easier knowing Tank was there. He wanted to be a part of the case and being a sniper was something he was qualified for.

At 3:35 the blue Ford Transit parked in front of me. A sedan stopped behind me, blocking me in.

My stomach churned out an extra squirt of acid, and adrenaline rushed into my blood. I reminded myself not to panic; maybe that was the way they did drug deals.

In the rearview mirror, I observed Ortiz exit the sedan with a small briefcase. He approached the passenger door of my rental car. I popped the lock and he got in.

"You brought the product?"

"Yes."

"Let's see it."

I pulled the cocaine from under the seat and handed it to him. "This product is as advertised. Analyze the last shipment from my cousin. Do not trust him. He will cheat you."

"I will pass your advice on to Don Jose." Ortiz made a short cut in the wrapping, scooped a sample on his knife blade, and dumped it in a baggie. He sealed the slit with tape and cut another at the opposite end of the package. He took another a sample and dumped it in a second baggie. He taped the cut and handed me the package. It now had his fingerprints on it in addition to mine.

He opened the car door. "Why did you pick this lot for the sample exchange?"

"You know I have men in Palm Beach County, right?"

"So?"

I gestured at the garage sixty yards away. "That would be a good position to station two off-duty Palm Beach County deputies and one off-duty City of West Palm Beach officer with sniper rifles, no?"

Ortiz's eyes narrowed. "Three sniper rifles pointed at me the whole time?"

I grinned. "You're not the only one with extra security, my friend. Sixty thousand dollars' worth of cocaine is a tempting target. Our relationship is new and untested, and I am cautious. I'll contact you in a few days. We'll arrange the price and delivery of the package and begin setting up my network."

Pete Martinez and Snoop arrived at my office five minutes behind Tank. We crowded around my coffee table in the conference room.

"Pete, what did you learn?"

"Salvador Ortiz and his driver drove to the same building off Hiatus Road that I followed him to a couple days ago. Once he turned into the lot, I went straight so they wouldn't make me. When I tailed him before, I didn't get photos of the building. This time I got video. Here are my videos and notes." Pete handed me a stick drive.

"Did you get pictures of the driver?"

"Sorry. I had rolled past the lot before he exited the car."

"Couldn't be helped. Good job on the tail though."

I swiveled to Snoop. "What do you have?"

"The blue Ford Transit went to the same address. Once the Transit entered the parking area, I spotted Pete's car ahead. My videos will show the same stuff he got, but here they are." He handed me a stick drive also.

"Anything on the men in the Transit?"

"Nah. Tinted windows. Couldn't see or photograph anything. Don't know how many were in there."

"That building is where the Garcia gang held me. I'll send this information to Wilma Leonard. She'll know best how to use it."

"You have further plans for the Garcias?"

"The Garcias are not my primary target. They are a means to destroy Tony Crucero. I intend to plant suspicion there—get them to whack Crucero for me. So far, I've struck out on that, but I'm working a Plan B for Crucero."

Lucifer

Losefa Topati hiked the sixth floor of the Bayfront Parking Garage. He found an unobstructed view into the second-floor conference room over the Royal Palms that lined the median and both sides of Bayfront Boulevard. He had cased the fourth and fifth floors when he first used the garage, but the crowns of the palms were too thick. The sixth floor was perfect. The late afternoon sun sank behind the building leaving the window in shadow. He observed the four men inside through his telephoto lens.

208

My god, that's Tank Tyler, Hall of Fame defensive end for the Port City Pelicans. Topati loved football. He recalled his own abbreviated career in the Broncos' training camp. He snapped several photos. *Tank Tyler. Who would have thought McCrary would know the great Tank Tyler?*

He couldn't make out the other two men's faces. The one with his back to the window had dark brown hair, cut short, and wore a beige jacket. The other one had gray hair, also cut short, and a pink-and-brown-striped golf shirt.

The young man and the middle-aged one stood. They shook hands with Tank Tyler and McCrary and left the room. Topati photographed the young man's face.

Topati swung the telephoto lens to the building's front door, obscured by palms. The door opened but he couldn't see who exited. A woman walked into view and descended the steps to the parking lot. A minute later, the door opened again. Good, it was the men from the conference room.

Topati videoed the two men shaking hands. He could see the gray-haired man's face. The younger man was in profile. The gray-haired man got into a Toyota whose license plate was hidden by palm fronds. Topati videoed the older man backing from the parking spot. After the license plate entered the viewfinder, he swung the camera to the younger man. Damn, he missed videoing the young man's car when it departed the lot. The frustration made his temples throb again. He slapped the concrete rail.

The young man's car accelerated north on Bayshore Drive. Topati tracked it, videoing until the license came into view. He smiled to himself.

He hoped he didn't need to kill Tank Tyler. Tank was his idol.

Antonio Crucero

"Come in, Luce." Crucero ushered Lucifer into his dining room and indicated a serving tray. "Would you care for a pastelito?" The pig was always hungry.

"Yeah, thanks." Lucifer selected two pastelitos and bit half of the first one in a single mouthful.

Crucero never got used to how freaking big Lucifer was. He must eat like three normal people to maintain his huge body, but that size allowed him to beat up McCrary when they fought. According to Lucifer, he would have killed McCrary if the cops hadn't arrived.

McCrary had humiliated him in front of one of his own whores. A whore, for God's sake. For that, there could be no clemency, no live-and-let-live. Crucero wanted one thing more than money, more than drugs, and more than women: He wanted Carlos McCrary dead.

Lucifer wiped his mouth with a napkin and spread several photos across the table. "Here's the license plate of the gray-haired man's Toyota. That's his picture there, shaking hands with this younger guy. Here's the young guy's license plate. Ask your contact in the police department to look up both owners."

"He's a private detective, not a cop." Crucero studied a picture. "I know him from somewhere." He stared at the wall and raked his mind for the memory.

"Nah. Don't worry; it'll come to me. Go on."

"Here's a blow-up of the men in the conference room. You can see McCrary and Tank Tyler's faces, but the two others kept their backs to the window."

"McCrary and who? Who's the black man?"

"That's Tank Tyler."

The fat idiot said that as if Crucero should know who the black man was. "Who's Tank Tyler?"

"You never heard of Tank Tyler?"

Did the freaky giant not hear the question? "Don't play games with me, Lucifer. Who is the black man?"

"He's the best defensive end to ever play the game, that's who. The guy is in the NFL Hall of Fame. He played on the Bigs Brigade defensive line for the Port City Pelicans with Bigs Bigelow, also a great player. You honestly don't know who Tank Tyler is?"

"I have heard of the Pelicans, but I don't follow American football."

"Tyler is rich, famous, and well-connected. I researched McCrary on the internet. Tank Tyler ain't his only friend what's connected. If we kill him, important people are gonna squeeze the cops until they find the killers."

Maybe Lucifer was not as stupid as Crucero thought. "So, don't get caught." Once Lucifer killed McCrary, Crucero would have Al put a bullet in his tiny little brain so no loose ends would lead back to him.

"Did you get a gun from Al?"

"Yeah." Lucifer yanked a Smith & Wesson Model 637 revolver from his coat pocket. The hammer snagged on his pocket lining and jerked it inside out. He struggled to free the pistol.

Crucero leaned across the table and forced Lucifer's arm down. "For crissakes, be careful where you point that goddamn thing."

Lucifer freed the weapon and clunked it on the table with the barrel pointed at Crucero. "Sorry, Tony. I'll be more careful."

What was the idiot thinking? Crucero rotated the revolver to point away. "Never point a weapon at anyone you don't intend to kill, Lucifer."

"I'm sorry, Tony. It won't happen again. Uh, Tony?"

"Yeah?"

"Al should kill McCrary. He has experience at that kinda thing."

"Al delivers product to our customers."

"Let me make those deliveries."

"Un-huh. Too risky. Al knows the customers and they know him. People don't want change, especially people who are afraid of undercover cops. It's gotta be you who kills McCrary."

Crucero snapped his fingers. "I know where I saw the old guy. He was standing next to McCrary's minivan when the cops arrested me. The bastard works for McCrary."

"This McCrary, he ain't no lone wolf, boss. I don't know whether I can do this alone."

"Then we'll let someone else kill him."

TWENTY

Tomaz Kopitar

Tomaz Kopitar glared across Tony Crucero's dining room table with ill-concealed loathing. Even after the uncouth crossbreed summoned him from Coconut Grove to Port City Beach, the barbarian did not offer him refreshment. "You say on phone you have information on cousin."

"Turns out he's not my cousin. His family has lived in Mexico for generations; mine in San Cristobal. His mother and my mother are both named Calderone, but that's coincidence. We are not related."

The fool had no sense of priorities. What else could one expect from a crossbreed? "As Americans say, BFD. Do you have *useful* information?"

"McCrary's office address is 3000 Bayshore Boulevard, Suite 250."

"That's on internet. What else?"

"He has an employee named Raymond Snopolski. Here's his picture." He laid two photos on the table. "This is his Toyota. I Googled him. Snopolski is a retired Port City police detective and a champion pistol shot. He was McCrary's partner when they were detectives. Here's the address on his automobile registration." He handed over a piece of paper. "It's his home. You might send men to learn whether he has a family. There might be leverage there."

Kopitar stuffed the photos and the paper in his pocket. Snopolski was an expert with a pistol. Niko was an expert with a sniper rifle. Kopitar would choose the rifle over the pistol in a firefight.

Kopitar preferred to capture McCrary or Snopolski and question him about Alena's three missing men before killing him. If that were not possible, he would lure one or both men somewhere in range of Niko and his sniper rifle.

"What else you have?"

Crucero lined up more photos in a row. "This is Tank Tyler, a rich American football player, or former player. His hobby is target shooting."

"Why is this important?" Kopitar asked. "Is he detective also? If he is rich, he do not work for McCrary."

"I don't know the nature of their relationship, but the two men are often together. McCrary has many powerful friends. If he is killed, they will pressure the police to find the killers. Keep that in mind."

"I will. What are other photos?"

"This one is Pedro Martinez, a Miami private detective who works with McCrary, a former Miami-Dade Deputy Sheriff." Crucero tapped another photo. "His car is registered at his office address in Miami. This is the address." He pushed a paper across the table.

"Where does McCrary live?"

"My man hasn't determined that yet."

"All you have new is names of three associates of McCrary?" Kopitar asked.

"Yeah, I guess so."

"You following McCrary?"

Crucero nodded. "Yes. I have a man following him. He searches for a chance to kill him, but the time and place have not, uh, presented themselves."

"You stop following now. I will send my people."

Kopitar had spent the week training his people and learning the changes in conditions while he had been in Europe. Now he was ready to hunt for McCrary, the crossbreed. He wished he could kill Crucero too.

Kopitar handed out photo sets. "Pass them around," he said in Serbian to the eight Blue-Eyed Devils crammed into his living room.

"The top three photos are Carlos McCrary. We think he killed Hugo, Bojan, and Edvard. He is very dangerous. The next two are pictures of texts that Alena received from Bojan's and Edvard's phones after the three men chased McCrary. Do you notice anything unusual about the texts?"

Viktor Kokot waved one of the prints. "The text from Bojan doesn't sound like him."

"How so?"

"He says: *Crucero send the man in Dodge Caravan. He not bother us again.* He used the present tense 'send' instead of the past tense 'sent.' Also, the word he used for 'bother' means 'to be difficult.' I knew Bojan for three years and never heard him use that word. He would pick the word that means 'trouble.' He often says that."

"You're right," said Kopitar, "but the context of both messages makes me suspect that McCrary sent them after he killed Bojan and Edvard. He used an English-to-Serbian translation app on his smartphone."

Kopitar gazed at the other men. "McCrary is smart. He won't be easy to capture. He has killed three of our best men. Look at the next two pictures."

Pavel Struna cleared his throat.

"Yes, Pavel," said Kopitar.

"Why capture McCrary? That could get more men killed. Let's kill him from a distance. Niko is a good sniper. I visited McCrary's office yesterday afternoon like you told me. The Bayshore Parking Garage is across the street. Niko could shoot McCrary through his office window or his conference room window or when he crosses the lot."

"Yes, but that wouldn't send a message. We have a reputation: Cross the Cernan gang, and there will be hell to pay. We must capture McCrary and question him about our missing men. Also, our missing Suburban. Afterwards we give him a barbed-wire necktie and drop his body in a public place. Everyone who does business with us should get our message loud and clear: Don't cross the Cernan gang."

Pavel Struna

Pavel Struna circled Chuck McCrary's building. Where was the white Grand Caravan? Was McCrary in his office?

He parked near the street and made a call.

"McCrary Investigations, this is Betty speaking."

"This is Victor Wilensky. Is Mr. McCrary in please?"

"Certainly, sir. I'll put you through."

Struna disconnected. Had McCrary driven a different vehicle? That would make it difficult to track him, but his men would cope.

He stationed one man a block south on Bayshore Boulevard and another a block north. When McCrary drove away, whichever direction he chose, one man would pick up his tail.

Struna drove to the Bayshore Parking Garage and spiraled up to the sixth floor in his Kia Sorrento.

He counted windows to locate McCrary's office. Peering through the telephoto lens, he recognized his quarry's outline through the blinds. He texted his men:

Objective is in office.

He waited. Whenever a car passed in the garage, he ducked down until they were gone, then watched McCrary again.

An hour later, McCrary passed through his conference room and switched off the lights. Good, he was leaving. Pavel shifted his camera lens to the entrance to the building. It wouldn't be long.

McCrary walked to a silver sports car. Struna zoomed the lens and focused on the trunk lid. *Studebaker.* He snapped a picture. He texted Drago Tajnic and Rudolf Novak:

Objective is in silver Studebaker sports car.

He returned to his Kia and began the long spiral descent to Bayshore Boulevard.

His cellphone rang once, and the Kia's Bluetooth picked it up. He punched the *accept* button. "Yes, Drago."

"Objective is travelling south."

"Got it. I'll call you once I catch up."

Struna drummed his fingers on the steering wheel while he waited for two cars to pay the cashier. He clenched his jaw. Was the cashier a complete moron? What was taking so long?

He turned south on Bayshore with a squeal of tires. He eased off the accelerator. It wouldn't do to call attention to himself. His phone rang again. "Yes, Drago. A bungling cashier delayed me."

"He took the Beachline Causeway."

"Okay. Watch for me when I pass, then drop back and let Rudolf replace you."

Struna caught Drago Tajnic's green Suburban stopped at the traffic light for Azalea Island Drive. He eased behind Drago. The light changed. Drago went left to Azalea Island and Struna picked up the tail.

Two minutes later, he called Rudolf Novak. "Objective is travelling west on Lenox Avenue. Hurry."

Rudolf caught Struna at 10th Street. Struna turned on 11th and Rudolf continued on Lenox.

"I'm 75 meters behind him, Pavel. He took 13th Terrace. It's a dead-end street lined with condos. He turned into the Waverunner Condos. The garage gate is raising. McCrary must have a remote in his car. I'll park at the Promenade Condos across the street."

Struna smiled. "Keep the phone line open while I catch up to you." Tomaz Kopitar would be happy. McCrary either lived in the Waverunner, or he was chummy with someone who did.

He turned at 13th Terrace. He studied the Waverunner building as he approached. He bounced into the Promenade guest lot and parked beside Rudolf.

Rudolf opened his door.

"No, Rudolf," Struna said into the phone. "Stay in the car. We'll talk by phone." He photographed the building and parking garage. "This visitor's lot is good for surveillance. Stay until six o'clock. Drago will relieve you then."

Tomaz Kopitar

Kopitar chewed his sandwich and studied the picture on his monitor. "The security is too good to capture McCrary at the Waverunner. There are cameras here." He clicked to the next picture. "And here... and here." He continued to click through the photos. "The parking entrance is too hard. That gate is steel like a warehouse door. No way to get past without noise and wasted time."

He turned to Pavel Struna. "Your team did well to uncover this place. Keep Drago on stakeout until eleven o'clock. If McCrary hasn't gone by then, we'll assume he's in for the night and you come back at six-thirty tomorrow morning."

Kopitar leaned back in his chair. "We must take him at a less secure location. Does he have a girlfriend?"

***

Kopitar paused the television and walked to the door. He would finish the Eleven O'clock News once Drago left.

Kopitar opened the apartment door and scanned the walkway behind Drago Tajnic. Empty. "Come in."

"Sorry to bother you this late, boss, but you said to call day or night when we located McCrary's girlfriend."

"Sit down and tell me what you learned."

Drago tugged a small spiral notebook from his pocket. "McCrary's girlfriend is Miyoki Takashi, age 26. She's an artist. Sells paintings at expensive art galleries in New York City and Chicago. Second-generation American citizen."

Kopitar waved him to stop. "I don't need to know everything on the internet. Where does she live?"

"Three miles from McCrary. She owns a penthouse in the Mariner Sands condos. Pavel and Rudolf followed McCrary's Studebaker to her visitor parking lot late this afternoon. The security is sloppy and Pavel rode the elevator with McCrary and several other people. Someone pressed the top button which is the 16th floor. Pavel got off on 14 with the last person other than McCrary. McCrary was still on the elevator. There are two apartments on 16 and one belongs to a couple whose mailing address is in Costa Rica. The other is Miyoki Takashi. We downloaded pictures of McCrary with her from her Facebook page."

"Is McCrary spending the night there?"

Drago smiled without humor. "He just left; she's alone."

TWENTY-ONE

Miyoki Takashi

Miyo rolled over in her sleep and tucked the sheet under her chin. Chuck's scent lingered on her pillow and she smiled in her sleep. Her breathing became even once again as she snuggled into the soft warmth.

A sound from the hallway infiltrated her subconscious. She stirred. The sound recurred. She rolled over and nuzzled her pillow.

The click of her bedroom door opening woke her. Did Chuck forget something? Maybe he had come back for his cellphone or wallet and didn't want to wake her.

"Chuck? Is that you?"

A rough hand seized her shoulder and flipped her onto her back. Another hand seized her chin and twisted her head. She struggled to sit up but someone sat on her legs. Another hand clamped a damp cloth over her nose and mouth.

She drew a deep breath to scream and smelled a sharp chemical odor. Her head swam and the scream died in her throat.

Miyo woke with her wrists and ankles bound, a piece of duct tape tight across her mouth, the truth slowly dawning—she had been kidnapped, but why? For ransom? Or was she going to be raped and murdered, then her body dumped in the Everglades?

She fought to break her restraints when the vehicle stopped and started and turned, flinging her body with every movement. She must be in the trunk but why was there not a sliver of light anywhere? Total darkness engulfed her. She thrashed about wriggling and kicking and, as her mind cleared, she realized she was in a wooden box inside the trunk of a vehicle that was hauling her God knows where. A shiver of terror ran down her spine. *Where is Chuck?*

Seconds later, the vehicle stopped and she heard two doors slam, then the tailgate of an SUV open. She felt the box being swung. Men's voices spoke a harsh language she couldn't understand. Then she skidded towards the end of the box when it began an ascent—metal stairs from the clanging sound of the men's footsteps. Was this the Serb drug gang Chuck had told her about? Why would they want her?

They stopped at the top of the steps, clunked the box down, and dragged it across a hard floor. She heard the sound of a key in a lock and the lid of the box swung open. The men staring down at her had not bothered to mask their faces. Her chest tightened. *They are not afraid of me identifying them because they intend to kill me.*

Her kidnapping wasn't for ransom; it was payback about Chuck.

Carlos McCrary

Miyo's picture flashed on my phone. *Multimedia message from Miyo* displayed below.

I hoped it wasn't another striptease video. After she sent a second one, I asked her not to do that anymore. In person was great, but not in a video. "You never know when someone will hack your computer or your phone and post embarrassing stuff on the internet."

When I clicked on the link, my heart leapt into my throat.

An R-rated video getting on the internet was the least of Miyo's worries.

Miyo sat in a plain wooden chair, her ankles duct-taped to the front legs and her arms behind her, so they were taped also. Other duct tape bands passed across her ribcage and her thighs. One strip covered her mouth. The screen showed her whole body and part of an unremarkable wall behind. The tee-shirt and old silk shorts were the ones she wore for pajamas. Other details in the photo were not clear on my phone screen, but her hair was a mess and she wore no makeup. She had been taken from her bed after she'd removed her makeup. The camera zoomed to her face; her cheeks were tear-streaked and her eyes were so wide the whites flared around them. She blinked rapidly, her nostrils flaring. She labored to breathe through her nose.

The video ended.

My phone signaled a text from Miyo's phone.

We have woman. $500,000 ransom. Do not contact police. Get money and wait for more instruction.

I forwarded the video and text to my other cellphone for backup.

While I headed to my bedroom closet to open the gun safe, I called Jorge and switched my phone to speaker.

"Chuck, *amigo, ¿Que pasa?*"

"Someone kidnapped Miyo. They texted me a video of her from her phone. Can you ping it to learn where they sent the message from?"

I dialed the combination, opened the steel door.

"I'm on vacation at the beach," Jorge said, "so I can't ping anybody. Call Kelly Contreras; she'll do it. I'll head for home right now and gear up. What do they want? Ransom?"

"The text says $500,000, but I suspect the ransom demand is cover for what they really want."

"What do they want?"

"They'll take the half million if I'm stupid enough to bring it, but what they want is me."

"Who are they?" Jorge asked.

"I'll have a better idea once Kelly pings Miyo's phone. I'll send you both texts for backup."

"Once I collect my gear, you want me to come to your office or condo?"

While Jorge talked, I strapped an ankle holster to my right leg and inserted my Browning .380 in it. That was my if-all-else-fails gun. I had neglected to carry it to the Everglades when I tailed Alena Cernan and that omission nearly got me killed.

I replaced the Glock 17 which I keep in a shoulder holster with the Glock I liberated from Edvard Oblak. Lifting down a footlocker from the closet shelf, I dumped Bojan Matic's Glock, the Serbs' three Kalashnikovs, and spare ammo for all weapons into it.

Tank and I had both practiced with the dead Serbs' Kalashnikovs and Glocks. I would never trust a weapon I had not inspected, cleaned, and test fired.

"Jorge, you can't be in on this. They said no cops. I'll call Kelly once I hang up."

"*Amigo,* in this case, I'm not a cop; I'm a friend. I'm in."

Closing the gun safe, I spun the dial. The footlocker strained my wounded forearm, but it was practically healed. I could haul the locker as far as my van.

"I know who these people are. I won't involve the police or the FBI, because they will never to go to trial. You understand what I mean?"

"You're not taking prisoners."

"Right. You shouldn't be involved."

"*Amigo*, I owe you my life. Deal me in."

I hesitated.

"If our positions were reversed, what would you do, eh? You'd be here in a heartbeat."

I couldn't argue with his logic. "Okay. Head home and gear up. I'll make a conference call in a half hour, once I talk to Miyo's parents."

"Got it," said Jorge.

Kelly Contreras was a Port City police detective I had worked with once on a case with Tank. She and Tank hit it off, and they had dated ever since.

I called her. "Kelly, this is Chuck. Miyo has been kidnapped. Jorge is at the beach and can't ping her phone. He suggested I call you. If I give you her number, can you ping it for the last fourteen hours?"

"I'm off this weekend. I'm in the Bahamas with Tank, but we'll catch the next plane back. Call Bigs."

A tight band gripped my chest. Tank would've been my next call, and he was out of reach too. Sure, I had Snoop and Jorge and others, but Tank was in a league of his own. He understood the dark universe I was in. Now I needed him, but he was on a beach a hundred miles away.

In the background, Kelly said, "It's Chuck. Miyo was kidnapped."

"Give me the phone... This is Tank. What happened?"

I drew a deep breath and struggled to control my voice. "Tank, bad guys have kidnapped Miyo. I was going to forward you a video and text that they sent me, but you're in the Bahamas. How soon can you come home?"

"I'll charter a seaplane and Kelly and I will fly straight to my dock. The pilot can clear it with customs. Hell, we could land at your marina if you want. We can be there in maybe two hours, three tops."

The tightness in my chest eased. I breathed again.

"Tank, there aren't any words... I'll arrange a conference call with you and Snoop and Jorge in thirty minutes. You'll need that long to check out of your hotel."

I called Bigs Bigelow next, Kelly's partner on the PCPD and a good friend of Tank's. "Bigs, I need a favor." I brought him up to date.

"Give me her number."

I did.

"I'll ping her phone and get back to you. Where shall I meet you?"

"Call or text me," I answered. "No need to meet."

"I want in on this. Kelly will too."

"Sorry, Bigs. If these guys are who I think, I'm not going to take them prisoner. No arrest, no trial, no prison. You and Kelly are cops; you can't be involved. Ping Miyo's phone and tell me everywhere it's been since eleven o'clock last night."

I thanked Bigs and called Snoop. "Miyo has been kidnapped. I'll forward you a video and text the bastards sent me from her phone. I'll conference call in twenty-five minutes if you want to back me up. It's okay for you pass on this. I'm diving into the cesspool you warned me about. Janet will be pissed if you get shit on yourself."

"Janet doesn't need to know everything, bud. I'll tell her you have a client emergency, which is true. That way I don't need to tell her what the emergency is. Want me to come to your office or home?"

"Not yet. Get your vest and armaments and head to your car and drive away. You won't want Janet or the girls to hear our conference call."

My phone rang. It was Bigs.

"Miyo's phone was at her condo when it was switched off at 3:30 a.m."

"I left her a little after eleven. They must've snatched her at 3:30. They used it to make the video and send the text. Where and when was that?"

"The phone came back online at 5:15 a.m. for seven minutes at a Miami address." He gave me the address.

"That's Alena Cernan's house in Coconut Grove. Is the phone still there?"

"I'm not finished. Like I said, it pinged for seven minutes, then went dark again. It came back on the network at 1:02 p.m. That must be when they sent you the ransom messages. It's still there at 22641 SW 326th Street in Homestead. That address mean anything to you?"

"Yeah. That's Jose's Auto Salvage. Last month the Cernan gang set up shop there to sell drugs. They must be tight with the owners."

"Or they are the owners."

"Could be. You say they left the phone on the network?"

"Yeah."

"They want me to know where they are."

Miyo's father was chairman of Takashi Holdings, an international conglomerate of marine construction companies, shipyards in three Asian countries, and dozens of container ships that transported freight all over the world. Daddy could afford the ransom, but I hoped it wouldn't come to that.

How the hell do I break the news to a father that his child has been kidnapped? And that it's my fault? This was a job for the FBI, or a minister, or a shrink—not an insensitive knuckle dragger like me. None of my training in Special Forces or the Port City Police covered this.

"Mr. Takashi, this is Carlos McCrary. I'm a friend of Miyo's."

"I know who you are, Mr. McCrary. Miyo told her mother and me about you when she visited us over July 4th weekend, and she mentions you whenever she calls. Is something wrong?"

"Something is terribly wrong, sir." I would give him a portion of the horrible truth.

"Is Miyo all right?"

"No, sir, she is not." *Break it to him gently.*

"Well, what is it?" His voice grew louder. "For God's sake, tell me what has happened."

"Miyo's been kidnapped, sir."

A woman's voice in the background said, "Why are you shouting? What is it?"

"It's Carlos McCrary. Something has happened to Miyo. Mr. McCrary, I'm going to switch the phone to speaker. Miyo's mother, Azami, is with me."

"Mr. McCrary, this is Azami Takashi. What has happened to Miyo?"

"She has been kidnapped, ma'am."

"Tell us what you know."

I wasn't about to tell them what I knew, at least not all of it. "I received a text message a few minutes ago with a video of Miyo attached. She was tied up in a chair, but otherwise appeared to be all right."

"Was there a ransom demand?"

"Yes, sir. $500,000."

"Why so little? That is suspicious."

"Yes, sir, I thought so too. I don't believe you and Mrs. Takashi are the targets. It's possible they don't even know who you are or who Miyo is, other than that she's my girlfriend. I believe the kidnappers are using Miyo to get to me."

"Can you send me the text? I'd like to see it."

"Sir, it would do no good for you and Mrs. Takashi to watch it. It is very upsetting. I am a former Port City police detective and I have numerous connections in the local police department. We are already working to get her back."

"I assumed that, Mr. McCrary. Once Miyo told us she loved you, we Googled you. We know more about you than you might think."

Why did I get the feeling that he didn't approve? *No time to think about that now.*

"The kidnappers said not to involve the police, so I am handling the kidnapping personally and involving the police unofficially. All this happened in the last half hour, so it's too early to have any more information. Give me your cell phone number and your wife's, and I will keep you up to date as things develop."

"We'll use the corporate jet and Azami and I will be in Port City before the day is out. I have your number here on my caller ID. I'll call you once we land."

I ended the conference call. Tank and Kelly would fly directly to Tank's mansion on Pink Coral Island. Snoop, Jorge, and I would meet them there. Best case, the five of us would assemble by four p.m.

Emotionally drained, I collapsed in a recliner. In the silence, I ruminated about Miyo and how terrified she must be. All because of me. The kidnappers hadn't identified themselves, but it had to relate to Alena Cernan's relationship with Crucero.

Another text arrived from Miyo's phone:

Take money to your office parking lot. Wait for more instruction.

I replied:

Okay. I need time to get money together. If you hurt her in ANY way, I will hunt you to the end of time and kill you.

Twenty minutes later, I pounded into the Mariner Sands visitors' lot and ran into the lobby. A young woman in a Mariner Sands jacket sat at a desk in one corner. I had never seen her before.

She beamed her best-trained smile. "How may I help you, sir?"

"I need to talk to your head of security. It's an emergency."

She frowned. Maybe emergencies were not part of her training. "Uh, I'm new. Nobody told me anything about any security."

Pointing at the ceiling, I said, "That is a security camera."

She stared at the camera for a few seconds. Perhaps she had never noticed it. "That's a camera? Cool."

"Who's in charge of it?"

She frowned again. Something else her training didn't cover. "Maybe our maintenance guy knows. He's been here longer than me."

"Where do I find your maintenance guy?"

She smiled. This was something she knew. "I'll page him, sir."

"Thanks." I stepped aside.

Three minutes later, a jowly middle-aged man in dark blue work clothes appeared. *Carl* was embroidered in white thread over his left pocket; *Mariner Sands* and a logo were stitched over his right. Carl wore a well-used leather tool belt. "You the man what needs maintenance?"

"I need your security videos from eleven last night to noon today. Where can I watch those?"

Carl crossed his arms. "Who wants to see 'em?"

I handed him a business card. "I'm a friend of Miyoki Takashi. She owns a condo on the top floor."

"Sure, I seen her around. Asian lady?"

My phone signaled another text. I glanced at the screen then at Carl. "This has to do with the emergency. Excuse me a minute."

I opened the text:

Why you not in office parking lot?

The kidnappers knew I wasn't there. That meant they could see the lot. I made sure no one tailed me from my office to Miyo's condo.

I texted back:

I want proof Miyo is alive.

I put my phone away. "Sorry for the interruption. Ms. Takashi is in trouble. Your security videos will help me discover what happened to her."

"We ain't needed to use them security videos for a long time. The condo office is closed on the weekend. I don't rightly know how they work."

"That's okay, Carl. I know how they work. Where is the control panel?"

"The control panel?"

"The room where the monitors show the pictures from the security cameras. You have five cameras; there must be a control panel."

"Oh, yeah."

I waited, but Carl didn't say anything else.

I asked, "Where are the monitors?"

Carl studied my business card so long that I thought maybe he didn't read well. "You a friend of Ms. Takashi or are you a cop?"

"Both. I'm her friend, and I happen to be a private investigator and a former police detective. I know how to run a security system. Where's the control panel?"

Carl stuck the card in his shirt pocket. "Follow me."

Carl led me through a side door and down a narrow hall with a concrete floor and bare fluorescent lights hung from the ceiling.

As we walked, my phone signaled a text from an unknown number with a Miami area code. It was a photo of Miyo with the front page of the *Miami Herald.*

They did not use Miyo's phone. I forwarded the text to Bigs with a request for him to ping the new phone.

I replied to the unknown phone:

I can't read the date on the newspaper and I don't take the Miami Herald. Send me a close-up of the date.

Carl stopped at the last door on the right and pulled out a key ring attached to his belt. He fumbled through the keys. "Maybe it's this one. Nope. Let me see."

He laughed with embarrassment. "Sorry, mister. Ain't got much call to open this door." He tested five more keys before he located the right one. "Here you go." He reached through the door and switched on the lights.

Shoving past him, I sat in a utilitarian desk chair in front of five security monitors. Two displayed pictures from the ceilings of the two elevators. Others covered the lobby, the driveway in front, and the door to the docks.

By trial and error, I ascertained the control for the first elevator. I ran it back to eleven o'clock the previous night. At 11:13, I watched myself enter the elevator on the top floor and descend to the lobby. I fast-forwarded the video until people flashed on the screen. I backed the video up. Two couples got on in the lobby and rode to floors 11 and 14.

Bigs texted me:

New phone pinged at Alena Cernan's house.

Fast-forwarding, backing up, fast-forwarding again, I scanned my way to 1:00 p.m., the time the kidnapper had contacted me. No one entered or exited the elevator on the penthouse floor after me.

My phone chimed with another text from the same Miami number. It was a close-up of today's date on the newspaper.

I replied to the last text:

I must talk to her.

Accessing the other elevator video, I repeated the process. Three men entered from the lobby at 3:27 a.m. with a large wooden packing crate on a dolly. They exited on the penthouse level. My heart flip-flopped though I wasn't surprised. Two kidnappers were Alena's Blue-Eyed Devils. The third man's face was hidden beneath a Port City Pilots baseball hat.

Fifteen minutes later, the men wheeled the crate onto the elevator. It seemed heavier when they bounced the dolly across the door gap and into the elevator. Maybe that was my imagination.

In the video from the lobby camera, the men maneuvered the crate out the door. The outside camera revealed a green Suburban. Freezing the frame, I wrote down the license plate. I pressed *Play* again. They opened the SUV's back doors and heaved the box into the rear. They were gone in seconds, with the woman I loved.

I made it to the Pink Coral Isle guardhouse at 4:40. "I'm Carlos McCrary. Tank Tyler is expecting me."

"Of course, Mr. McCrary."

The gate rose and I cruised down Pink Coral Way.

My phone rang. The call was from the Miami number that had sent Miyo's photo with the newspaper. I stopped at the curb. "Miyo, is that you?"

"You hold. I put her on." A long silence, then, "Talk to him. He want proof you alive."

Another long pause, then I heard a vague noise over the phone.

"You talk. Talk or I hit you again."

Another silence, another noise, then, "Chuck, come kill these five bastards."

The phone went dead. I texted the number:

You harm her in ANY way and I will hunt you down like a rabid dog.

God, what a brave woman, I thought. I admired her for taking the risk, but I wished she hadn't. I continued to 96 Pink Coral Way.

The ornate wrought-iron gates swung open on my approach. *Gregory must be monitoring the security camera.*

My phone announced another text from Miyo's phone.

Drive alone in Dodge Caravan to office parking lot 3000 Bayshore Drive. Wait for instruction.

I replied:

I will be there when I have the money. That will require a few hours. Maybe even to Monday. Banks are closed on Saturday. If you harm her, you and all your friends are dead.

I trotted up the porch steps as Gregory opened the door. "Good afternoon, Chuck. Mr. Snopolski and Lieutenant Castellano are in the conference room."

I would've shaken Gregory's hand, but that makes him uncomfortable. I had just recently convinced him to call me Chuck. "Where's the conference room?"

Tank's house was large enough to need a guide and pack mules. It had twelve bedrooms, and I had seen two or three of them. He converted some rooms to other uses, like his home office on the second floor. It was logical he had a conference room. After all, he had a house God might have built if He had the money.

"Follow me, sir." Gregory led me across the foyer to the elevator. He gestured me to precede him. "Third floor."

This was my first visit to the third floor. From the pool, I had noticed the spacious deck that jutted from the slope of the tile roof, but I had not paid much attention to it.

The elevator door rolled open.

"Here you are, sir."

The room might have been built as a squash court where part of the attic would have been. A mahogany conference table with twelve chairs sat in the center of the carpeted floor. Corkboards, whiteboards, and a projection screen were mounted on two of the white walls.

The sloped ceiling and half-wall had two pairs of French doors thrust out in a wide dormer on one side. The doors were open to the deck I had noticed from the pool area.

Snoop stood at the rail on the deck. I stepped through the French doors onto the Spanish-tiled floor.

"Miyo is at Alena Cernan's house in Coconut Grove, held by at least five Devils." I glanced around. "Where is Jorge?"

"Not so fast, bud. How do you know there are five men?"

"The kidnappers called and let me talk to her. She said, and I quote, 'Chuck, come kill these five bastards.'"

"That's quite a gal, bud."

"Yeah, she is. Where's Jorge?"

The seaplane's engine noise swelled in the distance.

"Tank and Kelly are on final approach. Jorge went to help with the baggage. Coffee's on the bar inside. Gregory made a fresh pot half an hour ago."

"In a minute. Let's watch this."

The seaplane emerged from behind a grove of sea grapes near Tank's seawall and descended, a giant swan gliding to a water landing. The engine's roar softened to a purr. The seaplane scarcely splashed on Seeti Bay. It glided toward Tank's finger pier jutting thirty yards from shore.

Ten yards out, the propeller stopped.

The pilot opened his door and stepped onto the float. The plane glided to the pier. He tossed a line to Jorge, who cleated it. Once Tank and Kelly disembarked, the pilot untied the line, tossed it into the plane, and fired the engine. He waved to Tank, who shoved the plane from the pier.

The seaplane eased away and circled into the breeze. The engine noise grew to a roar and the plane leapt across the water. It climbed into the air and banked west. It passed from sight behind Gregory's bungalow.

"Let's go inside, Snoop. We have work to do." I headed toward the coffee.

I crept from the shelter of one car to the only other car on the sixth floor.

Two Devils leaned on the concrete rail in front of their green Suburban with their binoculars focused on my Caravan across Bayshore Boulevard.

If Alena wanted me dead, her men would have shot me through my office window from the Bayshore Parking Garage. Lord knows it had been tried before. Alena's gang wasn't chintzy with their armaments. They would own a sniper-quality rifle.

Snoop had driven my minivan slowly down the last block of Bayshore. The rest of us advanced up the garage ramps. Tank drove Jorge's pickup truck first. None of the Cernan gang had even noticed the truck. He spotted the green Suburban on the sixth floor, continued to the seventh floor, and texted me. Kelly had come over my objections. I rode with her and she parked her Buick on the fifth floor. Jorge did the same in Tank's BMW.

Snoop drove the Caravan from one parking spot on the empty lot to another. He rolled into a space, then backed out. He backed into another slot, then out and spun in a tight circle.

The two Devils conversed in a language that sounded like clearing their throats. I didn't speak Serbian, but they probably said: *What is that lunatic doing? Is he nuts?*

The late afternoon clouds over the Everglades had thrown Port City into shadows. The garage's interior lights were set to come on at sunset in 45 minutes. For now, the sixth floor was gloomy enough for my purpose.

I peered up the ramp toward the seventh floor. Tank hid behind a concrete pillar with the sound suppressor on the Rock River varmint rifle peeking out.

I crept up the opposite side of the ramp until I crouched behind the Devils' SUV. Drawing Edvard's and Bojan's Glock 17s, I advanced on the driver side of the Suburban. Tank covered the other side from a distance.

Both Devils held binoculars to their eyes. I pressed the barrel of a Glock to each of their necks. "One move and you're dead."

Both men dropped their binoculars. The man on the left whirled and the other man jumped sideways. I squeezed both triggers. The left-hand man collapsed faster than an imploded building, his neck blown away. The man on the right pulled a gun and the sniper rifle coughed twice. He fell in a heap, his gun skidding under their SUV.

Jorge and Kelly reached the scene first. They opened doors of opposite sides of the SUV.

"Clear," said Jorge.

"Clear," Kelly echoed. "Hey, look what I found." She lifted two Kalashnikovs from the back seat.

"Great," I said. "Leave them in the back seat. We'll use those later."

I retrieved the first dead man's weapon from his shoulder holster.

Kelly knelt beside the SUV and fished the second man's gun from behind a wheel. She surveyed the gun I held. "Both Glock 17's."

"What well-dressed killers wear to a gunfight."

"Also, well-dressed cops and PIs." She handed me the other Glock and I laid the newly acquired weapons on the Suburban's hood.

Pistols are for close-up work, not sniper rifles. Alena wanted me alive. I shuddered to think why. Visions of barbed wire and the odor of gasoline came to mind.

I handed Edvard Oblak's and Bojan Matic's Glocks to Kelly and Jorge. "Use these instead of your own. If you shoot someone, the ballistics will match a dead man's weapon. I inspected, cleaned, and test-fired both of them."

Kelly stuck the pistol in her belt holster. "I'll lock my own in my trunk. Where did you get these?"

"It's better you don't know."

Jorge handed his own pistol to Kelly. "Lock this with yours; my pickup is too easy to break into." He peered at me. "What will you carry?"

"One of these new ones." I picked the Glocks off the SUV's hood. "The other Glocks were well-maintained. I bet these two took care of their weapons also."

Tank joined us.

"Sorry, guys. I missed the first shot."

"Could happen to anybody," Kelly said. "The second shot was on target."

The man on the right was familiar. I twisted his chin from side to side. "This one rode the elevator with me at Miyo's apartment yesterday."

"Casing the building," Kelly said.

Rifling his wallet, I extracted a tourist visa for Pavel Struna. I folded it in my pocket and tossed the wallet to Tank. "Spoils of war."

He fished out a cluster of bills. "You're kidding."

"Nope. You need a few hundred extra dollars the way the Sahara needs more sand, but it's an ancient custom: To the victor belong the spoils. Consider it a souvenir you can use to buy a nice evening out for Kelly and you."

I hefted the man on the left's wallet. I pocketed another tourist visa for Drago Tajnic. "I'll save this wallet for Snoop. God knows he took a huge risk down there. These guys might have drilled that van like Swiss cheese. Let's access their phones."

Drago's phone showed an outgoing text in Serbian sent when Snoop arrived in my Caravan. I recognized my name. I showed it to Tank. "Must be telling the boss I arrived."

I called Bigs. "This is an anonymous tip that there are two dead Blue-Eyed Devils on the sixth floor of the Bayshore Parking Garage. I'll give you a statement tomorrow. We're pressed for time. Could you wait a half hour for us to leave before you send a response team?"

"Since it's sunset on a Saturday in the business district, the bodies won't be discovered until Monday. If you like, I could wait for someone else to report them."

"Two other cars are parked on this level. Either driver might come back any time. I don't want to freak out anybody."

"I'll send a black-and-white in thirty minutes unless one of those other drivers reports the bodies earlier."

"Thanks. I found phones on the bodies, both with Miami area codes. I will send the numbers to you. Ping their locations since eleven last night."

By the time we reached my office, Bigs had emailed a report on the two phones' locations for the last twenty hours. One dead Devil had been on the kidnap team. They were equally guilty, but I still felt better that he was one of the dead ones.

Correction: One of the *first* dead ones.

TWENTY-TWO

I drove the Devils' green Suburban west on SW 334th Street, the road that ran a half mile south of Jose's Auto Salvage. Jorge and Kelly trailed me, Jorge in his pickup truck and Kelly in her Buick. There were no vehicles other than our small convoy. Two farmhouse lights gleamed to the south. Crossing 222nd Avenue, I kept my speed below the limit.

My phone rang. The caller ID said it was Hideo Takashi. I had more pressing demands than comforting a nervous father. Better if I could rescue his daughter first. I let it go to voicemail.

Jorge's pickup truck stopped. His headlights went dark in my mirror after he parked on the grass a hundred yards west of the avenue. He would approach the junkyard across the fields from the southeast.

I consulted my GPS and stopped due south of the junkyard. Kelly passed in her Buick. She would park a hundred yards this side of 230th Avenue and approach the target from the southwest.

I texted both of Miyo's parents:

I am following a lead that will take all night. Get a hotel and a good night's sleep, if possible. Will call you in the morning. I will not rest until your daughter is safe.

Regards, Chuck

I called Bigs. "Ping Miyo's phone and the new phone again."

"Hang on." A keyboard clicked in the background. "Miyo's phone is still at that junkyard. The new phone went dark at 5:09 p.m. It was at Alena Cernan's house before that."

After thanking him, I disconnected.

They used Miyo's phone to draw me to the middle of nowhere in the middle of the night. A place with no witnesses. Alena wouldn't be there herself. Whenever my Dodge arrived, her gang would shoot out the tires or block it in with their vehicles. Since they wanted me alive, they wouldn't shoot into the minivan, and Snoop should be okay. I hoped. If not, that's why we wore armored vests.

The moon was three-quarters full in a partly cloudy sky. We could cross the fields and orchards with no trouble. That meant the bad guys could spot us if they watched the fields and orchards around them, at least once we moved within shooting distance.

The gangsters we ambushed in the garage would have spotted us too, if they hadn't fixated on Snoop driving my Caravan like a crazy man.

Well, that ruse worked once. Why not use it again?

I texted Jorge and Kelly to move out.

Tank Tyler

Tank Tyler rolled west on SW 318th Street. He consulted his GPS and stopped due north of the fruit stand at Buddy's Berry Farm. A half mile in the dark to cover on foot. *The first quarter mile I slog through a dirt field, maybe mud, with no light but the moon. Sounds easier than NFL training camp.*

He popped the trunk, donned his armored vest, and locked the BMW. The sole artificial light came from a distant farmhouse. He let his pupils dilate before he started across the vineyard.

He called Chuck. "I'll text you once I'm in position."

"You have plenty of time. You'll hit easy going once you reach the landing strip."

"Okay. I'll set my phone on vibrate. Talk to you on the flip side." He ended the call.

In the moonlight, the espaliered vines loomed like monstrous scarecrows or the Whomping Willows of the Harry Potter books he read to his nieces and nephews. Tank glanced at the three-quarter moon emerging from behind a small cloud. He tripped over a guy wire bracing the espaliers of the row of vines. He held the rifle at arm's length above him and tumbled into the sandy dirt. *That's what I get for admiring the moon and killing my night vision. Gotta be more careful.*

He traversed another row of espaliered vines, dodged the guy wires at the end, and stopped at a four-foot welded wire fence separating the vineyard from an avocado grove. The spaces between the wires were too narrow for Tank's size fifteen feet. His three hundred pounds would crumple the fence anyway, and he didn't want any evidence he had been there.

Crabbing sideways, he encountered a truck gate. He eased the steel gate open enough to slip through.

Another welded wire fence ran south at right angles to the first one. A one-lane dirt road ran arrow-straight between the fence and the first row of avocado trees.

Tank hiked down the road for four minutes. Another truck gate blocked his way, this one padlocked. It was either climb over or crawl under. He didn't think the hinges would take his weight if he climbed over.

Tank chucked his backpack over the fence. He shrugged out of his armored vest and dropped it beside the backpack. He reached under the gate and laid the rifle on the grass. Scrunching on his back in the deeper of the two tire tracks, he sucked in his gut and snaked under the gate.

The dirt runway's wind sock hung limp, its orange and white stripes appeared black and white in the moonlight. A line from *Nights in White Satin* came to him. *Cold-hearted orb that rules the night/ removes the colors from our sight.*

Tank brushed himself off, donned the vest, and slipped the backpack over his shoulders. He retrieved the rifle and screwed the sound suppressor on the barrel.

Carlos McCrary

After picking my way through an orange grove under the moonlight, I climbed a fence, then threaded my way through a tropical plant nursery.

My phone vibrated. Stepping behind a row of potted plumbagoes, I shielded the phone screen from the junkyard ahead, and read the text.

Tank was in position.

I replied:

We're not. Wait until you hear fireworks.

My screen was too bright. A bad guy might spot the light when I used it later. I dimmed the brightness to 20 percent, then 10 percent.

The junkyard's seven-foot concrete block wall stood twenty yards away across a two-lane dirt access road used by both the yard and the nursery. Trees and shrubs grew in the strip between the road and wall. With the moonlight and the white-painted wall, the vegetation was obvious. The back wall had two sheet-metal-covered steel gates flanking the overgrown area.

My Google Earth and Google Street View research showed two buildings in Jose's yard. The building against the back wall was 75 feet on my left. Another was in the center of the yard 150 feet from the main entrance.

I texted Jorge and Kelly that I was in position.

Jorge replied that he was two minutes out. Kelly was at her post at the south wall.

I texted Snoop:

Start dancing.

I shinnied up a sabal palm and stood on the wall. The trees behind me hid my silhouette. A stack of squashed-flat cars lay beneath me. With the trees behind me, I sidestepped until I reached an aisle between the junk cars. Nothing moved in the yard except the leaves of scattered trees growing at random. A dog barked in the distance. No, there was more than one dog. There was no way to tell whether the dogs were in Jose's yard or a neighbor's.

Jorge signaled he had reached his position.

I texted them both:

Go, go, go.

Vaulting into the driveway between two rows of stacked, flattened junkers, I cat-footed to the storage building jammed against the back wall. It had to be for equipment, but I needed to prove it. I didn't want a gunman to emerge at my back once I had passed the building.

The steel building's walls had been pristine white thirty years before. Now they were dented and rusted the same as the double entrance doors.

Behind me, the barking grew louder. Damn, those dogs didn't belong to a neighbor; they were part of local security. I had seconds to find refuge.

The two windows on the front wall were dark. So were the windows in the double doors. I tried the left doorknob. Locked. I tested the other one. Also locked.

The barking redoubled and I sneaked a peek over my shoulder. Two black shadows rounded a stack of squashed cars at top speed and galloped up the driveway toward me, barking and snarling in full cry. Doberman demons in the moonlight. A Doberman sprints up to 40 mph, and these two were hauling ass in my direction.

There was no time to pick either lock and no room for me to run. I twisted and jerked on both knobs like my life depended on it, which I guess it did unless I shot the dogs, which I did not want to do. The poor dogs were doing what they were trained to do.

The thirty-year-old doors peeled open with a shriek of stressed metal. By now, I practically smelled the raw meat on the Dobermans' breath as they sprinted the last few yards toward me. Jumping inside, I slammed the doors behind me.

Seconds later, the dogs thudded against the doors. The glass was reinforced with wire mesh. Their claws scratched the doors. The disappointed Dobermans bayed their frustration.

So much for our stealth entry.

Drawing the Taser from my backpack, I opened one door wide enough for the dogs to enter single file. *Zap, zap.* Both dogs collapsed on the concrete floor. I dragged them aside. They would revive before morning, and the employees would hear them howling. Or the cops.

Squatting below the level of the dirty windows, I shined a dimmed flashlight around the building. Forklifts and cranes in flaked industrial yellow paint filled the room. No Miyo. And no Blue-Eyed Devils.

I texted Jorge and Kelly:

I tased two guard dogs and locked them in building. Bad guys know we are here. Use your thermals.

After pulling a thermal monocular from my backpack, I slipped out, shut the double doors behind me, and scanned the yard for any heat source. Everything on the screen was ambient temperature. The main building near the front gate was not in my field of vision.

In the distance, my Caravan's horn sounded. Snoop had arrived at the front gate.

Hefting an AK-47 formerly owned by a dead Serb, I headed down the center driveway. Cars stacked on each other rose high above my head on either side. The next row was shipping containers stacked three high on one side and a collection of ancient panel vans side by side on the other.

Ahead was the main building's back wall. My thermal monocular showed a diffuse glow that flared at the metal wall's north end. A smaller glow bloomed at the south end. Was it two people to the north and one to the south?

Scanning south, I recognized Kelly's glow as she walked from between the metal mountains fifty yards away. We exchanged waves.

I scanned north. Jorge was not visible.

The Caravan honked three more times.

To the north, a man walked into view holding a rifle. It wasn't Jorge, so he was a hostile. He shouted and raised his weapon.

Dropping the monocular in the dirt, I fired a three-round burst from the Kalashnikov as the hostile launched a fusillade my way. Behind me, a dozen slugs clanged and echoed off the stacked metal.

Leaping sideways, I rolled across the dirt.

The hostile kept shooting. More metallic bangs sounded beside me when I dove behind another stack of junked cars. Sparks flew off the rusted metal and landed on my cheek. To the north, I saw a muzzle flash from a second man firing from further down the driveway. Dirt spewed into the air at my knees, and a slug slammed my vest as hard as a baseball bat.

I fired three more bursts. The second hostile slumped to one knee and fired again. Another shot hit my vest. I fired twice more. A Roman candle of muzzle flashes painted an arc in the night as he fell sideways.

Inserting a fresh magazine, I duckwalked back toward the gap. A sliver of the main building's corner became visible between two pancaked cars stacked between me and the first two men. A body sprawled in the dirt. I must have hit him before I jumped.

Gunfire sounded from the north. Another fusillade echoed from the south. The Caravan horn sounded shave-and-a-haircut.

I found my monocular and scanned the building. The two glows I had observed earlier had faded. The heat sources inside the building were now outside. I scanned north and south. Nothing.

Pocketing the monocular, I advanced around the south wall. A dead man sprawled at my feet, an AK-47 in his slack grip. First, I kicked the rifle away from the dead man. Then I felt his pulse. Dead. Later I would come back and add the rifle to our collection of unregistered weapons.

A muzzle flash pointed northwest. Kelly fired her AK-47 at someone I couldn't see from my angle.

Edging my finger to the trigger, I advanced again, sidestepping past the corner of the building. A bad guy was firing a handgun at Kelly.

I fired two bursts from forty yards at his center mass. He staggered but didn't fall and he exchanged fire with Kelly.

This was bad. The bad guy was wearing an armored vest. That meant that more Devils might be wearing them. Armored vests require a head shot; I hate head shots. And the muzzle flashes had damaged my night vision.

The hostile ran toward the front gate. Kelly kept firing until he passed through the gate. It's hard to hit a man running at right angles. I hoped Tank was paying attention. If he wasn't, the guy might carjack Snoop and escape in my Caravan.

More gunfire came from the north. Kelly changed magazines. "Reload, Chuck. They're wearing vests."

"I noticed."

"I'll cover this side," she said. "You stay over there."

"Right."

We crept along the wider road that fronted the main building, paved with pot-holed asphalt. The gunfire noise increased when we rounded the corner. One man slumped on the pavement. Three men crouched near them, backs to us, pouring fire to the north. They must have spotted Jorge.

I nailed the one on the left. A baseball hat flew off his head as he fell. The middle man tumbled like a box of rocks. Jorge or Kelly had nailed him.

The last man sprinted toward the front gate. I used the strobing muzzle flashes to track him with the AK-47 but I missed in the dark. The running man cleared the front gate. He was Tank's problem now.

"Everybody stay where you are," I bellowed. If there were more gunmen we had not neutralized, I didn't want us to bunch together. My own ears rang from the gunfire, and my voice sounded far away. "By my count, we killed seven, but we don't know whether that's all. Kelly, you clear the building. Jorge and I will walk the driveways with our thermal scopes."

We separated. The building was clear. So was the yard. We frisked the bodies and collected wallets, phones, weapons, and more ammo. We had captured an arsenal big enough to arm a small revolution.

I stuck the baseball cap back on the head of the last man I shot. He was a Port City Pilots fan. They say Hitler liked dogs too. I wondered whether he was the guy I had seen in the security videos at Miyo's condo. I hoped so.

Kelly, Jorge, and I walked through the front gate, and I gave Snoop the all clear. Two men had run through the front gate, but there were three bodies beside the Caravan. Tank had shot one I had missed counting. I collected three more sets of wallets, phones, weapons, and extra magazines.

Waving Tank in, I handed him the three wallets. "Good shooting. Here are more souvenirs. How loud was the gunfire? Can we expect the cops?"

"Nah. The concrete walls and the piles of crushed cars act like the sound walls along I-95." He glanced down the empty street. "The nearest houses are a half mile either direction. I doubt they heard a thing."

"Okay. Let's drag these three inside and shut the gate. Someone will discover them in the morning."

Alena's crew was down by ten. Hell's population was up by ten. No, counting the two in the parking garage, hell was up twelve. Bad day for the Blue-Eyed Devils; good day for the real devil.

And a horrific day for Miyo.

One tire on the Caravan was flat and the rear fender was riddled with bullet holes. Smelling gasoline, I peered under the chassis with a flashlight. The last drops fell onto the sand, then stopped. The gas tank had drained. "No matter, people. We'll use their SUVs. Tank, you and Snoop frisk the bodies for car keys."

Jorge, Kelly, and I carried the phones into the junkyard office. We scoured all ten call logs and glanced at the texts they had sent. All were in Serbian. Or maybe Klingon. Nah, had to be Serbian.

No phone calls had gone out in the last two hours, but all ten phones missed incoming calls from Tomaz Kopitar. I didn't bother to listen to voicemails. They would be in Serbian, and they would say *What's going on out there?* and *Where is McCrary?*

The outgoing texts on nine of the ten phones were at least three hours old. We attacked so fast just one message went out, a text Niko Iva sent to Alena Cernan and Tomaz Kopitar. It had two Serbian words plus my name. I ran it through the translator app on my smartphone. The message said *McCrary is here.* Iva sent it when Snoop parked out front in the Caravan.

Tomaz Kopitar sent a group text to all the phones a half hour later. I ran the message through the translator app.

What is occurring? Call me immediately.

Tank and Snoop walked in. Tank handed me a key fob. "Niko Iva had the keys to the Lincoln Navigator."

"Take off his shirt," I said, "and rinse the blood out."

"What about his hat?" asked Tank.

"Iva was the guy in the Pilots baseball hat?"

"Yeah."

"Great. Get it."

Snoop tossed another key fob on the table. "Franc Widmer had the key to the Hyundai. You want his shirt?"

"We need five—no, wait—four shirts." I turned to Jorge and Kelly. "Pick three more distinctive shirts off the bodies and rinse out the blood."

Snoop grinned. "It's time to play dress-up."

"Niko Iva sent the text, and he had the fancier vehicle. He was in charge." I did another quick translation and used Iva's phone to reply to Kopitar:

We capture McCrary.

That was the best I could do since I didn't know how to make the past tense in Serbian. I switched off the phone and removed the battery in case Tomaz Kopitar had installed locator apps on his crew's phones. Then I removed the batteries from all the captured phones. Let Kopitar and Alena Cernan stew on that.

I tossed Snoop the key fob to the Navigator. "Bring everything we need from the Caravan and stick it in the Navigator." We transferred the extra ammo, a first aid kit, a box of energy bars, and assorted goodies.

"What about this?" Snoop held up the cloth bag with my gun-cleaning gear.

"Bring it to the office. We should clean our weapons before we use them again. Would you shut those outside gates first?"

"Sure thing."

The office building contained a wood-paneled conference room that had been new in the 1950s. The routine motion of cleaning weapons on the long table let me unwind a little. The adrenaline flushed from my bloodstream. I figured the others could use the break too.

Hideo Takashi texted me that he and Mrs. Takashi had arrived at the Port City Palace.

Despite the antique decor, Jose's Auto Salvage had a new coffee maker and a modern computer. Snoop brewed coffee, and I connected my phone to the computer so I could play video on the 27-inch monitor.

"I recorded this video of Alena's house last month after I planted a tracker on her Mercedes. I scouted the rear of her house, but I had to avoid security cameras. The cameras are mounted under the eaves here... and you can see the ones on the house through the opening in the bamboo."

"Wait," said Jorge. "Zoom in."

"Show me what you mean," I answered.

"There. The back door. Freeze the picture and zoom in."

I did.

"That's a wireless video and audio doorbell. There's a security camera and a monitor inside that door. The whole thing is battery-powered and cellphone-accessible."

"That's not good."

"Never mind that," Jorge said. "We'll think of something. Tell us the rest."

"When I picked the lock, I stuck to the rear alley and the side the cameras don't cover. There are windows on all sides of her house and, of course, front and back doors. No bars or wire reinforcements on the windows that I could see. It's hard to defend, so I figure Alena wouldn't hold Miyo in the house."

"What's that?" Jorge pointed at the monitor.

"That's the metal stairs to the garage apartment. These stairs are the sole access."

"It's too narrow for two men—pardon me, Kelly—for two *persons* to run up at the same time."

Kelly smiled. "Yeah, and metal steps will ring like a gong when we climb them."

Jorge said, "The porch at the top is four feet square. Too small to get momentum for a door kick-in."

"The door is probably steel too," I said, "you couldn't kick it in anyway."

"We would need a police battering ram like we used on the bordello raid," Jorge said.

"I put one in the green Suburban when we stopped at my office earlier."

Kelly grinned. "You sly dog. Did you bring a riot shield too?"

"Nah, they won't stop a bullet."

Tank cleared his throat. "Not to throw a dose of reality on your plan, but do you know the story of Horatio at the bridge? One Roman soldier held off an army by defending a bridge maybe six feet wide. Alena's porch is four feet, and the door is narrower than that. We can breach the door, but we gotta enter single file. One guy could hold us off; they had five at the time Miyo talked to you. Could be more by now."

"Could be less too. Don't worry about it; we'll think of something."

"Start thinking, *amigo"* said Jorge. "One other thing, they could have a wireless video and audio doorbell on that apartment door too. They will see us coming while we're at the bottom of the stairs. We have to find another way."

No one said anything. The silence lengthened.

The idea hit me so hard and so fast that I slammed my cup down. "They'll see us coming." I pivoted to Jorge. "You said, 'They'll see us coming.'"

"Yeah, so?"

"What if they can't see us?"

"With a wireless video doorbell and a window beside the door, they'll see us."

"Not if it's dark."

Jorge pointed at the monitor. "Hello. Earth to McCrary. What about those yard lights and landscape lights? You gonna shoot them out? They would still know we were coming."

"If we cut the power," I said, "the whole building goes dark."

Snoop shook his head. "Nope. When the power goes down, they'll go on high alert."

"Not if the power fails in the whole neighborhood. This is South Florida. Every time there's a thunderstorm, the power goes out somewhere. Imagine they look out the window and the whole neighborhood is dark. They'll think it's a power company problem."

"That might work," Kelly said. "The electricity went off at my building last weekend for two hours."

"The wireless doorbell system is battery powered," Jorge said. "Cut the power off and it still works."

"Not in the dark. There's no light to see."

"Next problem: How do you blow the power to the neighborhood?"

I pointed at the rifle leaning against Tank's chair. "We use the varmint rifle to blow the neighborhood transformer."

"What about the bottleneck climbing the stairs?" Kelly asked.

"I'll be the Trojan Horse," I said.

Snoop set his cup down. "What does that mean?"

"You'll see when we get to Coconut Grove."

TWENTY-THREE

Tomaz Kopitar

Kopitar drank his Scotch and studied Alena Cernan as she paced her living room with the endless rhythm of a caged tigress. He knew how his beautiful boss felt: tight chest, shortness of breath, acidic stomach. He felt that way too, but he hid it better. He realized at a visceral level that he was going to die tonight.

Alena held her phone at arm's length like it would bite her any moment. "Where are they? First Drago says McCrary is at his office at 7:30, then Niko says he is at Jose's Auto Salvage at ten o'clock. Then he says he captured McCrary, but he won't answer the phone." She laid the phone on the cocktail table and stepped away, staring at it.

"There must be a logical explanation." Kopitar didn't dare tell his boss what he thought. *The explanation is simple,* he thought. *McCrary killed them all the same way he killed Hugo, Bojan, and Edvard. The way he will kill everyone here, including Alena and me.*

"You sent texts to all ten?" Alena asked.

"Twelve," Kopitar corrected. "I sent texts to all twelve, including the two men I sent to the parking garage. No one responded. I also telephoned all twelve within the last hour. The phones go to voicemail." *Of course, they go to voicemail; McCrary has their phones and their weapons.*

Alena frowned. "If McCrary killed them, we have only Viktor, Jakob, Stefan, you, and me remaining. You are head of security, Tomaz. I don't feel secure."

"And Rudolf. You forget Rudolf. Viktor, Jakob, Stefan, and Rudolf are in the apartment with McCrary's woman. That makes six of us." He had posted ten men at the auto salvage. If McCrary survived that ambush, he was a demon and not a man. They were doomed. More importantly, *he* was doomed. And, of course, Alena.

Kopitar swirled his Scotch in the glass and listened to the ice cubes clink. It was such a lovely, musical sound. He chugged his Scotch and went for a refill. He was a dead man walking; he should enjoy his last night on earth. Alena served fine Scotch. He wondered whether hell had Scotch. He smiled and filled the crystal glass half full.

"Why do you smile, Tomaz? Our situation isn't funny."

"My dear, life is funny." He drank half the Scotch. He hooted and guffawed. "Life is funny."

Kopitar's phone vibrated in his pocket. He glanced at it when it announced in English, "New message received from Niko Iva."

He read the text. His gut tied itself in knots.

"What did Niko say? Did they capture McCrary?"

Kopitar handed the phone to Alena.

She read the message. Her face lit with a broad grin. "We were worried for nothing, Tomaz. Niko says they have McCrary."

Kopitar swirled his drink. Despite her intelligence and European education, Alena saw only what she wanted to see. Niko would never use that word for *captured*. That word came from the same translator app McCrary used to send the other fake texts.

"Niko didn't send that text. McCrary did." He poured the rest of the Scotch down his throat and banged the glass on the bar. The glass top shattered. *It's all right,* Kopitar thought, *our world is shattering. Why not the bar top?*

"I don't understand, Tomaz. It's from Niko."

Kopitar swallowed his Scotch and said nothing.

Her voice climbed higher. "It's from Niko."

Her voice broke. "It *must* be from Niko. It must be." She dropped the phone onto the carpet and covered her face with both hands.

"It is from Niko's *phone,* but McCrary sent it."

Kopitar walked over to his boss and clutched her hand. "Come with me. I will tell you something."

He led her to the bedroom. The faint smell of her perfume mixed with the Scotch on his tongue and made him feel sick for a moment. He must tell her now, because he would never have another chance before the demon killed them all. He grasped Alena's other hand in his.

"Are you drunk, Tomaz? Now, when I need you most? Why bring me to my bedroom to tell me something? Let's sit in the living room." She attempted to disengage her hands.

Kopitar tightened his grip and lifted her hands to his lips. "Alena, I love you. I have loved you for years. You and I should be together, not you and that Crucero crossbreed." He kissed her fingers. "We could have beautiful children."

Alena jerked her hands free and slapped him hard as she could. "You forget yourself, Tomaz. You're a fool to think we could be together."

She tried to shove past him.

Kopitar wrapped his arms around her and lifted her off her feet. "Don't you understand, my dear? You and I will die tonight. Or tomorrow. Or whenever McCrary comes for us. We can't stop him. Let's at least enjoy one night in heaven before McCrary sends us both to hell."

He tossed her on the bed and fell upon her, clawing at her blouse.

She fought him for a moment, then clutched his hair in her left hand. "You're right, Tomaz. You know me better than I know myself. You are the one I need." She smiled at him, kissed him with her mouth open, and spread her legs.

Kopitar's dreams had come true. He thought it was ironic that she had seen the light after it was too late for them to build a life together.

She ripped open her blouse with her right hand, and buttons flew across the room. She wasn't wearing a bra. Tugging his hair, she pressed his head to her breast.

As Kopitar drew her nipple into his mouth, she opened the top drawer of her nightstand and felt for the Browning .380 she kept there. She stuck it against his temple. "Are you enjoying yourself, Tomaz? I am not."

She squeezed the trigger.

Alena Cernan

Alena rolled Kopitar's body off onto the floor and got out of bed. She wrinkled her nose at the sight of brains splattered over her bed, walls, and floor.

No matter. Alena had survived worse situations than this. She recalled her family's escape from Slovenia. She was six years old when the civil war upended her world. Her father gunned down four partisans who came to arrest him in their palatial home. The partisans locked her father's own iron gate to keep him from escaping. He rammed through the gate with the family Mercedes and made it onto the residential street. He ran over the curb to bypass a roadblock and fired through his own windows at more partisans trying to block him. She would never forget the mad dash through the countryside with the windshield and side windows blown away. The wind messed her hair and stung her eyes. Her father gunned down six more men who wanted to stop their car as it sped toward Switzerland with three gold bars and a small sack of diamonds hidden in her Mickey Mouse suitcase.

Her father survived that. She would survive this.

She stripped off her clothes and walked to the hamper. No, she must wash the blood out before it set. She hauled her clothes to the laundry room and started the load with cold water.

She returned to her bedroom suite, showered, and examined her body in the mirror. No blood spatter marred the smoothness of her evenly tanned skin. Humming a tune to herself, she shaved her legs. Mustn't let these little setbacks upset her. Satisfied, she dressed and returned to the laundry room to examine the damp clothes. Yes, the stains came out. She transferred the load to the dryer.

Alena replaced the spent cartridge in the Browning and tucked it into her purse. She retrieved Kopitar's phone from where she had dropped it on the living room floor.

She flipped on the backyard lights, the pool lights, and the landscape lights.

She studied the monitors next to the back door. Banana plants and palm fronds swayed with the night breeze. Was McCrary hidden behind that banana plant? Insects swooped and soared in High Definition, drawn to their deaths by floodlights on the eaves. Or did McCrary spook them from their sleep beneath the undergrowth? The center screen showed the coral stepping stones arrayed around the swimming pool from the back steps to the apartment stairs. Or did McCrary hide beneath those stairs?

Niko was on his way with McCrary. He must be. Unless Tomaz was right. McCrary could hide a half dozen men in the lush tropical plants that protected her nude sunbathing from the view of neighbors on either side. If he killed her men at Jose's Auto Salvage, he would bring more men with him.

She must not think such negative thoughts. No matter what Tomaz feared, McCrary was one man. Even if he brought backup, Tomaz had sent her best people to the junkyard to ambush him. Any minute now, Niko would call to say he was on his way with McCrary.

She shuddered. Any minute.

She armed the alarm system, drew the Browning from her purse, and held the handgun at her side. Stepping onto the back porch, she locked the deadbolt behind her and crossed the Spanish tiles. A frog sounded in the moist undergrowth, echoed by another across the garden. When the frogs croaked, did that mean someone had disturbed them? She knew so little about her adopted tropical home.

She crossed the stepping-stones. Casting one last scan around the garden and pool area, she climbed the stairs. She rapped the metal door three times with the butt of her Browning. The pistol made a dull bong. She stepped back so the man inside could observe her in the security camera.

The dead bolt clunked and Jakob hauled the steel door open. "Come in, Ms. Cernan."

She opened the screen door and stepped inside. Jakob swung the heavy main door shut with a *thunk*.

She surveyed the room. An upholstered couch with two matching chairs sat in a living area. Viktor, Stefan, and Rudolf occupied three of the four chrome-plated chairs at the Formica dinette table near the small kitchen. Four mugs sat on the table. Empty takeout boxes heaped on the kitchen counter. The bathroom door stood open.

Alena paced the room, the Browning still in her hand.

Five AK-47s leaned against another corner. *Tomaz does not need his anymore,* she thought.

Alena marched to the stacked guns. She stuck the Browning in the waist of her pants and selected an AK-47. She laid it on the couch, strode to the kitchen counter, and poured another Scotch. Just one, she told herself, to settle her nerves. She held it up, then poured another inch before she added ice from the freezer.

The Browning pressed hard against her abdomen. A disadvantage of wearing tight pants, but she felt more secure with the Browning touching her body. She adjusted its position. It still wasn't comfortable, so she carried it in her hand.

McCrary's girlfriend was duct-taped to a straight-backed wooden chair from the dining room in the main house. She appeared groggy, like she had awakened from a deep sleep when Alena banged on the door.

"Why is her mouth not taped?"

"She removed the tape when she used the bathroom two hours ago. She had trouble breathing. She promised not to cause trouble."

Alena swallowed a slug of Scotch. "Did she eat?"

"She ate two pieces of pizza at eight o'clock."

She swirled her glass and listened to the ice cubes clink. Somehow that soothed her. "Niko texted. They captured McCrary."

"Are they bringing him here?"

Alena nodded. "By the way, I had to shoot Tomaz. You and Viktor fetch his body from my bedroom and stuff it in the trunk of the Mercedes. Spread a plastic sheet; I don't want blood on the carpet."

Jakob's eyes widened. "You shot Tomaz?"

She waved a hand dismissively. No need for the men to know about Tomaz's ridiculous notion that McCrary had won at the junkyard. "Tomaz forgot who was boss."

She gave Jakob a cold stare. "Never forget who is boss. You and Viktor do what I say."

"Should we be carrying a body in the open? A neighbor could spot us and call the cops."

"Don't be stupid, Jakob. The garden is surrounded by a wall of bamboo and bougainvillea, and it's the middle of the night. But make sure no one is in the alley before you carry him from the back gate to the garage."

The two men walked toward the door.

"Take your AK-47s too."

She trailed them to the door and bolted it after them. While her back was to Rudolf and Stefan, her chin trembled. She bit her lip, then tightened her chin into submission before she turned back. No need for the others to know what Tomaz said. Or what he tried to do.

Miyoki Takashi

Miyo gave up trying to break loose from the duct tape on her wrists and ankles. All she gained from the effort were bruises and abrasions. She had convinced her captors to leave her mouth free after the last bathroom break. *That was progress, wasn't it?*

She had spent her first hours of captivity more worried about Chuck than about herself. *Well, that's what love is, right? You care more about another person than you do about yourself. If I don't survive this, at least I found love. If I die, I will not die unloved.*

When the head man had instructed her to speak to Chuck, she refused. She didn't know much about police procedures, but she knew that the longer the phone call lasted, the better chance that Chuck or his friends with the police would trace the call. After the thug hit her a second time, she managed to tell Chuck how many men were holding her. The satisfaction was worth the bruises to her cheek.

For the entire day, Miyo studied her captors. She studied their body language and tone of voice. She learned the cadence of their speech, even though she didn't understand the words. She figured out the pecking order among the men who came and went, fetching pizza, coffee, beer, and whatnot. She had even figured out their names.

The banging on the door woke her.

The tall blonde entered and all four men snapped to attention. Chuck had described Alena Cernan well. She had a fashion model quality even in her jeans and silk top, except fashion models didn't have breasts that large. *Must be implants; she acts the type to want silicone boobs.*

Alena walked into the apartment clutching a pistol. She looked ready to use it. It was hard to be certain the way she waved it around, but Miyo thought Chuck carried a similar one in an ankle holster. It was smaller than the big pistols the men carried in their shoulder holsters. None of the other gangsters held a weapon in his hand inside the apartment. They even stacked their AK-47s in the far corner.

Yet the blonde gripped her pistol like a lucky rabbit's foot, refusing to part with it. She paced the room with jerky steps, almost panting, her nostrils flaring. She drank too much and shivered when she thought no one was watching.

To Miyo, it was as obvious as a newspaper headline that the wild blonde was disintegrating, though none of her goons seemed to care that their boss was coming unglued.

Miyo smiled inwardly. Something had spoiled Alena's plans. Something bad. Did Alena know that Chuck was coming?

Miyo knew.

TWENTY-FOUR

Carlos McCrary

I hid in the tropical foliage between the alley and the fence of the house across from the back of Alena's cottage. Streetlights at each end of the alley shed enough light for Tank and me to walk from the next street, where Snoop had parked in the Navigator.

Two windows on the south wall of the garage apartment overlooked the three-car parking area off the alley. Two on the west wall overlooked the alley. All four were the same size. The bathroom window would be smaller; therefore, the bathroom was on the north side where we couldn't see it.

"Light behind the curtains," I whispered. "Someone's inside."

"Is that the door you used when you mounted the GPS tracker?" Tank asked.

"Yeah. I picked the lock. The garage isn't alarmed either. *Shh.*" Footsteps clanged down the stairs.

Two men rounded the corner of the garage and angled toward the house, holding Kalashnikovs. They disappeared behind the curtain of vegetation that surrounded the back garden. I sidestepped along the alley and crossed Alena's alley parking area. Approaching her cyclone fence, I kept them in view through a crack in the curtain of bamboo. They climbed the back steps. One man unlocked the back door and entered. The alarm panel inside beeped. The first man disarmed the system.

The first man said something in Serbian and the second man entered, closing the door behind them.

I motioned Tank to join me. "Maybe they went for more beer."

"Or maybe Miyo is in the house and not the apartment."

"Un-huh. If she wasn't in the apartment, why were they there? And why are the lights on? No, she's there. It's a more secure location. We'll watch for a few minutes and see what develops."

We discovered a hidey-hole in the jungle of the alley to watch and listen from the shadows. It was opposite the parking area beside the garage.

Ten minutes later, the back door opened and the alarm beeped when it was armed. I sneaked back to the thin view between the bamboo. The two men carried a body wrapped in plastic, their Kalashnikovs slung across their backs.

Hefting a leather sap, I whispered, "Chance favors the prepared mind."

Tank waved his own sap and grinned, his white teeth glimmering in the distant light, his black face barely visible. He pointed at the rear man, then at himself. He pointed at the front man, then at me.

Nodding my agreement, we eased back to our watch post in the alley.

The men stepped from behind the bamboo and set the body on the ground. The front man unlatched the gate in the cyclone fence. Kicking the gate open against the spring, they boosted the body and lugged it across the parking area to the garage door. The gate clanged shut behind them. They laid the body down again, and we tiptoed across the alley.

The front man unlocked the door and reached inside to switch on the lights. He said something in the strange language, and they lifted the body again.

The rear man struggled through the door, and I entered on his heels. Swinging the sap at full power, I banged him in the temple. Before he hit the floor, I leapt at the front man and swung the sap again. The second thug crumpled in a heap.

Tank whispered, "He was supposed to be mine."

"Sorry, pal. Target of opportunity. Hit him again if you want."

"Can't do it, bro. If he's not dead already, it would be murder."

Kneeling beside the front man, I felt for his pulse. "He's alive. My plastic ties are in the Navigator. You see anything to tie him?"

Tank scanned the garage. "There on the workbench. A box of duct tape." He grabbed a silver roll.

A wooden box sat on the concrete floor beside the workbench. "That's the crate in the security video at Miyo's condo."

"They smuggled her out in that crate?"

"Like a sack of potatoes."

After I slipped the AK-47 strap over the man's head, I rolled him onto his stomach. I stuck the rifle under the bench and drew his hands together. Tank peeled off three feet of tape and wrapped it around the unconscious man's wrists.

"Tape his ankles in case he comes to," I said. "I'll check the other guy."

Tank taped the first man's ankles, and I felt for the second man's pulse. "He's dead." Slipping the dead man's AK-47 over his head, I set it beside the first one. "We don't need any more weapons. Text Snoop. It's time."

Alena Cernan

Alena glanced at her watch. She had sent her men to fetch Tomaz's body a half hour ago. How long did it take to haul a body to the garage? She had heard the gate in the fence clang shut earlier. "Shouldn't Jakob and Viktor be back by now?"

Stefan and Rudolf both regarded her. Rudolf shrugged. "You want me to help them?"

"No, let's give them ten more minutes." She sipped her Scotch. One good thing about Tomaz: He had introduced her to single-malt Scotch.

Kopitar's phone signaled a text. Alena tapped the screen. It was from Niko.

We arrive in five minutes with McCrary. We park in rear.

Alena smiled. Niko was alive. Tomaz was afraid for nothing. She drained the Scotch.

Rudolf sat at the kitchenette table drinking coffee. "You heard from someone?"

"Niko will be here in five minutes with McCrary. Call Jakob and ask what's keeping him and Viktor."

Once Niko Iva arrived with reinforcements, she would be safe. As far as the men knew, all was proceeding as planned.

A distant explosion rattled the windows and the lights went out. Alena sighed. Another transformer had blown. The power had gone out during a thunderstorm two weeks before for seven hours. She loved trendy, chic Coconut Grove, but living with a century-old infrastructure was a bitch. The power company was replacing the aging equipment, but much of the old gear was still in service.

Rudolf's voice carried through the darkness. "I called both Jakob and Viktor. Both calls went to voicemail. Maybe the power outage affected cellphone service."

"Look out the window. See whether the neighbors have power."

Rudolf tapped the flashlight app on his phone and stepped to the north window. He extinguished the light and fingered the curtain aside. "I don't see anything. Their power is out too."

"What about the house on the other side?"

Rudolf crossed the room, tripping over a chair in the dark. He cursed in Serbian and tapped his phone light on again. "Turn your light on, Stefan." He gazed out the window on the south. "All dark. Shall I call the power company?"

"No, you idiot, we have a kidnapped woman. Don't call any attention to us or this house. We'll wait it out. It's a cool night. Open the windows and it won't get hot."

By habit, she glanced at her watch again. "Shine your phone here, Stefan. Let me see my watch." She read the time and frowned. "Jakob and Viktor should have returned by now."

Lights flashed across the curtains on the south windows. She positioned her hand on the stock of the rifle beside her. "See what that is, Rudolf."

Rudolf crossed the room and fingered the curtain aside. "It's Niko. I recognize the Navigator headlights."

She relaxed. "Let them in."

Rudolf Novak

The light from Rudolf's cellphone reflected in the window and he tapped it off. "Lights off too, Stefan. I can't see through the glass."

Stefan extinguished his phone light. "Rudolf, open that window. Without the air conditioning, it's getting stuffy. I'll open the ones here."

The moon sank behind the two-story garage and threw the back garden into shadow, darkness within darkness. The back gate clanked. Seconds later, Rudolf glimpsed movement in the garden and his breath caught in his throat.

The first man in the garden aimed his cellphone screen at the stepping-stones. "That's Niko, I recognize his hat. He's lighting the way with his phone. Wait, he's limping. Two other men are hauling a body. Maybe they wounded McCrary. One more of our men is behind, also with his phone lit."

His colleagues had McCrary, Rudolf thought. He had been afraid for nothing; everything would work out the way Alena had planned.

Rudolf unbolted the steel door. He propped a chair to hold the door open. The breeze cooled his sweaty skin. He swung the screen door outward and stood sideways in the opening to hold the door.

Alena spoke harshly to Stefan. "Ask whether he needs help. Shine your cellphone over there."

The man in the Pilots cap switched off his cellphone light and heaved himself up the stairs with one hand on the steel railing. He climbed quickly, though he limped badly.

Rudolf stepped onto the porch. "Are you wounded, Niko? Do you need help?"

The man groaned while he struggled up the stairs, head down in the dark. "Umurbumblesnort," he grunted.

"What did you say, Niko?" Niko must be wounded to not be able to talk better than that.

"Scratchski pocketa whiskey butcheroff." The man reached the top of the stairs, still looking down.

No, that man wasn't moving the way Niko moved. Something wasn't right. Rudolf drew his weapon.

259

McCrary hit Rudolf's wrist and wrenched it aside as the Serb fired, then he stuck a pistol in Rudolf's gut and fired twice.

Miyoki Takashi

Miyo hollered. "Over here, Chuck.

Alena jumped from the couch with an AK-47 in her left hand and wrenched the small pistol from her waistband with the right. She squared toward Miyo's voice which came from the shadows.

Omigod, Miyo thought, *she's going to use me for a human shield.*

Chuck threw Rudolf's body across the room, knocking Stefan aside like a bowling pin, his cellphone spinning across the floor, its light reflecting on the walls and ceiling like a disco ball.

Stefan's phone cast Chuck's shadow across the ceiling as he bulled through the door, shooting at Stefan. The Serb bounced to his feet and sprinted toward the AK-47s stacked in the corner.

In the strobing light of muzzle flashes and the footlight of Stefan's phone, Miyo saw Stefan jump. Bullets filled the room. He skidded across the tile floor and crashed into the stacked weapons.

Tank followed on Chuck's heels, firing at Stefan, who struggled to grasp an AK-47 as he sprawled on his back on the floor.

Stefan rolled onto his side and twitched into stillness, his arm stretched across the Russian machine gun.

Alena skidded on her knees into the shadowy corner and halted behind Miyo. Miyo heard the AK-47 clatter on the tile when Alena released it to free her left hand.

Wrapping her arm around Miyo's neck, Alena jammed the pistol muzzle into her captive's ear.

Miyo called out, "Alena's behind me, Chuck. She has a gun barrel in my ear."

Alena shouted, "Drop your weapons, or I shoot the woman."

Carlos McCrary

Snoop crowded into the room behind Tank and me. I fired two insurance bullets into the men on the floor. Neither of them would rise from the dead.

Sirens sounded in the distance. Gunfire had awakened the neighbors.

Alena made herself small behind the woman I loved. Her right eye peeked from behind my beloved's head.

I kicked the cellphone across the room toward Miyo in the corner. If things went sideways, I wanted all the light I could get. The cellphone light shining from the floor transformed Miyo's visage into an eerie mask from a horror movie.

Assuming the Weaver stance, I leveled the Glock at Alena's eye an inch above Miyo's ear. Closing one eye, I lined up the white dot on the Glock's front gunsight with the slot at the rear of the pistol. "All your gunmen are dead, Alena. You are alone. Give it up. Let Miyo go."

Alena repeated her demand. "Drop your guns or I kill the woman."

"Alena, do you hear the sirens? It's over. Lay down your gun and step away from Miyo."

"No, you drop yours, and let me escape. Otherwise, I kill her."

"Alena, you don't need to die. You can surrender and cooperate, and you might avoid the death penalty."

"I have nothing to lose, McCrary. You and your friends drop your weapons and get out of my way, and I'll give you the woman. I walk out before the police arrive and take my chances."

I kept my right eye riveted on Alena. "Do you believe her, Miyo?"

"We are witnesses to kidnapping. If you drop your guns, she'll shoot all four of us. *Then* she'll run."

"You think I can talk her into surrendering?"

"Not a chance."

I covered Alena's right eye with the white dot. No pressure; the only thing depending on the shot was Miyo's life. And maybe mine. *Easy squeezy, nice and easy.*

Alena's head exploded on the wall behind her with a starburst of blood and brains.

The coppery odor of blood pervaded the room. It felt so thick I could almost taste it.

I knelt beside Miyo to remove the duct tape. It wasn't easy with my own body shadowing her from the one light shining from the floor. "Tank, shine your phone light over here."

He did, and I peeled away the tape. "Snoop, call 9-1-1 and tell them where the shots came from. No point in the cops waking the neighbors and scaring them half to death hunting for a shooter."

Snoop made the call.

Peeling the last of the tape from Miyo's wrists, I took her arm. "Can you stand, honey?"

Miyo wrapped her arms around my neck.

Lifting her to her feet, I embraced her. "I was scared I would lose you." The tears felt wet on my cheeks. "I don't know what I would do if anything happened to you."

Miyo whispered in my ear. "I knew you would come."

I squeezed her hand. "Sit and wait in here until the cops get here. You shouldn't be outside with all these guns around. Accidents happen."

"Okay." She sat.

"Tank, Snoop, give me your weapons."

I walked to the door and hollered to Jorge and Kelly. "Here come our weapons." I dropped the captured weapons one at a time to Jorge. "Put the Serbs' guns inside the garage, and stuff your rubber gloves in your pockets. Kelly, you and Jorge flash your badges." I shoved my own gloves in my pocket too.

"We weren't born yesterday, Chuck," Kelly said. "Lay your weapons down and keep your hands visible until the cops get control of the scene. We don't want any unfortunate incidents."

After setting my Browning on the porch, I stepped back into the apartment to wait with Miyo. The adrenaline rush was fading, and I felt as drained as I ever felt following a mission in the Middle East.

"The cops are on their way. I should go outside and act non-threatening." I touched her cheek. "I love you."

Miyoki Takashi

The Miami police lieutenant agreed to let Miyo wait until the next morning, which was a Monday, to make her statement. By five a.m. Miyo threw herself into Chuck's arms. "Take me home. I'm gonna sleep for three days."

"Not yet," Chuck said. "You need to call your parents. They're at the Port City Palace."

After a late breakfast, Miyo and Chuck drove to the Port City Palace in Chuck's Avanti.

Miyo clutched Chuck's hand as they entered the elevator to the penthouse. "In spite of being a naturalized US citizen, Daddy is still old-fashioned. I didn't say this before, but Daddy has reservations about our relationship."

"What sort of reservations?"

"Daddy says your work is too dangerous. He's afraid that we'll get married and I'll become a widow and our children will be orphans."

"Is that all?"

She punched his shoulder. "Don't make light of this, lover. I'm a modern woman and all that, but I do care what my parents think."

"Sorry. So, I should win them over?"

"No. You need to let *me* win them over. I had planned to work on my parents for a few weeks. Maybe a few months. Someday they will appreciate you the way I do. Then, *poof,* no more objections. I hadn't planned on them meeting you this way."

"The kidnapping blew that plan out of the water."

"You can shut up and sit there and act, uh, *eligible.*"

"Eligible, as in eligible bachelor?"

"You got it, honey bun. You're not as dumb as everyone says." She poked him on the arm playfully. The elevator doors opened.

She clutched his hand. "Let me do the talking, okay?"

Chuck made a zipping motion across his lips. "Got it. Speak when spoken to and act like an eligible suitor."

He stopped at the double doors to the suite. "How old-fashioned is he? Should I bow the way people do in the movies?"

She punched him in the shoulder again. "Oh, you weren't kidding, were you? No, don't bow; you shake hands." She rang the bell.

Miyo peered over her parents' shoulders and smiled at Chuck as he shifted his weight from one foot to the other. Father, mother, and daughter cried and hugged in the entryway. Her parents ignored him as if he were a piece of furniture.

I should have warned Chuck that they aren't the stereotypical inscrutable Japanese, Miyo thought. *Their emotional tide is flooding now. It will take some time to ebb.*

She gave them each one more pat. "Mom and Dad, this is Chuck."

"I am Takahiro Takashi. This is my wife Azami." They shook hands.

He father gestured at the table. "I ordered a brunch buffet sent up. It's still around noon in San Francisco. Have you eaten?"

Between bites of food, Takahiro interrogated Miyo on the facts of the kidnapping. Miyo soft-pedaled the worst parts and omitted the gunfight at Jose's Auto Salvage, which Chuck had told her about over breakfast.

Takahiro glanced at his wife, then swiveled to Chuck. "How did you ascertain where Miyo was being held?"

"My contacts with the Port City Police were able to ping her cellphone location."

Good, Miyo thought, *keep your answers short.*

"And how did you overpower the five men who kidnapped her?"

"My friend Tank Tyler and I ambushed two of them after they left the apartment to run an errand. Then I masqueraded as one of the gang members to gain access to the apartment. We had to deal with three."

"You killed two men and a woman in the apartment?"

"To save Miyo's life and the lives of four of my own people, yes."

Takahiro steepled his hands and frowned.

Miyo had seen this before. Tears gathered in her eyes.

"Mr. McCrary, I know a great deal about you, perhaps more than you realize. In addition to what Miyo told us about you, Azami and I studied everything about you we found on the internet. You had a distinguished military career, replete with heroism and medals, but you brought your militaristic predilection for violence home to your civilian life. Since resigning from the Port City Police, where you also served with distinction, you exhibit a history of vigilantism whenever you think it is convenient. Dead bodies accumulate in your vicinity like fallen leaves."

Chuck returned Takahiro's gaze without expression.

Beneath the table, Miyo held his hand. Tears spilled down her cheeks. When Daddy acted this way, he was as implacable as a tsunami.

Her father stood, scooting his chair from the table. "You have an affinity for savagery. This kidnapping is evidence that your fondness for violence is a danger to those around you, including our daughter."

He bowed his head to his wife, who rose from her chair and walked to his side to seize his hand.

"Azami and I oppose your relationship with Miyo. The fact that your enemies used Miyo for a weapon against you proves that our opposition is justified."

Miyo had experienced her parents' rehearsed theatrics many times. This was far worse than she had imagined. Next, they would make a spectacle of stomping from the room.

"Azami and I thank you for rescuing our daughter, but we point out that you were the cause of the kidnapping to begin with." He glanced at his wife and they half-stepped away from the table.

"We hope to never see you again. Miyo will show you out." They about-faced and marched from the room, closing the bedroom door behind them. Daddy's exit line was his message—no, his *demand*—for her to stay after Chuck left.

Miyo sat at the table in silence, tears tracking her cheeks.

Her parents had staged a similar exit at their home in San Francisco when Miyo was a senior in high school, the first time she dated a boy who was not Asian. The vision echoed in her mind—young love thwarted by her parents.

Screw that. I'm not a child anymore; I'm a grown woman. She wouldn't fall for that drama queen exit again. Holding Chuck's hand, Miyo stood up from the table and tugged him with her to the door. "You and me, babe."

The phrase *forsaking all others* ran through her mind. She slammed the door behind them.

TWENTY-FIVE

Antonio Crucero

C rucero mixed a drink and watched the Six O'clock News.

The television reporter stood in front of a parking garage with the Bayfront Boulevard and NE 30th Street signs visible over her shoulder. Crucero recognized the Bayshore Parking Garage that Lucifer was using to surveil McCrary.

He pointed the remote at the TV and cranked the volume. The previous night, a gun battle in that garage claimed two men's lives. Two mug shots flashed on the screen. Crucero's stomach lurched when he recognized them both from Alena's house.

The next segment reported ten fatalities at another gun battle west of Homestead. That reporter stood in front of Jose's Auto Salvage. More mug shots flashed on the screen. Crucero recognized two more dead men.

His stomach worsened. Acid rose in his throat and his vision whirled. He leaned against the bar for support.

The third segment reported that a kidnap victim was rescued from a Coconut Grove house. A glamour shot of Miyoki Takashi posed at an art gallery in New York City flashed on the screen. The reporter called her a well-known artist living in Port City Beach, who was abducted from her condo early Saturday morning.

During her rescue, five kidnappers were killed and one arrested. Crucero recognized Tomaz Kopitar's picture. The other four dead men were strangers.

Crucero staggered to a chair and fell into it. Who had survived?

If Alena talked to the cops, those drugs would lead back to him. If one of her thugs survived, he might not know where the cocaine came from. No, Crucero couldn't count on that. His diplomatic status would protect him from the cops, but not from his father's wrath. The old man would blow a gasket when he found out about this, and, with his old-boy network, Crucero had no doubt that he would find out. This time the old man would do more than threaten. This time, he would revoke Crucero's diplomatic credentials.

Crucero would be forced to return to San Cristobal and live like a peasant. *No,* he thought, *I would rather die.*

Crucero slugged a long drink and contemplated the end of his sweet life on Port City Beach, vacation playground for the international set. It was that goddamn McCrary's fault. If Crucero went down in flames, he wouldn't go alone.

He called Lucifer. "Come over after dark."

Miyoki Takashi

Miyo clutched Chuck's arm as they walked from the Miami police conference room. "I could not have survived that interview if you hadn't been there to hold my hand."

"Was it as bad as your father's interrogation yesterday?"

Miyo felt her face flush. "I'm sorry about that. Give them time. Give *me* time. I'll bring them around. Let's not talk about my parents anymore." But would she ever bring them around? She wondered.

"Okay."

Chuck led her through the squad room. "It must've been hard to relive every second from the moment they invaded your bedroom to when the cops arrived."

Which time? Miyo thought, *With my parents or with the Miami Police?* But she didn't say that.

Chuck held the door for her.

"Those bastards didn't merely invade my bedroom; they invaded my *bed.*" She stopped in the hall. "Which way?"

"The elevator is around that corner."

Chuck wrapped an arm around her waist. "You're shivering, babe."

"Am I?"

"Giving a statement to police can be stressful to a victim. The good news is that you don't need to go through the ordeal of telling it again. You can forget about it now."

Miyo recalled her father's accusing expression when he questioned her in their hotel suite. She shook her head and thrust the memory aside.

"I'll never forget it, Chuck. One kidnapper survived, so there could be a trial of that one thug."

"The one we taped up in Alena's garage? He'll plead guilty to avoid the death penalty. There won't be any trial."

The elevator arrived. Chuck mashed the button for the garage and slipped his arm around Miyo again. "I can't keep my hands off you. It's like I crave to hold you all the time. I came so close to losing you."

She brushed her fingers across his cheek. "You'll never lose me." *Forsaking all others* popped into her head again. She shook it off.

Chuck positioned his hand on the small of her back, a simple affectionate gesture. "Yesterday morning I walked onto that porch and saw those police lights flashing, and I realized the danger was over. Then I grasped that the whole kidnapping was my fault."

Miyo took his other hand. "Daddy didn't need to say that. If it hadn't been for you, I'd be taped like a mummy in that horrid garage apartment, or I would be dead."

The elevator stopped, and he held the door for her. "If it hadn't been for me, those thugs never would have kidnapped you. Your parents were right: The kidnapping was my fault."

They headed toward Chuck's Avanti. He opened the door but didn't release her hand. "If anything had happened to you because of me, I couldn't survive it. I love you."

269

"I love you too." She held him close.

"You're still shivering."

"Maybe it's because I'm scared shitless."

"Still?"

"Let's talk in the car." Her fear was of breaking with her parents if they wouldn't accept Chuck, but she didn't mention that. Let him think she felt the aftereffect of the kidnapping. Perhaps some of it was.

They got in.

Chuck backed the Avanti from the parking spot.

Miyo planted her hands on her knees, bracing herself. "I stopped shivering. I think."

"That's good."

"Those horrid men were able to kidnap me because you weren't there. If you were there, you would have stopped them." She crossed her arms.

"I can't always be there, babe. We live three miles apart." He handed the cashier a parking ticket and swiped his credit card. The gate rose and they accelerated onto the street.

Chuck peeked at his outside mirror and changed lanes. "One reason that I bought my condo was the security. Before we met, gunmen invaded my rented townhouse twice, and my landlady cancelled my lease and threw me out. Since I was relocating anyway, I wanted better security. Our condo security isn't perfect, but it's pretty good."

Miyo smiled. "The first time I came to dinner at your condo, a guard in the lobby scanned my driver's license."

Chuck climbed the ramp to I-95 north. "Like I said, pretty good security."

"At my condo, those guys waltzed into my apartment in the middle of the night, stuffed me into a wooden box, and hauled me out without anyone the wiser. Our security must be the pits."

"I told you that on our second date."

"It didn't seem important then, but, boy, it does now."

"There's a simple answer to that."

Miyo smiled at him. "What are you thinking?"

"If you lived with me, this whole nightmare would never have happened. Either that or I'd be dead, because they couldn't get to you unless they literally stepped over my dead body."

Miyo's breath quickened. "Are you serious? Living together, that's so... so *long term.*"

"Didn't I already break the longevity record for relationships with you? Five months, right?"

"Are you sure about this?"

"I'm in this relationship for the foreseeable future, but I don't expect that level of commitment from you with your parents opposing us the way they do. It's a good beginning though."

"Okay, then. I'll do it."

Miyo and Chuck spent the next few days at her condo getting to know each other from the perspective of a relationship instead of an easy love affair. Miyo asked him to sit for a portrait, and they talked for hours while Chuck posed in her studio.

Miyo would move in with him, but should she rent her condo or put it on the market?

Chuck helped her make that decision. "Honey, keeping your apartment will make your parents feel better that you've got an easy out. Besides, you need an art studio and there's no room for that in my condo. If we decide later to get married, we'll buy a bigger home together. I don't want to rush a lifetime decision for either of us."

They talked about children. How many would they want? What about religion? She was Buddhist; Chuck was Presbyterian. Did God really care which? What were their political views and how important were they?

Underlying all was an unspoken commitment between them. *We're doing this,* she thought. *We're really doing this.*

Chuck returned to his own condo Friday night with Miyo's portrait. He promised to hang it in the entryway.

Miyo fell asleep with a smile on her lips.

Carlos McCrary

By Saturday morning, I needed to deal with the mail and messages at my office. I had last visited the office for our strategy session the previous Saturday evening before we rescued Miyo.

Saturday morning in August. My Avanti was alone in the office parking lot. The other tenants were on vacation or at the beach.

Something jolted me to a halt at the front door to the building. If I were a *Star Wars* Jedi knight, I would've said there was a disturbance in the Force. Lucifer wasn't lurking in my parking lot, but something whispered that he was near. Call it the Force, or intuition, or a sixth sense. Or paranoia. I loosened my Glock where it was clipped on my belt and bent to feel the reassuring bulge of my Browning in the ankle holster.

Better cautious than dead.

When I exited the elevator, the second floor was as silent as fog and as empty as a church on Monday. There was no hum of distant printers, no murmur of conversations, no beeping of phones.

My sneakers made the only sound.

The click of unlocking my door sounded like a hand clap in a mausoleum.

Leaving the conference room lights off, I avoided going near the windows.

If I were Lucifer, I would surveil me from the Bayshore Parking Garage across the street. But would he be there on a Saturday? Even if he had been lurking in the garage all week waiting for me, would he have given up by now? Everything depended on how badly Crucero wanted me dead. And why had Crucero not put Al Tegumbre on the chase? Tegumbre was the logical assassin to send.

An ideal solution popped into my head. I punched my phone. "Snoop, sorry to interrupt your Saturday."

"You kidding? It's so hot my teenage daughters won't venture outside, not even to the beach. I mowed the lawn yesterday morning and melted into a big puddle of sweat. At breakfast, Janet hinted she has something planned, like a trip to the mall. You know I hate to shop. I would rather watch TV and wait for football season. I'm desperate for a diversion. What do you need? I'll walk your dog."

"I don't have a dog. You know that."

"That just shows you how desperate I am to get out of here before Janet grabs me."

"I'm at the office to catch up on paperwork. Lucifer would have recognized your Toyota on one of his stakeouts. Drive Janet's car and cruise the parking garage. Tell me whether he's there spying on my office. If he is, I'll lead him to the old phosphate mine in the Everglades and you can follow as backup. That's a safe location for us to hold him for the cops without endangering bystanders."

"Let's hope he surrenders. Give me 45 minutes. I'll call you when I'm close."

After closing the blinds in both rooms, I opened mail, answered emails, and listened to a voicemail I would return on Monday. I worked on my computer and made routine phone calls.

Snoop called. "I'm entering the garage. You ready?"

"Lucifer drives the same maroon Taurus every time I see him, but don't count on that. Scan every car for anyone inside. I'll hold the line open."

"Got it. On my way up... Making the first turn on the ramp... The cars on the first floor are empty... Second floor has a few cars, but they're empty... Third floor..."

A few minutes later he said, "Top of the garage. He ain't here, bud. Must've taken the weekend off like everyone else."

"Or he's staked out someplace else. Okay, it was worth a try. Thanks. Enjoy your television."

"Or Janet's shopping trip. Call if you need *anything*. Maybe you could buy a dog and I'll walk it."

I had to chuckle. "Enjoy the mall, Snoop."

The disturbance in the Force must have been an attack of paranoia.

I called Miyo. "You fancy a ride on the *Gator Raider?* The wind in your hair, a Margarita in your hand, and loving on your mind."

"I'm in."

"We'll eat at the Crazy Lobster after."

"Can I go topless?"

"On the boat, you bet. In the Crazy Lobster, they might have a problem."

"Meet you at your condo in an hour. An art buyer gave me a bottle of tequila available only in Mexico. I'll bring the tequila and a couple of suitcases. I may as well move some stuff in."

"Sounds good."

I locked the conference room door, my mind on Miyo.

The click of the lock echoed in the empty hall. The whole building exuded that empty, holiday-weekend atmosphere even though it was two weeks to Labor Day. Once I cranked the twin engines, I would switch on the stateroom air conditioner. The stateroom would be nice and cool by the time we anchored in Seeti Bay.

I curved toward the reception area daydreaming about Miyo, topless on the bridge of my boat. We would drop the hook and retire to the stateroom...

My sneakers made a faint *shoosh* when I walked toward the elevator.

I rounded the corner from the hall to the reception area, and Lucifer Topati pointed a pistol at my head.

———

I leapt toward the receptionist's desk as Lucifer fired the pistol. The desk wouldn't stop a bullet, but if the huge Samoan couldn't see me, he might aim at the wrong spot.

Two more shots rang out while I rolled across the floor. My jacket tangled around the holster clipped on my belt and yanked it off, dumping my Glock on the floor as I skidded to a halt behind the desk. There was less than an inch of veneered plywood between me and a bullet. Feeling for the Browning .380 on my ankle, I drew it.

Another shot shattered a desk drawer. Splinters thumped my face and ears. I scooched sideways, and more shots punched holes in the desk. One bullet punched through my right hand and knocked the Browning across the room.

Lucifer's empty revolver *click, click, clicked.* The floor vibrated and I raised my head to see Lucifer charging toward me. The floor shook with his 350-pound footsteps.

He threw the revolver at me and lunged. I ducked sideways and it *thunked* into the wall behind me.

My Glock tantalized me from ten feet away. The Browning was nowhere in sight. Lucifer grasped the shoulders of my jacket and wrenched me across the desk.

My wounded right hand wouldn't make a fist. I slapped my palms into a wedge and thrust my arms up. The action would knock an ordinary man's hands loose. Lucifer's hands could have been welded to my jacket. The jacket seams ripped instead.

I pummeled his midsection hard and fast, left-left-left. It felt like punching the heavy bag at Jerry's Gym, except Jerry's heavy bag moved when I hit it.

I tried to kick him in the balls, but he was so close that my shin made contact with little momentum. He grunted and jerked me closer. This time I kneed him in the groin. That hit the target.

He roared and released my shredded jacket, going for a bear hug. I ducked out of reach and hopped back.

Lucifer stood between me and the Glock. He snorted like a bull in *la plaza de toros,* but I had no cape, no sword, and one good hand. He lunged toward me. Sidestepping, I slammed my right elbow into his kidney while I danced out of the way.

He grunted and skidded to a stop. "You're a dead man, McCrary. This time there's no cops to rescue you."

"You've got it backwards, loser. There's no cops to rescue *you"*

His cheeks and nose displayed bruises where my backwards head-butt whacked him during our first fight. Maybe his nose was tender, but everything else was as tough as a truck tire.

Lucifer crouched—a tiger ready to spring, nearly as big, and just as deadly.

I feinted left. He half-stepped to his right, and I aimed a kick at his knee. Damn, but he was fast. My kick caught the back of his knee, bouncing off his rock-hard hamstring. Maybe I bruised him, but I missed the kneecap. In the weeks since our first fight, any kneecap damage I had inflicted had healed.

I feinted at his midsection. He dropped his hands and I caught his nose with a left cross. Blood spurted down his lips and chin.

He roared and charged.

If he captured me in a bear hug, it was game over.

Ducking under his outstretched arms, I sidestepped again and slammed a left to his kidney. He grunted and his momentum swept him two steps past me. I kicked his hamstring again. His knee buckled and he grabbed the desk.

He growled. Lucifer could bench-press a small truck, but he couldn't sprint as far as a frog can hop. His breath rasped in noisy rushes through his broken nose.

"You're... dead... McCrary."

If I stayed alive, I would wear him down. If I stayed alive.

I feinted at his midsection with my worthless right hand and followed with a quick left toward his nose. This time, he didn't fall for it. He caught my wrist in his lightning-quick right hand and hauled me nearer. I didn't fight it; I jammed toward him.

Ignoring the pain, I seized his crotch with my right hand and crushed his *cojones* as best I could. Lucifer screamed loud as a banshee. Even with a shot-up hand, I could squeeze hard enough to hurt.

I drove with my legs, and we both slammed into the wall. He released my left and wrestled for my right hand, Our combined 600 pounds smashed against an office wall built only for privacy. We crashed through the wall and into the suite next door, knocking over a credenza.

We slammed an office chair aside and tumbled to the floor with Lucifer on the bottom, still screaming when I grabbed his crotch again, this time with my left hand. I squeezed like I was cracking walnuts while he gripped my right wrist like a vice.

Clenching his privates harder, I head-butted his nose again and again. His cheekbones broke and bone chips and blood filled his sinuses. He stopped screaming and released my right hand. I butted his face twice more.

His eyes rolled back, either dead or unconscious, but he stopped moving.

I eased my right wrist from his limp hand and groaned. My wrist was broken, and he had shot a hole in my hand, but I was alive.

Levering myself upright, I stumbled through the broken wall and retrieved my Glock with my left hand. I couldn't use my right.

I rested on a chair in the reception area to catch my breath. Holding my Glock in my lap, I kept a wary eye on Lucifer while I called 9-1-1.

TWENTY-SIX

Miyoki Takashi

Miyo's cellphone rang while she was driving to Chuck's condo. She didn't use her cellphone while driving, so she let it go to voicemail. A block later, she paused at the curb and played the message. "Miyo, this is Snoop. Chuck's been in another fight with Lucifer. An ambulance is running him to the ER at Cedars of Lebanon. I'm gonna call Clint now and tell him too. I'll meet you both at the ER."

Should I call Snoop for more information or should I head straight to the ER? The ER won.

On the frenzied trip, she imagined all kinds of gloom. *How do cops' and soldiers' wives take this for years on end?*

Her throat tightened and her gut had overdosed on stomach acid by the time she reached the hospital parking lot. The glass ER doors hissed open when they sensed her approach.

She hurried to the receptionist. "I'm here to visit Carlos McCrary. Where is he?"

"Are you a family member?"

"I'm a, uh, a close friend. How is he?"

"We can't discuss a patient's condition with non-family."

"Can you at least tell me whether he's in the operating room?"

The nurse referred to her computer. "Mr. McCrary is in a treatment cubicle, not an operating room." She smiled and whispered. "It's not life-threatening."

"Can I visit him?"

"I'm sorry, ma'am. Immediate family members."

Forsaking all others... "I am his fiancée."

"That's different." She handed Miyo a visitor badge. "Cubicle 7. That door. I'll buzz you through."

The walk down the tiled corridor calmed her stomach, but she dreaded what she might find behind the curtain. *If the wives of cops and soldiers do this, so can I.*

She tugged the curtain aside; Chuck was propped up in bed. Her heart swelled when he grinned. "The nurse at the reception desk wasn't going to let me in, so I told her I was your fiancée."

"Is that a proposal?"

Everything's going to be all right, she thought. Tears flowed. She sat on the edge of the bed. "You don't get off that easy, lover. I want the music, the candlelight, and you on one knee—after I meet your parents."

Chuck tugged a tissue from the box beside the bed and wiped her tears away. She threw her arms around his neck and buried her face on his shoulder.

"Clint and I visit my parents in Adams Creek over most holiday weekends. This Labor Day we could leave Clint home for a change and the two of us go."

"Clint is part of the family too. All three of us will go."

She released his neck. "What happened to you? Snoop was vague on the phone. He's on his way. So is Clint."

Chuck lifted his right wrist to display a bright green fiberglass cast. "You should see the other guy."

She smiled. "Did you win this time?"

"I'm alive."

"What about Lucifer?"

"He was unconscious when they loaded him into the other ambulance."

Rebecca Tinsley walked in wearing a light blue nurse's uniform. "We have to stop meeting this way, Chuck."

She smiled at Miyo. "I understand you are Chuck's fiancée. I'm Rebecca Tinsley. I've treated Chuck before. Too often, in fact."

"I'm Miyoki Takashi. My friends call me Miyo."

They shook hands.

"Rebecca treated my gunshot wound a few weeks ago."

"And before that, it was broken ribs," Rebecca said.

Chuck pointed his chin at Rebecca. "If the doctors are through with me, can you get me released?"

"You're not my patient. I heard you were here, so I came over. I'll speak to your attending physician and ask whether she can release you. We need the room for real emergencies. Nice to meet you, Miyo."

She winked and left.

Clint eased his head around the privacy curtain. "Taking the day off?"

Miyo stood and Clint hugged her. "This guy will do anything for a little sympathy."

"How did you get in?" Miyo asked. "I told her I was his fiancée."

"I said I was his little brother. The receptionist looked at me funny, but she didn't say anything."

"She was afraid you'd call her a racist."

"That must be it." He patted Chuck on the leg. "You gonna tell me what happened?"

"Yes but wait until we get home."

A stocky, middle-aged woman with a clipboard came in. "I'm Dr. Winters, the orthopedist. Your X-rays came back. Your radius is cracked, not broken. The bullet that went through your hand was a ten-to-one shot: It missed all the metacarpals. We only needed to stitch you up."

"What is a metacarpal?" Miyo asked.

"The bones between his wrist and fingers." Dr. Winters pointed at the back of her own hand.

"That's why we used a fiberglass cast instead of plaster. Wear the cast for two weeks. Remove it to shower, then replace the surgical wrapping to prevent chafing. The nurse will give you extra wrapping. You can buy more at any drugstore. Don't lift anything heavy or put any weight on it and you'll be good as new in two weeks."

"Does that mean I can't do any pushups?" Chuck asked.

"Not for two weeks." Dr. Winters glanced at his chest. "And no bench presses either. Nothing that puts weigh on the wrist or hand."

Chuck nodded. "Got it, Doc."

"Can he go home?" Clint asked.

Dr. Winters perused the young black man up and down. "And you are...?"

"Clint Watkins. Chuck's brother from another mother."

Dr. Winters smiled back. "I'll tell the nurse to discharge Mr. McCrary."

She shook hands and left.

"What happens now?" Miyo asked.

"Someone brings paperwork for me to sign and someone else wheels me out in a wheelchair."

"How come you're so familiar with hospital procedure?"

"This is the third time this year I've been treated here."

Miyo's expression clouded and he added, "But this is an unusual year."

"Let's hope so."

"How do you feel?"

"They gave me pain pills and told me not to drive. I'm loopy."

"I'll drive you home. Clint, how did you get here?"

"Uber."

"You'll ride home with us, won't you?"

"Oh, yeah. Chuck needs *serious* nursing."

Carlos McCrary

Miyo was cooking in the Japanese dressing gown I had given her for her birthday. Black silk with hand-embroidered cherry blossoms from the Kyoto Boutique in Chinatown, $319 plus tax. I watched her from my stool at the kitchen island in my short pajamas. Blue, 60% cotton, 40% polyester from Walmart, $14.95 plus tax.

The pain pills made me woozy, so I couldn't join in the cooking. Lucky for me, watching Miyo was my favorite hobby.

She opened the refrigerator and surveyed the contents. "Let's discover what our breakfast choices are." She swung toward Clint. "Break a dozen eggs into that mixing bowl."

She winked at me. "Where are your chopsticks? *Our* chopsticks," she corrected and blushed.

With my head unsteady from the pain meds, I concentrated on the answer. "Our chopsticks are in the wide drawer to the right of the stove. What are you cooking?"

Clint cracked eggs into the bowl.

"*Tamagoyaki.* It's an old Japanese recipe my grandmother taught me. In Japanese *tamago* means egg."

"What does *yaki* mean?"

"When I said *tamago*, I exhausted my Japanese vocabulary. Anyway, it's a rolled omelet. Where's your whisk?"

"*Our* whisk is in the other wide drawer over there." My brain was starting to function even amidst the brain smog. "Soy sauce is in *our* spice cabinet on the top shelf."

She found the chopsticks and whisk. "How did you know I needed soy sauce?"

"I'm the World's Greatest Private Investigator. Besides, I never knew a Japanese or Chinese dish that didn't use soy sauce."

"In other words," Clint said, "a lucky guess."

"The secret of my success. Promise y'all won't tell Snoop."

The doorbell rang.

I made the mistake of turning my head and the room spun like a merry-go-round. I clutched the edge of the island. "Wow, these drugs are making me woozy. I'm not taking any more. I'll bite on a belt the way they do in Westerns."

Miyo laid the chopsticks and whisk on a spoon rest. "Clint, you keep breaking eggs. I'll get the door."

Something wasn't right. I coaxed and prodded my fuzzy mind to figure out what.

Miyo walked through the dining room.

What was off? I concentrated, but the narcotics had scrambled my brain.

Too late, the reason flashed like a neon sign in my mind: Security in the lobby announces all visitors. Whoever was at the front door had not been announced, because they didn't go through security.

I bolted toward the entry. "Miyo! Get away from the door."

Rounding the corner, I saw Miyo lean forward to look through the door viewer.

I shouted again. "No. Get back!"

She turned to look at me and I barreled into her with a bear hug as bullets thundered through the front door. Her body shuddered in my arms from the impact of the bullets, followed a heartbeat later by a bullet hammering my side.

We landed on the tile and slid across the foyer slamming into the far wall. Miyo collapsed like a puppet whose strings had been cut. I glimpsed the splintered hole where the door viewer had been. The assassin had waited until the lens darkened, then fired through the door.

Miyo's father had been right. He said I was a danger to those around me, including his daughter.

Stumbling to my feet, I fought to keep my balance. And my sanity. Damn those pain pills. Miyo lay crumpled against the wall, a pool of blood growing where she lay.

The unknown gunman would kick open my door any second to finish the job and I was unarmed and wounded.

The shots had been no louder than hands clapping—fired through a sound suppressor. No one else on the floor heard the shots, and no one would call the cops.

I lunged back toward the kitchen. "Clint! Run to your room. Lock the door and hide under the bed."

I galloped toward my bedroom, bouncing off the walls as my eyes played tricks with my balance. No time to open the gun safe. I jerked open the nearest nightstand drawer and grabbed for my Smith & Wesson Governor .45. My right hand wouldn't close around the weapon because of the bandages.

I clutched the revolver with my left hand. A cold shower might have cleared my mind, but I didn't have time to even wash my face, let alone tend to Miyo's wound. Now was not the time to think about Miyo. If I did, Clint and I might both die with her. Fight now; call 9-1-1 later. *Focus, man. Three lives depend on you.*

From the other room, the door protested as someone kicked it again and again.

If Clint weren't home, I would wait behind my bedroom door and shoot the gunman through the gap between the door and the jamb when he opened it. But Clint was home. The invader would ransack the apartment, and he might find Clint instead of me.

Praying that Miyo would survive until I could neutralize the gunman, I tiptoed down the hall, my bare feet gripping the tile like sneakers.

The door groaned one more time and the latch began to yield with a shower of wood chips.

My thoughts were jumbled. Yes, I could shoot through the door; two could play that game. But the shooter had known where his target stood, even though it was the horribly wrong target. If he were smart, he wasn't standing by the door waiting for me to shoot back.

I had six shots. I didn't sleep with spare bullets in my pajamas. Plus, my .45 slug would go through the door, the bad guy's body, and the wall of the condo across the elevator lobby. Too risky for innocent people. I could only take a sure shot.

A Spanish voice filtered through the damaged door. "One more kick ought to do it." He was talking to someone else; that meant there were two invaders. At least.

"Well, finish kicking it open. Then confirm that McCrary is dead and let's get out before someone calls the cops."

The second voice was Tony Crucero's. That meant the Spanish-speaker was Al Tegumbre, maybe carrying his Colt M1911A1.

If I couldn't ambush the invaders from my bedroom door, maybe I could from behind the entrance door. When I crossed the foyer, I saw Miyo lying there—her life slipping away. The coppery stink of blood filled my nose. It resurrected the image of Alena Cernan lying dead on the floor of her garage apartment. That smell and that image were engraved in my mind forever. *Focus, man, focus.*

I backed against the wall and aimed across my body with my left hand.

Another kick and the door opened a foot.

"Shit, it's not McCrary. I must have shot the woman instead. She's dead, but McCrary's still alive. He might be listening to every word we say."

The door opened another foot, and I spotted a piece of Crucero's body through the gap between the hinges. My vision steadied just long enough to fire twice then I squatted on my heels. I had four bullets left.

Crucero shrieked and jumped inside the door.

The door slammed open, banging against my knee and obscuring Crucero from my sight.

Bullets slammed through the door above my head, showering me with splinters. I counted four shots. That didn't mean anything if the shooter carried a Glock 17. Worst case, he had twelve shots to my four, and there were two invaders at least. If the first shooter was Al Tegumbre, he carried the Colt .45 he'd pulled on me when I broke into Crucero's apartment. It held seven shells. Maybe he had two bullets left, but if he had changed magazines, he was fully-loaded.

"The bastard shot me in the leg. Did you get him?"

"I must have. Peek around the door."

"You peek around the door. You're the professional. Besides, I'm wounded."

Crouching, I braced my left hand with my bandaged palm under it and focused on the door as best I could. *Easy squeezy, nice and easy.* My eyes burned, my vision blurred, and my cheeks felt wet. *I must be crying.*

Down to four shots, I waited for a good target. If either invader peeked around the door, my target would be an inch wide but less than three feet away. If he leapt into the room ready to shoot, I had his whole body to aim at, but he would be jumping sideways. A tough shot either way and my vision was already spinning.

Seconds dragged on. I imagined the kidnappers exchanging hand signals as they planned my death.

The unmistakable sound of a magazine being ejected echoed off my tile floor, followed by the click of another one thumping into firing position.

Any second now... I realized I was holding my breath. I exhaled, inhaled. Slowed my heart beat.

Tegumbre leapt from behind the door, spinning like a figure skater to land backwards facing me. As he jumped, he slammed the door shut so Crucero could catch me in a crossfire.

I hit Tegumbre twice, center mass, and his shot smashed through the wall above my head.

I swung the Smith & Wesson and fired my last two bullets at Crucero as he fired high also—a typical amateur mistake. My first bullet hit the wall near his right shoulder. The other struck his shoulder and knocked him off his feet. His Glock skidded inches from his right hand.

He moaned and twitched as he waffled on his back.

My revolver was empty; Crucero was alive and lying just inches from his Glock.

Rolling right, I pushed with my right hand. My arm collapsed from the weight on my cracked bone. In the chaos and brain fog, I had forgotten not to use my right hand. Abandoning the useless Smith & Wesson, I straightened with my left hand far enough to crawl. Rising from my knees, I lunged across the tile toward Tegumbre's Colt, which lay between him and Crucero.

Crucero levered himself to a sitting position with his left arm. He scanned the floor, and his gaze locked on the Glock. He stretched with his right hand and grasped it. He gasped in pain from the bullet I had put in his shoulder and dropped the gun again.

I snatched the Colt and challenged Crucero. The weight of the sound suppressor made it front-heavy. I struggled to boost the barrel higher.

Crucero reached across with his other hand and grabbed the Glock. He fired and missed.

Firing left-handed, I hit him twice in the gut. I fired again for Miyo. Then once more for Liz Jenkins. I squeezed the trigger until the pistol snapped empty.

Clint came running into the room carrying another pistol from my nightstand.

"You okay, Chuck?" Then he saw Miyo's body and leaned against the wall. His legs collapsed and he slid to the floor.

"Call 9-1-1, Clint. Miyo may not be dead."

The smell of blood and gunpowder filled the room. My ears rang so loudly that I barely heard the clatter when I dropped the empty pistol to the floor.

Clint pulled his phone from a pocket and called 9-1-1. As he relayed the need for two ambulances and gave our address, he moved across the foyer to aid Miyo.

"Make a compress from Miyo's gown and apply pressure to her wound until the EMTs get here."

Holding my left hand against the wound in my side, I leaned against a wall, and surveyed the foyer. Miyo's new portrait of me rested on the tile floor, speckled with blood. One of my bullets had punched through Tegumbre's chest and knocked it off the wall behind him. On my portrait, there was a bullet hole in my heart.

If Miyo didn't make it, the hole in my heart would be real.

Clint knelt in a pool of Miyo's blood and pressed his hand on my beloved's wound. So much blood…

I maintained the pressure on my own wound until the EMTs arrived. I pointed at Miyo. "Take care of the woman first."

The room still spinning, I clung to consciousness until the first EMT team had strapped Miyo to a gurney and headed toward the elevator.

TWENTY-SEVEN

I awoke in a hospital room at Cedars of Lebanon Hospital. Ironically, this was where, the day before, I had become the acknowledged fiancé of a woman who had been wheeled out of my home—no, it had become *our* home—on a gurney. A woman who wanted to have three children with me and might never have any. A woman who wanted to meet my family and might never see her own family again. A woman who would not have been in this ghastly trouble if we had never met.

Snoop stood when he saw my eyes open. "Miyo's still in surgery. They told me it's touch-and-go. She lost a lot of blood."

My brain was still drug-addled even though the room had stopped spinning. Weird thoughts pushed into my mind. My body breathed, but her breath was in danger of being stilled forever. My parents had all their children and grandchildren, but Miyo's parents could lose their only child and, with her, their only chance for grandchildren. Her parents had warned us both about this. They foresaw danger for Miyo from being around me. Did I attract death like a magnet?

Distant voices sounded. Someone was talking, maybe to me, or maybe about me. It didn't matter; I didn't listen. They were background noise to my personal hell of despair. Background loud as the lap of the surf, or soft as the *shush* of the air conditioner, or subtle as my own blood pulsing through my body. Not important, just background noise in hell. I was afraid to lose Miyo.

"Chuck, Chuck." A hand touched my shoulder. "Drink this."

I stared without recognition at the plastic glass with a tan liquid and ice cubes. It didn't register.

Snoop shoved the glass into my hand.

"It's iced coffee. Your system is still full of painkillers. The doctor said caffeine will help."

I lifted the glass to my lips. The caffeine hit my bloodstream, and I raised the glass in a toast. "Thanks."

"The detectives on the case are Tim Cowan and Samantha Gutierrez. They want to get your statement. You ready for that?"

"Are they here?"

"No. The doctors told them your surgery would last a while and you would be in the recovery room after that, so they left. I promised I'd call them when you woke up."

"Thanks. Call them now. How long have I been out?"

"About three hours."

"The last thing I recall is emptying a Colt .45 into Tony Crucero. I seem to recall that Clint was there too. Was he there, Snoop?"

Clint moved into my field of vision. "I was there, Chuck. I ran to your nightstand and grabbed a pistol. By the time I got back to the front door, the fight was over. I rode with Miyo in the ambulance to the hospital. Then I called Grandpa Magnus and Uncle Felix. They said they would contact the rest of the family."

My grandfather Magnus McCrary lived in Adams Creek, Texas. He would get word to my kinfolk in Houston and Austin. Uncle Felix would tell all my Mexican kin.

Snoop called the detectives and I listened to his side of the short conversation. I drank coffee and let the tumbled building blocks of my memories sort themselves out.

Snoop disconnected. "Tim says they'll be here in twenty minutes."

A hospital volunteer carried flowers in. "I'll set these on the windowsill with the others and go get another table to hold all the flowers. There are several more waiting to be delivered." She handed me a fistful of cards. "These came with the flowers."

As I thumbed thru the get-well wishes, Snoop gestured to the cards. "The nurses will only let two of us in here at a time. Everybody else is in the waiting room."

"Who's out there?"

"A dozen or more people. Tank and Kelly and Bigs Bigelow," Snoop answered. "Jorge, Mother Weiner, Vicky and Hank Ramirez. A few others that I can't think of right now. Oh, and Renate Crowell, of course. She wants to interview you."

Clint stood up. "I'll go out now so the nurses will let someone else come in. Who you want to see next?"

"Miyo, as soon as she's out of surgery." I lifted a hand. "I can't play favorites, so ask them to come in in the order they arrived. Can you handle that, Clint?"

"Sure. Then I'll camp out by the surgical center so I can get the first word on Miyo when the surgeons finish."

Clint left the room.

"Snoop, has anyone called Miyo's parents?"

"Samantha Gutierrez did. She told me they plan to fly here in their company jet."

It was inevitable that Miyo's parents would come. I knew without asking that my families in Texas and Mexico would be here soon.

I dreaded the thought of seeing Takahiro and Azami Takashi, Miyo's father and mother. I could only imagine the "I-told-you-so" conversation they would have with their daughter when I was not present. On second thought, my presence would not stop the recriminations anyway. Takahiro had made his opinion of our relationship quite clear when we first met.

All I could do was hope that Miyo would remain steadfast in the face of their disapproval. Then I thought again—perhaps her parents were right. Maybe I was too dangerous for the woman I loved. Maybe I was too dangerous for *any* woman to love.

Renate Crowell walked in. "How are you feeling, Chuck?"

"I told Clint to send in the first visitor who arrive in the waiting room. What are you doing here?"

"I was the first of your friends to arrive. Hey, don't look so surprised. You know *The Pee-Jay* has spies everywhere. We monitor the emergency radio frequencies. Can I sit down?"

When Renate called herself a "friend," she was stretching the word far beyond it dictionary definition. Every interaction we ever had related one way or another to her journalism career. Even the few times we had slept together had always arisen from one of her newspaper stories.

"Renate, this is no time for an interview. I am told that a lot of my friends are waiting to see me. If you will leave now and let one of them take your place, I'll talk to you tomorrow. Fair enough?"

Detectives Cowan and Gutierrez walked in. Tim Cowan showed his badge to Renate. "We need the room, miss."

Renate touched my shoulder. "I'm glad to see that you're at least out of surgery, Chuck. I'll go wait for word on Miyo." She left.

Cowan pulled over the chair that Renate had abandoned. "How you feeling, Chuck?"

"About as well as you might expect, Tim."

Gutierrez took the last chair. "The docs told us you were lucky. The bullet missed an artery by less than an inch."

"I just hope Miyo winds up being as lucky as I was."

Cowan held up a digital recorder. "Okay if I record your statement? Then I'll have it transcribed and sent to you for signature."

"Sure."

Cowan led the interview for the better part of an hour. Then Gutierrez had a few questions.

As the interview progressed, I became more aware of my surroundings as the passage of time flushed the drugs from my system. The caffeine didn't hurt either.

Cowan ended the recording and stuck the recorder in his jacket pocket. "Anything we can do for you, Chuck?"

"Yeah. How did Tony Crucero and Al Tegumbre get past security at the building entrance?"

Cowan nodded to Gutierrez. "Al Tegumbre came here yesterday the same time that Lucifer ambushed you in your office," she said. "He came with a realtor to look at a condo for sale, and he stuffed a wad of tape in a fire exit door latch. Cops found it on a security video from yesterday. Must've been Plan B in case Lucifer missed. He and Crucero snuck in that way this morning."

After a few minutes of small talk, the detectives left.

Snoop handed me my cellphone. "I snatched this when you arrived at the ER. It rang constantly once word got out. All those folks in the waiting room still want to see you. You feel strong enough?"

"Any word on Miyo?"

He shook his head. "Clint is camped out where the surgeons will be when they finish."

"Then I want to see the folks who were kind enough to come down here to wish me well."

After my third set of visitors, I managed to convince the nurse that it would be physically easier on me for the dozen people still waiting to see me come in at one time. I could spend ten minutes showing them that I was alive and convincing them that I had everything I needed and was going to be okay. Then they could all go on about their business and I could get some much-needed rest.

I had just finished my hospital dinner when Clint returned. "Miyo is out of surgery. She's still unconscious. Her parents arrived about an hour ago, and they are with her in her room. Mr. Takashi told me to tell you that Miyo is not receiving visitors, including you."

That was what I had feared. With Miyo unconscious, her parents were making her healthcare decisions, including who could visit her. I did not expect to see Miyo until she regained consciousness and asked for me.

My hospital visitors had included my family from both Texas and Mexico along with most of the cops from the North Shore Precinct and a dozen more from downtown. The contrast of my dozens of friends and family with Miyo's parents, who were allowing no visitors, made my heart ache for Miyo and her parents even more.

When I was released from the hospital two days later, I still had not seen Miyo. Nurse Rebecca Tinsley took mercy on me and managed to find out that the flowers I sent to Miyo's room had been refused by her parents and given to another patient who had no family or friends. Then I learned that she had been flown to California with her parents to recuperate.

Rebecca also learned that Miyo's prognosis was for full recovery.

At least she was alive.

Three weeks later, Miyo sent me a *Dear John* letter with her key to my condo enclosed.

I kept telling myself at least she had survived. So long as she lived, she might change her mind.

TWENTY-EIGHT

Wilma Leonard walked around her desk and hugged me. "How are you doing, Chuck? The physical therapy going okay?"

"Thanks, Wilma. Yeah, I'm back to about 90 percent." I sat in a side chair in her office.

"What brings you here so soon after getting out of the hospital?"

So soon? So much had happened since Miyo had left that it didn't seem soon to me.

After her *Dear John* letter, she sent me a get-well card with a note that she would return to Port City after she healed, maybe another four weeks. I checked with Miyo's condo office and learned she was now back, but she hadn't contacted me.

All this raced through my mind. So soon after the hospital stay? If felt like months had passed.

Wilma waved her hands. "Chuck, are you okay? I asked what brings you here so soon."

"Sorry, Wilma; I was thinking about Miyo." I shrugged. "Life goes on."

"Which brings us back to my original question. What can I do for you?"

"My, uh, my project has one loose end. I came to talk about the Garcias."

"You gotta be kidding." She spread her arms. "The entire Cernan crime family is either dead or in jail. So are Tony Crucero and both his thugs. Lucifer Topati can look forward to an attempted murder charge to add to kidnapping once he's discharged from the hospital. What more do you want? World peace?"

"I want the Garcias."

Wilma shook her head. "Have you lost your freakin' mind? Your fiancée breaks up with you, and now you have a death wish? You don't know when to stop, do you? Or is this your way to commit suicide?" She stared at me, then stood. "Let's get a cappuccino. I'm buying."

We walked to a Java Jenny's a block from the precinct. Wilma picked a table in the back corner. "Chuck, face the facts. Alena Cernan's gang had at most eighteen guns, split into three locations: the parking garage, the junkyard, and her house. You had Jorge, Kelly, Snoop, Tank, and Bigs. And you ambushed them at the garage and the junkyard."

"Bigs wasn't there."

She showed me her palm. "Don't confirm or deny. I wasn't fishing for the inside scoop. I don't know what happened and I don't *want* to know. I'm just setting the scene. You follow me so far?"

"Yeah."

"The Cernan gang was ruthless and powerful in their limited area. Overall, they were too small for their elimination to upset the Miami-Dade County criminal ecosystem. The other gangs, the Ochoas, the Taylors, and the Jacominos, they are as happy as pigs in slop that you eliminated their competition."

"I never kidded myself that no one would step into the vacuum."

"They should send you a thank you note and a Candygram." She enjoyed her cappuccino and waited for me to say something.

"Your point is that I hurt the Cernans but helped the other gangs. Zero-sum game."

"Pretty much. Before the Cernan gang's bodies were cold, the other gangs absorbed their territory like sponges. A local Mexican-American gang has already claimed Homestead. Cernan's gang disappeared—a piece of driftwood that washed out to sea again."

"That's what I expected. What's your point?"

"The other gangs occupied the vacated part of the Miami-Dade criminal ecosystem without a gang war." She stared at me. "There was no gang war over the vacated territory and *no civilian casualties!*"

"That's good news." I bit a chunk of pastelito.

"Moving along—Tony Crucero had five men, and we arrested three in the bordello bust. Crucero was down to two men, and Al Tegumbre was the one experienced gunman. Neither Crucero nor Lucifer Topati knew doodly-squat about guns or you would be dead. I read the CSI report on Lucifer's ambush in your office. He was a stupid amateur or we would have been attending your *funeral* instead of visiting you in the hospital."

My heart fell like a stone down a bottomless pit. Wilma was right: If Lucifer had killed me, Crucero wouldn't have invaded my home. Saving my own life had caused the gunfight that almost killed Miyo. I felt toxic—like I was poisonous to any one I got close to.

I bit another chunk of donut to chase the bitter taste from my mouth.

Nothing would remove the bitter taste from my soul.

Wilma twisted a napkin in her hands, making it into a white paper rope.

"When you killed Crucero and Tegumbre, you also saved Clint's life. If you hadn't been there, no one could have protected him."

"Clint would have protected himself. I have been teaching him to shoot. I put Clint in danger by bringing the killers to my condo in the first place."

Wilma smoothed her napkin.

"You never bought the cappuccino in all the years I've known you. Whatever point you want to make is important, or you wouldn't buy. Make your point."

She straightened her back. "In your home invasion, you encountered one real shooter. Granted, Al Tegumbre was a first-rate killer, but he was one man."

"Agreed. With that cast on my right wrist and bandaged hand, I got lucky."

"Crucero was a mid-level drug wholesaler to the Atlantic County gangs. No big deal. When he was killed, the price of cocaine rose for a week, but it came back down. Again, his elimination left no vacuum in the criminal ecosystem in Atlantic County. You with me?"

I waved a hand dismissively. "Nature, even criminal nature, abhors a vacuum and compensates."

"And the criminal ecosystem has adapted already. The good news is: The gangs made the adjustments peacefully with no drive-by shootings to cause civilian casualties. There was no gang war in either Miami-Dade or Atlantic County."

Wilma's point hit home with the force of a heat-seeking missile. *No civilian casualties* after I eliminated the Cernan and Crucero gangs. "The Garcias number over a hundred guns. You told me that the first day we talked about them."

"A hundred guns," she repeated.

"And they control one hundred percent of the drug trade in Broward County."

"One hundred percent," she said again.

She might as well have slapped me in the face with a wet mop. "Broward County is a huge prize—two million potential drug addicts. If I succeeded against the Garcias—which would be pissing on a forest fire— even if I succeeded, there would be a bloody gang war over the vacated territory. Dozens of civilians to get killed by stray bullets."

Wilma smiled. "Send what you have to the DEA or the FBI and take the win. Would your parents want you to throw your life away fighting a hundred guns? Would Miyo? And what about Clint? You're the one parent figure in his life."

"He has my parents and grandparents."

"Who live in Texas and Mexico, smart guy. You don't want to upset his life any more than you must." Wilma leaned toward me. "Life is for living, Chuck. Get on with it. Like that old Bob Seger song says: 'Turn the page.'"

"I always liked Bob Seger."

Vicky Ramirez called. "Come over for dinner?"

Vicky was an A-list partner in a boutique law firm. She had sent me clients from the first week I started McCrary Investigations. The first time Vicky invited me to her condo for dinner, I had known her professionally for three years. I had thought she was inviting me over to discuss progress on a case she had referred to me.

When I arrived to pick her up, she met me at her door dressed for an intimate dinner at her home. We flirted back and forth a bit until she asked why I had never asked her out.

One reason was that I didn't want to jeopardize our professional relationship. She was the sister of my best friend and former commanding officer when I was in Special Forces.

Vicky didn't want a conventional romance, because it would interfere with her career. She asked me to be her friend with benefits whenever we both were between relationships. We'd seen each other occasionally ever since.

The benefits part was nice, of course, but I valued her friendship more than anything. She stuck by me after I was arrested for murder and my steady girlfriend at the time deserted me like a sinking ship.

A month had passed since Miyo had returned to Port City. By now it was apparent that she never intended to return my calls. Vicky had come that first day in the hospital, of course, with my other friends. She had brought more than one casserole to my apartment in the weeks following while I grew stronger. I guess she thought a month was long enough.

Either that or Wilma Leonard had talked to her.

I couldn't help but smile. "I'd love to come over."

"I'm serving Chicken Marsala."

Vicky had served Chicken Marsala the first night we spent together. Some couples have "our song." Vicky and I had "our dish."

"Yeah, I'm ready for Chicken Marsala."

The End

YESTERDAY'S TROUBLE

CARLOS MCCRARY PI, BOOK 7

We kept searching for Lynch. Catch him before he killed again.

Morris Martinez's picture flashed on my phone. "Chuck, Lynch is here at High Five Jai-Alai Fronton and Casino."

I made it there in an hour.

Morris joined me in the lobby. "There are eight tables in the room. Lynch is at the high-stakes table. His back is to the entrance so he won't see us when we enter."

"Is he armed?"

"I watched his jacket when he bought chips. He has a knife up his sleeve. He's not wearing a shoulder holster or a belt holster; that I do know."

I sent Morris back inside and waited.

The longest ten minutes of my life later, Detectives Beltran and Feldman appeared with two uniforms. "He in the poker room, Mac?"

Don't call me Mac. "Yeah. There are over thirty customers and dealers in the room. Morris is playing at a low-stakes table. He's unarmed. Lynch carries a knife up his sleeve and possibly an ankle holster."

Beltran nodded. "Why isn't he armed?"

"He's off duty. He can't carry his weapon into a casino. I'm unarmed too."

Beltran glanced at Feldman. "Let's move the other gamblers out, one at a time. Quietly."

Feldman and Beltran pushed through the double doors. Customers and dealers straggled out one and two at time. I counted twenty-two customers and five dealers out through the doors before I slipped in.

Lynch sat where he could see two other tables. One was Morris's table. Beltran and Feldman had emptied the other tables with Lynch none the wiser.

I circled my finger at the people at Morris's table and gestured over my shoulder with my thumb: *Get them out, now.*

Morris murmured to the dealer, who closed and locked her bank. She and the other players stood and straggled toward the exit.

Lynch gazed to his left, his right, and craned his neck to see the other tables around him. Realizing they were empty, he leapt to his feet, threw his cards at Beltran and his chair at Feldman. He jumped around the table faster than I considered possible for a man his size. He grabbed the dealer's long blonde hair, and jerked her to her feet.

The remaining players stampeded toward the exit, bowling over the two uniforms entering the room.

Lynch slid a stiletto from his left sleeve, wrapped his arm around the dealer's neck, and dragged her toward the service door reserved for cocktail servers. He pressed the point of the stiletto to her throat. Her eyes rolled back and she screamed.

Lynch throttled her to silence with the crook of his elbow. "One move and she's dead." She was more than a foot shorter than Lynch and her feet dangled above the carpet. Her shoes dropped to the floor and she kicked her legs futilely.

Lynch was surrounded by four cops, Morris, and me. He scanned the room until his stare locked on me. "Carlos McCrary, the Mexican macho man. How do you feel now, spic? Do you still think you're smarter than me?"

He lowered the dealer until her feet reached the floor. She tugged on his forearm. Lynch didn't seem to notice.

"The bitch dealer and me, we're leaving. If anybody follows us, I'll slit her throat. Don't anybody do anything stupid."

He backed through the service door, dragging the dealer as a shield.

I rushed the door and peeked through the window.

Lynch punched the woman on the temple, stunning her. He threw her over his shoulder like a sack of potatoes and ran through the service bar. Lynch slammed through another set of doors into the casino kitchen.

I pushed through the service door and followed.

In seconds, I reached the kitchen doors and stared through one of the windows. The dealer lay on the floor, blocking our way, writhing in pain.

I lunged through the door.

Lynch yelled in the distance. "The nigger is a dead man, McCrary. If I can't have Katie, I'll take both of them to hell with me. And you too."

Lynch left his ceramic knife stuck in the dealer's neck. She'd bleed out in seconds if I pulled it out. Blood bubbled from her wound and ran down the side of her neck, soaking her hair like red paint. Her frightened eyes seemed big as poker chips.

I knew she wouldn't last more than seconds. I held her hands. "Help is on the way, sweetheart. Don't leave me, okay? Don't leave me."

She tried to speak, but bloody bubbles were all that came from her lips. They left red streaks down her cheeks. She groaned like a wounded animal, squeezed my hands, and sagged like a deflated balloon. Her eyes stared sightlessly into mine.

She was gone.

Available in Paperback and eBook from Your Favorite Bookstore or Online Retailer

ABOUT THE AUTHOR

Dallas Gorham's books combine murder, mystery, and general mayhem with a touch of humor—all done with a PG-13 rating. His Carlos McCrary, Private Investigator, Mystery Thriller Series can be read and enjoyed in any order.

Dallas writes in the mystery, thriller, and suspense genres. (Take your pick: His novels have all three elements) His stories will get your heart pounding and leave you wanting more. He writes to hit hard, have a good time, and leave as few grammar errors as possible (or is it "grammatical errors"? Hmm.)

In his previous life, Dallas worked as a shoe salesman, grocery store sacker, florist deliverer, auditor, management consultant, association executive, accountant, radio announcer, and a paid assassin for the Florida Board of Cosmetology. (He is lying about one of those jobs.) If you ask him about it, he will deny ever having worked as an auditor.

Dallas is a sixth-generation Texan and a proud Texas Longhorn, having earned a Bachelor of Business Administration at the University of Texas at Austin. He graduated in the top three-quarters of his class, maybe. He has also been known to lie about his class ranking.

Dallas, the writer, and his wife moved to Florida years ago to escape Dallas, the city, winters (Brrrr. Way too cold) and summers (Whew. Way too hot). Like his fictional hero, Chuck McCrary, he lives in Florida in a waterfront home where he and his wife watch the sunset over the lake most days. He is a member of Mystery Writers of America and the Florida Writers Association.

Dallas is frequent (but bad) golfer. He plays about once a week because that is all the abuse he can stand. One of his goals in life is to find more golf balls than he loses. He also is an accomplished liar (is this true?) and defender of down-trodden palm trees.

Dallas is married to his one-and-only wife who treats him far better than he deserves. They have two grown sons, of whom they are inordinately proud. They also have seven grandchildren who are the smartest, most handsome, and most beautiful grandchildren in the known universe. He and his wife spend waaaay too much money on their love of travel. They have visited all 50 states and over 90 foreign countries, the most recent of which was Indonesia, where their cruise ship stopped at Kuala Lumpur.

Dallas writes an occasional blog post at http://dallasgorham.com/blog that is sometimes funny, but not nearly as funny as he thinks.

If you have too much time on your hands, you can follow him at the following social media links:

www.DallasGorham.com

facebook.com/DallasGorham
twitter.com/DallasGorham

www.ingramcontent.com/pod-product-compliance
Lightning Source LLC
Chambersburg PA
CBHW051333020726
47501CB00007B/2069